Praise for the Novels of Susan Donovan

THE GIRL MOST LIKELY TO...

"An exceptional novel with humor and pathos and rich in detail, and the finely put-together characters make this a story worthy of our Perfect 10 award and a must-read. You'll laugh, cry, and your heart will break over this brilliant story of a man and a woman—what most wondrous stories end up being about."

—*Romance Reviews Today*

"A wonderfully convoluted tale of love lost and found, secret pregnancies, and spousal abuse, Donovan's latest shows us the healing power of forgiveness and the strength found in the love of family. It's peopled with complex characters who learn much about themselves and those they love through the course of this compelling story."   —*Romantic Times BOOKreviews*

THE KEPT WOMAN
A RITA Award Finalist

"Sexy and funny. Donovan takes the marriage-of-convenience plot and gives it a fun update that will leave readers grinning....these characters are filled with genuine warmth and charm."

—*Romantic Times BOOKreviews*

HE LOVES LUCY

"A great book...terrific."   —*Fresh Fiction*

MORE...

"A fun and sexy 'feel good' story and a 'must' title to add to your current romance reading list."

—*BookLoons*

"A story of rioting emotions, wacky weight challenges, and lots of love. This is one story you will be sad to see end. Kudos to Donovan for creating such a believable and realistic story."   —*Fallen Angel Reviews*

"*He Loves Lucy* has everything: humor, sweetness, warmth, romance, passion, and sexual tension; an uplifting message; a heroine every woman…can empathize with; and a hero to die for."

—*Romance Reviews Today*

"An extraordinary read with intriguing characters and a wonderful plot…fantastic."   —*Romance Junkies*

"Lucy is a humorous delight…fans will enjoy this fine look at one year of hard work to find love."

—*Midwest Book Review*

"A great romance…a top-rate novel…with its unforgettable characters, wonderful plot, and excellent message, *He Loves Lucy* will go on my keeper shelf to be read and re-read a thousand times…Donovan proves that she will have serious star power in the years to come."   —*Romance Reader at Heart*

TAKE A CHANCE ON ME

"Comic sharpness…the humorous interactions among Thomas, Emma, and Emma's quirky family give the

book a golden warmth as earthy as its rural Maryland setting. But there are also enough explicit erotic interludes to please readers who like their romances spicy."
—*Publishers Weekly*

"Donovan blends humor and compassion in this opposites-attract story. Sexy and masculine, Thomas fills the bill for the man of your dreams. Emma and Thomas deserve a chance at true love. Delightfully entertaining, *Take a Chance on Me* is a guaranteed good time."
—*Old Book Barn Gazette*

"Full of humor, sensuality, and emotion with excellent protagonists and supporting characters…a wonderful tale. Don't be afraid to take a chance on this one. You'll love it."
—*Affaire de Coeur*

"Impossible to put down…Susan Donovan is an absolute riot. You're reading a paragraph that is so sexually charged you can literally feel the air snapping with electricity, and the next second one of the characters has a thought that is so absurd…that you are laughing out loud. Susan Donovan has a very unique, off-the-wall style that should keep her around for many books to come. Do NOT pass this one up."
—*Romance Junkie Review*

"Susan Donovan has created a vastly entertaining romance in her latest book *Take a Chance on Me*. The book has an ideal cast of characters…a very amusing, pleasurable read…all the right ingredients are there, and Ms. Donovan has charmingly dished up an absolutely fast, fun, and sexy read!"
—*Road to Romance*

"Contemporary romances don't get much better than *Take a Chance on Me*...Such wonderful characters! You want sexual tension? This book drips with it. How about a love scene that is everything that a love scene should be? There's humor, a touch of angst, and delightful dialogue...*Take a Chance on Me* is going to end up very, very high on my list of best romances for 2003."
—*All About Romance*

KNOCK ME OFF MY FEET

"Spicy debut...[A] surprise ending and lots of playfully erotic love scenes will keep readers entertained."
—*Publishers Weekly*

"Donovan's blend of romance and mystery is thrilling."
—*Booklist*

"*Knock Me Off My Feet* will knock you off your feet... Ms. Donovan crafts an excellent mixture to intrigue you and delight you. You'll sigh as you experience the growing love between Autumn and Quinn and giggle over their dialogue. And you'll be surprised as the story unfolds. I highly recommend this wonderfully entertaining story."
—*Old Book Barn Gazette*

"From the beginning I was hooked by the author's fast-paced writing and funny situations...I highly recommend this debut book by Susan Donovan. You'll just have to ignore the ironing and vacuuming and order pizza for the family until you've finished being knocked off *your* feet by this saucy, sexy romp."
—*A Romance Review*

AIN'T TOO PROUD TO BEG

SUSAN DONOVAN

St. Martin's Paperbacks

This is a work of fiction. All of the characters, organizations, and events portrayed in this novel are either products of the author's imagination or are used fictitiously.

AIN'T TOO PROUD TO BEG

Copyright © 2009 by Susan Donovan.
Excerpt from *The Night She Got Lucky* copyright © 2009 by Susan Donovan.

Cover photograph © Maria Teijeiro/Digital Vision/Photolibrary

All rights reserved.

For information address St. Martin's Press, 175 Fifth Avenue, New York, NY 10010.

ISBN: 978-0-312-36604-9

Printed in the United States of America

St. Martin's Paperbacks edition / November 2009

St. Martin's Paperbacks are published by St. Martin's Press, 175 Fifth Avenue, New York, NY 10010.

10 9 8 7 6 5 4 3 2 1

This book is dedicated to my dear friend, Arleen, with appreciation for the thousands of miles we've trekked with our dogs, our double strollers, or dogs and double strollers. Frische Luft, *baby!*

The more I see of man, the more I like dogs.

—Madame de Staël

CHAPTER 1

The photo album crackled with age as the page was turned. "This is it," the widow said, tapping a ridged fingernail onto the edges of a black-and-white snapshot. "I know he'd want the world to remember him this way, in this moment."

Josephine Sheehan placed her reporter's notebook on her lap and leaned in close to the old woman, peering at the photo of Ira Needleman on his 1947 trek to the North Pole. His young face was frozen in triumph, frozen in time, and probably just plain frozen. His huge, toothy smile and iced-up goggles were all she could see of a slight man buried inside a fur parka, both arms raised in triumph against the vast white horizon, a U.S. flag flapping above the permafrost. It was a photo of a guy who'd made it to the top of the world, literally. No wonder his widow had chosen this photo to accompany his obituary.

"It's a wonderful picture," Josie said, smiling at Gloria Needleman.

"He was so young, and everything was ahead of him." With a sigh, Mrs. Needleman gently peeled the photo from its yellowed page.

As she'd already told Josie, Ira would return to San

Francisco just months after this photo was taken, where he'd meet Gloria and fall in love. They'd get married. They'd have kids and grandkids. Ira would run a successful Bay Area electrical supply company. He'd mentor four inner-city kids and pay for their college educations. He'd compete in his first triathlon at the age of seventy. The young man in the snow had just begun the grand adventure of his life.

The widow handed the photo to Josie, giggling. Josie waited patiently for Mrs. Needleman to bring her in on the joke.

Gloria shrugged and offered up a pensive smile. "My Ira had a very good time while he was here. He made the most of every day." She patted Josie's hand. "And when you get down to it, is there anything else a person can ask for?"

That's when Josie had her epiphany.

Okay, maybe it was just an epiphanette. But at that moment, right there on Gloria Needleman's plastic-covered couch, it dawned on her that if you lead a life chock-full of relationships and adventures and sorrows and celebrations, like Ira Needleman did, then the people you leave behind can focus on how you lived rather than the fact that you died.

But if you died before you had a chance to live? Josie knew there was nothing worse. In the news business they called it a "tragic death," as opposed to a nontragic one. Josie herself had been known to use that phrase now and again in her obituary feature stories for the *San Francisco Herald*.

And suddenly it all became clear to her—if Josephine Sheehan, thirty-five, dropped dead right that second, her own newspaper would put her demise in the "tragic" category.

She'd never married. She didn't use all her vacation

days. She still rented. Josie didn't do triathlons or biathlons or any athlons at all. And her most stable interpersonal relationships were with a too-hairy Labradoodle named Genghis and the women in her dog-walking group. Yes, she had parents and siblings and nieces and nephews, but no kids of her own.

And her love life? It was nothing but a series of starts and stops that hadn't taken her anywhere. She'd had eleven boyfriends since college, six of whom had moved into her place only to move out again. Her sister once glibly suggested she install a turnstile at her front door. She'd been so offended by that remark that she got out her calculator and did the math. Bad move. It seemed her average relationship lasted 4.2 months, followed by 7.6 months of unattached limbo. In other words, one of her romances had the shelf life of a container of bacon bits. This would be information she didn't plan to share with her sister, or anyone else, ever.

And right there, with Mrs. Needleman staring at her, Josie knew that if she died that day there would be several people more than willing to say that her life had sucked, but there wasn't a single soul who could claim that Josephine Agnes Sheehan had sucked the marrow out of life.

Her vision began to swim.

"Are you all right, dear?" Mrs. Needleman's voice had a charming warble to it. She put her hand on Josie's knee and studied her face with concern. "Do you feel sick? Can I get you some water?"

Oh, man. Josie envisioned the headline on her obit, courtesy of the jokers on the copy desk:

SPINSTER EXPIRES;
DOG ALERTS NEIGHBORS TO DECAYING BODY

"Should I call someone at the paper and tell them you're not feeling well?"

And my God! What photo would be scrounged up for her obit? The picture of Josie at her sister's wedding, in that bridesmaid's dress her brother said made Josie look like an eggplant with boobs? Or the one from eighth grade, where Josie sported the Cyclops zit? Or how about the one of her stinking drunk in Cancún after college graduation, falling out of her beach chair, digging through the sand trying to locate the lime wedge that had fallen from her Corona bottle? Because really, those were the choices. Josie had never gone to the North Pole, and the world had recently learned that the permafrost was anything but, and now she couldn't reach the top of the world unless she took a raft!

Josie began breathing too fast.

"Is there anything I can do for you?"

She blinked at Mrs. Needleman, embarrassed. Josie needed love in her life. She needed deep, true connection—the kind of grand adventure that only seemed to happen to other people. And unless this eighty-four-year-old widow from Cayuga Terrace was some kind of mystical matchmaker, there wasn't a damn thing she could possibly do for her.

"Thank you so much for your time." Josie tucked the photo into the pages of her notebook and crammed everything into her bag, then stumbled to her feet. "You and your late husband shared a beautiful life together, and again, I'm sorry for your loss." She headed for the door. "I'll call to let you know the day we plan to run it."

"Stop right there, Miss Sheehan."

Gloria was fast for an old lady. When Josie turned, she was already right behind her. The woman examined Josie's face with a fierce curiosity that had nothing to do with the obit and everything to do with her odd behavior.

"I apologize," Josie sputtered, letting her shoulders droop. "I just . . . I'm . . . look, I just figured out that I'm really, really late for something."

"Another interview?"

"A life."

Gloria's pensive smile returned. She took one of Josie's hands in both of hers and gave it a friendly squeeze. She looked Josie right in the eye. "I've always believed that if you're breathing, it's not too late."

Josie laughed. That's what her dog-walking friends always said, usually after they'd reamed her for stumbling into yet another going-nowhere relationship.

"Great. Thanks again." Josie reached behind her and fumbled for the doorknob.

"Ask the universe for what you want, dear girl." Mrs. Needleman's face turned serious. "Be very precise in your request. Put it in writing and wait for it to come to you. It always does."

Josie frowned. She'd seen that garbage on TV once—some woman claimed she wrote a list of all the qualities she wanted in a man and then met her soul mate in thirty days. Josie had laughed long and hard at that, seeing as how the universe couldn't even get her order right at the Dairy Queen window.

"That's very sweet, Mrs. Needleman. Thank you again."

The friendly squeeze turned into a grip. The widow scanned Josie's face, demanding her attention. In a voice that had lost all its charming warble, the widow said, "In your case, I suggest you do it before daybreak."

Josie gritted her teeth while trying to smile politely. The old lady wasn't done. "And, I must be honest with you, I think it's going to take great courage to embrace what you ask for."

Josie yanked her hand away and retreated out the door. She backed out of the Needleman driveway, tires squealing, wondering what the old lady meant by that remark about courage. Plus, why the hell did everything—including her love life—have a deadline?

Josie was so disconcerted that she nearly caused the tragic deaths of several pedestrians.

CHAPTER 2

She was half awake when the light began to find its way west to San Francisco, peeking around the edge of the Transamerica Pyramid. They'd made it, and Josie was proud of their tenacity. After thirteen hours of loitering, she and Genghis had ended up fourth in line at the grand opening of the newest Celestial Pet Superstore, where they soon would claim their prize of an entire year's worth of free dog grooming.

Josie looked at the group that remained. Weaker and less disciplined individuals had voluntarily thinned the herd as the night dragged on, complaining of exhaustion or boredom. But Josie and Genghis had come prepared for a sidewalk vigil—iPod, laptop, blanket, folding chair, chew toys, and a thermos of coffee. The coffee was for Josie. The chew toys were for Genghis. So was the folding chair, as it turned out.

While most people and dogs slept in the pale sunlight, Josie took out her laptop and decided to get it over with. All night she'd been mulling over the slightly scary Mrs. Needleman and her suggestion that she write down what she wanted in a man, then send it out to the universe—before daybreak. And sunrise was just minutes away.

What was the worst thing that could happen? She'd not find her ideal man? She was already there. Besides, creating this kind of list would show the women in her dog-walking group that they were wrong about her. Bea, especially, was always telling Josie that she didn't have the life she wanted because she didn't *know* what she wanted.

Ha! She'd show Bea! She'd show them all! Josie knew exactly what she wanted, and she started typing.

MY MAN
Is kind
Funny
Respects himself and others
Loves dogs
Is intelligent (though not necessarily an Ivy
    League graduate)
Is passionate about his work, whether he's a
    garbage man or a CEO
Is generous to a fault
Is a deep thinker
Has overcome obstacles in his life
Appreciates nature
Believes in a force greater than himself (but
    doesn't even need to call it "God")

Josie stopped there because the next few things that popped into her head weren't so noble. They were downright pornographic. She'd gone three months without actual sex so that was to be expected. And so what? No one would ever see this list, right? It's not like the universe would tattle to her mother. Besides, Mrs. Needleman said to be precise. Josie wrote on.

My man loves the feel of skin on skin and can't
   get enough touching, snuggling, caressing
He has eyes that reveal his true soul
He kisses so good I get light-headed
He has a wild imagination in bed
He is well endowed (not circus-act material, but
   something on the largish side)
Can go all night
Wants to have babies with me

She stopped again, looking up and down the side-walk furtively. She met the eye of the man next to her in line, a skinhead with a long-haired wiener dog. She quickly looked away. Had he noticed her heavy breathing? That she'd started to sweat? Josie adjusted her position on the blanket and recrossed her legs. She changed gears.

He'll love old houses
He'll be a safe and courteous driver
He won't mind cooking every once in a while
He'll rub my feet and ask me about my day
He'll go to the North Pole with me before it's
   too late

"Hey! You just spilled your bloody fuckin' coffee all over my bloody fuckin' spot!"

"Oh, God, I'm so sorry!" Josie scrambled to her feet and used the corner of her blanket to sop up the spill before it reached the skinhead's camouflage sleeping bag. She smiled sheepishly. Since she'd detected a British accent, she added, "Cheers, mate."

Josie plopped back down. She decided the list was as complete as it could be, so she hit the save key and placed her order with the universe.

It was done. The sun came up.

Suddenly, she felt a prick of discomfort and looked toward the skinhead again. He wagged a pierced eyebrow in her direction. She gave him the benefit of the doubt—maybe this guy had "courteous driver" written all over his face but she just couldn't see it because of all the other tattoos.

She silently amended her list. *Dear Universe, I'd really appreciate it if my man were tattoo-free. Thank you.*

The lights of Celestial Pet flickered on at precisely seven-thirty. Employees scurried about, taping down helium balloons, turning on cash registers, adjusting elaborate product displays. Through the glass, Josie could see the sign for the grooming salon, just off to the right. Victory was in sight.

At eight o'clock sharp, a smiling woman in a deep blue vest came to the front and ceremoniously used a set of keys to open the doors. Josie had already packed up the coffee-stained blanket, the laptop, folding chair, iPod, chew toys, and empty thermos. However, as the doors opened, it dawned on her that she'd neglected to look in a mirror. She hadn't freshened her lip gloss or run a brush through her curls. Surely she looked like a woman who'd pulled an all-nighter on a sidewalk.

The group cleared the doors and made a beeline to the grooming center. Three small reception desks were set up, and the three people ahead of Josie were immediately registered for their freebies. She had to wait patiently. When it was her turn, a young blond girl waved her and Genghis over, then promptly left her station. Josie was pissed! If that girl didn't hurry up and get back, numbers five through eleven would get the coveted spots, and she hadn't been waiting outside for thirteen hours for nothing!

The skinhead was being served ahead of Josie. Same for the guy who was behind him!

In her mind she began to compose a letter to the Celestial Pet corporate offices. *The slipshod organization of your grand opening robbed me of my hard-earned year's worth of free dog groomings . . .*

"Looks like we have a winner. May I get your name?"

The blond girl had been replaced by . . . *him*. The cheap blue vest looked ridiculous on the man. He was well over six feet, solidly built. Somewhere in his mid-thirties. Sandy brown hair cut in short waves. Eyes so green and luminous it was like staring up into an enchanted forest. His smile was deadly—white teeth and full lips that promised a kiss of cosmic magnitude. If it weren't for the elaborate tattoo peeking out of the left side of his shirt collar, the guy could have been a male model.

Or the man on her list.

Josie cursed herself for looking like a shopping cart lady on what was obviously going to be one of the biggest days of her life. Then the most extraordinary thing happened.

Josie couldn't move. She couldn't speak. All she could do was stare at him. And a strange, heated energy began flowing through her body, looping to the gorgeous dog groomer and back to her, gaining power with each pass. She felt as if she were on fire inside, a liquid molten fire that left her tingling everywhere.

The energy disappeared as suddenly as it had started. Genghis jumped up and put his paws on the counter, and the man reached out and gave his head a rub.

"Okay then," he said to the dog as he sat down at a

computer. "Since your owner seems to be on the shy side, maybe I'll get started with your name."

"Genghis," Josie said, answering for her dog.

The groomer peered at the panting, happy-as-hell dog, trying to find a pair of eyes under all the hair. "He doesn't strike me as the marauding-warlord type."

"My sister named him," Josie said, as if that explained everything. The synapses in her brain started to fire again, and she gave herself a mental face slap. This was her moment to shine! Her physical appearance might be middle-of-the-road on her best day, but her wit was consistently sparkling, and Josie would not walk away from this counter without this megafine man being aware of that fact.

"You see," Josie continued, running a hand through her snarled curls, hoping to appear carefree in the process. "My dog's a Labradoodle, and my brother-in-law made fun of me for paying good money for a mongrel, but my sister thought he said 'Mongol,' hence Genghis, as in Genghis Kahn, but I see you already got that."

She knew her whole future was riding on his response. She waited. She wanted him to laugh. Actually, she wanted him to press her to his muscular chest and kiss her like a man possessed, but she'd settle for a laugh. So what if he was just a dog groomer? Like she'd said on her list, it didn't matter what he did for a living as long as he approached it with passion. And she could see passion beneath that calm surface. Plus, she was sure she could find a way to live with the tattoo. Josie Sheehan was nothing if not flexible.

After a brief pause, the man's eyes crinkled and a corner of his mouth twitched. "That's a great name," he said. "And do you have one just as unique?" His large, well-kept fingers hovered over a computer keyboard, waiting for the generic information he'd want from any contest winner.

She sighed, aware that she'd failed to impress. "My name is Josephine Sheehan." Then she proceeded to spell it for him. Also, she gave him her e-mail, home address, work address, home phone, cell phone, work phone, and her parents' phone, though she'd noticed he'd stopped typing a while back.

He handed her a brochure. "Here are the rules for the free year of grooming. Please keep in mind that there's a once-a-month limit, and there are additional charges for specialized services. Feel free to call and make your first appointment at any time. Thanks for coming to the newest Celestial Pet."

Josie clutched the glossy paper in her sweaty hand. *That was it? It was over?* That couldn't be right.

"You know," she said in her most casual voice, "you probably just made it possible for me to retire."

The man's eyebrows rose in surprise.

"See." She stroked her dog's fur as she spoke. "Genghis has this soft retriever undercoat with the kinky poodle hair on top, so he's a magnet for anything that's not glued down—twigs, dirt, dust, dryer lint, grass, burrs, thorns, carpet fibers, bugs, whatever. And if he gets rained on or sits in his water bowl or jumps in the shower with me, it all gets matted together. And you know those little steel combs are worthless, so I end up spending over a hundred a month for grooming. So this will really help."

The man cocked his head, as if seriously considering everything she'd just said. Which of course he would do, being a deep thinker. Then he asked, "Your dog showers with you?"

Josie felt her face redden. She laughed awkwardly.

"Oh, you know, on special occasions." Then she squeezed her eyes shut in mortification. Did she just say she showered with her dog *on special occasions?* The truth was that Genghis jumped in uninvited sometimes. That was it. That was all she had to say. So why didn't she say it? *What was wrong with her?*

The man laughed, too, then tweaked Genghis's beard. "Well, my man, at least you'll be squeaky clean while kickin' Chinese ass."

Josie told Genghis to get off the counter. "Thanks," she said, turning to go. She reached the doorway, but had to glance behind her to see him one last time. He was looking at her! Unfortunately, his expression was a combination of sadness and amusement, so, of course, she figured he must have found her pitiful in an entertaining way. And after that exchange, what man wouldn't? He thought she showered with her dog! She kept going.

But she looked again—maybe it wasn't so simple. His eyes showed interest, so the sadness might be about something other than her. Suddenly, he smiled, and she smiled back. Then she left the store, a spark of hope flickering in her heart.

Damn! Josie spun back around, charged through the front doors and back toward the grooming salon counter, where her man was already entering someone else's information into the system.

"Pardon me," she said, smiling at an older gentleman and his Afghan hound. "This will just take a second."

Josie looked directly into the groomer's kind, deep-thinking eyes. "I'm not usually this forward and I have no idea what's come over me, but you know everything about me and I know nothing about you and I couldn't leave here without knowing your name."

He nodded, a faint smile pulling on his lips. Then, very slowly, he raised his right index finger to the upper left pocket of his blue vest. He pointed to his embossed nametag.

"The name's Rick," he said.

"Lordy," the elderly man said.

The whole point of Josie's return had been to redeem herself, to reveal her bold and decisive nature. Instead, she'd just crowned herself Queen of the Dorks.

"Nice to meet you, Josephine," Rick said. He reached out his hand to grasp hers.

"My friends call me Josie." His hand was hot and smooth and the palm-to-palm contact was so thrilling that her knees threatened to buckle. Okay, so she might have grasped his hand a little too tightly, but he managed to retrieve it.

The old gentleman groaned. "For God's sake, girlie, just hurry up and ask the boy for a date so I can go home and get some shut-eye!"

Rick lowered his gaze toward the keyboard and Josie couldn't tell if he was laughing or embarrassed, but she did notice he had incredibly thick, long, dark eyelashes. She stood in awed silence, realizing the universe had filled her order not within thirty days, like that schlubby woman on TV, but within thirty freakin' *minutes!*

She'd just been served at the drive-through of true love!

Yep, she was still breathing all right, and according to Mrs. Needleman, that was the only prerequisite for finding a life. But could she be brave enough? She took a deep breath and went for it.

"Rick, I'd like you to join me for a cup of coffee sometime."

The skinhead chose that moment to walk past with his wiener dog. "Be careful, *mate,* or she'll spill it all over you."

Rick nodded, obviously trying not to laugh, then he looked at Josie square-on, those magical green eyes cutting her to the core. "I think I'd enjoy that, Josie. I'll give you a call later."

"Thank God," the old man said.

She was about to ask Rick at which number she could expect to receive the call and his specific definition of the term "later," but she restrained herself. "Great!" A huge smile spread across her face. "I'll talk to you later, then!"

"Is this a pet store or a singles joint?" the elderly man with the Afghan snapped at Rick impatiently. "That's the problem with business today—all anyone thinks about is sex! What happened to customer service?"

Rick blinked, stunned, watching Josie Sheehan and her Labradoodle clear the double glass doors of the store. What had just happened to him? His skin was tingling and his face felt hot and his head was spinning. His heart felt as if it were filled to capacity— and he didn't even know he *had* a capacity. It felt as if part of his spirit had just cracked open, and he didn't know whether to fear the breach or welcome it.

For a man who had long prided himself on being impenetrable to women, the whole encounter had left him off balance. Rick heard himself laughing. The sound of it surprised him.

"Son, get your mind out of the gutter and do your job or I will have to speak to your boss."

Rick gave his head a quick shake and focused on his customer. "I'm very sorry about that," he said, smiling.

"There's no need to involve my boss. Now what can I do for you?"

He registered the old man's Afghan hound and then a King Charles spaniel before his stint at the grooming counter was done. Next, Rick helped in the stockroom and attended the sales associates meeting, but all he could do was think of her, the woman with the hair as wild as her dog's. Rick shared a pizza with the manager of the fish and aquarium department, but afterward, he couldn't remember a single word he'd said during the meal. Late that afternoon, while helping set up chairs for the evening's free dog-training introduction class, Rick wondered if he might be coming down with the flu. That had to be it.

A little before five P.M., his cell phone rang. It was a call he had expected sooner or later, but the news was a horrible shock nonetheless. All thoughts of Josie Sheehan and her funny dog vanished.

She stopped checking her e-mail and voice mails just before midnight. But, just in case, Josie took her portable home phone and cell phone with her into the bathroom while she brushed her teeth. By the time she began flossing, Josie felt like kicking herself. Did she really think that list on her laptop was some kind of magic bullet, that millions of tiny electrical impulses turned into little black letters on a digitized screen would somehow change the course of her life?

"Schtupid, schtupid, schtupid," she slurred through the double-waxed thread. While rinsing, she decided that if she wanted a man like Rick the dog groomer to find her irresistible, it would help to feel that way about herself, first. Hadn't that been her problem all along—that somewhere deep down she thought she deserved the kind of losers who had populated her past?

Josie turned off the water and stared at herself in the mirror. She was thirty-five years old! What was she waiting for? It was time to put an end to that old insecurity forever.

She felt a warm and fuzzy bump against her right calf, and looked down to see Genghis leaning against her, tongue out, beady eyes gazing lovingly at her. He was funny that way, always knowing when she needed a little reassurance.

"You think he'll call?" As an answer, Genghis licked her knee. "Seriously? You do? So you think I should just chill?"

"Errrrummph."

"Maybe you're right. I'll think positive." Josie flicked off the bathroom light. Her dog toddled down the hall ahead of her, jumped in bed and waited, immediately assuming his preferred spooning position against her tummy once she joined him. She pulled the covers over them both.

"Good night, Doodle Man." Josie kissed Genghis's big fluffy head, so glad she had her dog. She closed her eyes and flopped an arm over her hairy bed partner. Yes, it might take a while for Rick to realize she was irresistible, but she could wait.

She had Genghis.

CHAPTER 3

The group was set to meet for their usual walk at six A.M. at the off-leash area of Dolores Park, just west of the Mission District. As always, they gathered at the Starbucks on Diamond Heights and continued on to the park, where they let the dogs run free for about twenty minutes of group play. Except for Ginger and Roxanne. Ginger's timid bichon frise often retreated to the safety of her owner's arms, and, because Roxanne's new dog had aggression issues, she wore a muzzle and stayed on a leash.

Typically, their outing was topped off by a brisk twenty-minute loop around the park (or an uphill route through the neighborhood) with the leashed dogs trotting at their sides. Then they headed back to the Starbucks for a morning cup. Except for Bea, who didn't drink coffee and believed the company's hidden agenda was global enslavement through caffeine intoxication. She expounded on that theory every time they met, Mondays, Wednesdays, and Fridays at six, plus the occasional Sunday afternoon at four.

On that memorable morning, Roxie's large brown dog was especially unpleasant, growling and lunging at every unfamiliar male—human or canine—that she spied. Josie, Bea, and Ginger were accustomed to Lilith's antics, but people who didn't know Roxie and her mixed boxer gave them a wide berth, avoiding eye contact while yanking their own pets to safety. Every once in a while, someone would make a disapproving comment and look at the pair with disdain.

"Bite me." Roxie leveled that insult to a passerby while giving Lilith's head a reassuring pat. "Can't people see I'm just desensitizing my dog as part of her socialization process? I mean, really, they act like she's foaming at the mouth or something!"

Ginger pointed a French-tipped nail toward Lilith's muzzle. "Actually, I do see some foamlike substance under her chin."

Bea snorted with laughter. "I don't know which dog guru you're all worshipping this week, but in my humble opinion, stuffing an aggressive bitch into a muzzle and dragging her out in public so she can get worked up to a froth doesn't do a damn thing to *desensitize* anyone, least of all the dog."

At that point, Josie looked around at their group and wondered, as she often did, how they had all ended up together. She would be the first to admit that the eight of them didn't create any kind of cohesive unit. Some days, like this one, the humans in the pack seemed to barely tolerate each other.

Roxanne, Ginger, Bea, and Josie were coworkers at the *San Francisco Herald,* and had known each other casually for many years. The dog-walking group was formed about three years before, when the women wound up in the break room at the same time and discovered they shared a common love of dogs. Since then, their commonalities had expanded. For example, all of them were currently manless. They didn't plan it that way, but that's what happened.

Roxanne Bloom, at twenty-eight, was the youngest. She was tall and lean, with glossy black hair and huge dark eyes set off by a pale complexion. She covered criminal courts for the *Herald,* so she wasn't in the newsroom much. As Roxie put it, she was usually hanging out in courtrooms with pervs, psychopaths, and folks with huge anger-management problems— and those were the lawyers!

Roxie had been knocked silly by her last boyfriend's betrayal, and hadn't bounced back. The guy was a hotshot criminal defense attorney thirty years her senior, and it had ended in a bigger train wreck than even Josie had anticipated. Josie was with Roxie the night her friend extinguished a burning cigar right smack in the middle of the older man's bald spot. Soon after, Roxie started blogging to deal with her fury, which grew into a kind of Web clearinghouse for boyfriend horror stories from around the globe. She'd developed quite a following at *www.i-vomit-on-all-men.com.*

Roxie's lovable old collie had died just a month ago, and she went out and adopted a dog from a rescue agency to keep her company. Roxie said she could feel Lilith's pain, describing her new pet as "needy." Josie knew Roxie could call it anything she wanted, but it wouldn't change the fact that the dog was just plain *kee-razy.*

Bea Latimer was the oldest of the crew, and the most eccentric. She was fifty-three and worked as an assistant sports editor at the paper. She was tall and solid with short gray hair and pale blue eyes, and she dressed pretty much the same every day—chinos, belt, and a golf shirt embroidered with a team logo or the name of some tournament or 5K run. She knew everything about the news business and even more about sports. Anyone who spent five minutes with Bea would learn she'd been a champion swimmer who earned a spot on the 1980 Moscow Summer Olympics team but missed her shot at glory because of the boycott. She'd never forgiven Jimmy Carter or the rest of the world.

Bea's Finnish spitz was named Martina, and Bea had her on a grueling schedule of training and competition as an agility dog. Bea had never been married, didn't date, and lived a couple blocks from her mother. All the standard alarm bells went off in Josie's head when she first met Bea, but she'd stopped wondering about her friend's sexual preference or even if she had one. It didn't seem to occupy Bea's attention, so why should it concern Josie?

Then there was Ginger Garrison, the *Herald*'s home and garden editor. Ginger was forty, divorced, and the mother of twin fifteen-year-old boys. After Ginger's husband left her for the first in what would become a cornucopia of skanky hos, she and Larry graciously agreed to share custody of the boys. They also hammered out the property settlement, alimony, and child support issues with relative ease. The dog was a different story. It took nearly a year and close to twenty-five thousand in legal fees, but Ginger got sole custody of HeatherLynn, a perfectly coiffed bichon frise who dined on free-range chicken and slept on a satin dog bed.

Ginger was gorgeous. She was always the one in the group who turned heads and caused men's mouths to fall open just by walking down the street or bending down to fix her ankle strap. But since she'd hit the Big Four-oh, Ginger had grown insecure about her looks, and had convinced herself she was in the beginning stages of menopause, though her doctors and everyone else in her life had told her she was imagining things. In addition to the self-induced hot flashes and crying jags, Ginger had become fixated on the crow's feet and frown lines only she could see. She'd made four appointments with the plastic surgeon for Botox injections, but had canceled them all because of her ongoing concerns about a possible link to brain tumors.

Then there was Josie herself. She was perfectly aware that she was the plain Jane of the group, that there was nothing remotely funky about her. She was a little too short and a little too curvy, with curly brown hair past her shoulders, and gray eyes. She had a master's degree in journalism from Stanford. No one in her family had ever gone to prison or appeared on a reality show. Her mother was an English Lit teacher at a community college and her dad was a plumbing contractor. Her older brother, Donald, was a single accountant and her younger sister, Beth, was a crazed wife and mother of two toddlers. Pathologically normal, the whole lot of them.

Josie knew she was a good person. She didn't get to mass regularly but she tried to make an appearance at Easter and Christmas. She gave to several charities. She tried to meditate every day even though she hated sitting still. She tried to eat right and usually did okay unless cocoa or phyllo dough products were involved. She had a life insurance policy, though she wondered why she bothered.

One thing Josie was sure of—she had the friendliest dog there was. Genghis was the Jay Leno of the dog park. Dogs and their people flocked to him, the people already laughing because he looked like such a goof. Genghis was a big, golden-brown clown who loved everyone, especially those with food. Genghis would walk off with anyone who offered him anything remotely bacon-flavored, and he'd sell his soul to Satan for a cube of cheddar cheese. This lack of fidelity used to make Josie feel insecure. She sometimes compared her dog to Ginger's HeatherLynn, who peed herself if Ginger left her field of vision. She knew Genghis loved her, and she was aware that canine incontinence wasn't anything to be jealous of, but sometimes Josie wished he was more of a one-woman dog.

So that morning, after Bea's sermon on muzzles and dog gurus, Roxanne stormed off without a word, the foaming Lilith in tow. The rest of them lured their dogs away from playtime and went after her.

"That might have been a little harsh," Ginger said to Bea as they walked.

Bea shook her head purposefully, her short hair spiked with so much gel it didn't move in the breeze. "It wasn't harsh—it was *true*. One of us has got to have the balls to tell Roxie the way it is—her dog hates males because *she* does! Isn't it obvious?"

The thought had occurred to Josie, of course, but saying it out loud was another thing entirely. "That's not really fair, Bea," Josie said, as they quickened their pace. "Lilith had aggression issues long before Roxie got her. She was a rescue dog—a stray—remember? And anyway, we could use the dog-reflects-owner formula with every one of us and paint any kind of picture we wanted."

Ginger frowned, but immediately used a fingertip to massage away any wrinkle that might have formed in the valley between her brows. "Exactly what are you implying, Josie?"

She shrugged, realizing she'd started a conversation she might not be brave enough to finish.

"Do tell, Joze," Bea said with a laugh.

Josie looked down at Genghis and his usual happy-as-hell expression and the way his hair-covered eyes darted around the park, going from person to person and dog to dog, clearly amenable to any kind of contact.

"Well, I'll start with me." She thought that was a diplomatic move. "Maybe my dog reflects my personality in some way. Maybe I'm too trusting. Maybe I'm just an easy-going person who allows herself to get seduced too often."

Bea snorted again.

Ginger, however, seemed intrigued. "Okay. I see where you're going." She mulled it over for a moment. "Let's do Bea next."

"Say *what*?" Bea's eyes got big.

"It's clear that Bea runs Martina ragged with training and competitions just like she used to do to herself. It's her way of proving her own worth, one more shot at gold-medal glory!"

Bea's mouth fell open, but quickly snapped shut. Her silence made Josie wince. Eventually they caught up to Roxie.

"May we join you?" Josie asked.

"Yeah," Bea said. "We were just having a fascinating conversation about how our dogs reflect our particular neuroses."

"Oh, Bea." Ginger sighed. "I didn't mean anything by what I said. Don't be so sensitive."

Bea continued, speaking only to Roxie. "For example, have you noticed how HeatherLynn is terrified she'll be abandoned? She clearly gets it from Ginger, whose biggest fear since the divorce has been that no one will want her."

Ginger gawked.

Roxie gasped. "Oh, my *God*." Her eyes sought out Josie. "Did you start this?"

She nodded, then shook her head to the contrary. "Wait. I think Bea did."

Roxie jutted her chin toward Bea. "And I suppose you've got a clever observation to make about Lilith?"

"Hold on a minute," Josie said, wedging herself between Bea and Roxie. "We're friends. We can be honest and kind at the same time."

"Ha! That's a mighty tall order for Ms. Latimer," Ginger said with a sniff.

"The Botox has gone to your brain, Ginger."

"I haven't had any . . . yet. But I have a consultation next week, and this time I'm really going through with it!"

A jogger ran by, annoyed that the women had blocked the park path with their impromptu group therapy session. Josie corralled everyone into the grass. "Let's calm down."

"Do you truly think I fear not being attractive?" Ginger peered into each of their faces, her voice reaching new heights on the shrieky scale. "Do you think I'm obsessed with looking good for men? That I have to be with a man to be whole? *Do you really think I'm that insecure?*"

Bea shrugged. "If the high heel fits . . ."

"So what was your theory about Lilith?" Roxie demanded. "C'mon, Bea. Bring it on."

"I simply observed that your dog reflects your own aggression toward men."

Roxie's lip curled, exposing her top teeth. "Aggression? What fucking aggression?"

"I could still get a man if I wanted one—I mean, if there was one I found interesting and worthy of my time." Ginger said this mostly to herself.

"And Joze, yours is probably the most blatant of all."

Josie looked at Bea, nonplussed. "My what is blatant?"

Bea softened her voice. "All I'm saying is that Genghis is a mirror to your dysfunctions."

Josie groaned. "Can we change the subject, please?"

"Oh, Joze," Roxie said. "You fall in love too fast. You're just like Genghis that way—walking around just waiting to love the next thing that comes along."

Ginger patted Josie's arm. "You need to be selective and proactive. You should really think about exactly what kind of man you want, then wait for him. When he comes along, you should be the one to take charge. You've never even asked a man on a date, have you?"

Josie was appalled at the inaccuracy of that comment. "I have so! Tenth grade. Scotty McCallister."

"What happened?" Roxie asked.

"He laughed and said no. That was enough for me."

Bea sighed. "All we're saying is that when it comes to men, you seem to have no detectable standards. You never call the shots in a relationship. From the first date to the day he walks out you just seem to be along for the ride."

"It's true," Ginger added. "I think it goes back to your sister, and how you always felt plain compared to her."

"Holy shit," Josie said. "I seem to have forgotten to bring cash for today's session. Would a check be okay?"

Bea patted her shoulder. "It's just that you've never fought for what you want because you don't even *know* what you want, or what you deserve."

"Oh, *really*?" Josie smiled at Bea, because, as of yesterday, she did, in fact, know exactly what she wanted and deserved. His name was Rick Something. And she was just about to inform them of that development when Genghis lunged toward a little sheltie with a dripping tongue and Ginger decided she wasn't quite done.

"I hate to bring this up, Josie, but just last week you said you'd do the dirty deed with any halfway decent-looking dog groomer who'd cut Genghis's hair for free."

Josie's mouth hung open as she struggled with the leash. How could Ginger take that comment out of context like that? "I was talking about the Celestial Pet grooming giveaway, which I won, by the way, though no one asked. And it was a joke, Ginger. You seemed to possess a sense of humor last week. Any idea what happened to it?"

"I don't know!" Ginger's arms went flailing. She jerked the leash around so much that poor Heather-Lynn looked like she was on a bichon carnival ride. "Maybe my sense of humor has flown out the window along with everything else I once had! Right along with my happy family! My dreams! My perfect skin! My estrogen!"

"Here we go," Bea said.

"I don't need a man in my life to be happy." Ginger suddenly pulled herself taller. "I want to establish that right here and right now. I, Genevieve Renee Michaels Garrison, being of sound mind and body, declare that I do . . . not . . . need . . . a . . . man . . . in . . . my . . . life . . . to . . . be . . . happy."

"Men are lowdown dirty dogs," Roxie said.

"Watch your mouth," Bea said.

"I mean, really—who needs a man when you have a dog?" Ginger said.

Josie stared at all of them. They were bitter and angry—for good reasons, she supposed—but she didn't share their convictions. Josie wanted a man *and* a dog. Was there anything wrong with that?

Bea suddenly shoved her outstretched hand into the center of the circle of women, palm down. "Pile on, girls," she ordered.

Ginger looked a little wary of the command, but Josie knew what Bea meant because she'd played high school softball. So Josie slapped her hand on top of Bea's. Roxie followed suit. Ginger tentatively placed hers on top, manicure gleaming.

The apologies erupted from all of them, almost simultaneously. The smiles followed. Ginger looked like she was about to cry. Josie felt relieved, and figured this was the perfect time to tell them about her strange encounter with Mrs. Needleman, the list, and Rick.

Roxie barged in before Josie could open her mouth.

"Repeat after me," Roxie said. "We pledge to be at peace without men in our lives."

Everyone echoed that sentiment and Josie was about to remove her hand and go ahead with her announcement when Bea said, "We are whole, powerful, and single pet owners by choice."

Everyone repeated that, too.

That's when Josie began to get nervous. Apparently, everyone was going to be required to say something profound and profoundly antiman, which had to be a cover for how, in their heart of hearts, each of them wanted a man more than anything. Except maybe for Bea, but even then Josie couldn't be sure. All she knew was that *she* did! Josie wanted a man! And as of yesterday, she knew there was one out there for her!

"We don't need a man to tell us we are beautiful and fabulous." That was Ginger's addition, and the group repeated it with fervor.

All eyes turned to Josie. Genghis began tugging at the leash again, intrigued by a pair of Pekinese. She felt pressured. Later, she'd wish she'd said something else—anything else—but this was the pledge that good old go-with-the-flow Josie made for the entire world to hear: *"We hereby vow to lead full, happy lives in the company of our dogs!"*

The women pumped their hands in unison and reached to the sky with a great *whoo-hoo* of empowerment. Lilith frothed at the mouth. People stared. The yelling frightened HeatherLynn so much she peed all over Ginger's shoe.

Josie's heart was quite heavy by the time they reached the coffee shop. She'd lied to her friends. The truth was that in a perfect world, Josie would be leading a full, happy life in the company of her dog *and* Rick the dog groomer.

So much for all the whoo-hooing.

CHAPTER 4

The hot wax felt soothing as the aesthetician applied it under Josie's brow and covered it with a strip of gauze. When she ripped that sucker away in one aggressive sweep of her hand, Josie saw stars.

"Aauughhhhh!" She jolted up in the reclining salon chair, panting. "You said people do this every week? Why would someone do that to themselves?"

The aesthetician giggled, gently pushing Josie back into the chair. "You get used to it."

Josie lay back and closed her eyes, dazed by the series of events that had brought her to this high-end torture chamber. Taking a deep breath, she had to admit it was impressive what a girl could achieve in just a couple of angst-fueled weeks.

She never did hear back from Rick. After a few days of compulsive e-mail and voice mail checking, she figured he'd dropped off the face of the earth. But a strange thing had occurred in the meantime—Josie lost her appetite. It had never happened before, and in days her clothes felt looser. So she decided it was the perfect time to hit the gym again, where she might be able to get more bang for her workout buck, kind of like going grocery shopping on double-coupon days.

Ten pounds later, Josie looked and felt terrific. Though Ginger didn't know the circumstances of this sudden slim-down, she applauded Josie for her will-power and gave her a gift certificate to her salon, where Josie had just been given a mani-pedi, a stylish new cut, and half of a hellish wax job.

When the procedure mercifully came to an end, she stood before a huge salon mirror. Her hair looked terrific, no question, subtle layers of soft curls just above her shoulder that gave definition to her round cheeks. And Ginger had been right—the eyebrow wax really did open up Josie's whole face and empha-size her eyes. All that and ten fewer pounds had re-sulted in an astounding change in her appearance.

"You like?"

Josie nodded, but peered closer to the mirror, not-ing a red stripe above her eyelid. She touched it.

"Don't touch it!" the aesthetician cried. "Let the aloe vera do its thing. The irritation will be gone within the hour."

Josie turned her head to get a side view of the welts. "You sure about that?"

"Positive."

Leaving the salon, Josie knew it was now or never. She had to take advantage of this convergence of fate. The perfectly styled haircut, the new eyebrows, and the cute new outfit she'd chosen to wear—a silk georgette skirt that ended in a sexy flounce right above the knee, paired with a form-fitting white cami and a cute three-quarter-sleeve jacket—she knew this was as good as it was ever going to get. It was time to make her move.

About a half hour later, Josie strolled from her car across the Celestial Pet parking lot, the dog-grooming salon in her crosshairs. She smiled, knowing the shopping cart lady was gone, gone, gone, and in her place was a vixen with some seriously emphasized eyes.

Her plan was to walk right up to Rick the dog groomer and demand an explanation for his lack of follow-through. The man didn't stand a chance.

A young woman with leather studs in her ears and a silver hoop in her nose looked up from a book. Her eyes took a second to focus. "May I help you?" She said this with the enthusiasm of someone who'd just been hit with a tranquilizer gun.

"Yes. I was wondering if I could talk to Rick. Is he in today?"

She scrunched up her nose like something smelled bad, but said nothing.

"You know, Rick," Josie repeated. "He's a groomer at this store? Light brown hair?" She hoped these details might jog the girl's memory.

"Sorry, but there's no groomer here named Rick. In fact, the only groomers who work at this store are women. Did you want to make an appointment or something?"

Josie shifted her weight from foot to foot, puzzling this out. Could she have imagined Rick? Had the lack of sleep that day, combined with that pornographic list, led to some kind of hallucination of wishful thinking? Had she imagined that whole conversation? Those emerald eyes and that luscious mouth? Her mother had always accused her of letting her imagination get the best of her. But not this time, Josie knew. No way. Rick was real.

"Of course there's a man here by that name," she said with confidence. "I met him. I spoke to him. He *touched* me."

The girl slammed her book shut with annoyance. "I don't think so."

Josie was becoming agitated. "But he was here on opening day. I was one of the first ten dog owners to come in the store. I won a whole year's worth of free grooming and he signed me up!"

The girl pursed her lips, then said, "I don't know what to tell you, lady. There's no groomer here named Rick. Besides, what's with your eyelids?"

Josie gasped, touching her brow, cursing herself for not checking herself in the mirror before waltzing in here. "Allergies," she said.

"Right. So if you want to schedule a grooming appointment, great. If not, I'm going to have to call security."

Josie sighed in exasperation, then leaned an elbow on the counter. Maybe she needed a new approach. "Okay, here's the thing—this man was so sexy I had to change my underpants when I got home, all right? Green eyes so deep you could take a bath in them. Diana Ross eyelashes. And there's a really wicked tattoo running up the side of his neck and when I saw it my knees got so weak I thought I'd fall down. And I don't even like tattoos."

"Dude!" The girl bolted ramrod straight in her chair. "Rick's not a groomer!"

"No?" Josie backed away, startled by the girl's sudden zest.

"No way. Rick Rousseau owns the place."

"Huh?"

"Yeah. Rick Rousseau owns all fourteen Celestial Pet Superstores in Northern California. He's the CEO! He always helps out in all the departments at a grand opening, and yeah, you're right, he was in here for a while that morning."

"I had no idea," Josie mumbled. This definitely

changed things. "How do you spell that last name?" Josie asked, pulling a notepad from her new bag.

"You said he *touched* you?" The girl looked at Josie with newfound respect as she spelled it. "Damn. I wish I were you."

Josie thanked her for her time. She used her car visor mirror to apply a dab of concealer to her eyelids. She located the Celestial Pet corporate offices on her GPS before either her nerve or her hairstyle could wilt. She was about to pull out of her shopping center parking space when she heard a tapping on the driver's side window.

"Josie?" A man's pale blond head appeared at eye level. "Wow—you look fabulous. I've really missed you."

Josie sighed. It was Lloyd, the latest man to break up with her. It had been nearly three months, and she couldn't say that she missed him. She rarely even thought of him. In fact, the last time he crossed Josie's mind was about a week ago when she found one of his CDs mixed in with her music stash. It was a Clay Aiken live bootleg recording.

She rolled down her window. "Hey, Lloyd. What's up?"

His eyes looked her over hungrily. "Have you done something different? Your hair? Your weight? Your makeup?"

"Nope. I've always looked exactly like this." Okay, it was probably impolite messing with his head like that, but so was the way he left her. She came home from work late one night and found a note that read, *"It's just not working for me. Take care."* No further details. Josie was ashamed to admit it, but at the time she actually appreciated Lloyd's correspondence, owing to the fact that the previous disappearing boyfriend—that would be Spike—hadn't left a note of any kind. It was as if Spike had been sucked into another dimension, along with his toiletries and clothing. She never saw or spoke to Spike again. Later she heard he'd moved to Los Angeles and was working at a Chuck E. Cheese's, so she'd been dead-on correct about the other-dimension part.

"What are you up to, Josie? Doing a little shopping on the *Herald*'s dime?" Lloyd laughed at his own unfunny joke, one of the things she'd never liked about him.

"I have every other Thursday afternoon off, remember? Because I go in every other Saturday morning, remember?"

He nodded. "Sure. Sure."

He didn't remember. A man had to care about the woman he lived with before he detected any kind of pattern in her work schedule. "Well, I need to go, Lloyd. Nice seeing you."

"Can you have lunch with me? My treat."

Josie shot him a look that said *hell no* but her mouth said, "Now's not a good time."

"We had something special, Josie. I think about you a lot." His eyes continued to scan up and down her person. "You sure you haven't done something different? Because you look great. I mean, you always looked nice, but you look, you know, *a lot* better. I hope you don't take that the wrong way."

Was that even possible? She shook her head and laughed. "Okay, Lloyd, I confess. You're right. I've done something radically different. I'm now choosy about the men I have lunch with. And the truth is, I wouldn't eat with you if I were a starving typhoon survivor and you were with the Red Cross."

She rolled up her window and put the car in reverse. She heard Lloyd cry out but she didn't catch what he said, and worried that she might have run over his foot.

Celestial Pet Superstores, Inc., was headquartered just outside Berkeley in a two-story office complex made of mirrored glass and shiny steel. A three-dimensional corporate logo hung over the entrance, big as a tractor-trailer. It was a globe orbited by cats, dogs, birds, fish, and small rodents that could have been either guinea pigs or gerbils, it was anybody's call. Josie entered, but before she could make it across the marble lobby, a security guard with a badge and gun headed her off. He inquired about her business.

"I've come to see Mr. Rousseau."

The guard's bushy eyebrows knitted together. "Do you have an appointment?"

"In a way."

He chuckled. "What way would that be?"

"Umm . . ." Josie began to question her plan. Maybe she should have just phoned. But you can't show off a kick-ass makeover over the phone, now can you? "Rick said he'd call me, but never did."

The guard looked at her quizzically. "So you're a stalker?"

"No, I'm a reporter."

Wrong answer. He marched over to the security desk and dialed up the public relations department. He checked Josie's press ID and her driver's license, made her sign a visitor log, clipped a temporary badge to the strap of her bag, and gave her directions.

She took the elevator but skipped the PR office entirely and headed toward a set of unmarked glass doors that screamed "executive suite." The reception area inside was empty so she headed down an interior hallway. A huge man nearly crashed into her.

"May I help you?" His eyes darted to her visitor's badge.

Josie looked up, up, and up some more. "Huge" really didn't cover it. The guy was a giant. Close to seven feet tall. Blackest of black skin. Shiny bald head. A diamond stud the size of a blueberry in his right ear.

"Rick Rousseau, please," she croaked.

The man stiffened, as though he were alarmed by her request. "I'm afraid he's unavailable. How did you get in here?"

"May I speak to his secretary?"

"That would be me."

She laughed. She didn't mean to be rude, and she knew it was well into the twenty-first century and there was no such thing as "typical" anymore, but she'd never seen a secretary of his proportions. "I just need a moment of his time," she said, composing herself.

"That's not going to be possi—"

A big mahogany door opened and out stepped Rick, focused on a stack of papers in his hand. He wore a pair of olive green hiking shorts—the kind with a hundred pockets—running shoes without socks, and a Barenaked Ladies concert T-shirt. His hair had grown a little longer, and he hadn't shaved.

God, the man was even hotter than she remembered.

"Hi, Rick." Josie peeked around the freakishly large secretary who'd just blocked her approach.

Rick's head snapped up, and he blinked at her with those ocean-green eyes. She watched as he flipped through his mental Rolodex in an attempt to recall who she was and why in the world she was standing in his hallway. She was about to help him but it turned out not to be necessary.

"Josie," he said, shifting from a look of surprise to outright curiosity. "Your hair is styled differently. And I can see you didn't sleep on the sidewalk last night."

"Nope. I've been sleeping indoors lately. And yes, my hair's different."

"I like it. A lot."

She touched the curls that now just grazed her shoulder. "Thanks."

"How's Genghis?"

"Great. He sends his regards."

At that point, Rick nodded to the big man, who immediately stepped aside, accepting the stack of papers from Rick's hand. There was a flash of something in Rick's eyes when he first saw Josie from head to toe. It looked like appreciation, but it disappeared instantly.

"Teeny Worrell, this is Josephine Sheehan, a devoted Celestial Pet customer. Josie, you've already met Teeny."

"A pleasure to meet you, Ms. Sheehan," Teeny said, extending his humongous hand for a shake.

"The pleasure's mine, Mr. Worrell." Her hand disappeared in the secretary's grip.

"Why don't you walk with me?" Rick placed a hand at the small of Josie's back and turned her toward the reception area. She stole a glance back at the extralarge Teeny, who was shaking his head.

"So," Rick said cheerfully, "do you invade the workplace of every guy you invite for coffee?" He held the glass doors open like a gentleman. An angry gentleman.

"I don't know—do you always promise women that you'll call but never do?"

He raised one dark brown eyebrow and looked down

at her. They'd stopped walking and stood very close in the elevator lobby. His hand slid from the center of her back to her hip, where it lingered. Chills raced up her spine, and that weird energy was back—Josie's body was flooded with it.

"Something came up on the East Coast." He studied Josie's cheeks, her chin, her lips, and then locked his eyes on hers, intense and somber. "For the record, I don't usually go back on my word."

"Fine. Also for the record, you're only the second man I've ever asked on a date in my whole life and the first one I ever tracked down at his place of employment, so it looks like it's near-virgin territory all around."

They glared at each other for a moment. Eventually, Josie shrugged. "It doesn't matter, anyway. I think this whole thing was a mistake." She took a step back and his hand fell away from her hip. She immediately regretted the move and wanted to slap it right back on her butt, but figured it would be awkward to orchestrate.

He cocked his head and asked, "A mistake? Why?"

"Because I went to the store to find out why the handsome dog groomer blew me off, only to discover you're the employ*er,* not the employ*ee.*"

A faint smile appeared on his lips. "Does that matter?"

"I guess not."

"Then where's the mistake?"

"Look, I convinced myself there was something special about you. It's a long story. But the bottom line is, I was trying to be more proactive about the whole dating thing and it seems I got carried away."

One of Rick's eyes squinted.

"Well, take care." She turned toward the elevator

but stopped, thinking she couldn't end things so rudely. "No hard feelings, okay? I'll still shop at Celestial Pet. I get all my dog toys there. And now I have the free groomings!" She forced a smile. "Good-bye."

Rick rubbed his beard stubble, obviously trying to hide a smile. "Wait."

"Yeah?"

"Out of curiosity, could you please describe Josephine Sheehan's usual approach to dating? I don't think I'll be able to sleep at night unless I know."

She caught the sarcasm in his voice, but it was a legitimate question, and Josie had to think through her answer. She recalled what Bea had said about her lack of initiative and standards. "I never had an approach before you."

"Is that so?"

She nodded with certainty. "Yep. But I took one look at you that day at the grooming salon and I said to myself, 'Make it happen, girl, or you'll always regret it.' But like I said, I think I just got carried away."

A shadow passed across Rick's eyes. "Please accept my apology for not calling you."

She shrugged. "It's okay."

"No, it's really not, Josie." His voice softened and he reached for her hand, cupping it gently. "Never accept that kind of bullshit from a man—*ever*. You deserve better. Every woman does."

She laughed. "Well, aren't you gallant!"

His expression narrowed and he shook his head almost imperceptibly. "I try my best not to hurt anyone, that's all." A look of puzzlement came over him. "What's wrong with your eyelids?"

Inside, Josie had curled up into a fetal position and wished to die. Outside, she sported a carefree smile. "Allergies."

Rick studied her cautiously. "Well, Miss Sheehan, how can I can make this up to you?"

Josie's eyes got big, her lips parted, and her mind began spinning with possibilities. A cup of coffee now seemed way too humdrum a request for such a charming and courteous pet-supply tycoon. Her imagination jumped around from a jaunt to Cabo aboard his corporate jet, to a weekend in wine country, to introducing him to her parents while on a private cruise down the Nile. But instead, she went for something really outlandish.

"You could start with a kiss." *My God, where was all this bravado coming from?*

He tugged on her hand until she bumped up against his body—full-frontal contact! Her thighs tingled. She got a head rush to end all head rushes. She raised a hand to his rough cheek. His gaze went directly to her mouth.

That's the moment he leaned in, angled his head, and the elevator binged. Three uniformed men burst through the door with their guns pointed at Josie's head. "Got her," one of them said into a radio clipped to his shirt.

She thought she'd pee herself.

"Stand down! *Now!*" Rick blocked her with his body. She hooked her arms around his waist and ducked. "She's not a security matter," he said. "She's a friend."

Josie's legs really did collapse at that point. She began hyperventilating at the idea that real guns with real bullets were pointed at *her.* Since when was she a security risk everywhere she went? Was it the makeover? Rick reached behind him and steadied her, preventing her from collapsing to the Berber carpet.

The guards holstered their guns, but Josie's buddy from the lobby didn't sound happy about it.

"Mr. Rousseau, sir, she was supposed to go to public relations. When she didn't show, I knew I had to stop her before she found a way to get to you."

Rick chuckled. He pulled Josie around and hoisted her up by her armpits. "Too late for that, I'm afraid."

Josie gazed up at him. He anointed her with a smile. She wanted to smile in return, but she was so nauseous from the adrenaline crash she decided not to risk it.

CHAPTER 5

"I really don't mean to hound you about this." Teeny took a slurp of herbal tea from his delicate china cup and sighed. "But Rick, I gotta ask you, man. Seriously . . . *what the fuck*?"

Rick laughed. He stretched his legs out over the porch railing, leaned back in the old rocker, and folded his hands on his lap. Twilight had begun its slide over Samhain Ranch, pushing the sun west beyond the vineyards, throwing gold light down onto the grapes and red streaks up into the sky. This was his favorite time of day. This was his favorite spot on earth. And he was counting on a weekend of Sonoma Valley solitude and silence to help him come up with an answer to Teeny's question.

"Point taken," he said.

"She's cute. Okay, fine, not my gender of choice, but I can appreciate cuteness when it shows up, despite the mark-of-Zorro eyebrow wax." Teeny held his teacup in midair. "But I'll be honest with you, man. I'm baffled. There hasn't been a woman in your life for almost seven years! I've watched you make an art form of turning women down! I mean, Gwen Anders is *still* trying to get in your chinos! After all these years!"

"Wax? She told me she had allergies."

Teeny chuckled. "Hell, no. That was a wax job gone terribly wrong, no doubt about it."

"Why are we discussing Gwen Anders?" Rick closed his eyes for a moment and searched for patience. "The woman runs my foundation. She's smart and conscientious. I don't want anything more to do with her, not now, not ever, as you are well aware."

"Yes. I am. Which brings us right back to my original question—why *Josephine Sheehan*? Are you sure about this?"

Rick gave his head a quick shake, closing his eyes to concentrate on his breath. In, out, searching deep for some kind of reasonable response. This wasn't a question for his mind, that much he was sure of. It was a question for his heart, and Rick and his heart hadn't been on speaking terms for a very long time, even before the accident. He opened his eyes and looked at Teeny. "Nothing's happened with Josie Sheehan."

"Yet." Teeny's frown deepened. When his dark brow crumpled it made the old football scars look all the more menacing. "Let's keep it real, Rick. I saw the way you looked at each other. *Damn*."

Teeny set his cup down into its fancy saucer, which was perched on a white wicker table. The eighty-year old Spode china had come with the place, along with the wicker table and the rockers they sat on and everything else the eye could see. When Rick purchased Samhain Ranch from a real estate investor a year ago, he bought a piece of Sonoma Valley history—three thousand acres of vineyard with its own manager, sixteen rooms full of antiques, vast gardens, a state-of-the-art horse stable, and a live-in family that had been running the Victorian-era ranch house and keeping the grounds for four generations. His Pacific

Heights house was fine for when he was in the city. But in the last year, Rick had come to see the ranch as home.

"What I'm asking is, are you chucking the plan?" Teeny turned toward Rick and braced his elbows on his knees. "Because if you are, we'll need to expand the background search—move further into her family and her friends and her job. All the old boyfriends, too, and that's a healthy list. We'll have to go deeper into her financials, as well. I want to be absolutely sure there's no connection to our man. You know Bennett Cummings is a sly muthafucka."

Rick blew out a puff of air. *Right. The plan.* It was nearly seven years ago that he made a pledge to himself, and he'd stuck to it. Since the morning he woke up in agony and heard the news about what he'd done to Margot Cummings, he hadn't let a woman anywhere near him. No dating. No flirting. No nothing. What was the point? He'd done enough damage to the female species to last several lifetimes.

His last hurrah was the accident. He'd smoked a joint, snorted some coke, and thrown back a few Sam Adamses, just in time to take his motorcycle for a spin in the dark and the rain. He'd convinced Margot to come along. He hadn't seen her since college, but, as he knew well, she was good-looking and a good lay. Back then, those were his only requirements.

He took the turn too fast, skidding into a guardrail. He died on the operating table—soared over his own twisted body and looked down upon the scene in awe. Then he woke up. Alive. On fire with pain. Bennett Cummings was at his bedside, telling Rick what he'd done to Margot. Cummings leaned close to Rick's face and whispered, *"Some day, you will pay for my daughter's life with your own."*

After seven years in a coma, Margot died. Rick had traveled to Rhode Island for her funeral two weeks ago. It was the right thing to do. Bennett Cummings approached him at the service. "It's time to collect," was all he said. Then he walked away.

Teeny cleared his throat. Rick looked up, noting the concern on his friend's face. He knew Teeny had a legitimate point—why now? Why Josephine Shee- han? What in the hell was he doing?

There was no way he could tell Teeny the truth— the way the energy had crackled through him the in- stant he saw Josie, how his heart sat up at attention when he first heard her laugh. Teeny was sensitive, but every guy had his limits.

"I like her," Rick answered matter-of-factly. "It feels different somehow with Josie, very strong, but good. Almost wholesome. I know that might sound ridicu- lous, but it's the truth."

Teeny blinked, his lips parting.

"I don't want to play her, Teen, I just want to get to know her."

Teeny seemed to recover from the shock. "So you're chucking the plan?"

"Yeah."

Teeny nodded. With some difficulty, he pushed him- self to his feet. He let out a deep groan and shifted his weight gingerly.

The media had once proclaimed it was a miracle that Syracuse University cornerback Timothy Worrell was up and walking six months after his injury. Rick knew better. He'd been there to see Teeny fight for every minuscule success, every bend of his knee, ev- ery raise of his shoulder. They never gave up on each other in the eighteen months they spent in rehab. They saved each other's lives.

"I'm hitting the barn. You coming?"

Rick had converted half of the cavernous old barn into a state-of-the-art fitness facility, complete with a steam room and Jacuzzi. In addition to being his personal assistant, security chief, and best friend, Timothy Worrell was his official ass-kicker. Rick wasn't up and walking because of a miracle, either. Like Teeny, his body was a testament to grueling rehab, orthopedic surgical skill, and cutting-edge plastics and metals. And all of it required daily upkeep. "Be there soon."

Teeny took a few steps across the wooden porch floor, then turned, laughing. His deep guffaw silenced the crickets, and his huge white smile lit up the twilight. "*Wholesome?* Damn, Rick. I can't believe you just said that. If it had been anybody else I'd say they were full of shit." Teeny winked before he limped off.

Maybe he was right, Rick thought. He could be fooling himself. But why? There was no reason. He'd been perfectly comfortable tucked away in his private world before Josie and her dog strolled into the store and zapped him. The way all that energy sizzled between them was bizarre, but not unwelcome. What was the word for that kind of reaction? Rick wondered. Smitten? All he knew was that after years of saying no to a string of beautiful, accomplished, and persistent women—of which Gwen Anders was the epitome—he'd said yes to a cute, funny, and awkwardly honest obituary writer who hadn't exactly been lucky in love herself.

Rick rose from his rocker and took one last look at the dramatic twilight world before him—rugged mountains, groves of towering live oak, vineyards as far as the eye could see. Maybe someday he'd bring Josie here. She struck him as the kind of person who'd appreciate it.

I will not hurt her.

The mantra was only in his head, but it came at him so hard it knocked his breath away. For seven years now, he'd been in hiding. Every moment had been about getting his life together, repairing the damage he'd done to the world and himself. For seven years, he hadn't dared trust himself with a woman. So why in God's name did he think he could be trusted with Josephine Sheehan?

When Rick reached down to collect Teeny's cup and saucer, the china rattled in his hand. He was trembling.

Josie's mother slammed down a wooden spoon and turned away from the stove. "Would you please put that dog out in the yard! And for God's sake, get that underwear away from him!"

Josie scrambled from a kitchen chair to catch Genghis before he wore out his welcome. Like he did most Sundays. She lunged, but missed, and the dog was off on another lap from kitchen to dining room to formal living room to family room to hallway. He flew back to the kitchen, ears blown back, delight shining in his little beady brown eyes, Fruit Of The Looms flopping from his jaws.

Josie's father shouted from the family room, his voice rising above the Giants game on TV. "If that damn dog keeps this up, I'll have to go to work commando!"

"Ohmigod," Beth said. "Not a pleasant visual." Josie's sister went back to tossing the salad.

Josie dropped to the floor and closed off access to the dining room. Genghis skidded to a stop and changed course, his claws flailing on the kitchen tile. Once he regained traction, he was greeted by Josie's brother, Donald, who had body-blocked the hallway in preparation for the dog's change of direction.

"Got him!" Donald laughed as Genghis lay down in defeat. "Give it up, dude," he said.

Josie felt a swell of pride as her dog dropped the drool-soaked boxer shorts on command. Maybe Bea had been wrong—those six weeks of dog-training classes had not, in fact, been a complete waste.

"Good boy." Donald ruffled Genghis's fur. "You really need to get this dog a haircut, Joze," he said, standing up. "The Tito Jackson look is so yesterday."

Beth chuckled. "And we all know how trendy Josie's gotten lately."

"I didn't think you noticed," Josie said sarcastically.

"Can't you girls spend an afternoon without all the snarky comments, for crying out loud?" Josie's mother bent down, rattled around in a cupboard, and continued talking, her reprimand muffled by clanking bakeware. "I don't think you're any better then you were as teenagers. Anyway, Josephine is looking stunning lately!"

Beth rolled her eyes. "Mom, did you want me to put the feta cheese on top of the salad or put it in a separate bowl on the table?"

Josie's mother straightened, turned, and stared at her youngest child in disbelief. "Your father has detested feta cheese all his life. Trust me when I tell you he hasn't changed his opinion and never will, not about feta, or politics, or the church, or sex, or anything else in this mortal coil." She picked up the wooden spoon and waved it around. "Men don't change. Mark my words."

Josie caught her sister's eye as she pushed herself up from the floor. "You know it's bad when she breaks out the Shakespeare," she whispered to Beth.

"I heard that. I'm not deaf." Ann Sheehan put the lid on the potatoes and leaned up against the kitchen counter, crossing her arms over her chest. She was still beautiful at sixty-three, Josie thought. The red in her hair had been washed out by silver, but it created a lovely frame for her smooth skin and gray eyes.

"Everything okay, Mom?" Josie walked to her mother and rubbed her upper arm. "Is everything all right with you and Dad?"

"I think I'll take Genghis for a walk." Donald grabbed the leash off the hook and snapped it to Genghis's collar.

"We're eating in twenty minutes!" Josie's mother called after Donald, then raked a hand through her hair with a sigh. "I hate the way you girls snap at each other. After thirty years, you think you could move on."

Josie patted her mom's shoulder. "Sorry. But everything else is okay?"

Her mother sighed. "I'm fine, Josie. Your father and I are fine. Perfectly fine. Everything's fine."

"Thank God there's one thing I can always count on to stay the same." Beth made this pronouncement as she walked out to place the wooden salad bowl in the center of the dining room table, then continued her thought when she returned. "It seems like everyone I know is getting divorced. I mean, it's not like I blame them. I think about divorcing Howie at least three times a day."

"Beth!" Josie's mother looked horrified. "Does Howie know how you feel?"

Beth shrugged, opening the pantry door and finding a small cut-glass serving bowl. "Oh, I change my mind by the time I get the kids to bed. Usually. I don't know . . ." She spooned the feta cheese into the bowl. "Maybe it isn't even about Howie. Maybe it's the kids.

Or maybe it's just me. All I know is sometimes I want to commit hara-kiri after a day of changing diapers and wiping off the kitchen counter." Beth looked up at her sister and mother, offering them a blank stare. "Seriously, I must wipe off the kitchen counter seventeen times a day. While cooking breakfast, then cleaning up after, then while preparing a mid-morning snack, then after, and the same process over and over again with lunch, snacks, dinner, snacks . . ."

As if on cue, Howard Fleischek popped his head into the kitchen. Josie was struck by what a sweet, open face her brother-in-law had. He walked over and planted a kiss on Beth's cheek.

"Anything I can do to help?"

Beth's head snapped back. "You're supposed to be watching Chloe and Calvin!"

"They're asleep on Grandpa's lap."

"What?" Beth stared at him in shock. "They're not supposed to nap now! They'll be off schedule! They won't go to sleep at bedtime if they're sleeping now!"

Howie's face fell and his voice sounded injured. "Jesus, Beth. They fell asleep on their grandfather's lap. It's a Norman Rockwell moment, not the Armageddon."

As tears welled in Beth's eyes, Ann intervened. "Let's go in and relax while the potatoes finish boiling," she told her son-in-law, guiding him out of the kitchen and into the family room. Howie glanced back at his wife, frowning.

"What's with you, Beth?" Josie returned to the table and sat down. She watched a wave of confusion wash over her sister's pretty face. Beth was four years younger. She was the Sheehan daughter who'd inherited the full monty of their mother's beauty, along with her auburn hair. When they were kids, Josie was always referred to as the "cute" one, while Beth was "such a beautiful girl."

Her sister collapsed into a chair with a groan. "I don't know what's wrong with me."

"This is all you ever wanted," Josie said to her gently. She stretched out her hand across the tabletop and Beth grabbed it. "You've got it all—a great husband, a beautiful house, healthy kids. You belong somewhere, Beth. You've got a wonderful life. There are a million women who would kill to have what you have."

Beth sniffled.

"Besides, if it's so horrible, why are you always on me for not being married with kids?"

Beth removed her hand from Josie's and wiped her eyes. "Because you're thirty-five and the only man in your life is a eunuch who eats underwear."

"And?"

"It's time to stop looking and start finding."

Josie laughed. She wanted to say something about Rick but she knew her sister wouldn't appreciate all that had happened with Mrs. Needleman, or the list. A person had to be somewhat whimsical to grasp the importance of those details. Beth wasn't that person. "So you're telling me to settle? Is that what I'm hearing?"

Beth's eyes brightened. "I'm telling you to get real, Josie. Lloyd was very nice. There was no reason it couldn't have worked out for the two of you."

Josie busted out with a guffaw. "Lloyd was a weenie, Beth. Plus, he wasn't the slightest bit interested in me. And he just flat-out hated Genghis. He wasn't the right man."

Beth rolled her eyes.

"But I do have some news . . ." Josie examined her

fingernails, pondering the best way to mention Rick Rousseau. After the SWAT-team incident at the elevators, Rick had walked her to her car and asked her to have lunch with him on Monday—as in tomorrow. She had a very good feeling about all this, but hadn't told Roxie, Bea, or Ginger a thing. What could she say? *"Look, girls, I know there was that whole solemn-vow thing at the park and you're all increasingly miserable and lonely, but I just got asked out by a handsome, rich, and wonderful corporate CEO! Try not to hate me!"*

"News?" Beth perked right up. "As in 'another boyfriend' kind of news?"

"He's not just another boyfriend." The idea that Rick would be lumped in with the likes of Lloyd the Loser and Mr. Chuck E. Cheese made Josie shudder.

"So?" Beth looked impatient. "When's he moving in?"

Josie pursed her lips with annoyance. "We have our first date tomorrow."

"So he'll wait till next week to move in."

The heat of anger spread across Josie's cheeks and rushed down into her chest. "Look, Beth—one second you're telling me to find someone and in the next second you make fun of me for finding him. You're worn down. I get it. But that doesn't mean you can be a total asshole to me, Howie, or anyone else. You need to get a grip before you really hurt someone."

Beth looked surprised by her older sister's outburst. She stared at her in silence.

"Besides, this man is different," Josie said, holding her chin high. "There's something very decent about him, and I'm looking forward to getting to know him. The least you could do is be happy for me."

Beth's mouth opened. After a moment she said,

"I've never heard you talk about a guy like that. You sound very sure."

"I do? Really?"

"Has he tasted your eggplant Parmesan yet?"

Josie sniffed, offended. "Why do you ask?"

"No reason."

"Right."

"Has he met Genghis?"

"He has."

Beth frowned. "Was this before or after he asked you out?"

"He happens to like my dog."

Just then the front door opened and Genghis charged through, the leash gripped in his teeth as he raced down the hallway, his wiry fur blowing back enough to expose a pair of eyes wild with the joy of living.

Beth looked from the dog to Josie. "You might want to hold on to this new guy—he sounds like one in a million."

"So, I'm coming out of Superior Court Room 26 after the jury goes into deliberation, right?" Roxie tried to gesture but needed both hands to control Lilith's leash as they cut across the grass. "And the dick brain walks right by me like I don't even exist! I couldn't believe it!"

"You had no business dating that dirty old bastard in the first place." Ginger dismissed the mention of Roxie's ex-lover with a flip of her wrist. "He was old enough to be your father."

"He's an egomaniacal criminal defense lawyer," Bea offered. "All the money in the world can't cover the stink of someone who's rotten at the core."

Josie nodded with conviction and touched Roxie's

arm. "No woman should have to put up with that kind of bullshit from a man. Every woman deserves better."

The women stopped walking and stared at Josie.

Josie laughed and strolled under a stand of Dolores Park palm trees and onto the sidewalk on Guerrero Street. She quickened her pace, hoping her friends' curiosity would wane. It didn't.

All three women raced to catch up.

"What was *that* all about?" Ginger said. Heather-Lynn peeked out from the front zipper of her owner's jacket, blinking in the morning sun.

Josie shrugged. "It's just something I heard some-one say the other day. I thought it was great."

"She was right on, whoever she was," Roxie said.

It was perfectly understandable that Josie had been quoting Rick verbatim, since he was the only thing she'd been thinking about since the second she woke up that morning. In just six hours, she'd be meeting him at John's Grill downtown. She felt her cheeks flush at the thought.

"So how are things with you, Josie?" Bea glanced over at her with a hint of smile on her lips. "You seem so happy lately. Bright eyed and bushy tailed. What's up?"

"Oh, nothing," she said. "It must be the meditation."

"You're taking medi*cation*? What are you on?" Gin-ger said, shocked.

"I said medi*tation*."

Ginger frowned. "But you hate meditation. You said it gives you hives."

"I've decided to develop my practice." Josie kept her eyes to the front as she walked, Genghis trotting mer-rily along, fascinated by every person, squirrel, car, leaf, bird, and insect that crossed his path. "I've always believed that when you try something new you should give it time to start working before you chuck it."

"Interesting," Bea said. "Which discipline? Calm abiding? Simple mantra? Empty mind?"

Josie swallowed hard, aware of her friends' attentive expressions. "Empty mind all the way," was her answer. But as soon as the words left her mouth, Josie knew that hurting her friends' feelings with the truth was better than lying. Anything was better than lying. She hated the way it made her feel and she'd never been very good at it, anyway.

Roxie sighed deeply, apparently absorbed by her own thoughts. "But for a guy with an AARP card, he sure has a great ass."

"What?" Ginger was outraged. "Roxie! Get a hold of yourself! Let the man go! He's a scumbag!"

"I know I'm just torturing myself." Roxie shook her head, embarrassed. "It's just so hard sometimes."

"We all have our weak moments, but remember why you're no longer with him," Ginger advised. "The man called you stupid. He called you a pack mule, for God's sake."

Josie knew that was only part of it. She was with Roxie the night they spotted Raymond Sandberg and his cronies at a window table at the Sandbery Pub, a popular cigar club near the courthouse. Raymond's back was to the door, and Roxie decided to surprise him. Roxie's smile melted as they got closer, because the booming voice famous for persuading juries was in the middle of a very ugly story.

"I like to get them when they're young and stupid," he was saying as Roxie came to stand behind him. One of the men at the table recognized Roxie and tried to get the loudmouthed defense attorney to shut up, but he

was on a roll. *"The girl I'm with now—the reporter— she's a pack mule. I just keep piling on the bullshit and she keeps coming back for more. If she could give a decent blow job, she'd be perfect."*

Raymond must have sensed something was wrong at that point, because his punch line got nothing but horrified stares. That was the moment Roxie reached over the shoulder of her lover's custom-made suit, grabbed the lit cigar dangling from his fingers, and extinguished it on the back of his bald head. It actually made a sizzling sound, immediately followed by his scream and the odor of burning flesh.

"I hate him," Roxie said, stomping her feet as she walked uphill. "So why do I keep thinking about him? Why does seeing him make me crazy like this?"

"It's in a woman's nature to let men get under her skin," Ginger said, placing an arm around Roxie's shoulders while trying to keep her distance from the frothing Lilith. "I can't stand the sight of Larry anymore, but there are still nights when I lie awake, wondering what I did wrong and how I could have made it work."

Bea hissed in disgust. "Larry was banging the boys' math tutor, Ginger. In your driveway. What was there to make work?"

The four women walked in silence for a moment. Suddenly, Ginger slapped Roxie on the back and held her head high. "But who cares? Right?" She waved her arm around. "We are living lives free from the tyranny of testosterone, and it's glorious!"

Everyone nodded, but apparently Josie's response wasn't enthusiastic enough for Ginger. "Am I right, Josie?"

Josie's eyes got big.

"Am I right?" It seemed Ginger's question wasn't rhetorical.

"Absolutely," Josie said, pasting a smile on her face. "In fact, I've gone the entire morning without a man."

They all laughed at that. When they reached the Starbucks a few minutes later and began to go their separate ways, Bea tapped Josie on the shoulder.

"The whole morning, huh?" she asked, a smile pushing her cheeks up into her eyes.

Josie nodded. "Every single minute of it has been testosterone-free."

Bea laughed. "Well, then. *Om* to you, my friend." She placed her palms together and bowed slightly.

Unsure how to respond, Josie clicked her tongue and gave Bea an enthusiastic thumbs-up. "Back at ya!"

Bea's laughter continued as she executed a flawless turn, Martina heeling at her left side, and headed toward her car.

CHAPTER 6

The knot in Josie's stomach grew tighter and heavier with each passing second. Rick was late. He'd called ten minutes ago and said he was on his way from a meeting in the financial district. He told her to mention his name to the maître d' and relax until he got there. So Josie sat tucked into a cozy two-person booth near the bar, her insides in shambles, her eyes glued to the door.

Maybe he was always late. Maybe it was a character flaw. But it could be worse, right? In the scheme of character flaws, it was even forgivable. But she worried—maybe it was one of those character flaws that seemed endearing at the start of a relationship but would bug the holy hell out of her a month down the line. She'd had a lot of experience with that sort of thing.

Then again, his lateness might be due to circumstances beyond his control. Maybe he'd been run over by a trolley car. Maybe he'd witnessed an old lady being robbed at gunpoint and then took off after the bad guys, tackled them, and was now giving his statement to the police while being hailed as a hero. Maybe he was . . . walking through the revolving door!

Oh, God. Rick smiled and chatted with the maître d' while he smoothed down his windblown hair. His eyes darted toward Josie as he began to stride his way to the booth. He was wearing a charcoal-gray suit with a tie of deep greens and blues. He had one hand tucked nonchalantly in his trousers pocket. The tip of his elaborate tattoo rose just above the collar of a crisp white dress shirt.

He was, no question, the hottest man she'd ever seen in her life. The knot that had been in Josie's stomach was now lodged in her throat.

Rick never took his eyes off her. His smile had mellowed as he walked, but it was most definitely still there. His gaze was locked on Josie like nothing and nobody existed but her.

Suddenly, he was at the table. He didn't sit down. Instead, he reached for Josie's hand and pulled her from the booth.

And he kissed her. No warning. Not a word of greeting. Rick simply pressed her body to him and put his mouth on hers. It wasn't the kind of kiss that would prompt the other patrons to suggest they get a room, but it sure wasn't a peck.

His lips were like hot silk. One of his hands gripped her upper arm and the other held her captive at the base of her spine. The pesky knot in her throat was history. It had been swept away by a tidal wave of sexual desire that just wiped out everything in its path. Including her brain function. She couldn't move. She was on fire. She'd been reduced to nothing but liquid lava lust. Rick's soft tongue opened her lips. She had forgotten how this felt. No, wait—she'd never *known* how this felt.

Josie let out a moan of wonder and delight, then the kiss was over. Rick slowly pulled away.

"I thought it would be nice to pick up where we left off," he said, grinning. "Hope that works for you."

Josie's pulse was crazy fast, and she felt dizzy. She stared into his sexy green eyes, mentally checking off another item on her list, because Rick Rousseau, pet supply magnate, was a sensational kisser.

"It works real good for me," Josie said, trying to remember where she was. A sudden jolt of panic hit her. She stole a peek at the door and amended her answer. "If no one's waiting to shoot me, that is."

Rick laughed. He guided her back to her seat and settled into the vintage leather booth across from her. "Again, I apologize for the gun incident." He rested his elbows on the table and leaned forward, lowering his voice. "My people are a little jumpy these days. I recently received a threat and I've had to bump up the security."

Josie felt her eyes bug out. "What kind of threat? Like a physical threat? What would somebody want from a pet-store owner?"

Rick smiled. "My thoughts exactly. And it's probably nothing. It's an unfortunate sign of the times, but most CEOs have their own private security detail. It goes with the job."

Josie frowned. "You have security with you all the time?"

"Most of the time, yes."

"So we've got an audience right now, as we speak?"

"Just Teeny. He's at the other end of the bar."

Josie lifted her chin to see over the booth. There he was, right next to the door, a large man teetering on a small stool. Teeny gave her a subtle nod and an equally low-key smile.

She was horrified. She looked back at Rick, who seemed unaffected. "You mean he saw us kissing?"

"Yes," Rick said, chuckling softly. "And the poor man's probably still in shock." Josie wanted to know what he meant by that but the waiter came by.

To say she enjoyed lunch with Rick would be the understatement of a lifetime. He was smart. His voice was gentle. He was handsome but didn't seem to be aware of his looks. It amazed Josie that she didn't feel intimidated by Rick, or worried that she was out of her league. He made her feel comfortable. He seemed to enjoy her company, too, and even stared at her approvingly when she walked back from a trip to the ladies' room. It made her blush.

While they ate, Rick asked Josie to tell him about her life. She was done by the time she finished her soup.

Rick then volunteered information about himself. He said he'd been a spoiled rich kid born and raised in Rhode Island. His mom died when he was at Yale getting his business degree. After school he wandered the globe trying to find himself.

"Did you?" Josie asked.

Rick's laugh was uncomfortable. "I lost myself instead," he said.

He told Josie that his only ambition back then was to attend as many wild parties as possible, and he managed to avoid a job for six years. With a stiff voice, he said, "When I was twenty-eight, I was in a serious motorcycle accident. It woke me up fast."

Josie could tell he was skipping over a few painful details, so she just listened, nodded, and enjoyed the view as he talked. It made sense that Rick was to the manor born, as the saying went. He had a noble jawline and an aristocratic nose. Perfect teeth. His eyes were friendly but keen, and framed in those extraordinary lashes. She decided he'd look at home in a smoking jacket, standing before the fireplace drinking champagne from fluted crystal. The image sent a shiver of excitement through her, since she was more accustomed to men in boxer shorts who drank beer from a can while watching cable.

"I came out here about six years ago, after my father passed away. He left me some money and property, which I liquidated, and I moved here to start my business." Rick smiled at Josie, and she saw a touch of embarrassment in his expression.

"So you started over."

"You could say that."

Josie sat back into the booth and cocked her head at Rick. It certainly was a lot to absorb. The fact that he had a colorful past wasn't a shock—most people in their mid-thirties had done some wild living. Except for her, of course.

She smiled at him. "So, let me see if I understand this fully."

"Okay." His left eye squinted.

Josie leaned forward. "You're a smoking-hot reformed bad boy with a fabulous sense of humor, his own corporate empire, and mad kissing skills."

Rick's lips parted but nothing came out.

"I'm sorry, but I'm not sure you're my type."

This time when Rick laughed it was full-bodied, loud, and genuine. Josie could see Teeny lean back on his stool to make sure all was well. She looked over the back of the high booth and gave him a salute.

"I like you, Josie," Rick said. "I'd like to do this again."

"Sure. Or maybe I could cook for you sometime."

His eyes widened. "Or I could cook for you."

With that, Josie silently checked off another item from the list. She was about to ask him how, in the name of all that was holy, he hadn't been snatched up by some woman a long time ago, but the waiter chose that moment to bring their check.

Rick asked if Josie had time to take a walk before she went back to the office. After a quick call to the newsroom and a check of her voice mail, she joined Rick on the sidewalk.

"Mind if we walk up Market Street to the Ferry?" he asked.

Josie grinned up at him, hoisted her bag on her shoulder, and said she'd love it.

It was a pleasant May afternoon in San Francisco, with a sharp breeze and a bright blue sky. Market Street was packed with the working crowd, everyone on a mission to get somewhere quick. By contrast, the two of them were simply taking a stroll.

It surprised Josie when Rick reached for her hand and gave her fingers a squeeze. She had to laugh— here she was, light-years away from listless Lloyd, strolling down the street hand in hand with a man custom-made for her by the universe, on a date so enjoyable it was scary. If it weren't for Teeny observing them from a distance of about twenty paces, the moment would have been perfect.

Bennett Cummings believed this was a private matter, a wrong that could be righted by his hand alone, with the utmost of discretion. The criminal justice system had failed him spectacularly. His civil case could be tied up in the courts for decades. He'd known for some time that if he wanted justice, he'd have to go out and get it himself.

He glanced over at his wife, sound asleep beside him despite the glare of his reading lamp. She'd aged so much in the last seven years. Grief would do that to a woman. He removed his eyeglasses, rubbed the bony bridge of his nose, and sighed. Years ago, he'd decided not to involve Julia in the details. It would be easier for her if she remained oblivious. Julia wanted it done, of course, but she had no interest in how he planned to do it. She'd suffered enough.

Cummings turned out the light and curled up on his side in the darkness, pulling the satin comforter close. He didn't know why he bothered. He hadn't slept well in seven years. And since that morning two weeks ago—when Margot slipped away from them forever—his mind had not stopped its weaving and churning, not for a second.

Richard Rousseau was no dullard. The young man was as thorough and cautious a businessman as his father had been, and Cummings had to admire how he'd gone about keeping himself and his assets safe. Both his hillside home in San Francisco and his wine country retreat were sewn up tight as a virgin—digital motion sensors, heat sensors, automatic lights, and a small army of highly trained security staff. Unfortunately, Cummings hadn't yet found a way to get to any of them—they were well paid, had great benefits, and were loyal to Rousseau. And because the whole Rousseau family was gone and the young man appeared to have no social life whatsoever, there was no one to use as leverage against him.

Rousseau also had taken advantage of every stateside loophole and every offshore safe haven that would protect his inheritance from civil litigation. In fact, Cummings had to admit that Rousseau had gone the route he himself would have taken had he found himself in a similar predicament—if he'd murdered an innocent girl, got off with a slap on the wrist, and fled across the country to hide like a coward.

Cummings shut his eyes tight, the rage pummeling his insides. He was well aware that Rousseau had "turned over a new leaf" as it was so blithely called, but it was for naught. A lifestyle of celibacy, good deeds, and hard work on the West Coast would never erase the devastation he'd left behind on the East Coast. A hundred anonymous charitable foundations and a thousand spiritual awakenings couldn't bring Margot back.

Cummings turned his face into the pillow and gritted his teeth against the pain. Rousseau had stolen his daughter's life and destroyed the lives of those who'd loved her. Rousseau had killed his baby girl, his precious, golden, happy daughter, the only child he'd ever had. The young man had suffered physically, but he'd survived. He'd healed. And it wasn't right. It would never be right until Rick Rousseau was dead.

Cummings allowed flashes of memory to pass through his mind. Holding Margot's hand on the beach. Teaching her how to drive a stick shift. Watching her walk down the center staircase that October morning, when he suddenly realized his little girl had grown into a beautiful woman, almost overnight.

Cummings cried freely. He knew Julia was so heavily medicated that he'd wake the dead before he'd ever wake her.

CHAPTER 7

Josie talked on the telephone headset while her fingers clicked at the keyboard. The leisurely lunch had left her short on time, and she had exactly twenty minutes to get her Tuesday obit feature to the city desk, and it was a big one. Paulie Patrakis, sixty-four, beloved owner of San Francisco's Olympia Kitchen restaurant, had keeled over that morning while taking a tray of baklava from the oven. Josie tried to remain objective during the telephone interview with Paulie's eldest daughter, but the truth was, news of Paulie's death hit her hard. He had been a kind and sweet man, and he made the best baklava this side of the Aegean Sea. Up until very recently, a triangle of his honey-oozing melt-in-the-mouth phyllo had been Josie's sensual thrill of choice. But that was before she met Rick.

"He worked hard and he loved his family and friends," Paulie's daughter, Issy, was saying. "He never needed anything fancy to be happy. He woke up every day happy."

Josie's fingers flew across the keys, relieved that she'd found her lead.

Just then, Ginger's head appeared in Josie's cubicle doorway. Bea's head popped over Ginger's shoulder soon after. Josie glanced their way, still typing, when they approached her desk. Since it looked like her friends were parking instead of merely passing by, Josie held up a finger to indicate she'd be a minute.

"Paulie Patrakis died," Josie mouthed to them.

Ginger's face fell. "Oh, how sad. He was such a nice man!" she whispered. Then panic hit her expression. "What am I going to do for baklava?"

Josie returned her attention to the phone call, trying to wrap up the interview. "Issy, I appreciate you taking the time to talk with me today. We received the photo, so we're set to run the article tomorrow. Again, I am so sorry for your family's loss. We'll all miss him." After a few more "thank you"s and "you're welcome"s, Josie ended the call.

"This is really depressing," Bea said. "He wasn't very old, was he?"

"Sixty-four," Josie said.

"I won't survive menopause," Ginger said, blinking. "I'm sure of it now."

Josie grinned at her friends. She couldn't help it. She was in love. Just forty minutes ago, she was in Rick's arms, his lips on hers and his hands in her hair, right in front of hundreds of tourists. And Teeny. He'd agreed to come to Josie's for dinner Thursday. The other reason she was smiling was because she knew something Bea and Ginger didn't—Issy Patrakis had just informed her that Paulie had had the decency to place the large tray of freshly baked desserts on the counter before he collapsed, and the restaurant was open for customers to pay their respects.

"You look awful perky for a girl who's just lost her baklava," Bea said, crossing her arms over her chest. "Been meditating again?"

"Give me twenty minutes," Josie said, holding up

her palm. "We'll get a taxi. Call Roxie and tell her to meet us there."

Ginger placed her fingers flat upon the center of her brow, intercepting the frown before it could cause any damage. "Where are we going?"

"Olympia Kitchen. Paulie's last tray." Josie turned back to her computer. "Meet me by the elevators in twenty."

Josie made her deadline with a whole minute and a half to spare, hitting the send key with that rush of accomplishment that always reminded her how much she loved her job. She'd managed to paint a picture of a person's life in under twenty minutes—father of six, grandfather of fourteen, a regular guy with an unusual work ethic, a restaurateur who for decades dished up spanikopita and moussaka with a story and a smile. Josie grabbed her purse and headed for the lobby, stopping by the city desk on the way.

"It's in," she told Kenny, the city editor. "I'll be on my cell if you have questions."

"Thanks, kid," he said, not even looking up from his computer screen.

She raced down the main aisle of the newsroom and waved to the receptionist as she reached the lobby, where Bea and Ginger waited. Just as Bea hit the down key, the receptionist's voice called, "Hold up, Josie!"

She spun around. Denise, the newsroom receptionist, was gesturing to a small figure perched on the edge of the lobby couch. "I just left you a voice mail—there's someone here to see you."

"You coming?" Ginger held the elevator door.

Josie stared at the gray-haired lady with the unmistakable piercing eyes. She hadn't spoken to Mrs.

Needleman since the day her husband's obit was published.

In ten years on the dead beat, Josie had known family members to stop by the newsroom for only two reasons—to retrieve a personal photo lent to the paper or to complain about an inaccuracy, and Josie knew she'd long ago returned the North Pole photo to Mrs. Needleman.

"Was there an error in the story?" Josie took a step toward the old lady, her stomach sinking at the thought of running a correction.

"Oh, no. It was lovely." Mrs. Needleman smiled up at her, as if there were nothing odd about her visit.

With an understanding nod, Josie remembered a third reason why someone might stop by—loneliness. Mothers who'd lost their soldier sons. Siblings or children of the deceased. Neighbors. Grieving friends. About three years ago, a widower arrived in the newsroom in a suit and fedora and offered to take Josie out for a beer, explaining that he needed to talk about his wife, and Josie had already proven to be an excellent listener.

Bea's voice sounded impatient. "I guess we'll just bring you back a piece."

"Make it two! Thanks!" Josie shrugged at her friends and sat down next to the widow, dropping her bag on the floor by her feet. "How have you been, Mrs. Needleman?"

"I'm getting along," she said in that wavering voice. "It's a little too quiet for my taste, of course. Ira was such a talker. He always had something to say to the TV people, especially that Bill O'Reilly fellow. He never cared for him."

Josie nodded.

"I hate to say it, but if Ira weren't already dead, last night's Fox News lineup would have done him in for sure."

"I see."

"I'm thinking about selling the house."

Josie glanced at Denise in a silent plea for help. The receptionist smiled.

"Conference Room A is open. Would you like me to send in coffee?"

Josie nodded at Denise in gratitude. "That would be fabulous."

"I'd prefer tea," Mrs. Needleman said, pushing herself from the sofa with little difficulty. She'd come to the paper dressed in a blue wool jumper over a beige polyester blouse tied in a bow at the neck. She had on pearl clip earrings, and carried a stiff patent leather bag with a huge snap closure, an accessory so ancient it had become ultrachic again. Her hair had been recently permed and styled. She wore an old-fashioned, flowery perfume. Josie watched her march toward Conference Room A as if she'd been there before, then flick the light switch inside the doorway. The fluorescent bulbs blinked on.

"This will be lovely." Mrs. Needleman motioned toward one of the swivel chairs. "Have a seat, Miss Sheehan, and you can tell me all about your progress over a nice cup of tea."

Gwen Anders slammed down the phone and paced in her office. Why had Rick distanced himself so? Was it Margot's death? Of course not. He'd started limiting his contact with Gwen long before that, as if he wanted their relationship to be less casual, less personal. She'd cried several months back when he told her, from that point forward, to make an appointment before stopping by the Celestial Pet offices. He said it was about keeping his corporation and his foundation separate. She knew it had nothing to do with any of that nonsense. He was trying to push her away. He was trying to avoid her.

Did he think she didn't notice? Did he think it was acceptable?

Gwen brought both hands to her chest and tried to steady her breathing. Now was not the time to panic. She couldn't allow emotions to cause her to be sloppy. Now was the time for precision and focus. With concentration, she could bring it all together. It was taking longer than she expected, but it could still go according to plan. If she could just hang on a little longer, Rick would wake up and see that Gwen was what he needed and wanted.

She'd done everything right. She'd been patient as a saint. Chaste as a nun. Discreet as a priest. Above reproach in her management of the foundation and in all her personal affairs. There was nothing—*nothing*—that Rick could find objectionable about her lifestyle. Even Teeny Worrell hadn't found anything on her. She'd made sure of it.

Gwen had been loyal to Rick in the extreme. She'd turned down several outstanding job offers and a very generous proposal from Rick's nemesis, Bennett Cummings, who was perpetually looking for a chink in Rick's armor. Of course she was above such bribery. She ignored Cummings.

Was it her looks?

Gwen smiled to herself, breathing easier now. She was flawless. That was the only word for it, really. Her weight and muscle tone were perfect. Her hair, skin, and teeth were in top form, radiant with health. Her clothing, shoes, bags, accessories—all impeccable.

Nothing overstated. Nothing that screamed money or status, which, of course, indicated she had both and needed neither.

So what had she missed in this equation? Why on earth had Rick Rousseau never once shown a flicker of interest, in all these years? She was well aware of his tragic past—in fact, it was an essential ingredient to his overall appeal—but *please*. The man was only flesh and blood. This couldn't go on much longer, could it?

Of course not. That would mean she'd miscalculated horribly. And Gwen Anders didn't miscalculate.

One by one, the senior managers of Celestial Pet Superstores rose from their buckwheat-hull sitting cushions and headed toward the rear entrance of the office building. It had been a productive staff meeting, as their outdoor gatherings under the ginkgo tree usually were. On the day's agenda were revising inventory, postponing construction plans for their fifteenth store, and brainstorming on whether they should offer a line of in-house organic pet care products. Rick also approved the month's broadcast, print, Internet, and direct-mail marketing plans and okayed a jump in the warehouse-to-retail delivery budget. As a last order of business, Rick agreed they had no choice but to fire a groomer at the newest store, a young woman whose lack of enthusiasm had drawn dozens of customer complaints. Rick's policy was to personally approve all employee firings, at all levels.

Only Teeny remained under the shade of the ginkgo tree. Rick watched him pile several of the cushions together to create a supersized chaise longue for himself. He stretched out his legs with a groan. "Bad news," Teeny said, folding his hands on his solid belly. "Cummings leased a private jet last week in Providence—put it on twenty-four-seven retainer."

Rick nodded. "He's getting sloppy."

"Or I've got friends in all the right places." Teeny smiled big.

"That goes without saying." Rick closed his laptop and leaned his back against the tree trunk. He looked up into the canopy of bright green, fan-shaped leaves and the pale blue sky beyond. After lunch with Josie, he'd changed out of his suit and into his real career wardrobe—shorts and a T-shirt. He took a deep breath, knowing that something about Teeny's news bothered him.

"If it was that easy to find out about the jet, it could just be a decoy."

Teeny grunted. "I wouldn't put it past our pal Benny, but I think it's for real. In my opinion, he's getting ready to make a visit to Shaky Town."

Rick smiled, remembering how hard it had been to persuade Teeny to move cross-country with him. He'd had to provide studies showing the statistical improbability of the big one hitting San Francisco within the next decade.

Teeny had studied the pros and cons of the move in the way he conducted all his business—concerns were based on hard facts and voiced in a no-frills fashion. "There's a flood, you camp out on the roof," he'd explained to Rick, counting off on his fingers for effect. "There's a hurricane, you evacuate as soon as the word comes down. There's a tornado, you go to the basement. But an earthquake? Shit, man, unless I learn to levitate, it's Barney Rubble time for my ass."

"What else is he up to?" Rick asked. He lowered his gaze to his friend. The truth was that Teeny had made the transition to San Francisco just fine. His right-hand man didn't talk much about his private life, but Rick knew Teeny had a significant other, and when he wasn't working, Teeny was with his lover in the Castro District. Teeny didn't hide the fact he was gay. He didn't advertise it, either. It was simply who he was. Rick was with Teeny that day in physical therapy, when his friend decided life was too precious to pretend to be something he wasn't. Soon after, he came out to his family and former teammates at Syracuse, and the world kept spinning.

"Cummings is doing his usual," Teeny said. "His Yalie pals. His broker. Golf at the club. Nothing much else—his semiretirement doesn't look all that semi to me." He cocked his head and looked at Rick with concern. "He hasn't contacted anyone in the freelance violence industry, if that's what you're getting at. I don't think he's planning to outsource this errand. It's personal."

Rick nodded.

"So if flight plans are filed for that jet, it means the man's decided to make good on his promise to fuck you up."

"Thanks, Teen. Keep me informed."

"Always do."

They sat under the tree for a few moments before either spoke. Rick let his eyelids slide shut. Eventually, Teeny cleared his throat. "We need to talk about Miss Sheehan."

Rick's eyes popped open. "Did you find something on her?"

Teeny's burst of laughter sent the birds scattering. "Not only did I not find anything on her, I didn't even know women like her *existed* anymore."

Rick rolled his head from side to side, hiding his smile as he stretched his neck muscles. "How so?"

"She's boring, is what I'm saying. Excellent work-performance reviews. No traffic citations, parking tickets, or library fines. No freaky shit on the Internet. No maxed-out credit. She spends most of her time at work, at home with her silly-looking dog, or with three women friends from the newspaper. None of them have lives so they hang out together at the dog park three to four times a week. It's sort of pathetic."

Rick chuckled.

"Your girl hasn't dated in a while. There's only the occasional movie or dinner out with friends and time with her family. She's enrolled in a yoga class at her gym, but her attendance is sporadic."

"Anything new on the Sheehans?"

"Nothing. No freaks. No fakes. And certainly no connection of any kind with Bennett Cummings. As far as I can tell, they're just as mind-numbingly normal as she is. And we're about done with all the old boyfriends."

"Anything interesting?"

Teeny hissed, shaking his head. "Aside from the fact that I've never seen a more pitiful group of slacker white boys in my life, they're pretty unremarkable. One dude has defaulted on his student loans. Another had a juvenile pot charge. One guy got arrested in some kind of militant environmental protest. But I'll tell you what—" Teeny's eyebrows arched high on his scarred forehead.

Rick waited. "What?"

"None of these guys lasted long, man. A lot of them moved in with her, but they didn't stay. Maybe she's lousy in bed."

It was Rick's turn to laugh. From what he could tell from those lunch-break kisses, whatever Josie Sheehan might lack in finesse would be more than made up for by her enthusiasm. Her soft skin was on fire when he touched her. Her pretty little mouth had sought out his with real hunger. Those sighs she made were incredibly hot.

"She'd be a quick study with the right teacher," Rick said.

Teeny shrugged. "Hey, man, this is your area of expertise, not mine."

Was it? Rick squinted, staring up at the sunshine punching through the ginkgo leaves. It was true that women had once been his specialty, but everything was different now.

When he thought back on those days, a sick knot of regret twisted in Rick's gut. The truth was that in the seven years between graduation and the accident, women took up most of his waking hours. If he'd had a job back then, he might have considered his pursuit of women an avocation. But because he'd had the freedom to live off his ample trust fund without the annoyance of actual work, womanizing became his profession, the outlet for all he learned getting his business degree from Yale. Rick had traveled the world looking for new opportunities—with women. Every night he observed the market. He made new acquisitions at regular intervals, only to plunder their natural resources and dump them back on the open marketplace in a matter of hours, days, weeks, or months, according to his whim, and at a much reduced value.

That was a long time ago. Now his vocation was Celestial Pet Superstores, Inc., and his avocation was an anonymous charitable foundation that paid the bills of uninsured or underinsured head injury patients. Women were no longer his area of expertise. They didn't interest him. They didn't even exist for him.

Until Josie.

And he was well aware that the free-market exploitation approach was not only wrong for Josephine Sheehan, it had been wrong for Margot Cummings and every other woman he'd ever messed with. In fact, it was just plain wrong—in a huge, karmic kind of way. He knew if he wanted something good with Josie, he'd have to do everything right, every step of the way. Besides, he owed it to Josie, Margot, all women everywhere, and himself.

His plan was to get to know her. He'd take his time with her, moving as slowly as possible. He'd make sure she felt comfortable and knew she was appreciated. Only then would he bring up the possibility of sex.

"I'm going to her place for dinner Thursday," Rick said, still looking up at the leaves,

Teeny said nothing.

"She's cooking for me. Seven o'clock."

Teeny still said nothing.

Rick returned his gaze to his friend, whose face was a mask of equal parts horror and hilarity.

"And you don't have to sit outside her apartment waiting for me, Teeny. I'll be fine."

Teeny's eyes widened, but he still had no reply.

"She said she'd like to make me eggplant Parmesan."

Apparently, Teeny had been holding in a huge guffaw for as long as humanly possible. When it finally exploded from him, he rolled off his organic buckwheat-hull cushions and flopped over in the grass, clutching his sides.

Rick could appreciate the irony. He'd instituted a no-alcohol, no-drugs, no-woman-no-way policy seven years ago, and had never veered from its confines. Not once. No matter how tempting the temptation. Even

Gwen Anders, the tall, cool, blond bombshell executive director of his foundation, didn't distract him. He'd lost count of her subtle attempts at seduction over the years, though he'd noticed an uptick in their frequency lately. In fact, she'd called him three times that morning alone, on foundation business she would need to discuss in person, no doubt.

So what had happened to Rick's resolve? Apparently, it was no match for Josie Sheehan and her goofy dog and her eggplant Parmesan. So as Rick watched Teeny roll in the grass laughing so hard he was crying, he couldn't really blame him. The whole thing must look pretty comical.

It didn't feel like a joke, though. It felt good. It felt right.

"My progress?" Josie plopped into one of the conference room chairs and stared at Mrs. Needleman. "Progress with what?"

Gloria Needleman folded her hands primly in her lap, studying the framed collection of the *Herald*'s historic front pages lined along the conference room walls—the 1906 San Francisco earthquake, Hiroshima and Nagasaki, the Bay of Pigs, Watergate, 9/11.

"With love, of course—the only thing that will ever save us." Mrs. Needleman moved her gaze from the greatest horrors of history to Josie's eyes, and Josie knew she couldn't fool this woman if she tried. Gloria Needleman was beyond eccentric, beyond being an odd bird. The woman had an intense otherworldly vibe. Josie wondered if it was the result of a long and interesting life, or if she'd been born that way.

Regardless, Josie had a feeling that Ira Needleman's achievements had been made possible by his wife's unusual strength.

Denise the receptionist entered the room, delivered the tea, and promptly left. Josie noticed how Mrs. Needleman turned up her nose at the refreshment's presentation.

The old woman dunked her tea bag, waiting for Josie to answer her.

"Umm, Mrs. Needleman?" Josie cleared her throat.

"Please call me Gloria."

"And I'm Josie."

"Of course you are."

"Umm, Gloria?" Josie took a deep breath. "Have you done this sort of thing before?"

The woman's eyes brightened with a devilish gleam. "Do you mean have I ever been forced to drink off-brand tea in a cheap Styrofoam cup?"

Josie laughed, surprised by the caustic barb. Bea would love this lady. "Actually," she said, "I was referring to the love-life thing. The list. The universe. Your matchmaking guidance. Do you do this often?"

Gloria shrugged and paused for dramatic effect. "I've dabbled," she said, then took a tiny sip of tea. "And I've had some success. I'm guessing by your response that it's working for you?"

"My God!" Josie jumped up and shut the conference room door. She raced back to her chair, lowered her voice, and leaned forward on her arms. "I did the list, like you said, and a half hour later, *bam*! There he was! And I'm talking everything on my list—well, the stuff I can tell at this point anyway—intelligence, humor, kindness, and, you know . . ." She wasn't sure how to convey the concept of "hot as hell" to a great-grandmother.

"A real hunk-a-hunk of burnin' love?"

Josie smiled. The old Elvis Presley lyric was hokey, but accurate. "You got it," she answered.

"Lovely," Gloria said, clapping her hands together in glee.

"He's coming to my house for dinner Thursday night."

"Excellent." Gloria took a cautious sip of her dark brown drink, then flicked her tongue at the bitterness. "What will you be preparing?"

"Eggplant Parmesan."

Gloria reached out toward Josie with both palms up, as if she were begging. "Why in God's name would you want to make that? Is the man a vegetarian?"

"Uh, no." In fact, Rick had ordered a huge steak at lunch. But Josie was baffled as to how her signature dish had suddenly lost all its street cred.

"I meant no offense," Gloria said. "It's certainly your choice what to serve. There are more significant things to worry about."

Josie cocked her head in curiosity. "Such as?"

Gloria's eyes narrowed, and Josie heard the old woman sigh deeply. "I came here today because I have something very important to tell you."

Josie sat up straight.

"I have an overwhelming sense that the young man who's recently entered your life is in some kind of danger."

"What?" Josie scooted her chair even closer and got a heady whiff of Gloria's perfume, which made her slightly dizzy. "Hey, let's back up—how did you even know I had a young man?"

"That's not especially important. What is important is that you understand what I'm telling you."

Josie frowned. She held the old woman's gaze and realized she was absolutely dead serious. "He has a lot of security guards around him," Josie said, hesitantly. "He says it's standard for today's corporate world. But what would make you think he's in *danger*? You don't even know him!"

Just then, Gloria's eyes closed. Josie held her breath. What was the protocol when an eighty-four-year-old woman went perfectly still and ceased moving? CPR? The Heimlich maneuver? A good pinch?

Gloria raised an arm and held up a pale and crinkled palm as if to keep Josie at a distance, but otherwise, she remained utterly still. Several long seconds went by. Josie took a sip of her tea. She couldn't help but think how delicious a slice of Paulie's baklava would taste right at that moment.

Josie worried about Rick. Was he in trouble? Was all the security about something other than work? How much did she really know about him, anyway?

"Your lover is a complicated man, Josie." Gloria opened her eyes to reveal a ferocity that seemed out of place on such an old face. "I believe he's going to need your understanding and forgiveness, and soon. I am telling you this so you can prepare yourself."

Josie frowned. "He's not my *lover,* Gloria. We just met!"

The old woman shrugged. "Thursday will be here before you know it."

Josie's mouth fell open. In a matter of minutes, Mrs. Needleman had belittled her eggplant, made her new boyfriend sound shady, and basically accused her of being a slut! She wouldn't even take that kind of crap from Beth—or Bea, Ginger, and Roxie! Josie sniffed and sat up straighter. "Pardon me, but you were the one who told me to be choosy—don't you think I should at least wait until the third date before I jump in the sack with him?"

Gloria giggled, her bony shoulders rising and falling under her polyester shoulder pads.

Josie leaned back in her chair, thinking that among the strangest experiences of her life, this conversation with Mrs. Needleman was right up there. Gloria was either crazy, putting on an act to get attention, or she had psychic powers of some kind. Maybe she was a witch. Or a guardian angel. Or an octogenarian vampire slayer. Josie crossed her arms over her chest and considered the giggling old woman, and realized that the only thing that mattered was what she'd said about Rick.

"All right, let's say I accept your claim that my lover—I mean, Rick—is in danger. Is there anything I should warn him about?"

Gloria stopped giggling the instant Josie posed her question. She shook her head sadly and reached out to touch one of Josie's folded arms. "He already knows, dear girl, and it's a heavy burden, indeed."

Bennett found her in the usual place. She'd moved the Queen Anne sitting chair to face the picture window, where she sat staring over the sloping grounds and out into the Newport Harbor. Every day, his wife moved the damn chair to the window. Every night, the maid moved it back beside the antique tea table. Why the hell bother? Bennett didn't know why anyone bothered with anything around here anymore—meals, dusting, flowers. It seemed as pointless as tending to a dollhouse.

He walked across the parquet floor to Julia, his feet feeling like blocks of cement. He wondered if this sense of dread was similar to how families of Alzheimer's patients felt—you went to your loved one, but you weren't sure they'd be there. You spoke to them, but you didn't know how much they heard. Julia wasn't whole anymore. Yes, her brain was intact, but her spirit was gone. Rick Rousseau had stolen that, too.

Bennett leaned down and kissed the top of his wife's head. Back when they'd met in school, Julia's hair had been a glory to behold, pale yellow waves that reflected light like a mirror. She was a beauty then. Tiny chiseled nose and pale eyes, a full mouth and small white teeth. She had elegant hands, long, slim legs, and firm breasts. She was from a good New England family, like his own, and possessed the social ease that would be required as the wife of a prominent industrialist. When the time came, she gave him a daughter. The child was as beautiful as her mother and as smart as her father.

Bennett had always maintained that, as parents, they'd done everything right. Julia stayed at home with their child, while Bennett built his company. Margot was loved. She was given freedom and opportunity. She had dance and piano and French lessons. She went to the most exclusive private schools and summer camps. She was given a brand-new red convertible BMW when she turned sixteen. A Yale education. A Fifth Avenue wardrobe.

But Bennett wasn't entirely delusional. He noticed early on that his daughter hadn't inherited all she'd need to be successful in life. She lacked an inner strength. She chafed at discipline. She didn't know the meaning of restraint. And so when she had an abortion at nineteen, it was a huge disappointment to Bennett, but not exactly a surprise. Up until the night of the accident, Margot's life continued to be an orgy of excess—too many parties, too many drugs, too many bad boys.

And Rick Rousseau was the worst of the worst. He'd gotten Margot pregnant at nineteen, and he'd killed her at twenty-eight.

Without taking her eyes from the ocean, Julia reached up and over her chest to pat Bennett's hand where it lay on her shoulder. She was silent.

"It's time," he said, staring out the window with her, searching for that elusive point in the distance that had fascinated her so, day after day, month after month, year after year. "I have everything in place."

Julia squeezed his hand in comprehension.

"He must be held accountable, darling," Bennett whispered.

Julia nodded, her hair brushing the top of his hand.

"Tell me again this is what you want."

Very slowly, Julia turned her body away from the sea and toward her husband. She raised her face to him. Her eyes were vacant. Deep crevices framed her mouth. Flesh hung from her once dramatic cheekbones. "Kill him," she said, the lack of expression on her face so chilling that Bennett took a step back. "Do it for me."

Bennett stifled a gasp. His beautiful wife was a hideous stranger to him now—eaten away by hate and loss. How had he let this happen? How had he failed his precious girls so miserably, so totally? How had he—a brilliant, powerful, respected man—let a pretty-boy punk like Rick Rousseau ruin their lives?

"I'm going to get caught," he said to her, matter-of-factly. "I fully expect to spend the rest of my life in prison."

Julia shrugged, an act that seemed to drain all the

strength from her thin body. She turned away from him and toward the sea.

Bennett knew he'd been dismissed. He retreated from the sitting room, the sound of his footsteps echoing through his empty house, the sound of his heart thudding inside his empty shell.

He would do what had to be done, though in truth, there was no passion in him—only exhaustion and a dull sense of duty.

Rick found her place with no trouble. She lived on the second floor of a white stucco apartment building in the Mission District, on a narrow one-way street off Seventeenth. Rick waved at Teeny as his friend pulled his Lexus from the curb with a shake of his head. He wondered how long Teeny would be entertained with how Rick had exchanged his solitude for the companionship of Josie Sheehan. He decided it could be a while.

Rick stopped on the sidewalk and looked up, admiring how flowers and greenery spilled from planters on Josie's small wrought-iron balcony. He glanced at the spring bouquet he held in his hand, hoping it didn't pale in comparison.

"Rhrrrr . . . umph."

The sound came from the balcony. Rick looked up again, seeing a bearded snout poke through the balcony railings. Two beady brown eyes zeroed in on him down on the sidewalk.

"Genghis, my man." Rick noticed that the dog had yet to benefit from any groomings, free or otherwise.

The Labradoodle's tongue lolled over his bottom lip and his tail began twirling like a hairy ceiling fan. *"Woomph,"* the dog said. *"Woomph. Woomph. Woomph!"*

Josie arrived at the set of French doors and made kissy sounds to get her dog to come inside. Rick saw how she'd pulled up her hair and clipped it onto the back of her head, with errant spirals of curls falling down around her face. She looked so pretty, in such an unassuming way. She was nothing like the women he'd pursued back in the day, and nothing like the women who continued to pursue him. She was sweet and funny and down-to-earth. There was something almost innocent about her. He knew he'd been right that evening at the ranch, when he'd told Teeny there was something wholesome about his feelings toward this woman.

"Get in here, you beast," she snapped.

"I'm coming as fast as I can," Rick replied, laughing at the shocked look on her face and how she blushed outrageously.

"Oh, my God! Not you! You're not a beast . . . are you?" Josie looked as flustered as she sounded. "You're early! How long have you been down there?"

"Long enough to know I'd rather be up there with you."

Josie scrunched her lips, clearly trying to tame an all-out, full-mouth smile of delight. She managed to reach the railing before her grin broke loose.

"What's up, Juliet?" Rick asked.

Josie wrapped her fingers around the iron rail and beamed down on him. Her round cheeks blazed and her eyes sparkled.

"Wooomph," Genghis said, rising on his back legs and plopping his paws on the rail.

"The door's open," she said, running inside.

Josie greeted Rick at the top of the stairs a moment later. She'd let down her hair, and it fell in soft curls at her shoulders. She was wearing a pair of jeans and a cute pink top that showed just a hint of freckled cleavage. She looked soft and round and he was drowning in the need to plant his face in the crook of her neck and sink his fingers into her flesh. But he thought better of it. It was an odd feeling, second-guessing himself like that. He couldn't remember the last time he'd ever done anything with a woman except exactly what he wanted, exactly when he wanted, for as long as he'd wanted. The last time he'd been this conflicted had to have been before puberty.

A large brown fur ball zoomed around the corner, sailed through the air, and body-slammed him. Rick nearly fell on his ass from the impact, which surely would have crushed the flowers he held behind his back.

"Sit!" Josie commanded. Genghis removed his paws from Rick's chest and assumed the position, though his entire body wiggled with excitement.

Josie wrapped her hand around the dog's collar and looked up at Rick, clearly embarrassed. "I'm very sorry. We're still working on polite greetings."

Rick laughed at the understatement, running his free hand over the front of his disheveled shirt, feeling for rips and missing buttons. Finding none, he smiled at her. "I have to admit it's been a while since I've been molested like that."

Josie grimaced.

"Maybe next time it can be you instead of your dog?" Rick whipped the bouquet from behind his back and held it out to her. "These are for you, Josephine Sheehan," he said, offering up the florist's creation. He'd asked for something seasonal and simple, yet pretty. He hoped it fit the bill.

"They're gorgeous!" Josie grabbed the bouquet with both hands and buried her nose in the fragrance—

exactly the way he longed to inhale the hills and valleys of her flesh. She rose on her tiptoes and planted a soft kiss on his cheek. "That was really sweet of you. Come on in."

Before he could take a step, Josie pointed sternly to the floor and ordered Genghis to lie down. Surprisingly, he did as commanded, for about three seconds.

Rick followed Josie into the apartment. He knew he should have used those first moments to respectfully look around her living room. Instead, he rudely ogled her round ass as she hustled into the kitchen for a vase. She had a firm, full bottom and thighs that looked like they'd be a handful of solid heaven.

When she turned the corner, taking her ass with her, Rick had no choice but to glance around the place. It wasn't huge, but it made a statement, and she'd obviously put a lot of thought into how it looked. The wood floors were polished to a sheen. The high ceiling was a dazzling white. And the far wall was the color of a ripe plum, so purple it was almost black. The other walls were a pale green, and there were plants, and lots of colorful artwork and pillows throughout an otherwise neutral room.

"This is a nice place. Did you paint it yourself?"

"Absolutely," she replied from the kitchen. "Do you like it? Most people find the color a little over-the-top."

"Oooh-whooaaaahhh!" Rick yelped, the sudden jab to his crotch catching him by surprise. With nose firmly in place, Genghis began snuffling at his trousers with unabashed enthusiasm.

"So you don't really like it, then?" Josie rounded the doorway with the flowers in a vase, a cute little frown marring her forehead.

Rick decided to cut Genghis some slack. He discreetly pushed the dog to the side of his leg so Josie wouldn't see his infraction. "No, no. I do like it. It's really different."

"Right. That's what my sister, Beth, said, and I *know* she hated it." Josie placed the flowers on the coffee table and sat on the couch.

Rick joined her, Genghis on his heels. As soon as Rick reached the sofa cushions, Genghis plunged his nose into his lap again.

"No! Down!" The dog withdrew his snout, crawled under the coffee table, and peered up at them guiltily. Josie shook her head and groaned. "I know he's obnoxious, and I apologize. I'm working on it. He had six introduction obedience classes, but I haven't been very consistent since, and I think he's regressing."

Rick chuckled, afraid to imagine the dog's interest in crotches prior to obedience training. "You know, Celestial Pet offers convenient classes right in the store. We have a staff of professional dog trainers. I'd be happy to set something up for you."

Josie nodded. "Oh, I know! They're great! Genghis graduated from the Level 1 program in your Daly City store."

Rick tried to smile, making a mental note to check into the standards of the obedience program, chainwide. In fact, he thought it might even be time to hire that animal behaviorist consultant everyone had been raving about. Rick took a quick glance down at Genghis, still peering up from beneath the coffee table.

"Beth said that if you can tolerate my dog, you're a keeper."

He laughed, thinking maybe Beth was on to something. "So you told your sister about me?"

Josie shrugged, the blush returning to her cheeks.

She had such creamy skin on her face and throat, and he allowed himself to study the contours of her neck and shoulders and collarbones. He stopped his eyes from continuing southward.

"Would you like to know what I told her?"

When Rick looked up, he found that a smile touched Josie's lips. "Sure," he said.

"I told her you were special, that there was something really decent about you."

Rick felt his body flinch. *Decent?* As unexpected as it was unwanted, the image of Margot flooded his mind, the gray face and skeleton-thin body. She looked dead even as the machines continued to beep and whir, doing what had to be done to keep her alive. Margot had ceased to be long before her body gave out. She'd vanished that June night seven years ago, after Rick grabbed her by the waist and plopped her down on the back of his Harley, insisting they leave the party together and go for a wild ride in the rain. They'd laughed and laughed as he spread her legs apart to straddle the bike. She'd kissed him hungrily and told him he could wear the only helmet—she didn't want to mess up her hair. Rick felt her breasts and belly push up against his back as he revved up the Harley engine. He put the bike in gear and she playfully bit him on the back of the neck. It was reckless. Crazy. Wrong. The pot and beer and cocaine coursed through him, along with the thrill of the hunt. There wasn't a single thing that was decent about that night in the Rhode Island rain. There wasn't a single decent thing inside his soul.

"Are you hungry, Rick?"

Josie's voice brought him back to the present, and the sight of her sweet and trusting face flooded him with conflict. He wanted to warn her to stay away from him. He wanted to take her to bed. Maybe Teeny had been right . . .

"Would you like a glass of wine?"

"No, thank you. I don't drink."

"Oh. Okay." Josie nodded.

Rick waited to see the comprehension spread over her face, laced as it usually was with pity or judgment. He saw neither. Instead she gave him a sweet smile and placed her satiny hand over his. "Then let's get some ginger ale and you can help me with dinner."

Before she could get up, he pulled her tight into his arms, feeling a hot rush of emotion welling up in him, nearly choking him. He squeezed her supple body. She squeezed him back. He held on for dear life.

Dear life—what a perfect description that was. Life was a treasure, and he'd thrown his away seven years before, only to spend every second of every day since trying to find it again, rebuild it from the inside out. And up until he met Josie, he was certain a woman could never fit into his new existence.

Rick felt Josie's warm breath against his ear as he squeezed her tight. He inhaled her hair and skin—so fresh and sweet.

"Is something wrong?" Josie's question came out in a gentle whisper. "Are you okay?" She pressed her body flush against his.

"I'm good," Rick croaked, determined not to crumble in her arms ten minutes into their date. He steeled himself. "I sure like the way you feel."

She giggled, and her flesh rubbed against him. "You feel pretty incredible, too. I noticed that when you kissed me Monday."

With a steadying breath, Rick relaxed his grip on Josie and gently pushed her away. He looked into pretty gray eyes clouded with concern. "I've always loved eggplant Parmesan," he said, obviously changing the subject.

One of Josie's eyebrows shot high on her forehead. "Seriously?"

"Absolutely."

While they'd been talking, Genghis had wandered off. He chose that moment to return, and dropped something in Rick's lap. It landed with a thud.

It took Rick a full second to get his brain to cooperate with his eyes, because he swore that balanced across his left thigh was a largish phallus, and it wasn't his. It was rubbery. And it had an off/on switch.

He heard Josie gasp. "Oh, my God," she whispered. "Oh, no." She scrambled for it, but Rick snatched it away and held it beyond her reach. Josie fell across his lap, clawing the air to get it from him.

Rick tried his best not to laugh. He held the dildo into the light and examined it, while Genghis came closer, his tail whirring and flipping and his beady eyes lit with delight. Clearly, the dog was interested in playing fetch—with the penis.

"I thought you got all your dog toys at Celestial Pet," Rick said, snickering.

"I'm going to die now." She buried her face in Rick's thigh.

"I'm pretty sure this gem was never in our inventory. I would have remembered."

Genghis jumped straight into the air and snatched the dildo from Rick's hand. His tooth must have flipped the power switch because as the dog ran off with the sex toy, it began to vibrate and wiggle in his jaws. The crazed look in his eye revealed just how much fun he was having.

Josie suddenly jumped to her feet and raced after her dog. "Drop it, dammit!" she called out. "Leave it! No! Drop it! Bad dog!" Then she let loose with a string of curses Rick hoped to hell hadn't been part of his store's canine obedience curriculum, all while the dog looked like he was having the time of his life.

At that point, Rick decided the hell with it, and allowed himself to laugh. He laughed harder than he'd laughed in seven years. Tears formed in his eyes as he watched the possessed, penis-chomping Labradoodle and his curly-headed owner racing in circles around the living room.

Eventually, Josie slowed down and slapped her hands to her thighs in frustration. "I'm going to wring your freakin' neck, you damn doodle brain!"

Rick laughed some more.

"Don't just sit there—do something!" Josie screamed, taking off again.

He didn't have to be asked twice. As soon as Genghis approached his next loop past the coffee table, Rick dived for him, grabbing him around his middle. He rolled to the floor with the dog cradled in his arms, a tackle so smooth that Teeny would have been proud. Josie tried to stop in time but she crashed into both of them, landing with a thump next to Rick on the rug. Maybe he was laughing too hard to concentrate, but Genghis wiggled from his grip, taking the dildo with him. Josie let her face flop down into the rug with a loud groan of defeat.

"I've never been so mortified in my life," she mumbled into the carpet.

Rick's hand found the small of her back. He placed his palm there, still laughing, as the realization washed over him—he was happy. Being with Josie made him happy. *This must be what it feels like to be happy.*

She rolled her head slightly to the side, and one of her eyes peered out from behind a curtain of curls. A tiny tear began to take a crooked path from the corner of her eye across her freckled nose.

"Oh, Josie, hey, it's no big deal."

She nodded, then sniffed. "Sure. Whatever. You should probably go now."

Rick leaned in, putting his face less than an inch from hers. He could smell her sweet breath. He pushed the curls away from her cheek, and when that little tear fell off the tip of her nose, he caught it in his lips.

"Please don't be embarrassed," he said.

She sniffed again. "Right. This happens all the time, I'm sure. Just your basic get-to-know-you kind of date. Nothing to be embarrassed about."

Rick's hand returned to the small of her back. He felt her arch into his touch. He felt the heat of her skin through her flimsy pink top. Without weighing the pros and cons of a single damn thing, he slipped his hand up under her blouse so that he could feel her skin on his. She let go with one of her little moans. He shoved his hand lower, into the waistband of her jeans, and laid his palm against her ass.

"Rick?"

He flipped her over. He got on top of her. She was opening her arms and opening her thighs to welcome him. He put his mouth on hers and she opened for him there, as well. God, he'd never felt a woman so ripe in his life. He'd never felt this kind of hot rush of desire—with all the trimmings. He liked her. He cared about her. He didn't want to hurt her.

He dragged his lips from hers. "Josie, oh, shit, I'm trying to be decent. I really am."

In response, one of her hands slapped down on his ass and her calves imprisoned his hips. "If you're any kind of gentleman, you'll keep kissing me." Then she grabbed his hair and yanked him back down again.

He got lost in it—the hot smell of her skin and the silky slide of her tongue and the way his body was being swallowed by the need to connect with her. He slipped his arms under her shoulders and rolled with her until he was on his back. She moved with him effortlessly.

A peculiar sound penetrated the sexual fog in his brain. Josie obviously heard it, too, because she went still in his arms. She took her mouth off his and straightened up, the shift in her weight causing her pelvis to grind into his. There was no way on earth Josie wouldn't notice the huge erection thrusting into her.

"Oh, this is just great," she said, putting her hands on her hips as she looked past Rick's head. The sound continued, a muffled, squeaky, back-and-forth sawing kind of noise.

"Err-eee-err-ee, grerr-eee-grerr-ee. Eng, eng, eng."

"Genghis is chewing on my vibrator," she said, looking down at Rick.

"Ah, so you prefer the more polite name for it."

Josie cocked her head thoughtfully. "What would you call it?"

Rick laughed. "It's a big-ass dildo, sweetie."

Josie bit her lip. "Well, whatever it is, it's the only one I have and it cost over twenty-five dollars."

Rick felt his erection pulse. Josie obviously felt it, too, because she squirmed a little.

"I wouldn't worry about it too much," he said.

"Oh, yeah? Why's that?"

"Because you're not going to need it anymore."

Josie beamed. "I was so hoping you'd say that."

CHAPTER 8

"I haven't done this in a while," Rick said, stroking the tops of Josie's thighs as she straddled him.

She laughed, wondering how long of a hiatus the handsome Rick Rousseau was admitting to—three days? A week? Two weeks? She was almost ashamed to tell him it had been three months for her.

"It's been almost seven years, Josie," he whispered.

She went still. She held her breath. She stared down at those deep green eyes curtained by long lashes. He had to be joking.

"It's the truth," he said.

Josie pushed herself off Rick's body and stood up. She reached a hand down for him and he pulled himself to a stand with an audible groan. Suddenly, it all made sense to her—Rick had suffered such a serious injury in the motorcycle crash that he wasn't able to have sex! That could be the only explanation. But if that were the case, then what was that giant erection doing in his pants? Maybe it was more of a musculo-skeletal issue than a blood-flow issue? She couldn't help it—she reevaluated his below-the-belt situation to be sure she hadn't been imagining things.

"Everything still works, if that's what you're wondering."

"Uh, no, I mean, that's really great news." Josie was helpless to prevent the red from flaming across her cheeks again.

"You look delicious when you blush," Rick said, eliminating whatever space had developed between their bodies. He cupped her face in his hands and kissed her again. It was brief, but it was hot and slick and Josie felt the bottom of her belly drop.

"Mmmmm," she hummed.

"It was my choice to be celibate," he said.

Josie nodded as the kiss ended, pretending to understand, though she didn't. "And you're choosing to decelibate yourself? With me? Now?"

A crooked smile pushed up the left corner of Rick's lips, and she stared at those lips, blinking in wonder. Oh, boy. She was doing it again—falling in love. She was falling for Rick Rousseau. And this wasn't some kind of accidental slide, either—the way it had been with Lloyd or Spike or any of the rest of them, whose names she could no longer remember. This time she was going down hard and fast and with such abandon that she swore she could hear a loud thump. Maybe it was just the sound of her heart banging in her chest.

"That's my plan, if you're okay with it," he said.

"Why me?" She raised her eyes to his, and found him looking at her thoughtfully through those glorious eyelashes.

"Because you are wonderful, Josie. Beautiful and sweet and smart and I feel happy when I'm with you. You make me laugh. You make me want to try."

She shook her head, confused. "Try?"

"To be the decent man you imagine me to be."

Josie slipped her hands around Rick's waist and rubbed his muscular back. "Where were you hurt, can I ask?" She let her hands roam, eventually bringing them to his firm butt.

"My ass is fine," he said with a grin.

"No kidding," Josie said, giggling. She moved her hands to his narrow hips.

"The left hip is man-made," he said.

She let her hands slide down along the back of his thighs, then around to the front, feeling nothing but solid muscle beneath her fingers.

"My left femur is held together with a titanium rod. My left knee is a testament to modern plastics."

Her stomach fluttered. She was frightened by what he was telling her. She squatted down and placed her hands gently on his calves, then his shins, waiting for anything else he had to say.

Rick's hand caressed her hair. "The right tibia broke in four places. My right ankle was crushed—trust me when I tell you that you don't want to go through airport security with me."

Josie remained in her squat, staring down at the wood floor of her apartment, suddenly overwhelmed. She knew her fingers trembled where they touched him. Eventually she rose to a stand, spreading her palms flat against Rick's shirt, feeling the rise and fall of his solid abdomen, eventually moving her hands along his ribs and chest.

"Three broken ribs. A lacerated spleen. A bruised heart. A punctured lung."

Josie felt the sorrow well up in her. How could one person go through so much and still be walking around?

"You can stop now, Josie. It's all ancient history."

She shook her head, not looking at his face. She

placed her hands on his shoulders, biceps, forearms, and hands. She needed to know everything.

Rick sighed softly. "Pretty much the same thing as my legs—a little bit of plastic or metal here and there."

With that, Josie placed her hands on his head and raked her fingers through his hair. The look on her face must have been horror, because Rick immediately comforted her.

"I was wearing a helmet. I had a minor concussion. Nothing more."

She nodded, not knowing what to say, and not sure she wanted to be the woman to put all the pins and plates to the test.

He tipped up her chin with his fingers and looked her in the eye. "I'm healthy now, Josie. It's been a long time and I'm healed. I run. I lift weights. I do yoga. I get stiff sometimes, but I'm good to go."

"But I . . . I don't want to hurt you accidentally," she whispered, trying with all her might not to blush or tear up. "I'm not a tiny woman. I could crush something. I could snap one of your rods or chip one of your plates."

He chuckled again. Gently, he took her into his arms, squeezed her, and whispered into her hair. "You're the woman I want, Josie. Just say the word when you're ready."

Josie melted into his hug, knowing that no man's embrace had ever felt this perfect, this complete. Rick's arms were strong but they cradled her gently. She could hear his heart beat in his chest. She could hear the patience in his voice. Sure, Rick Rousseau might have a few synthetic parts, but he was more of the real thing than any man she'd ever encountered.

Josie decided to skip the words. Instead, she took his hand and led him through the living room toward the bedroom. Genghis stopped chewing and looked up at them with curiosity, giving Josie the two seconds she needed to swoop down and grab the now disfigured vibrator. She tossed it in the bathroom trash can on the way down the hall.

Josie's home phone began to ring. Whoever—and whatever—it was would have to wait.

Bea snapped her cell phone closed and turned to Roxie and Ginger. "Well, she's not answering. Now I'm sure something's going on."

"Good Lord, Bea!" Roxie said, laughing. "Josie is a grown woman. She can choose not to answer her phone if she wants—that's the beauty of living in a democracy."

Ginger leaned forward on one elbow, whispering as if spies were lurking at the outdoor bistro. "As much as it pains me to say this, Bea may be right. Think about it—it's more than the usual scatterbrain stuff with Josie lately. She may be avoiding us."

As if shocked by the accusation, HeatherLynn poked her head out from the cocoon of Ginger's jacket, little black button eyes popping from her white pom-pom head.

"You guys are nuts," Roxanne said.

"She didn't show up for our walk yesterday," Bea reminded Roxie, lowering her hand to stroke the top of her own dog's head. As usual, Martina slept peacefully by her owner's side, content and well behaved. "And now she can't meet us for a drink tonight? So I ask, since when does she have so many scheduling conflicts?"

"Maybe she's babysitting for her sister's kids," Ginger offered.

"See? I'm sure that's what it is," Roxie said. "You

know how Beth's always dumping her kids on her at the last minute."

"Of course I'm right."

"You're wrong," Bea told Ginger with finality.

Ginger sighed. She took a soothing sip of her lemongrass Mojito. "Whatever you say, Bea."

"So you agree there's something going on with Josie?"

Ginger laughed. "Not necessarily, but I'll say anything to get you to drop the subject."

"Not gonna happen," Bea said.

For the next few minutes, the three women sat quietly at the small wrought-iron table. Lilith tugged at her muzzle and growled at a man strolling down the sidewalk. HeatherLynn retreated back into her hideaway. Martina slept.

Roxie took a long drink from her margarita and sighed. "Have you ever noticed that we get on each other's nerves more when Josie's not with us?"

Bea nodded, taking a swig of her Michelob Ultra. "All the more reason to find out what's going on with her, and get her back on track."

Roxie shrugged.

"Hey, Ginger," Bea continued. "Remember that woman who came to the paper to see Josie the other day? When we were heading out to grab some of Paulie Patrakis's last baklava?"

Roxie's mouth fell open. "You got some of his last baklava? You went *without* me?"

"We tried to reach you but you were covering that double-murder thingy." Ginger frowned when she said that, then groaned in exasperation and smoothed out her brow. "What about the old lady, Bea?"

"You think Josie has something going on with an old *lady*?" Roxie's face froze in shock.

"Oh, for God's sake," Bea said, dropping her head into her hand.

"Not everyone is turned on by senior citizens, Rox," Ginger said.

"What*ever*." Roxie rolled her eyes. "So who's this old woman and what does she have to do with Josie avoiding us?"

Bea settled back in her bistro chair and looked around at the hip city crowd, pondering the question. "Josie was in a very serious conversation with the woman. It looked important."

"I think she was the widow of one of Josie's obits," Ginger said, pursing her lips. "As usual, Bea, you're looking for intrigue where there is none—maybe you should buy a spy novel or something."

"I can sense these things," Bea said, her conviction growing. "Josie has something going on in her life that she's not telling us about, and I'm sure it's a man."

When Ginger gasped and stiffened in surprise, HeatherLynn popped out of her owner's jacket again.

"No way," Roxie said, her voice louder now. "Josie would have told me if there was someone in her life."

"Oh, really?" Bea arched her eyebrows. "You don't think Josie would be the tiniest bit embarrassed about a new boyfriend considering that little no-man-no-way vow we all just took?"

Nobody had a response for that.

Bea turned to Ginger. "Do you really think she'd be anxious to tell us about her latest selection from the primordial slime pit of men when all we do is talk about the joys of living in a testosterone-free zone?"

Ginger's lips parted, but she stayed silent.

Bea raised her bottle toward Roxie. "And Roxie, do you really think she'd be running to the proprietor of the infamous i-vomit-on-all-men.com Web site to brag about the wonderful new guy who's stolen her heart?"

"Well, if you put it that way . . ."

Ginger interrupted them both. "You know, I took that vow seriously. I've completely changed my way of thinking. I will never again worry about pleasing a man. From here on out it's all about pleasuring myself!"

When she got two silent stares, Ginger amended her comment. "Wait—that didn't come out right."

Roxie turned to Bea. "I don't get it—what would the old lady have to do with Josie's new man?"

Bea's eyes narrowed. She drummed her short fingernails on the bistro tabletop, not answering right away. After a few moments of contemplation, she looked up with a smile. "What's the one thing we all have in common?" she asked, sounding pleased with herself.

"Dogs, of course," Ginger said with a sigh. "Plus, none of us are having any sex, and, let's face it, the more time that goes by the less likely I am to ever have it again, because in a few years I'll probably have a dried-up hoo-hah and more chin hair than the Unabomber, and then where will I be?"

Roxie choked on a mouthful of margarita.

"Actually," Bea said, rolling her eyes, "I was alluding to the fact that we're all experienced journalists." Bea folded her hands in front of her on the table. "We are trained to track down information. We know how to put together facts to reveal an accurate and balanced snapshot of the truth."

"I write about trends in bathroom design," Ginger pointed out.

"Reporting is reporting," Bea snapped.

Just then, a shiny black Lexus cruised by. The

equally black man behind the wheel slowed the car, then nodded at the women before he drove on.

Lilith growled.

"Do you know him?" Ginger asked.

"Nope. Just a friendly guy, I guess," Roxie said.

"Anyone who drives that slow is on the prowl," Bea said.

"I swear I've seen him before," Ginger said.

"So let me get this straight, Bea." Roxie crossed her arms across her chest. "You're suggesting we *spy* on our friend? You want us to go undercover on Josie, start asking questions of her neighbors? Family? Sources? How about we sit outside her apartment and watch who comes and goes? Maybe root through her garbage?"

"There's no need to get carried away," Bea said.

"You're the one who's been carried away!" Roxie was clearly upset. "Josie is my friend. I would never do that to her."

"It is pretty smarmy," Ginger said. "I wouldn't want you guys doing that to me, not that you'd find anything. I say we just ask Josie. If she wants us to know, she'll tell us."

Roxie nodded. "Of course. We'll just ask her what's going on. We'll remind her that we're her friends and she can tell us anything."

Bea shrugged. "Fine. Ask her, then. Go on."

Roxie pulled out her cell phone. She dialed Josie's home number. No answer. She called Josie's cell. No answer. She tried both again. No answer.

"Here, let me," Ginger said, rooting through her oversized pink leather bag to find her cell. She placed the phone on the tabletop and put it on speaker. The three women waited patiently through four rings.

"See?" Bea said. "She's not going to pick—"

The phone sparked to life. The call had gone through but the only sound was of shuffling and mumbling, followed by a high-pitched yelp and a deep-voiced laugh. Then there was the sound of something smacking the receiver a few times, with a little more laughing thrown in. Then the line went dead.

Ginger tossed the phone back into her purse and, without comment, drained the rest of her mojito.

Bea bowed her head humbly, as if acknowledging the roars of an imaginary crowd. "My work here is done," she said.

"I don't freakin' believe this!" Ginger waved her hands around. HeatherLynn panicked and popped back inside the jacket. "Josie took a vow! She was the one who told us to go out and lead full and happy lives in the company of our dogs! No one forced her to say that! She came up with that all on her own!"

"Let's not jump to any conclusions, here," Roxie said, glaring at Ginger. "We don't know for sure what we just heard on the phone. It could have been anything."

Bea nodded. "Sure. Hey, in fact—" She started laughing. "I bet all that giggling was part of her empty mind practice!"

Ginger pursed her mouth tight. Roxie stared out into the street. Bea chuckled some more.

"I do worry about her," Ginger said, shaking her head. "You know how she is—all a guy has to do is buy her a bacon cheeseburger and the next day she's at Macy's picking out her stainless pattern. We can't let her do this to herself again. We can't let her waste her time with another überloser."

"Amen, sister," Bea said.

"But who are we to interfere?" Roxie leaned forward on her elbows again, quite serious. "I love Josie.

She's my best friend. But she's an adult. I know I wouldn't appreciate you guys doing that to me!" Roxie flashed her dark eyes at them. "I mean, it's my life! I can make healthy choices for myself! Who are you to say what's good for me?"

Bea nodded. "Okay. Well, I got two words for you—*Raymond Sandberg.* Any further discussion?"

Lilith growled as the black Lexus cruised by again, headed in the opposite direction.

"I've got a real bad feeling about this whole business," Ginger said, letting her voice trail off as she watched the car drive away. "Strange old ladies. Mystery boyfriends. The idea of spying on our friend. And what's with Super Fly in the Lexus? Am I paranoid or is that the second time he's driven by?"

Roxie shook her head emphatically. "I'm not rooting through anybody's garbage. That's where I have to draw the line."

CHAPTER 9

"You sure are popular," Rick said through his teeth, which were clamped down on the elastic neckline of Josie's little pink top. He would have used his hands to remove her blouse, but they were busy springing her left hip from the prison of her bikini underwear.

"The damn thing's turned off now," she said, tossing her cell phone onto a basket of folded laundry. "My friends can be persistent." Josie returned her attention to the metal buckle of Rick's jeans, frowning in concentration. "They're probably wondering why I didn't meet them for a drink tonight."

"Why didn't you just tell them you had a date?"

Josie smiled in triumph, pulling the belt strap loose from the buckle. Then she looked at Rick, biting her bottom lip. "Um, they don't know about you yet. I haven't found the right time to tell them."

Rick laughed. "Ah. You're ashamed of me."

"What?" Josie's gray eyes went big and her cheeks reddened. "Of course not! It's just that—oh, jeez, it's a really long story, but none of my friends are in relationships right now, and we kind of promised each other that we'd be happy without men, that we could have wonderful, satisfying lives in the company of our dogs."

"Whoops."

"Yeah." Josie glanced down at her own below-the-waist bareness, and when she looked back at Rick, her cheeks were flaming. "Whoops big-time."

Even while they laughed, Rick felt the weight of the moment descending on him. He was beginning to see all that was happening here, in stark clarity. There was a beautiful, funny, half-naked woman straddling his legs, looking down on him with trust and adoration. Her satiny thighs were spread. Her shiny curls fell around her face. Her creamy, freckled breasts were practically falling out of her top. And if all that wasn't erotic enough, the entire scene was backlit by evening sun spilling through the bedroom blinds, which gave the entire vision an ethereal glow. And as he stared in wonder at this apparition, he felt the light of her smile and the warmth of her laughter cut through seven years of cold darkness.

It dawned on Rick that he was about to hold the door open and welcome a woman into his life. He was on the verge of telling her to make herself at home and prop her feet up right smack in the middle of his heart and soul. He was about to surrender to the possibility of a relationship—with a good woman who deserved only goodness in her life.

Rick smiled to himself, amused by his own big-time whoops moment. Seven years of hard absolutes had begun to soften the morning Josephine Sheehan walked off the sidewalk and entered his grooming salon. By now, Josie's pretty face and easy laugh had begun to chisel away at every wall he'd ever built around himself.

Rick watched Josie's happy smile fade. He reached

up and stroked one of her cherry-red cheeks. "Tell your friends about me whenever you're ready, if you ever decide you want to. It's completely your decision."

She frowned. "You're having second thoughts. I can tell."

Her question took him by surprise. "You mean about you and me? About us?"

"Yes."

He laughed at the irony, shaking his head emphatically. "Josie, there are a thousand thoughts racing through my brain, but none of them are second thoughts about us."

Rick pulled her down to his chest. He opened his fingers wide and spread them though her curls, capturing the back of her head in his grip. His mouth found hers. It was like a secret language, the way his lips spoke to hers, how she responded, coaxing him and soothing him at exactly the right intervals. It was a language he'd never known, one he'd never had any interest in learning—until now, with Josie.

His hands explored her tender neck, shoulders, back, and wound their way down to the rounded globes of her butt. She was so warm everywhere, so silky and solid, that his hands couldn't get enough of her. He found himself kneading her flesh while his kisses escalated.

Rick realized that Josie was tugging at his shirt buttons, her kisses growing wild. He knew she wanted to feel skin on skin as much as he did, but it was a moment he also dreaded, because the instant the shirt came off the kissing would stop. He was sure of it. There wasn't a woman in the world who wouldn't be shocked—if not outright horrified—by the tattoo on his torso.

He gave her bottom a friendly pat and put his hands

on her shoulders, slowly pushing her away. Josie let out a mewl of protest when their lips parted, then she reached for the buttons on Rick's shirt again.

He sighed, knowing the moment was unavoidable. He allowed her fingers to pop one button at a time. The cotton of his shirt slowly opened, revealing everything he had been and everything he still was.

"Oh." That's all Josie said as the image was revealed. She stayed silent as she shoved the shirt off his shoulders, untucked it from his pants, and threw it to the floor. For a long moment, she studied the image permanently imbedded in his skin, saying nothing. Eventually, she raised her wide eyes to his.

"Holy freakin' shit," she whispered, her gaze darting from the tattoo to Rick's eyes and back again, several times. She let out a long breath of air and her shoulders fell.

"I thought this might ruin the mood," Rick said, fully stretching out on the bed, arms at his sides, giving her a complete view. There was no point in trying to minimize the impact. He lay still, letting her study him. "I guess it's a little late to be asking, but are you okay with tattoos?"

Josie bit her lip the way she did whenever she was carefully choosing her words. "I knew you had a tattoo, of course," she said quietly. "A little bit of it shows above whatever shirt you're wearing. And I thought it looked interesting, but I just . . . well . . . I had no idea . . ."

Rick smiled sadly. "Remember that globe-trotting past I mentioned?"

Josie nodded.

"This is a little souvenir I picked up in Asia. It started in India, continued in Sri Lanka, and got its finishing touches in Thailand."

A small frown wrinkled Josie's brow. "It's incredible, really. The colors. It's so complex. But it's kind of, I don't know, intense. Maybe even intimidating."

"You're quite good with words, Josie. But I think you're trying to be kind. It's just plain scary—you can say it."

When she looked up at him again, Rick saw clean, simple understanding in her eyes. Again, no judgment. No sense of condemnation. And certainly no fear. "We all do things we wish we hadn't," she said softly. "I'm sure if I'd ever been anywhere more exotic than Petaluma I'd probably have done something wild, too."

Rick laughed. "My wild Josie," he said tenderly, reaching for her hand. Her fingers felt soft and small cradled in his. "I just don't want to scare you away."

"You haven't," she replied immediately. She brushed the curls from her face.

Rick believed her. There was something reassuring about the steadiness in her lovely gray eyes. "The thing is, I wouldn't want to get rid of it now even if I could," he said. "It's a reminder of lessons learned, I guess. And I've done a lot of research on the symbols over the years, and I realize it's like a road map of my life. I think those tattoo artists knew more about my destiny than I did."

"But your accident—" Josie said haltingly. "I can see the scars on your arms, but there aren't any marks on your tattoo."

Rick laughed. "Funny how that worked out."

Without a word, Josie crossed her arms over her waist and pulled off her shirt. Next she unhooked her bra at its front closure, displaying a pair of full, pink breasts. With the same calm sense of purpose, she reached forward and undid the fly of Rick's pants, then pulled them low on his hips. It was a move Rick knew would expose every small detail of the tattoo.

Slowly, Josie crawled across the bed, all that silky firm flesh for him to gaze upon, and climbed over him. She gently lay down on her side, put her head on his stomach, and, with her fingers, traced the journey of the two winged serpents as they snaked their way up the left-center of his body, a passage through a map of the seven prime chakras, the energy centers of the human body.

She caressed the elaborate lotus symbols that marked each chakra, her touch curious and respectful. She brushed her fingers along the length of the serpents' bodies, the lighter one representing his spirit and the darker one his psyche. She laid her hand on the two sets of dripping fangs.

Rick wondered if someday he'd be able to share the entire tale with Josie, the story of how the battle of his inner serpents had nearly killed him.

"Josie," he whispered, his hands stroking her soft curls.

"Yes?" She didn't look up at him. Her fingers continued their expedition up and down. They brushed his skin from the first chakra at the edge of his pubic hair up to the seventh chakra just above his left collar-bone—a journey that took her from the most base to the most evolved elements of the self. He felt himself growing hard again. There was something so maddeningly innocent about this woman. She was smart and intuitive, but she was kind. Hopeful. It was like all the world's harsh bullshit hadn't ripped away her innocence. And though he wasn't quite sure how she'd remained that way into her thirties, he was drawn to that quality, perhaps more than anything else about her. He wanted to be near her goodness. He wanted some of that for himself. He wanted *her* for himself.

"You're a very special woman, Josephine Sheehan."

He felt her hair tickle his hip as she nodded. "You're special, too," she said. Then she laid her cheek against his belly and gently kissed him, right on his second chakra. "I want to make love to you, Rick. Right now."

His breath went shallow. He buried his fingers in her curls. "I want that more than anything, but—"

Josie raised her eyes. "Yes?"

"Only if you're ready."

She laughed. She pulled herself up along the side of his body, giggling and kissing along the way. When her eyes were level with his she hovered over him. She put her lips on his and gave him a kiss so hot and sweet he feared he'd explode before he even got inside her. He wasn't exactly used to this.

"I want to show you how ready I am," she said, flashing a wicked grin as she threw her leg over his belly. "Touch me and see."

Rick slid his hand between their bodies, the need in him so fierce he worried he couldn't stop now even if she told him to. His fingers grazed over the curls at the opening to her pussy, and he let them dip inside, ever so gently. Instantly, his fingers were covered in her honey.

Rick closed his eyes and savored the power of that sensation. He had a woman, naked, wet, wanting him. And he wanted her more than anything he'd ever wanted in his life. He tried to steady his breath as he moved his fingers along the luscious, wet opening.

Suddenly, his mind reeled with memories. Sex from his past—raw and hard and wild, usually with women he barely knew and always with women he didn't love. How would he be with Josie? Could he let himself go without returning to all that ugliness? Could he trust himself? He wanted to make love *with* Josie, not do something *to* her, and he wasn't sure he was capable.

She obviously sensed his hesitation. "I promise I'll be gentle with you," she whispered, kissing him again. When Rick opened his eyes and saw that she was perfectly serious, he laughed.

"Uh . . ." he said, his fingers still playing in her slickness. "That's not exactly what I'm worried about."

She frowned. "You're worried?"

He nodded. "It's just that it's been so long and I want you so badly, that I'm afraid I'll—" Rick shook his head. "Josie, I'm scared that I'll rip you apart, eat you alive. I was never the most sensitive lover in the world. I've had more experience with fucking than loving, if you know what I mean."

She smiled.

"And then there's that seven years of deprivation to consider."

She smiled bigger.

"I am worried I'll be too much for you."

Josie nodded slightly. "I see," she said.

Before he knew it, she was on top of his thighs, legs spread, and curls spilling down as she brought her mouth to him. He jolted with the sensation, her hot, wet mouth enveloping him. She hummed and licked and sucked, as if she were in a trance. As the minutes rolled by, Rick's body began to shake from the concentration it took not to erupt in her mouth. *Fuck*, he kept thinking. *Fuck, she's good.* Had it felt like this with other women? It had been a long time, but he didn't think so. He would have remembered this marvel of pressure, heat, connection.

Josie was making love to his cock with her mouth. He couldn't stand it another second.

He reached for her head and raised it up. She licked her lips, then smiled at him. "Am I too much for you?"

"Hell, yes," Rick said. In an instant, he'd captured her in his arms and flipped her on her back. He got on top of her, the need in him quite simple. He had to get inside her. Now.

He dropped his mouth to hers, devouring her as she moaned and squealed and opened her legs to him. It happened so fast—he was in her, up to the hilt, completely sheathed in her pulsing flesh. He kept his mouth on hers, licking inside her lips, slowly moving in and out. She was heaven—a hot, snug heaven—and he never wanted to stop.

"Yes," she hissed. *"God, yes, Rick."*

He got lost. Whatever happened in his past was gone. Those hard memories had been replaced by Josie's softness, her kisses, the sounds of her pleasure. They twisted and rolled in passion. He held her down. She rode him. He came inside her with a roar, like a volcano exploding after a long, cold dormancy.

Seven years, to be exact.

The hours had been a blur for Josie, a whirling tide of lust, magic, and pleasure that felt almost supernatural. At the same time, though, she noticed how every instant was firmly rooted in her body. The truth was, she felt wholly alive, intensely aroused, and completely connected. Her everyday human body had become a surprising delight to her, a vehicle taking her to exotic places she'd always figured were for other—well, sexier—women to visit.

She smiled to herself, knowing that she'd just gotten her first taste of grand adventure, right there in her double bed in her little apartment off Seventeenth Street. As it turned out, there were no parkas or airline tickets required. All she'd needed was Rick Rousseau.

Josie was glad she was lying on her stomach with her face buried in the sheets, because she was building up the nerve to make the most downright ballsy request of her life, and she didn't want Rick to see her embarrassed or blushing, or both. But of course she'd blush! She was already blushing from her hairline to her toes due to the fact that she'd had more orgasms in the past two hours than the last two decades, and her skin was still on fire, everywhere.

"Rick?" she whispered.

"Mmm?" She felt him raise his head from the small of her back, where'd he'd been for several long moments, obviously resting and maybe even sleeping.

"I know it's been seven years and you're probably tired—"

"Mmm?"

"But can we do it again?"

Without warning, Josie was scooped up from the mattress, Rick's arms wrapped around her belly from behind. She yelped in surprise as she was unceremoniously flipped over on her back by a laughing, smiling man.

When she regained her wits, she noticed he was not only happy, he was hard again. Very, very hard again.

Rick descended upon her and hovered, his face just inches from hers, his hands planted at either side of her head. God, she loved the way the muscles of his upper arms bulged when he did that.

"You were already raring to go, weren't you?" she asked suspiciously. "You were just waiting for me to catch my breath."

"It was the gentlemanly thing to do," he said, giving her one of those bewitching smiles again, his full-lipped mouth curled up at the corners, his green eyes dark with desire. "But I've got to be honest with you—I think we have a problem, Josie."

Her eyes went wide. "We do? I thought everything was going great!"

Rick nodded, chuckling softly. "The problem is, I can't get enough of you. The problem is, I never want to leave this bed. I never want to do anything in my life again except kiss you and stroke you and smell you and bury myself up inside you and hear you cry out when you come, over and over again."

"Oh," she breathed. "But we'll have to feed Genghis eventually."

"And I have a business to run, you know."

"Right," she said, breathing fast. "And people are always dying in this town, so I have to show up at work."

She ran her palms up and down the ridges and swells of Rick's biceps and triceps and whatever those long lean muscles were called on his forearms. In addition to the feel of soft body hair, smooth skin, and hard muscle, she'd occasionally detect the bulge of a bolt, plate, or pin, and would marvel at how graceful he was, how strong and flexible his body remained despite what he'd been through.

"I've got to have you again. I can't wait."

Rick lowered his mouth to Josie's throat, and she raised her chin to give him access to what he wanted. She'd already decided he could have whatever, however, whenever. In fact, she'd made that decision the other day over lunch at John's Grill. The usual worry began to waft through her mind—she'd fallen for a man she barely knew. Again. So was she simply repeating her tried-and-true pattern? It couldn't be. This wasn't the same. Not anywhere near the same. Rick was a wish fulfilled. Rick was a miracle. Rick wasn't Lloyd or Spike or Randy or Billy or . . .

"Oh, my God!" she cried out, the intensity of the pleasure bringing her right back to the moment, the man.

"Did you like that?"

"Oh, oh," she breathed. "Don't stop. Please don't stop."

Rick returned his mouth to her left nipple, biting down harder this time, sucking with more desperation, all in perfect concert with the way he pushed his cock up into her, burrowing deep. Josie writhed under him. The pleasure was sharp and originating from the deepest part of her, and it was building, spreading from her belly to her toes and fingers, and she knew it wouldn't be long before she went over the edge one more time.

"No," Rick said, his voice firm and low. "Not yet."

Josie opened her eyes to the most wondrous sight— the gorgeous, intense stranger who'd arrived in her life via special delivery, courtesy of the universe, was no longer a stranger. His face was alive with passion and affection. It had opened—to her. He truly cared for her. He wanted her. He wanted something special and real with her. She would have no more doubts.

"Please, my sweet Josie, feel me," Rick said, his eyes scanning her face. "I need you to stay right here with me. Feel exactly what's happening between us." With that, Rick reached beneath her and gathered her close to his chest, all the while pushing himself farther inside her body, rotating and thrusting and rubbing, all of which made Josie wonder—*how am I supposed to be the orgasm crossing guard here, holding up a big red stop sign smack in the middle of Ecstasy Street?*

Rick suddenly cupped her face in both his hands, pushing one last time, his eyes locking onto hers with seriousness, with purpose. "Now," he said.

She exploded. She heard him call out her name, as if from a distance. And in that suspended moment, where it felt like they were perched together on the very top of the world's biggest roller coaster, there was nothing to do but hold on to each other and enjoy the ride. The sensations began to roll through them, first a fireball, then a wave, and next a river, flowing on and on until it calmed, spreading heat and peace through them both.

After several long minutes, Rick was the first to move. He stroked the side of Josie's face, then placed quick little kisses all over, from her nose and forehead to her neck and shoulders. When he finished, they both sighed, held on even tighter to each other, and listened as their breathing found a perfect rhythm.

Suddenly, Rick's body went rigid, as if he'd felt a stab of pain. Josie stilled, too, wondering which steel plate had shifted or which pin had sprung loose inside him.

"Where does it hurt?" she asked, her hands firm on his upper arms. "What should I do? Tell me what to do!"

His back began to shake. Was he crying? "Rick, please, tell me what's wrong!" Josie pushed him away so she could determine if the pain had left him speechless. She discovered he was laughing, not crying.

"Someone is licking my toes," he said.

"Genghis?"

"God, I hope so," he said, before he burst into laughter.

Josie peered down Rick's bare body to the foot of the bed. Her dog had both front paws on the mattress, and the gleam in his beady brown eyes revealed how he longed to join them.

"Down, boy!" she commanded.

Genghis didn't budge. His pink tongue flopped out of his mouth as he panted happily.

"Get off the bed, Genghis. Go on," she told him. "Please."

More happy panting. No moving.

Rick nuzzled his nose into the crook of Josie's neck. "It appears your dog doesn't take you seriously, sweetie," he whispered, kissing her collarbone.

"Story of my life."

"You've got to be firm—say it like you mean it." He nibbled his way down her right shoulder. "Give it another try."

Josie glared toward the foot of the bed, where Genghis waited, his furry helicopter tail revving up for a takeoff. She made her voice as low and serious as she could. "Down!" she barked. "Get off! Now!"

The dog hopped down.

"See?" Rick was busy licking her cleavage, unaware that all Genghis had done was trot around to the side of the bed, where he now crouched in his ready-to-play position, butt up in the air and paws stretched straight out in front of him. A pair of shredded boxer-briefs dangled from his teeth.

"He just needs to know who's the boss around here." Rick stayed buried in her breasts. "Dogs want to know who's the leader of their pack. It's a relief to them when they know someone is in charge."

Josie leaned down and kissed Rick's tousled hair. "Of course," she said, trying not to laugh. "We'll discuss this further when we're out shopping."

Rick raised his head, frowning. "We're going shopping?"

Josie leaned her head in Genghis's direction. "Seventh floor, men's undergarments," she said cheerfully.

"You're going to have to put her in the car if she can't stop growling," Bea said, thoroughly annoyed with Lilith's antics. "We're trying to remain incognito, remember?"

"If I put her in the car, then she'll be whining and barking in addition to growling," Roxie said.

"Doesn't somebody manufacture a soundproof muzzle?" Ginger asked. "I mean, for God's sake, they've invented everything else. I was surfing the Web the other day and found this new poop scoop that scrapes it up, bags it, and ties it closed without you ever having to bend over or touch anything."

Bea squinted at Ginger in the shadows. "Your dog's doo-doo is the size of a Lincoln Log. You could pick it up with a pair of eyebrow tweezers. What do you need a contraption like that for?"

"Shhh! Here comes somebody!" Roxie waved her hand in the darkness under the huge old elm tree. "It's a guy! It's a guy!"

"Oh, my God," Ginger whispered. "She had a man up there. You were right, Bea!"

"But wait," Roxie said. "How do we know he came from Josie's apartment? He could have come from anywhere. He might even live there."

Bea nodded. "You're right, Roxie. Excellent point."

A door opened on the second floor of the white stucco building. A curly-haired woman came to the railing of her balcony with a big scruffy dog at her side. Though they didn't need it, the porch light provided some beyond-a-reasonable-doubt illumination.

The three women under the tree turned to each other and nodded in silent agreement.

"Good night, Rick," Josie whispered in a voice loud enough for anyone to hear.

The man turned around on the sidewalk and blew Josie a kiss, saying, "Till the morrow, sweet Juliet." Then he headed back up the street, hands in his pockets, a swagger in his stride.

"I do not freakin' believe he just called her 'Juliet,' " Ginger whispered. "No one's ever called me 'Juliet'!"

"My God. Did you get a good look at that man?" Roxie craned her neck around one of the lower tree branches. "He's absolutely gorgeous. Hottie McHottness."

Bea glowered at her.

"I meant that in an objective-reporter kind of way," Roxie added.

"And he just called her 'Juliet'!" Ginger repeated. "I think I'm going to cry!"

"For God's sake," Bea said.

They watched the man stroll up half the block before a shiny black Lexus pulled to the curb.

"That's the same car!" Ginger said, her voice getting squeaky.

Then the man Josie had called "Rick" walked around the front of the Lexus and got in the passenger side.

The women watched in silence as the shiny black luxury car drove past them quite slowly, the driver acknowledging their hiding place under the elm with a barely discernible nod of his head. The car came to a stop at the intersection before it turned north. Lilith's growling escalated.

"I got the plate," Roxie said, already whipping out her cell phone to jot down the numbers. "I have a buddy in major crimes who can run it for me tomorrow."

"Good work," Bea said.

"What is going on here?" Ginger said, shaking her head in disbelief. "We're being followed! That guy in the Lexus is following us! He followed us from the bistro to Josie's!"

"Or he thinks we followed him," Bea said.

Ginger took a step back from the tree, pulling her jacket tighter around HeatherLynn. "I'm scared. I think we should tell Josie she's in some kind of danger, that her so-called Romeo is some kind of criminal or something. We should call the police. This isn't something we should be involved in."

Bea sighed, straightening from her crouch under the tree. "Ginger, we don't know what or who that Rick guy is. He could be on the board of supervisors or a congressman, for all we know. He could be a professional athlete or a friend of her brother's, for crying out loud. But we're going to find out."

Roxie clicked her cell phone shut and took a step toward the sidewalk, pulling Lilith along with her. "I've had enough for one night. I'll see you all at the park in the morning," she said.

"Do you think Josie will show?" Ginger asked.

Bea looked up toward the now empty balcony and nodded emphatically. "Oh, yeah. She'll show. She'll want us to think everything is status quo, which ought to be more fun than a barrel of monkeys."

CHAPTER 10

The gardener looked shocked to see his employer standing in the doorway, which was understandable. If Bennett's memory served him correctly, and it usually did, the last time he had spoken to Esteban Jaramillo in person was in 1998, when the Newport Garden Club wanted to include the Cummings estate on the annual garden tour. The topic at that meeting had been pruning and mulching, as Bennett recalled. That's not what he was here for today, however.

Esteban's dark eyes went huge. He removed his baseball cap and wiped his forehead. "Good morning, Mr. Cummings," he said, moving away from a workbench and taking a few tentative steps toward the doorway.

Bennett extended his hand to his employee and tried to smile casually.

"Is there something wrong with the grounds, Mr. Cummings?" Esteban swiped his palm on his dirty jeans before he accepted his boss's outstretched hand.

Bennett sensed how nervous he'd made the man and felt guilty. "No, no. Nothing's wrong, Esteban. Everything's wonderful." He glanced around the meticulously organized building euphemistically called "the potting shed." In reality, the two-story structure was twice the size of a typical family home and featured a greenhouse, two studio apartments, and a six-bay garage that held everything from backhoes and dump trucks to riding mowers, tillers, and stump grinders.

"I . . ." Esteban swallowed hard. "We . . . Carmelita and me . . . we were so sorry to hear about Miss Margot."

Bennett straightened and nodded. He rarely pondered what his house staff thought of him and his family, but he'd always assumed they observed them with disdain and fear in equal measure. The rich were always a puzzle to those who worked for them.

"Thank you." Bennett cleared his throat. The truth was, he felt as awkward as Esteban. "And your family? How is your family?"

"Oh!" Esteban's eyes lit up. "Excellent, Mr. Cummings. Thank you. Rodrigo, our oldest, is in his second year at the Rhode Island School of Design. He's getting straight As."

"How fabulous," Bennett said, not knowing who the hell Rodrigo was but feeling vaguely proud that his gardener's son had made it into the one of the country's premier art schools. "And his field of study?"

Esteban's eyes went wider. The man was obviously growing suspicious of the conversation, since Bennett had never given a rat's ass about him, his wife, or his kids during the more than two decades he'd been under his employ.

"Computer animation," Esteban said, shifting his weight awkwardly, then shrugging. "You know—cartoons."

"Of course. Wonderful." Bennett cleared his throat again. "Well, Esteban, do you have a moment? I have a proposition for you. It may sound rather strange, but I was hoping we could come to an agreement."

Esteban's eyes narrowed. He shoved his ball cap into the front pocket of his jeans and motioned for Bennett to have a seat at the long wooden table in the main room of the shed. Bennett imagined this was where the crew ate their tortillas and whatnot for lunch.

His head groundskeeper took a seat across from him, and Bennett noticed that the change of venue had created a sense of equanimity between the two men, which amused him.

"Esteban, I appreciate all your years of service."

The gardener fell back against the chair. "You're firing me."

"No! No!" Bennett laughed awkwardly. "Of course not."

Esteban put his palms flat on the surface of the table, his face losing much of its earlier friendliness. "What, then, can I do for you, Mr. Cummings?"

Bennett took a deep breath. In all his years of business he had never underestimated an adversary, and that approach had served him well. He had a feeling that this little arrangement with Esteban Jaramillo the gardener would require nothing less.

"I want your car, Esteban."

For a second, the man's face was blank. Then it lit up with amusement and he laughed. "The *Buick*?"

"Yes."

"But—" He stopped laughing. "I hadn't really thought about selling the Buick, Mr. Cummings. Me and Carmelita are still using it because we gave our Jeep to Rodrigo, you know, to take to school."

Bennett waved the details away. "You won't be

without transportation." He reached into the inner pocket of his sports jacket and pulled out the folded papers. "This is the title to my 2009 Escalade. It's already in your name."

Esteban's mouth turned to stone. He blinked. His shoulders went rigid. "Why?"

Bennett pushed the title toward his gardener. "I'm giving you the Escalade in appreciation of your fine work over the years."

"Twenty-six years, Mr. Cummings," Esteban said.

"Exactly."

"And then what?"

"You put your Buick in Bay Number 6 and forget about it. You never even notice if it's no longer there."

Esteban said nothing. He made no move toward the title. His eyes stayed focused on his employer's face. "The Escalade plus ten thousand dollars in cash," his groundskeeper said, his voice as flat as the tabletop. "Trini, our daughter, is going to college next year. She got accepted to Princeton. The money would come in handy."

Bennett had to laugh—it seemed everybody was a hustler at one level or another, even out here in his own potting shed. "I'll have the cash to you in three hours. Now, I'd like the keys to the Buick, if you please."

Esteban got up from the straight-backed chair and walked to the pegboard near the door. He snagged a key ring dangling from the top left hook, then came back and tossed it onto the table. "You have to jiggle the shift when you put it in reverse," he said.

Bennett nodded.

"And—I'm not going to lie to you, Mr. Cummings— it needs a new alternator."

"Doesn't matter."

Esteban looked down on his boss, smirking. The

gardener picked up the paperwork, scanned it, then held out his palm. Bennett dug into his pants pocket for the Escalade keys. He handed over the gaudy platinum key fob, enjoying the huge smile that spread across Esteban's face at the sight of it.

"Two hours for the cash, right?" Esteban asked.

"Actually, I said three hours."

"Make it two."

Bennett chuckled. "A man named Milton will be here in two hours. He's my attorney."

"Will you already be gone?"

Bennett stood, meeting his gardener's steady gaze. "I am not feeling well, Esteban. The flu, I believe. I'll be recuperating for a couple of weeks and won't be seeing anyone." He turned and headed out the door.

"Get well soon, then, Mr. Cummings." Esteban waited till he got a few yards away and added, "And have a safe trip."

"Oh, I guess I just fell asleep reading," Josie said aloud, pulling into the first parking spot she found near Dolores Park. No. She didn't like the way that excuse sounded—too flippant.

"Drinks were *last* night? Oh, my God! I thought it was *next* week we were getting together!" No, she hated how snooty that one sounded, like she had so many obligations that she couldn't keep track. Besides, no one with an iPhone could get away with that, not when alarms were going off every fifteen minutes to remind you to call your mother, or stop off at the grocery after work, or to start your period every fourth Sunday.

Josie cleared her throat and gave this one a try: "I am so sorry. I should have called you guys. I think I got food poisoning from a bad batch of eggplant."

Yuck. Besides, her recipe had a bad enough rep as it was.

With a sigh, Josie got out of her Honda CR-V and fetched Genghis from the back, hoping a perfect excuse would come to her spontaneously. She spied Bea and Ginger waiting at the top of the hill, and prayed her spontaneity would be the instant kind.

"This is ridiculous," she mumbled to herself, gathering up the leash. She'd just tell them the truth. Sure, they'd be hurt and angry, but they'd get over it. Eventually her friends would have to be happy for her.

Suddenly, Roxie was at her side, joining her for the walk up the hill. Genghis tried to give Lilith a friendly sniff but the muzzled she-devil growled.

"Morning, Rox. How are you?"

There was no response. Josie peered closer into her friend's face, her chances of getting any information severely reduced by the oversized dark sunglasses.

"Rox? You okay?"

By that time, Ginger and Bea had reached them at the hill's halfway point. With a shaky hand, Roxie ripped off her sunglasses to show them that, no, everything was not okay.

"The paper's going to fire me," she said, her lips trembling.

"What?" Ginger put a hand on Roxie's arm. "Why? That's ridiculous! You're one of the best reporters we have! Are we into another round of newsroom layoffs?"

Roxie shook her head. "Kenny called me last night at home. It's just me, no one else." She sniffed. "It seems the board complained about my Web site again."

"Just ignore the little weenie," Bea advised.

Roxie shook her head and choked back tears. "Kenny

is the city editor, Bea—my boss. And he's dead serious. He already warned me once and I blew him off."

Josie's eyes went wide. "Really? When did that happen?"

Roxie shrugged. "Last month. Kenny told me the board decided my Web site *'jeopardizes the integrity of the newspaper'* or some shit like that and, more importantly, they think it violates my contract."

"How?" Ginger asked.

"You know—everyone on staff agrees not to work for a competing media outlet, and that's what they think I'm doing."

Bea laughed. "The last time I looked, i-vomit-on-all-men.com wasn't a general-circulation daily newspaper."

Ginger agreed. "All you do is provide irrefutable evidence that men are pigs, not just in America, but all over the world. You're providing a vital public service."

Roxie sniffed. "Yeah, well, thanks. Unfortunately, the board doesn't see it that way. They told me last month to shut it down and I said I would, but, obviously, I didn't. So I have a meeting with them next Wednesday at ten."

"That's just like them to make you sweat bullets for a week," Bea said, shaking her head. "I'll sniff around and see what I can find out—they might just be blowing smoke up your ass."

"Thanks, I guess," Roxanne said, looking into the faces of her friends. When she reached Josie, she tilted her head slightly and gave her a quizzical frown.

Josie knew this was her opening. "Listen, guys, there's something I need to—"

But Roxie chose that moment to burst into tears. "First Raymond and now this!" she cried. "In a few days I'll be unattached *and* unemployed! What have I ever done to deserve such a craptastic life? Somebody tell me!"

Josie followed her friend's lead and plopped down to the grass. Bea and Ginger followed, and the women gathered close as Roxie cried. They sat like that for about five minutes, watching as the sun cleared the rooftops, spilling light onto the brand-new day.

Bea was the first to speak. She put her hand on Roxie's shoulder and said, "We're right here, Rox. Whatever you need, you let us know."

"That's right," Ginger said, patting Roxie's back. "We're all going to get canned eventually, with the way the newspaper business is floundering. So we'll be strong together. We'll get through this together."

"Do you want us to go in there with you next week?" Josie asked.

Roxie shook her head and laughed. "I don't think having my girl-power posse along would improve the situation."

Just then, Lilith let loose with a snarling growl, low and intimidating despite the muzzle. A dog park regular had just arrived with his male husky.

"Shhh, girl. Quiet." Roxie stroked Lilith's short wiry hair. "Give it a break, why don'tcha?"

Lilith began frothing.

"I've got an idea," Ginger said, sounding cheerful. "Take little ole Lilith here into the board meeting with you—but forgo the muzzle. Let her release all her pent-up aggression once and for all!"

Their laughter rose and fell, then faded into a round of sighs, Roxie's the loudest. After a few moments, they rose from the grass and continued their walk. With every step, Josie saw how Roxie teetered on hysteria even as she talked on and on, preparing for the battle that lay ahead.

Josie figured her confession could wait a few days, at least until Roxie's crisis had blown over. The last thing her friend needed to hear right now were the details of Josie's miraculous discovery of her soul mate, the millionaire tattooed love god who'd introduced her to true passion and mind-blowing sex. Josie figured a girl needed to be in a stable frame of mind to hear that kind of news from her best friend— especially when that friend had taken a vow of solidarity to be done with men forever.

"Ready for a refill?"

Rick dragged his gaze from his laptop screen to find Teeny hovering over his desk, yet again. This time he'd brought in the coffeepot. Ten minutes ago the interruption had been about a problem with the security cameras at the ranch. Ten minutes before that, Teeny had come in to inform him that they'd set a date for the corporate backpacking retreat.

Rick sighed deeply. "All right. I surrender. Shut the door, man. I can't stand this another second."

Teeny ran a flawless pattern to the door and back, then slid into a chair by the window, where he crossed his legs casually and asked, "So, is there something in particular you wanted to talk about?" His eyes twinkled as much as his diamond stud earring.

"You should have been in a sorority," Rick said, shaking his head and laughing.

"Tell me about it."

Rick closed his laptop and laced his fingers behind his head, still chuckling. It must have been torture for poor Teen last night, because the instant Rick got in the car, he told his friend he wasn't going to talk about his evening with Josie, that he needed some time to think things over first.

Teeny had shrugged like the topic was the furthest thing from his mind, and he'd driven Rick to Pacific Heights in silence.

"You want to know about Josie," Rick said. It wasn't a question.

"Okay, sure. Is that what you called me in here for?"

"I didn't call you in here for anything, Timothy."

Teeny laughed, his mountainous shoulders shaking as he let go with a high-pitched snicker. He stomped a size 14 Italian loafer on the bamboo floor a few times for emphasis.

"You need a life, Worrell."

"Hey, man, I got a life. A really, really good one. But right now, I'm interested in hearing about *your* life. Were you right? Was Josie Sheehan a wild thing up under that librarian's wardrobe?"

Rick unhooked his fingers and swiveled around in his chair to face Teeny. "She doesn't dress like a librarian."

"Fair enough. A kindergarten teacher, then."

"She doesn't dress like a kindergarten teacher, either."

"You're right. My bad." Teeny held out a palm in concession. "Let me start over." He cleared his throat. "So, was Josephine Sheehan a wild thing up under that obituary writer's wardrobe?"

"Yup."

"Damn!"

"But I don't kiss and tell."

"Hey, man, up until recently, you didn't even kiss."

"This is very true."

"So what's next?"

"I have absolutely no idea."

That's when Rick got up from his desk chair and walked to the glass wall of his office. Beyond he could see the UC Berkeley campus, the Bay, and the city of San Francisco spread out before him.

"Uh . . ." Teeny rubbed a hand over his shiny bald head. "Are you saying you may not want to see her again? Because we've got some serious man hours invested in Miss Sheehan."

"Oh, no. I'm sure I want to see her again. She's all I've been thinking about this morning. In fact, we're having dinner tonight. And I'm thinking about bringing her to the ranch."

"Okay." Teeny nodded soberly. "Then it's the tattoo—she must have hated the freaky snake shit, huh?"

Rick turned to his friend and shook his head, laughing softly. "She doesn't love it, but she didn't run out of the room screaming, either."

"It's a start."

"It is."

"And did you tell her about—?"

"No." Rick didn't need to hear the whole question. He knew Teeny was asking if he'd told Josie about how he acquired the tattoo—his six-month, hallucinogenic journey through the Asian subcontinent that ended with the last-minute reprieve from a Thai prison sentence, not the first time his daddy had saved his ass, nor would it be the last.

"See, that's where I'm stuck, Teeny," Rick said with a sigh. "I don't how much truth she can hear and still want to be with me. And I don't know when to start telling her. And I know that I can't have a real relationship with a woman unless she knows where I've come from."

"I hear you," Teeny said.

"All I know is that last night was not the time to mention any of it."

Teeny nodded. "I can see how the serpents would be plenty for one night. You got to ease the girl into the situation, right?"

Rick laughed outright. "I don't know *what* I'm supposed to do! That's the point! And I've got to tell you—" Rick looked at his friend and shook his head in consternation. "I'm starting to think the self-denial routine all these years wasn't just about going straight— I'm thinking maybe I shut myself off from the world to avoid facing my past."

Teeny uncrossed his legs and leaned forward in the chair, a deep frown creasing his forehead. "I'm not following you, Rick. All I've seen you do since I've known you is make amends for your mistakes, fix all that can be fixed, do the right thing at every turn. I haven't seen you avoid a single damn thing, man—not once."

Rick paced back and forth in front of the glass wall. He'd already made the decision to let Josie into his life, and he didn't regret it. He'd already made the decision to trust her and be good to her—it was a done deal. But those decisions weren't based on his feelings for Josie alone. He also had reams of information about everything in her life—her relationships, her credit score, her family and friends, her driving record—there hadn't been a single thing untouched by those "man hours" Teeny mentioned.

But what did Josie know about *him*? She knew what he told her. And even if she Googled him, she'd only find old newspaper clips about the accident, the charges that were dropped, and the pending civil case. Unfortunately, the juicy details would have to come from Rick himself, details he feared would send a woman like Josie out the door.

Teeny rubbed his hands together in agitation. "She'll see you've changed. If she cares for you, she'll keep the past where it belongs."

Rick scratched at his beard stubble, then let his hand run down his throat. It reminded him of all the kisses he'd left on Josie's neck last night. How warm and soft she was. How damn good she smelled—like cinnamon rolls from the bakery, like sweet, hot woman flesh. And that laugh of hers! He hoped that he'd hear that joyous, free laugh a million times before his time on earth was done.

"Rick?"

"Huh?"

"Damn, dude. You weren't joking."

"About what?"

Teeny got up from the chair and joined Rick at the glass wall. "You know, one of the things I've always admired about you is that when you set your mind to something, you make it happen. No hemming and hawing—you just do what you have to do to get it done. Celestial Pet is a perfect example. You've built it from nothing to a successful company in just six years. It's amazing."

"Thanks. But it's not like I did it alone—you were with me. And so were my father's resources."

Teeny put his hand on Rick's shoulder. "What I'm saying is you've taken the same approach to Josie."

Rick looked sideways at him, shoving his hands into his shorts pockets. "How so?"

Teeny smiled. "Well, my friend, once you made your decision to deviate from the plan, you deviated the living fuck out of it."

Rick chuckled.

"I think you're already in love with this girl."

Rick didn't say anything, mostly because there wasn't

enough air in his lungs to speak. He coughed instead. And blinked a few times.

"You've gone from zero to ninety in a matter of days, Rousseau."

"I know I have."

"No more crashes for you, got it? That's all I'm saying."

Rick looked up into his tall friend's face and saw moisture forming in his eyes. "Teeny, I wouldn't have survived without you."

"No shit," he said. "Same for me." Teeny wiped his cheeks and took a deep breath. "Okay. So while we're on the subject of friends, we really should talk about the dog ladies."

Rick was baffled. "The *who*?"

"Josie's friends, you know—the girls' gym teacher, the movie star from *Gilligan's Island,* and the young Demi Moore."

"As I recall, they have names, Teeny."

"Yeah, well, they were hanging out under a tree next door to Josie's place last night, waiting on you to come out. And I spotted them earlier at an outdoor table at Biko's. More importantly, they saw me see *them.* So they're probably scratching their heads right about now, trying to figure out why the chauffeur for Josie's new boy toy has been spying on them."

Rick grimaced. "This could be awkward."

"Mark my word, Rousseau." Teeny gave Rick's back a friendly slap. "The dog ladies are going to start yanking your chain."

"Why would they do that?"

"Because you just busted up their all-girls club, man! And besides, they got nothing better to do."

The sound of the door opening made Rick and Teeny turn in tandem. Instinctively, Teeny reached for the semiautomatic pistol tucked inside his waistband.

"It's just little ole me," Gwen Anders said, her golden hair spilling over her shoulder as she peeked in the door. She smiled at both of them. "Hope I'm not interrupting."

CHAPTER 11

"Good afternoon! Welcome to Wal-Mart!"

Bennett Cummings wasn't certain of the protocol here, due to the fact that he'd never set foot in a big-box discount store in his life, let alone this particular establishment in Worcester, Massachusetts. But he smiled at the man in the vest, said thank you, and carried on with his mission.

He'd come for clothing and a few necessities for the road. Within seconds of entering the huge structure he'd spied a pharmacy, a hair salon, a floral shop, an optometrist's office, a bank, a tax preparation kiosk, a McDonald's, and a manicure shop, not to mention the giant supermarket operation in the other half of the building. *My God,* Bennett thought, *the Waltons of Arkansas will own the country outright within five years.*

In the men's department he selected a cheap vinyl belt and two pairs of dungarees of dubious quality, plus a plaid overshirt with a polyester quilted lining. He chose a baseball cap that proclaimed GOD BLESS THE USA! in red, white, and blue script. He selected a few T-shirts, one of which featured something called a "monster truck," which had the most grossly ill-proportioned tires he'd ever seen on a vehicle. He chose some sneakers, socks, and undershorts.

He grabbed a first-aid kit from the camping department. He selected a small cooler that would fit a few cans of soda and a sandwich or two. He found a pine-scented air freshener in the auto department and a Rand McNally Road Atlas in the aisle of books and magazines.

Somehow, as the purchases began to fill his cart, he felt jubilation. Perhaps it was because he was finally moving forward. Regardless of how it would end, the process had begun.

"I'm gonna knock your fuckin' ass to kingdom come if you don't put that shit down! *Now!*"

Bennett stopped and spun around in his tracks at the sound of the shrill female voice. The object of her scorn was a child no more than five, who was clutching some kind of action figure in his hand, eyes wide from the harsh scolding.

"Put it down, you moron! Didn't you hear what I said?"

Bennett's heart cracked. He couldn't help but recall Margot at that age, all golden perfection and smiles, one hundred percent human potential. In essence, no different from the little snotty fellow whose own mother just called a moron.

The woman caught him staring.

"Take a picture, why don't you?"

A pitiful wail rose from an infant car seat perched precariously on the handle of the woman's shopping cart.

Bennett continued to stare at the trio.

"Look, asshole, don't fuck with me. I'm not exactly having the best day of my life."

"We all have bad days," Bennett said softly. "But

we should do everything in our power not to take it out on the children."

The woman was so offended she nearly spat. She rested a fist upon a roll of flesh that may have once been her hip, then gave him a fierce once-over, from his four-thousand-dollar custom-made lamb's wool sport coat to his Gucci moccasins.

"What the fuck do you know about bad days?"

This was exactly why Bennett had come to Wal-Mart—he wanted to tone down his look. He wanted to be just another person on the road, sitting in a rundown Buick, going somewhere or nowhere with his sodas and his sandwiches and his USA baseball cap, not registering in anyone's memory for any reason, whatsoever.

"Pardon me for intruding on what is clearly a private matter," Bennett said. "It's just that I recently lost my daughter. It's been difficult."

The mother, who was hardly more than a child herself, gave her neck a few back-and-forth rotations, then huffed. "She die or something?"

"Yes."

"She get the cancer?"

"She died from injuries sustained in a motorcycle accident."

The woman ran a hand through her rather greasy-looking light brown hair and nodded. "My kids' daddy has a bike. He's gonna kill himself one day, I keep telling him."

Bennett nodded. He noticed that the little boy had put down the action figure and cautiously moved closer. "Hello, young man," Bennett said.

"Whazzup?" the youngster said.

His mother thought her son's disrespect was hilarious. When her laughter subsided, she looked at Bennett thoughtfully, then said, "Well, mind your own business, is all I'm saying."

He had no idea what possessed him, but he reached in his wallet and pulled out a crisp hundred. "Buy your son the toy," he said.

She frowned. "You some kind of sick fuck or something?"

Bennett had to laugh, because, technically, the answer to that exceedingly vulgar question was a resounding *yes*. He was on his way to commit premeditated homicide, after all. But he meant the child no harm.

"Here." He handed her the money.

The young woman squinted at him. "Are you shitting me?" She took it in her hand, turned it over, examined the bill for signs of forgery. By this time, her baby was flat-out screaming.

"Have a good day," Bennett said, steering his cart in the opposite direction and walking away. He heard the little boy ask if he could hold the money.

Bennett moseyed into the grocery area and picked up some peanut butter and a six-pack of single-serving mixed fruit. He got some bottled water, some root beer, a loaf of whole-wheat bread, and some sliced turkey breast. He paid for his purchases with cash, then went into the men's room where he put on his new ensemble, including the ball cap. He stuffed his expensive clothing into a trashcan overflowing with damp paper towels.

His destiny called.

"I wasn't expecting you, Gwen."

Regardless, the executive director of his charitable foundation was now standing in the middle of Rick's office, so he motioned for her to take the seat recently occupied by Teeny.

"Timothy, a pleasure to see you as always," she said.

"Miss Anders." Teeny acknowledged Gwen with a nod, then shot Rick a sharp look. "Talk to you later," he said, walking out and closing the door behind him.

"I had no choice but to barge in on you, Rick. You've been avoiding me." Gwen made herself comfortable in the leather-and-steel side chair, crossing her legs for maximum effect. Gwen was dressed, as usual, in a flawless custom-tailored pastel-colored suit, three-inch-high pointy-toed pumps that fell somewhere between basic business and overtly sexy. She'd worn her hair down, however, which was unusual for her, as she usually pulled it back in a bun or put it up in some kind of twist at the nape of her neck. Rick wondered if Gwen had something special planned for this particular visit.

"I haven't been avoiding you, Gwen." Rick returned to his desk chair. "I've been a little preoccupied lately."

"Haven't we all?" Gwen gave him a tolerant smile. Then she reached into the portfolio case at her feet and pulled out an ultrathin laptop. She placed it on the surface of her tight skirt, opened it, clicked a single key, and spun it around to face him. On the screen was a colorful bar graph with a pronounced downward slope.

"The Meadowbrook Foundation has lost eleven percent of its net worth in the last six months, due to the volatility of the market. I've desperately needed your direction these past three weeks but you've ignored all my calls, e-mails, and text messages. So, I'm here today to inform you that in the last thirty days alone, you've lost seven million dollars. In all good conscience, I should probably tender my resignation."

Rick shook his head slowly. "Spare me the histrionics, Gwen. You know you've done nothing wrong."

Rick sighed. When his father died, he became the sole beneficiary of an estate so huge that seven million seemed like loose change. At first, all Rick could do was stare at the stack of papers his father's legal team had delivered, baffled by the gibberish. He was still in severe pain and going to outpatient physical therapy five days a week. He had no idea what to do with all the money. In fact, he hadn't decided what to do with his life, or even if he deserved to have one.

The size of his father's estate—and the responsibility it entailed—was mind-boggling. It took Rick a few months, but he eventually decided to sever all ties with his past. His parents were gone and he had no brothers or sisters, so there was no reason to stay in Rhode Island. He sold the importing business to his father's lifelong competitor. He cashed out his father's investments, stashing most of it away in offshore accounts. And he began the long process of healing—body, mind, and spirit.

Even before his move out west, Rick took fifty million off the top to establish his foundation. He named it for the country road where he wrecked his bike and his life. One of his father's attorneys recommended Gwen Anders to run it and Rick heartily agreed. She was brilliant, impeccably honest, and willing to do whatever was necessary to keep his name out of the public domain. His only interest was in helping people with traumatic head injuries receive the care they needed. He did it to ransom his spirit. He did it in Margot's honor, because it was the only thing he'd ever be able to do for her.

"Well?" Gwen waited patiently as Rick studied the graph. Then he met her gaze.

"We start from here and do the best we can," he said. "It's only money."

Gwen laughed, tossing her hair back as she did so. Interestingly, when he'd hired her six years before, Rick barely noticed her beauty. It was as if he'd cut himself off so thoroughly from the world of women that her stunning looks didn't register. Of course, his respect for her business acumen had grown over the years, and he'd long ago privately acknowledged that she was extraordinarily good-looking.

But Rick hadn't been interested in Gwen. He hadn't been interested in women, period. So Gwen had taken it upon herself to change his mind with one barely suggestive comment or subtle tactical strike after another, for six years now. Her approach was so understated that he sometimes wondered if he were imagining it, but Teeny was always there to shed light on the truth: Gwen was determinedly, irrevocably, hot for her boss.

"I've made arrangements for us to have dinner with our team from Staunton and Blalock tonight." Gwen turned the laptop away from Rick and closed it shut, obviously annoyed that he'd barely glanced at her hard work.

"Tonight?" Rick sat up straight. "I can't."

Gwen laughed softly and shook her head. "You have no choice, Rick. I know you say you've been preoccupied—and the nature of your distraction is none of my business—but surely you've noticed that Wall Street is burning and we're all choking on the smoke?"

Rick nodded his head, pleased as ever that Gwen Anders was in charge. "I'm well aware of that, Gwen."

"Good. Then you're also aware that Staunton and Blalock's client list is comprised of San Francisco's most elite investors, who are currently their most frantic and pissed-off investors. I had to throw a fit to get us this emergency meeting."

"Tonight isn't good for me, Gwen. I have plans."

In silence, Gwen packed up her laptop and closed her portfolio, her hair hanging down across her face as she did so. She uncrossed her long legs, flipped her hair back, and stood. Rick stood with her.

"Excuse me, Rick," she said matter-of-factly. "But I was under the impression this foundation meant a great deal to you on a personal level. I assumed that you were dedicated to providing long-term care to as many underinsured and uninsured head injury patients as possible. I believed your mission was to help everyone who needed it."

"It is," Rick said, his jaw tightening.

"That mission takes money. The seven million we lost because of your preoccupation could have provided long-term care for a dozen patients, perhaps even giving back a life or two in the process."

Rick nodded, shoving his hands deep into his shorts pockets. "Gwen, you know I have always appreciated your dedication to Meadowbrook."

"Thank you."

"However, I do not appreciate your attempt to manipulate me with guilt or any other emotion. It isn't working and never will."

One of her pale eyebrows shot high on her forehead. "I would never attempt anything of the kind."

"Good." Rick remained outwardly calm but inside he was fuming. "Go tonight without me. Make the most prudent decisions possible. I am confident the foundation is in good hands."

Gwen beamed, as if their exchange had been tension-free. "Thank you for your confidence, Rick.

So, if I may ask, what plans do you have tonight that are so important?"

He paused a second, wondering how to answer. On one hand, if Gwen knew he had a girlfriend, it might put an end to her fishing expeditions. On the other, knowing Rick had changed his policy on women could spur Gwen to double her efforts. It didn't matter, Rick knew. The truth was the truth. It was that simple.

"I'm getting takeout pizza with my girlfriend. Then we're going to walk her dog around the neighborhood."

Gwen froze. It was as if her living flesh turned to solid ice before his eyes. She didn't flinch or breathe, but Rick knew what had to be flashing through her mind—all those times he'd turned down her invitations to chic picnics, black-tie fund-raisers, the opera, box seats at AT&T Park, quaint restaurants . . . the list had grown long in six years. In her stillness, Gwen was probably trying to grasp the fact that Rick had not only been disinterested in women as a matter of principle, but he'd also been disinterested in her, specifically.

She blinked, the ice sculpture beginning to thaw. "Did you say *girlfriend*?" she asked.

He nodded.

"Pizza?"

"Yes."

"And a *dog*?"

"A Labradoodle."

Gwen put a hand to her throat, as if she were literally trying to stop a rise of bile.

"I—" She laughed uncomfortably, shaking her head. "But I thought . . . I'm sorry, just a moment." She took a steadying breath and pasted on a cool smile. "Is this a recent development?"

"It is."

"Well, this comes as quite a shock, Rick. I've always assumed . . ." She stopped suddenly, tucking her portfolio under her arm. "I'll send you a summary from the meeting," she said, her words clipped. "If there's any recommendation you don't agree with, let me know immediately. We can't afford another day of fiscal hemorrhaging."

"I will."

"Good-bye, Rick."

With that, Gwen Anders strolled to Rick's office door, her hips and her straight yellow hair swaying as she moved. The instant her hand reached the doorknob, she looked over her shoulder. A set of pale blue eyes scanned Rick's face for a last-minute clarification, an explanation—*something.*

"See you, Gwen," he said. "Thanks again."

Gwen Anders wasn't the type who slammed doors. So it surprised Rick when she did.

"Beth?" Josie couldn't believe her eyes. Her sister hadn't once come to see her at work in all the years Josie had been at the paper, and the day she decided to visit, she brought their mother! "Mom? Oh, my God, what's wrong?"

Josie heard the voice of Denise the newsroom receptionist from behind her shoulder. "Conference Room A again?" she asked kindly.

Josie nodded and mumbled her thanks, showing her sister and mother into the room. The things that went through her head were in this order: *Dad has had a heart attack; Donald has died in a plane crash; one of the babies has just been diagnosed with a terminal illness.*

Her mom's face was lined with exhaustion. Beth couldn't look Josie in the eye.

"Just spit it out," Josie said. "Don't torture me like this."

"Well," Josie's mother began, glancing quickly in Beth's direction. "Howie has asked your sister for a separation. He's already moved his things out of the house and rented himself an apartment in town, close to work."

Josie shook her head as if to unplug her ears. This couldn't be right. *"What?"*

Beth looked up, her eyes unnaturally bright as they latched on to Josie. "So? Aren't you happy? Aren't you going to say you told me so?"

Josie fell against the seat back, speechless. She had to remind herself that her baby sister was probably in shock and that a *whump!* upside her head might not be in her best interest.

"That's enough, Beth," their mother said, her voice as tired as her face. "You said you needed Josie's help and advice, so let's forgo the bitterness."

Beth looked down, wringing and twisting her hands in her lap.

Josie turned to her mother for some context. "Want to fill me in?"

Ann Sheehan sniffed. It was obvious she'd been crying, so Josie reached out and touched her mom's arm. "Are the kids doing okay? Just answer me that."

"They're oblivious, thank God. They think Daddy's at work. They're with Grandpa right now."

Josie nodded, feeling some relief. "Did the two of you have a fight, Beth?"

"A whopper," she said, still looking at her hands.

"What about?"

Beth shrugged, slowly raising her face. "He came home late again and forgot to stop at the store like I'd asked him to. I was really mean to him. I said some really awful things that I shouldn't have."

"Okay." Josie looked to her mother, who rolled her eyes heavenward. "What exactly did you say, Beth?"

"Well . . . I don't remember the *exact* words."

Their mom blew out a hiss of air. "That's such a load of bullshit, Beth. Just tell her what you told Howie. How's your sister supposed to help you if she doesn't know what you did?"

Josie tried not to look shocked. She'd never heard her mother say anything more than an occasional "hell" or "damn," and every once in a while a "Sweet Mother of Jesus" would pop out, which, along with Shakespeare's Greatest Hits, was reserved for times of true crisis.

Beth rolled her head around, looking at anything and everything in the conference room except her mother and sister. "I told him he was as sexy as left-over meat loaf," she said very matter-of-factly. "I told him I'd be perfectly happy if he never touched me again as long as I lived. I told him he was useless as a father and I couldn't stand the way he smelled."

Josie shut her eyes for a second and thought, *Sweet Mother of Jesus.* "Okay. Anything else?" She couldn't believe she dared to ask.

"Yeah. I told him I only married him because I knew he'd take care of me financially. I told him I settled when I married him. That he didn't excite me and never really had."

Josie bit her bottom lip so hard she tasted blood. She glanced briefly at her mother, whose mouth was pulled into a narrow white line of distress.

"Okay. So did you mean any of it?"

Beth let out a groan. "No! Maybe some of it. I don't

know. I just—" She looked up at Josie with an expression of bewilderment. "I think something's wrong with me, Josie. I've been so unhappy. Miserable. I ache all over. I'm exhausted. Some days I can't even walk up the stairs. Some days I don't . . . I can't . . . I don't even like my own babies! I've been too angry and tired to love my own kids!"

Josie reached out and caught her sister as she fell forward into her arms. Josie's mom leaned over and kissed the top of Beth's head and handed her youngest child a stack of tissues. Beth cried and cried. Eventually, Josie patted her sister on the shoulder and asked, "When's the last time you went to the doctor, Beth?"

She blew her nose in a tissue and shrugged. "Whenever Chloe's last checkup was, when she had her last round of vaccinations. I don't know—three months ago or something?"

"Was that the pediatrician?"

Beth nodded.

"No, Beth. I'm talking about *you*. When is the last time you went to a doctor and had a complete physical?"

She looked at Josie like she was speaking a foreign language. "Uh, when I was in college? I don't know— it had to be before I got pregnant with Calvin. But I've been to the obstetrician more times than I'd like to remember."

"Calvin is almost four," Josie said.

Beth nodded, then blew her nose again.

"Mom, she needs an appointment to see her doctor. In the meantime," Josie looked at her sister, "I'll talk to Howie if it's okay with you. I'll explain what's happening and ask him to hang in there."

Beth blew her nose yet again. "I think it might be too late, but thanks, Josie. That would be great." Then

Beth mumbled, "I'm sorry if I've been mean to you, too."

Josie nearly laughed. She'd been waiting for that particular apology for thirty-one years, and now that she'd gotten it, it didn't seem important. She walked her mother and sister to the elevators and headed back to the newsroom.

As she passed Denise's desk, Josie said, "Listen, if anyone else comes up here looking for me, tell them I'm at a funeral home convention or something."

"Will do," Denise said.

Josie made a sharp U-turn. "Oh, unless it's a really handsome man with gorgeous green eyes and a serpent tattoo that runs up the left side of his neck—you can send him right on back to my cubicle!"

"Yeah, right." Denise laughed like that was the funniest thing she'd ever heard. "You are such a riot, Josie," she said.

CHAPTER 12

Bennett Cummings opted for the northern route. There was no particular reason, other than it was spring, and on a northern route he'd be able to witness the earth coming alive one last time. It would be his sixty-seventh cycle of change—not bad, really. It wasn't as long a life as the fellows in the actuarial department might have selected for him—with his excellent health and impeccable lifestyle habits—but not too shabby, either. Sixty-seven springs had been his to treasure, no matter what happened.

Besides, he'd never really taken the time to see the country. In his forty years of business travel he'd only become familiar with five-star hotel suites, private airstrips, Michelin-rated restaurants, and the inside of banks, boardrooms, and manufacturing plants. Their exact geographic location had rarely mattered to him.

And so it was that he found himself just west of Albany around dinnertime. It was a rather cloudy day, with a few sprinkles hitting the windshield, when he stopped at a family restaurant off the interstate. He ordered the fish special. He should have known better, of course, considering how far inland he'd come. But he topped it off with a piece of warm cherry pie with vanilla ice cream, accompanied by a strong cup of coffee, which more than made up for the fish.

Bennett didn't know how many hours he'd be able to drive after sundown. His eyesight wasn't as keen as it had once been, and he found the reflection of headlights on wet pavement especially distracting, but he decided to keep going until he absolutely had to rest.

There was something thrilling about this kind of existence, Bennett decided. He was an everyman, a shadow among shadows, guided only by his preferences and the limits of his physical stamina. It was freeing. He wished he'd tried this sooner.

The sky turned completely black by eight P.M. The rain was coming down harder, and he squinted between sweeps of the windshield wipers. He and the gardener's car had become old friends in the last couple hundred miles, and he'd decided the situation was comical, really. The tires were just shy of dangerously worn. The shift did indeed stick, and not just when putting it in reverse. The alternator needed to be replaced, yes, but so did the wipers and a dozen other components. The heater was intermittently overzealous and the defrost had a mind of its own. And here he was, Bennett Cummings, suffering through all this inconvenience while he owned seven luxury vehicles and had reserved a private jet that, along with its three shifts of personnel, sat idle in a Providence hangar at the rate of seventy-six thousand a day.

The cat-and-mouse nature of all this made Bennett smile. Of course Rick Rousseau was keeping an eye on him. He knew that Rick would know the second any flight plans were filed for that jet. All the financial and technological resources at Rousseau's disposal would make it easy to track Bennett's cars, as well. But a 1991 Skylark with a bum defrost? A guy in a ball cap eating substandard fish at a diner outside of Albany?

No. Rick Rousseau would be blind to Bennett's movements.

The rain continued, and Bennett couldn't help but recall that it was a night like this one that had changed his life. The phone call came just before midnight. The Rhode Island State Police said their daughter had been injured in a motorcycle crash on a rainy country road. She was still alive, but she'd suffered what the doctors called a traumatic brain injury. The driver of the motorcycle had just died in surgery, they added.

It was one of those moments in a man's life that went beyond rational explanation. The police hadn't said who owned the motorbike, but Bennett instinctively knew it was Rick Rousseau. The truly strange thing was that Rousseau hadn't been in Margot's orbit for a decade or more, not since he'd gotten her pregnant in college. But Bennett had recently heard that the young man was back from his travels, and somehow, he put the two events together in his mind. As Bennett and Julia drove to the emergency room that night, he took some comfort knowing that justice had been handed down by the universe. Rousseau had been punished—he was dead! But Margot was alive, and Bennett would spend every dime he had to ensure she'd be as good as new, as quickly as possible.

He'd failed, of course. Margot was never good again. The ultimate betrayal was that doctors had the skills to drag Rousseau back from the dead, but they left Bennett's little girl to wither away in a coma. He'd remained hopeful during those long seven years. Bennett never gave up, not like Julia did with her pills and her private world. Bennett visited the nursing facility twice a week, every week, and with each medical consultation he demanded his daughter be kept alive with every trick in the book. He knew a miracle was just around the corner.

He'd been wrong about that, too.

Bennett peered through the rain and pulled into an inexpensive chain motel, his eyes and throat burning from the memories. He paid cash and registered with his fake ID. He took a shower in the flimsy bathtub, and got under the scratchy sheets. That's when he turned on his BlackBerry. Bennett knew that making calls or texts from the device would leave a trail of digital breadcrumbs along his route, so he would use his cheap pay-as-you-go phone for that in an emergency. But he would allow himself to use the Black-Berry to look at old photos, to remind him why he was on this journey.

He clicked through dozens, including Margot as a golden-haired toddler, running down to the boathouse with her favorite stuffed rabbit clutched in her hand. Then there was Margot as a ten-year-old snowflake in the winter pageant. The dressage competitions of her early teen years, with her beloved Thoroughbred mare. Their father-and-daughter excursion to New Zealand. The Yale years.

There was one last photo of Margot, and it was the most heart-wrenching of them all. It was taken just months before the accident. Bennett had caught Margot unawares as she sat in the morning sun on the east veranda. She looked up from the newspaper, erupting in an openmouthed smile of surprise.

She wore no makeup, yet her face glowed. She was a woman in the prime of her beauty, with plenty of time to turn things around, if she would only apply herself.

She'd shooed Bennett away, laughing. "Go away,

Daddy! I'm sorry I ever got you that stupid thing!" She'd smoothed a hand over her mussed-up hair and gone back to her newspaper and morning coffee.

Bennett zoomed in on the image displayed on the small digital screen. He studied it carefully. As always, he recognized the veiled sorrow in his only child's eyes. It was a sadness she'd carried since the abortion.

Margot had never forgiven herself for getting rid of the baby. She never would. She'd told him so.

Bennett powered down his BlackBerry and turned off the bedside lamp. He lay there in that cookie-cutter hotel room, in the darkness, listening to the rumble and whine of the interstate. The stinging in his eyes and throat started up again, and this time he welcomed the hot rush of grief it carried in its wake.

"Bea, can you just let it go? Please? I have enough on my mind at the moment."

Bea understood completely; that's why she told Roxie not to worry about it—if she'd just read aloud the license plate numbers from the previous night, then Bea would take care of everything.

It took Roxie a moment to respond. "I hate to say this, Bea, but I think there's some kind of weird rescue fantasy of yours at work here. Josie is a thirty-five-year-old woman and she doesn't need us to rescue her! Maybe you should get a second dog or something."

Bea chewed on the pencil she held between her teeth. "So you're not concerned about her?"

"I want nothing but the best for her," Roxie said. "But I know that if she let a guy in her apartment, then she already knows who he is. Josie may be a little too gullible at times, but she's not entirely stupid."

"Okay. Fine," Bea said, then changed the subject.

"So are you ready for your meeting with the board next week?"

Roxie groaned. "I'm meeting with a labor lawyer today. He's going to review my contract and tell me what options I have, if any. Plus, I have the forms I need to apply for food stamps."

Bea laughed. "You're not going to need food stamps, woman. Think big! Your Web site is already burning up the Internet. If the bozos here fire you then you can focus on turning your site into a real moneymaker."

"Yeah, I've thought about that."

"Then do it," Bea said. "You could sponsor a contest for the worst boyfriend of the week. You can sell T-shirts and coffee mugs and bumper stickers. You can go on the self-help lecture circuit. You can become the mouthpiece for the spurned and burned from every corner of the globe." The phone was dead silent. "Did I lose you? Hello?"

"Bea," Roxie said breathlessly. "You're a freakin' genius! *I-vomit-on-all-men.com—a cyber haven for the spurned and burned.*' How rockin' is that?"

"Pretty rockin'," Bea said, grinning. "So, weren't you going to read me the license plate numbers?"

"Oh, hell, why not? Just promise me you won't go launching some intervention without me and Ginger."

"Girl Scouts' honor."

Roxie read the series of numbers and letters to Bea and they hung up. Within five minutes, Bea was finished chatting with an old friend at the Motor Vehicles Administration.

She looked down at the chicken scratch in her notepad: *CPS Incorporated of Berkeley, California.*

"Hello there, Romeo," Bea said under her breath, staring at her handwriting. "I sure hope you're on the up-and-up, otherwise, you're going down."

* * *

The sun was setting as they walked the last few blocks to Josie's place.

"I had a great time tonight," Josie said, looking up at Rick's handsome, smiling face. "Thanks for bringing the pizza."

Rick wrapped his arm around her shoulder and squeezed tight. "I've loved every minute," he said.

It was a sweet enough moment, but Josie had been sensing a soft hum of uneasiness between the two of them all evening, while they ate their vegetarian thin crust and laughed, while they sat on the balcony and talked, and all during their hour-long walk with Genghis. It was nothing she could put her finger on, really, just an occasional look in his eye or twist to his voice. It could be that Rick was experiencing one of those "Oh-my-God-what-have-I-done?" day-afters. But it could be something worse.

One thing Josie knew for sure: If she were truly taking a different approach to dating this time around, she'd need to come right out and ask Rick what was up. She had to ask even if she was afraid of the answer. It was a bold move she'd never managed with Spike or Billy or Wayne or Lloyd or Troy or any of the others, so she'd never had a clear sense of the status of the relationship on any given day. No wonder every one of her liaisons had been a road to nowhere. No wonder the end was always a surprise to Josie—a *Starsky and Hutch* swerve down an exit ramp she didn't even see coming.

Josie smiled back at Rick and squeezed him around the waist, thinking that Rick might not be troubled by their brand-new romance at all. Maybe he was distracted by his work. Or, God forbid, he could be thinking about the "danger" Mrs. Needleman had warned of.

"There's something I'd like to talk to you about, Josie."

Guess I better buckle up.

"I really like you. I think you're wonderful and fun and beautiful."

Josie sighed, wondering which breakup cliché Rick Rousseau would select, because, if she didn't count Spike's alien abduction, she'd never had a relationship end without one of the Big Three: *This is not working for me. I really think we should see other people. It's not you, it's me.* God, did she ever hate that last one.

Rick took a breath. "What I wanted to tell you was that I've thought about it, and . . ."

He was going to pick the last one, she just knew it!

"I'd like you to come spend the weekend with me at my ranch. I've never invited a woman there. But I want you to see it because it's the place I love more than anywhere else in the world."

Josie turned very slowly and looked up into Rick's face, dumbfounded. Her arm fell away from his waist.

"Oh," Rick said. "You have other plans. That's cool."

Josie shook her head.

"Look, if I'm going too fast, all you have to do is let me know. I completely understand."

Josie grabbed his hand. Her heart was kicking up its heels under her breastbone.

Rick laughed. "Oh, man, this is pathetic—I've lost my game, Josie. I don't know what the hell I'm doing."

She laughed, too. "You don't need a game with me," she said.

"Good, because I'm feeling about as suave as a

twelve-year-old right now." He raked his fingers through his wavy hair. "Look, I know I'm going fast, but I'm crazy about you and all I want is to spend time with you."

Josie nodded, so overwhelmed by this man's honesty and goodness that she thought she might cry. She averted her eyes momentarily and checked on Genghis, who was peeing on a tree.

"Can I bring Genghis?"

Rick chuckled. "Absolutely."

"Because I can have my parents watch him if it's not convenient. He can get wild sometimes."

"I'll remember to pick up my boxers from the floor," Rick said, giving Josie's chin a little pinch between his thumb and forefinger. "The G-man is always welcome. There are a couple dogs up there to keep him company, so they'll have the run of the place."

"Really?" Josie didn't know what excited her more—that Rick had invited her to his ranch or that he owned dogs! *He loves dogs! Another item from my list!* "I had no idea you had pets."

"Of course I do. What kind of pet store owner would I be if I didn't?"

"Excellent point."

"There are about sixteen barn cats up there, too, but only one of them finds humans worthy of his time." Rick paused, letting his fingers brush the side of her cheek. "So you'll come with me?"

"When do we leave?"

"How does now work for you?"

"Perfect."

Rick grabbed her and hugged her so tight she couldn't breathe for an instant. Even without oxygen, she'd never been this happy in her life.

* * *

It was a shame that the Sonoma Valley was blanketed in darkness by the time they pulled into the automated wrought-iron gates at Samhain Ranch. The hour drive from the city was always spectacular, and Rick had never forgotten the impact of the first time he drove up the lane to the property. *Magic.* That's all he thought. He'd even said it out loud. "This place is magic."

Teeny had turned to him and said, "I'll tell you what—with this listing price they better have Houdini himself doing the valet parking."

Because they'd called ahead when they left the city, the main house was lit up from the inside and all the porch lights were blazing. Rick looked in the rearview mirror to see the headlights of Teeny's SUV right behind him. The gates closed and locked once both vehicles were in.

"Sweet Mother of Jesus," Josie gasped, rolling down the passenger-side window of the Lexus and sticking her head all the way out. "This place looks like a resort or something!"

Rick smiled. "It is. But it's just for us."

She popped her head back into the car and looked over at him, her curls messed up from the wind. "I had no idea," Josie whispered. "I mean, you told me what to expect, okay, but I had no idea it was this amazing. I can already tell the place is magical."

Rick didn't bother to hide his huge grin. He'd known that she'd appreciate the place the way he did. "Maybe you brought the magic with you, sweet Josie," he said.

As always, Chen and Tara started their barking frenzy to welcome Rick home. Genghis barked his reply, which made his own dogs double their racket. Then Genghis spun out of control, running back and forth on the rear leather seat, barking nonstop in a high-pitched yelp of excitement, as if he were about to have the greatest adventure of his life.

Rick knew how he felt.

Josie didn't bother trying to control Genghis. She opened the back passenger door of the Lexus and let him fly out, a big ball of brown fluff that hit the dirt running, the other dogs in pursuit.

"You sure they're friendly?" Josie asked, trying not to sound like an overprotective mother.

Rick chuckled and slid his arm around her waist. "Absolutely sure. Since Genghis arrived with me, they'll be cool. They're really sweet dogs."

Just then, three blurred shapes charged down the dirt lane, sending dust through the dark air. First was a mid-sized fur ball, followed by a much bigger dog, and then a little creature barking so fast it sounded like a toy machine gun.

"First thing I did after I bought this place was go to the pound for a couple mutts to keep me company," Rick said, getting their bags from the trunk.

Josie nodded and bit her lip, trying to keep track of Genghis as the dogs looped around gardens in front of the house. She couldn't help it—her little guy had never needed to protect himself from an aggressive dog. Not even at Dolores Park. Would he know how to defend himself? He could get hurt.

Rick pointed toward the dogs. "Tara's the little one. She's a sheltie with terrier thrown in. Chen is the big one. He's a combination of Rottweiler and a cement mixer, I think."

Josie laughed nervously, still not convinced of the sweetness level of Rick's dogs, especially the cement mixer. When she heard a terrified yelp a second later, her spine stiffened. The pack returned, racing just as fast, the machine-gun barking still at full volume at the rear. Only this time, Chen was out in front of Genghis in a flat-out run, yelping as if fleeing from death itself. Josie smiled.

"I think we're good," she said. Then she got up on her tiptoes and gave Rick a gentle kiss. "I'm really glad to be here. I can't wait to see everything."

Before her heels could hit the ground again, Rick dropped their bags and wrapped her in his arms, a clear signal that her little peck hadn't satisfied. He lowered his mouth to Josie's with confidence, as if he were sure she'd know exactly how to respond. And she did. It was a mystery, really. With most men, kissing had felt like some kind of test to Josie, an intimate gesture that was supposed to convey passion but usually only resulted in a torturous Ping-Pong match inside her mind—*does he want me to open wider? Is that wide enough? Does he want a taste of my tongue? Was that too much? He's just clamped down on my upper lip, but was that a slip or on purpose, and does he expect me to return the nibble?* Obviously, it was difficult to enjoy kissing when she thought she was being graded.

There was no such torture with Rick. Just pure pleasure. Pure relief. Josie let go with a deep sigh as her body melted against his, as his lips captured hers, caressed hers, responded in warm welcome to anything she might give him in return. Now this was kissing, Josie knew. This was bliss.

Her fingers twisted in the curls on the back of Rick's head. She wrapped one leg around his and pressed her belly up against his belt. She didn't worry about making a wrong move with Rick, because there were no wrong moves. They were speaking to each other with honesty. They were connecting. And that energy was swirling and looping through Josie and into Rick and back into her, entering and exiting her body, driving her forward, pushing her on and on and—

"Pardon me," a deep voice said.

Josie staggered away from Rick's embrace, trying to pretend she wasn't horrified.

Teeny gave her a sweet smile. "Welcome to Samhain Ranch, Miss Sheehan." Teeny lowered his voice and looked toward Rick, his eyes big. "Sorry about that, man, but Rosa wants to know if you prefer the guest cottage, or your suite, or both, or what. I'll fill her in and then I promise you won't see me till tomorrow."

Rick chuckled. "No problem. Let's ask our guest which she'd like." Rick pulled on Josie's hand until she was touching his side. "Any preference?"

"Uh . . ."

"The suite is closer," Teeny offered helpfully.

"We'll take it."

Rick smiled down on her, laughing. Then he said to Teeny, "Tell Rosa not to worry about us—we won't be needing anything until breakfast."

"Will do," Teeny said, then he nodded Josie's way. "Enjoy, Miss Sheehan."

"Call me Josie, *please*." She took a step closer to the huge man and touched his arm. "Only the lady at the dry cleaner's calls me 'Miss Sheehan.'"

Teeny's smile widened. "You got it, Josie. 'Night."

Rick cradled her hand as they watched Teeny walk around the side of the main house. "Shall we start our weekend, then?" he said, smiling down at her in the dark.

"I thought we already had."

"We've not even begun," Rick said. "I've got big plans for you, Josephine."

My girlfriend. With those two words, Gwen Anders's world had collapsed.

The dinner meeting had been an utter waste of time. The swinging dicks from Staunton and Blalock didn't know a damn thing more than she did. They were just fumbling around in the dark like everyone else. It wasn't about the thrill anymore. It was only about survival. In the world of finance, the line that separated the heroes from the villains had always been somewhat blurry. Now it had been obliterated. The rules had changed on everyone, overnight.

Just like in her personal life.

Gwen took another gulp of wine, ashamed that she was slamming down a three-hundred-dollar bottle of California cab like it was Welch's grape juice. She'd been saving that bottle for the evening Rick would finally be sitting here with her, in front of the fireplace on a cool San Francisco night, the lights of Fisherman's Wharf twinkling below.

Girlfriend.

Gwen had known for a few months now that Rick was ready to have a breakthrough. He'd been laughing more. Talking more. His life seemed to have a robust quality about it that she'd never seen. He was about to emerge from his cocoon, and why? Gwen herself, of course. Her presence had coaxed Rick out of hiding—her beauty, her steadfast devotion, and her quiet support. He was about to admit his hidden attraction for her. And she was waiting for him with open arms.

Girlfriend? Absurd! She and Rick were destined

for each other. She'd known it from the start, the afternoon she'd been brought in for the interview. She was his perfect match, his equal in all respects, the man she'd been created for. Perfect. Perfect. Perfect. Fucking *perfect*.

Girlfriend! How could this have happened? Who was she? How did she get to him? Just how beautiful *was* this woman?

Gwen jerked to attention, her wine nearly spilling. There wasn't anyone more beautiful than she was. That wasn't her ego talking. It was simply the truth.

She threw her wine glass across the room. The crystal shattered. The ruby-red liquid dripped like tears down her off-white walls and splashed on her white carpet.

Gwen dropped her face into her hands. She'd saved herself for him—nearly six long years of deprivation. Living like a fucking nun! Turning down hundreds of offers from men—many of them very rich and handsome men—because she was waiting for Rick Rousseau!

Bastard. Liar. Traitor.

She heard her own voice cry out. When she began to slide off the sofa it was like she couldn't prevent it—her bones had melted in the heat of his betrayal. Her knees hit the plush carpet. She fell forward, pounding her fists into the rug. *Bastard! Liar! How could you do this to me! You were supposed to be mine!*

Gwen regained consciousness when the morning light slipped through the slats of her miniblinds. Her mouth felt as if it were stuffed with sand. Her head pounded. She opened her eyes to find herself crumpled on the living room floor. When she raised her head she was treated to the horrific sight of cabernet sauvignon on the wall, dried like trails of blood on pale skin.

Instantly—seamlessly—her thoughts turned to Bennett Cummings.

CHAPTER 13

It didn't happen often, but Josie was rendered speechless the moment she stepped from the outdoor balcony and into Rick's suite.

"The bathroom is right through there," Rick said, carrying the bags through the room and nodding his head to the left. He disappeared into what looked like a huge dressing room with walk-in closets. Josie heard the thud of the bags hitting the floor.

"We should have everything you need," Rick called out, "but let me know if there's something extra you might like."

Josie remained silent, staring. The first eye-opener had to be the bed. It was quite old, and quite large. It was made of a dark wood like mahogany, and the headboard was carved in an ornate pattern of ocean waves and dolphins and sea birds, and it stretched all the way to the ceiling, which had to be ten feet high. The footboard was carved in the same motif and was about four feet high.

The whole vision was covered in what looked like decadent cotton and silk in a muted blue—pillows of every size, sheets, down comforter, coverlet. The bed was so high up off the floor that there were his-and-her step stools on either side.

A dresser and mirror took up most of the opposite wall. Made of the same mahogany and carved in the same fancy design, the dressing table was topped with gray marble and the mirror frame stretched all the way to the ceiling.

The room was rounded out by a huge fireplace, several groupings of settees with tables and lamps, six floor-to-ceiling windows, and an antique Persian carpet.

"You okay?"

Josie's mouth must have been hanging open unattractively. She tried to collect herself. "Dear God, Rick," she whispered.

He laughed, moving toward where she stood in the center of the huge room. "Most of the furniture in here is original to the house," he said, kissing her cheek. "This place has a pretty colorful past—would you like me to tell you the story?"

"I love stories," Josie said.

"Then let's get comfy." Rick guided Josie to the bed and helped her up one of the step stools, kind enough to steady her by placing his hands firmly on her ass.

"You're a true gentleman," she told him.

"I'd hate for you to injure yourself," he said, patting her behind protectively.

Rick laid Josie on her back, propped her up comfortably on pillows, then stretched out beside her. He cleared his throat. "Once upon a time—well, in 1883, to be precise—this place was built as a hotel for travelers from the Sonoma Valley train station up the road." Rick played with Josie's hair for a few moments, then dragged a fingertip down the length of her nose.

"About ten years later, a mysterious woman bought the property. She was a biracial daughter of a former slave with some bad-ass entrepreneurial skills—she turned the hotel into the region's premier bordello."

"No!" Josie tried to sit up but Rick soothed her shoulders back down.

"Oh, yes. Just relax and let me tell you all about it." He kissed her lips softly and continued. "So Madame Toulouse, as she was called—"

"You're making this up."

"I am not." Rick kissed the side of her neck. "Madame *Too-loose* made sure there was always plenty of live music, liquor, and immoral babes to go around. Apparently, she did a bang-up business."

"Okay—now I know you're making this up," Josie said, rolling her eyes at the bad puns.

"She became a very rich woman," Rick continued, as he unbuttoned the first three buttons of Josie's shirt. "Local law enforcement turned a blind eye to the shenanigans, mostly because they were blind drunk and holed up behind locked doors like the rest of the regulars."

"Ah, yes—the birth of undercover work."

Rick nodded. "You're the funniest woman I've ever met, have I told you that?"

"You only say that because I'm letting you unbutton my shirt."

He leaned forward and kissed the now exposed tops of her breasts, moaning in delight. Rick looked up at Josie. "You've also got fabulous breasts."

Josie smiled, grabbing one of his hands and placing it on her breast. "So how exactly did you get your hands on all this splendor?"

Rick chuckled. "Well . . ." He grabbed one of her hands and pressed her palm against the front of his jeans. "An upstanding and hardworking family bought the property in the 1930s."

Josie moved her hands up and down his erection. "Is this a long story?"

"Yes, and getting longer by the second," he said. Ricked yanked off his jeans and boxers, then his shirt went flying. He returned his attention to Josie, pulling her top down so that he could unhook the front closure of her bra. When one breast popped free, his mouth was there to catch the nipple. He repeated the process on the other side.

All the while, Rick had somehow managed to un-button the top of Josie's jeans and his fingers were already exploring the outside of her pussy lips.

Josie arched her hips in need. "Are we getting to the climax of your story?"

Rick laughed. "You're so impatient, Josie." Then he ripped off her shirt and bra and threw them to the floor. Next, he pulled down her pants and underwear and tossed them aside. They got hung up on the edge of the footboard.

Rick then dragged his lips down the front of Josie's body, leaving little electrical shivers of pleasure as he went, stopping only at the rise of her mound. He be-gan nibbling on her flesh.

"You know," he said, already laughing, "the family who bought this place from Madame Toulouse turned out to be real busy beavers."

Josie shook with silent laughter. "Please. I'm beg-ging you. No more."

"Really, they were!" Rick returned his attention to between her legs, a region he obviously considered his own personal playground. The idea excited Josie so much the muscles in her thighs began to tremble. He was torturing her!

"The land here was very fertile," he said, letting his fingers push open the plump and wet outer lips. When his fingertips found her swollen little clit she began to pant. When he put his mouth on her and dragged his tongue back and forth from her clitoris to the entrance of her wet opening she nearly swooned.

"The wine flowed," he said, nuzzling her. "They plowed thousands of new acres of vineyard land—" One finger entered Josie.

She gasped.

"And they added an olive grove that produced gallon after gallon of slick, golden liquid—" He inserted a second finger. Josie shuddered.

"For three generations it just kept getting better and better and better . . ." Rick slid in a third finger while simultaneously placing his tongue on her clit and licking and sucking on the hard little pebble of nerve endings. That was it—Josie was gone.

It took a moment, but Josie eventually returned to earth. "That was the best fucking bedtime story I've ever had in my life," she mumbled. When Rick didn't reply, she opened her eyes. He was sitting straight up, frowning. Then she heard it.

"Is that somebody at our door?" she whispered.

Rick groaned. "Yeah, and I know exactly who it is."

Still reeling from having her fertile ground plowed, Josie watched the magnificently naked Rick Rousseau stride toward the door without a care. He obviously didn't mind if the entire wine country population saw him naked, but Josie sure did, so she struggled to get under the covers.

He opened the door, none too graciously. "Well, hurry it up then," he said impatiently. "Get in here."

Three dusty dogs ran into the room. After a moment of excited sniffing, circling, and shaking, they sat at

Rick's feet. Josie realized Rick's dogs were pretty cute when they weren't running like hounds from hell.

"These are the rules," he said in a stern voice. Josie watched as all the dogs' eyebrows twitched, as though they were hanging on his every word. "No jumping up on the bed. Do not get on the couches. No drinking out of the toilet—and I'm talkin' to you, Chen— your water bowl is in the usual spot."

Genghis had begun to inch closer to Rick's naked body, ready to sniff at the man parts on display. "Don't you even *think* about it," Rick growled. He then pointed to a corner behind one of the sofa and table groupings. "All of you, lie down and leave us alone."

The dogs toddled over to the corner and collapsed next to each other, Tara sandwiched between the two bigger dogs, all three obviously exhausted from their play. Genghis yawned. He looked like he'd lived there forever.

Josie was extremely impressed with Rick's take-charge attitude, and when he turned her way she smiled. "I kind of like it when you're bossy," she said, wagging an eyebrow. She pulled back the coverlet and patted the sheets.

Rick got a running start, jumped, and flopped on his back on the bed. "Good," he said. "Now where were we?"

Rick lay awake in the darkness. Josie was dozing off, floating away on a postsex cloud, her soft thigh thrown over his hip and her head resting on his chest. Chen was snoring. The crickets and tree frogs performed their nightly concerto, a sure sign summer was just around the corner.

He stared at the ceiling and toyed with Josie's curls. After about four hours of lovemaking, he was sated down to his bones, warm and loose and at peace. He felt a kind of childlike hope taking root in him, as if all things were possible and the next grand adventure lay just around the bend.

Of course, all this was because he was falling in love with Josie—he was falling in love with a woman for the very first time in his thirty-seven years on the planet. He might have been living in an emotional wasteland of late, but he was astute enough to know love when it hit from point-blank range.

And he could tell it was going to be a love so good and so big that it would make up for lost time.

He looked down at Josie's face, innocent and sweet, and knew that she was falling in love, too. It was in her eyes when he was inside her. It was in the way she held him in her arms. Her love was a miracle.

But there was a reason he was lying there awake in the middle of the night. Something was very wrong. He knew he was misleading Josie. He owed her some information, and fast. He owed her a complete picture of who he was. Without it, he would be using her like he'd used every other woman in his life. And he knew that if he ever did anything to hurt sweet Josie Sheehan, then everything would come crashing down around him.

If he hurt her, the sweat and tears and pain of the last seven years would become meaningless. The goodness he'd managed to salvage from his life would disappear in a puff of smoke. There would be no balancing the scales. There would be no repair to his karma, or to the world. He would be right back to his old self, creating suffering and pain wherever he went.

Rick closed his eyes briefly. He knew there was only one path for him, in all things. Truth. He took a deep, steadying breath and, in the stillness of his heart, he asked the universe to give him courage.

"Josie? Are you awake?"

"Hmmm," she said.

"I need to talk to you."

" 'Kay," she said in a sleepy voice. She kissed his chest hair and then began breathing deep and slow again.

"Baby, I'm sorry, but it's important. Please wake up."

"I'm awake."

"You sure?"

"Yeah." Josie pushed herself up and sat cross-legged on the bed, facing him, looking a little unsteady. A silly smile suddenly spread over her face. "I was having the weirdest dream," she said, yawning. "It was *The Best Little Whorehouse in Sonoma*—the musical—and my friend Bea played the role of Madame Toulouse and Teeny was the sheriff, so, technically, that would make it a nightmare, right?"

Rick laughed. "Sounds like a real crowd-pleaser." He took a moment to simply gaze at her. Her hair was all jumbled. She was sleepy and cute and naked.

A lump formed in his throat.

"Is something wrong, Rick?"

He decided he needed light for this conversation, and reached over to the bedside lamp, turning it on to its lowest wattage. "Nothing's wrong, really. I just need to be completely clear with you about everything—I don't want there to ever be dishonesty or misunderstanding between us."

Josie's eyes got big. "You're married."

"No!" Rick sat up, too, grabbing one of her hands. "No, Josie. God, no! Nothing like that." *But I wish it were that simple,* he thought.

She frowned, then slowly slid her hand from his grasp, as if putting a buffer zone between them. Rick knew he needed to hurry and get this over with, because the truth might be better than what Josie was kicking up in her outrageous imagination.

"I mentioned my wild days, when I traveled the world trying to find myself, right?"

She nodded quickly, then brushed her curls away from her face. The way she sat, the way she held herself, he could tell she was bracing for bad news. She was so lovely there in the soft yellow lamplight. Josie was soft, curvy, beautiful. She was kind. She possessed a sunny, joyful spirit that she'd generously shared with him. He could not damage that spirit.

"I left out the details," he continued. "I didn't know how to tell you about just how bad it really was. I still don't—but I know I have to."

Josie said nothing, but she nodded soberly, her eyes following the serpents' twisted path up the front of his body.

"When I got out of college, I was a pompous ass who didn't respect anyone or anything—I thought the world owed me. I treated women badly, and I mean spectacularly badly. I used them for sex and I manipulated them and I left them without a word of good-bye, all for sport."

Josie took a deep breath. "I'm familiar with the type."

"I got into drugs, Josie. Coke and Ecstasy and psychedelics. Lot of pot. I drank. I had access to what amounted to an unlimited trust fund, and I wasn't anywhere near mature enough to handle it. When I was twenty-eight, I ended up getting arrested for narcotics possession in Thailand, and would have spent the rest of my life in a rat-infested cell if it weren't for my dad's money and international connections. I have no doubt about that."

Josie's eyes got big again, but this time they were brimming with fear.

"You'd think that event would have scared some sense into me, but it didn't. I got back to the States and just kept doing the same shit here. I was ruled by my ego—I didn't want to hear anyone tell me that I was headed for disaster, but literally, I was on a collision course with it."

"I have to stop you right here," Josie said, waving her hands above her head. She looked panicked. "When's the last time you were tested for HIV?"

Even before she'd asked, Rick knew that's where she was headed. It made perfect sense, considering the picture he was painting for her. "I've tested negative twice a year for more than seven years, ever since the accident. My last test was about two months ago. I know this is nothing to be proud of, but I did practice safe sex most of the time."

"Thank God," Josie said, shaking her head and slapping a hand to her mouth. Rick thought she might cry.

"I'm telling you this because you have to know where I've come from, Josie. I care about you a lot, and I'd like to have something real with you, and the only way to do that is with a foundation of full disclosure."

"Jesus," she whispered, laughing in disbelief. "I have another question I need to ask. Right now. Before you say another word."

"Sure."

"Did you ever get anyone pregnant? Do you have a bunch of kids running around the world?"

Rick was pleased he could answer her with certainty.

"No. To my knowledge I never got anyone pregnant nor do I have any children. I would know if I did."

"You're sure."

"Absolutely. I would have been hit up for child support."

"And rightly so," Josie snapped.

"I would've moved heaven and earth to be in my kids' lives." Rick could see the relief on her face. "Josie, that's not a responsibility I would take lightly."

"Okay. Thanks," she said, looking away and biting her bottom lip. She tucked the comforter under her arms and pulled her elbows close to her sides, as though she were building a cocoon.

At this point, Rick half expected her to demand Teeny drive her home and tell Rick to never contact her again. He wouldn't blame her.

Josie turned back to him, her head held high. "What else? Let me have it."

He paused a moment and studied Josie, a spark of hope growing in him. Maybe she was stronger than he dared imagine. Her eyes were flashing with hurt and anger, but maybe she would come out the other side of all this in one piece.

"The motorcycle accident. I wasn't the only one injured. There was a girl on the back of the bike."

"Uh-huh," Josie said without emotion, as though it were too much for her to process.

"There was only one helmet and I was wearing it. She suffered severe brain trauma and was in a coma for the last seven years. When I went back East a few weeks ago—when I didn't call you for coffee—it was because she had died. I went to her funeral."

"Tell me about her." A single tear slipped down Josie's cheek. She didn't wipe it away.

"Her name was Margot Cummings, a girl I'd known

for most of my life. Our parents were in the same social circles. I dated her for a short time at Yale. When I got back to the States I ran into her at a party and decided to take her for a ride on my bike."

Josie's mouth was pulled tight. "What happened, exactly?"

Rick told her. He told her about the drugs and the beer and the rain. He told her how he died on the operating room table and looked down on his own mangled body, only to wake up the next day, alive and in agony. He told her about rehab with Teeny, the dropped criminal charges, the pending civil lawsuit. He told her about his father dying and leaving him money. He told her exactly how much.

He talked for so long that the sun had started to come up. Every question Josie asked—and she asked a lot of them over the hours—he answered truthfully. When she wasn't asking questions, Josie sat still in her little cocoon and listened intently.

Rick heard a rustling sound and looked over his shoulder to find all three dogs sniffing at the bed, tails wagging. Chen nudged his nose against the small of Rick's back.

"I should let the dogs out," he said.

"We should all get some fresh air." Josie got out of bed and disappeared into the bathroom. He watched her as she moved—pink and round and female from tip to toe. He wanted to think of her as his—his woman, his love, his partner—but he wasn't sure she'd permit it now. Though she'd been an amazing listener, he had no idea what Josie would do with all the information he'd unloaded on her. He half expected her to come out of the bathroom fully dressed, with her bags packed.

It would take an extraordinary leap of faith for a woman to stick around after all he'd just laid on her. It would take an extraordinary woman. But, in truth, that was the only woman he would want to share his life with.

Josie reappeared, glanced at him briefly, then went into the dressing room. She came out a few moments later wearing a pair of jeans and a worn Stanford sweatshirt. She was the sexiest creature he'd ever seen, and his heart felt as if it would break.

The dogs ran to her. She bent down and rubbed their heads, then picked up Tara and held her out at eye level. "Look at you, you little cutie! Let's go outside, everybody!"

Josie opened the door and the dogs fled. She stayed in the open doorway, the sun spilling down on her. She shook her head slowly. "So incredibly beautiful," she whispered.

Rick threw the covers off, hopped out of bed, and went to her. He stood behind her, pressing his body into her back. He wrapped his arms around her. "Josie—"

She shook her head to cut him off. "We're all human, Rick. We're all imperfect. We all make mistakes . . ."

He was about to agree but she cut him off with a shout, *"And some of us just make huge fucking whopper mistakes that go on for years and years and end in catastrophe!"*

Rick remained still, his heart banging in his chest. He was terrified. He was terrified of losing her, and he'd only just found her.

"You know, Beth—my sister—she got mad at her husband the other day," Josie continued in a much softer voice, still looking out on the ranch. "She told him he was as sexy as leftover meat loaf and a terrible father. She told him she didn't like the way he smelled."

Rick wasn't sure if he was expected to comment, so he stayed quiet.

"Howie packed up and left, but he'll be back," Josie said. "People can do really stupid things when they're depressed or have lost their way, you know?"

"I know," Rick whispered into her ear.

"Howie will forgive her, because he loves her. They'll work it out. But Beth will have to do her part to earn his trust again."

Rick pulled her tighter and closed his eyes.

Josie sighed. "I guess all we can do is wake up every day and start over." Her voice faltered. "So, what I need to know . . . I guess what I'm asking is . . ." Rick felt her breath catch on a sob.

"Every day, sweet Josie—you're exactly right about that." He leaned down and left a kiss on her cheek. "I wake up every day and I know I'm privileged to have one more chance to make things right."

She nodded softly and sniffled.

"I can never change the past. All I can do is live today with integrity and balance."

"That sounds like a laxative commercial or something," she said, sniffling again.

Rick smiled to himself, realizing how that could sound like mumbo jumbo, though it was anything but. If explaining his own personal credo helped Josie understand him—and trust him—he was glad to do it. "No matter what else is going on in my life, I wake up every day with the same three objectives: *Do no harm. Dwell in compassion. Train my mind.* If I'm following that formula, I know I'm living honestly and not ruled by ego or negative thinking."

"I see."

"I look at it as a daily dose of grace, but that's all it is—a twenty-four-hour reprieve from my old ways.

And I have a routine that I follow to keep me on track."

Josie turned her head to the side, just barely glancing over her shoulder. "What kind of routine?"

"I abstain from alcohol and drugs, obviously, and I meditate for at least ten minutes a day, sometimes up to an hour."

"Wow," Josie said.

"I take care of my body with rest, good food, and hard physical work. I connect with nature in some way, every day. I also make a list in my head of all the things I'm grateful for first thing in the morning and the last thing at night."

"Okay," she whispered.

"And, most importantly, I perform one act of service for someone else—it doesn't have to be a big thing, maybe just return somebody's grocery cart or pay their parking ticket or something, but I do it every day and I never do it wanting something in return."

Josie was still in his arms.

"It reminds me that we're all connected, that my actions affect others." Rick paused. "I'm not saying I do any of this perfectly, but I do it."

"I understand," she said softly.

"You do?"

"Yes. It's your way of balancing out the damage you've done to yourself and others."

Rick smiled. "You do understand."

Josie took a giant breath. Rick felt her rib cage expand under his embrace.

"That was a big sigh. Want to tell me what you're thinking?"

She turned in his arms, and when her eyes met his, he was immediately flooded with relief. Josie still wanted him. It was written all over her pretty face. She was going to give him a second chance.

"I've been so afraid I was falling for you too fast, that I was repeating my same old pattern, getting all ga-ga for a guy before I even knew who he was."

Rick nodded.

"But now I know this isn't the same thing at all," she said, laughing uncomfortably.

"No?" Rick smiled.

"Nope—it's worse. You've just laid out your messed-up life in a high-def, big-screen, surround-sound kind of way, and here I am, falling harder and faster than I did with all those other guys combined!"

"Oh." Rick lowered his forehead to hers and he held her there, waiting for her breathing to slow. "At least you know exactly what you're getting with me," he said.

"Ha."

Rick tucked his fingertip under Josie's chin and tilted her face. He kissed her. It felt like a first kiss, tentative and sweet and full of hope. Maybe, Rick thought, that's exactly what it was—their first real, true, intimate kiss.

When their lips separated, Rick asked, "Do you want to try this with me? Do you want to see where our relationship goes?"

"Yeah, I do." Josie's gaze was steady. "Do you?"

"More than anything."

"Then that's what we'll do," she said, giving him a cautious smile. "We'll follow your formula—we won't hurt one another, we'll be honest and kind, and we'll keep our thoughts positive."

He hugged her close.

"I can't meditate worth shit, though," she mumbled into his chest.

"We'll work on that together," he said.

He held her for a long time, all the while thinking, *This is one extraordinary woman.* In the silence of his heart, in the morning sunshine, Rick was grateful for Josie Sheehan and second chances.

He'd covered a lot of ground in a short time. New York, Pennsylvania, Ohio, and Indiana were already behind him. Bennett decided to exit the highway outside a town called Peru, Illinois, grab some lunch, and see if he could spot a coin laundry. He wanted to run some of his new Wal-Mart wardrobe through a wash cycle.

He ate his tuna salad on white from the corner restaurant while his clothes went around and around in the dryer. He couldn't help but notice the young girl at the opposite end of the laundry, alternately watching *Judge Judy* and staring at him. She looked to be just barely out of high school. Too thin. Dirty blond hair parted in the middle. A top that barely covered the bottom of her small breasts and a pair of jeans that barely covered the crevice of her behind. It was scandalous the way young women dressed these days. When he was a young man, one could only see this much flesh at the beach, in the pages of *Playboy* magazine, or, if fortunate enough, in the privacy of one's own bed.

"Like what you see? We could go to your car."

Bennett blinked, his mouth full of tuna salad. The young lady was sauntering over to him. She leaned a hand on the back of his orange plastic Laundromat chair. Bennett swallowed, then patted his mouth with a thin paper napkin.

"I am not interested," he said, looking away.

Her laugh was hoarse, which made sense because her skin and clothing—what little she wore—smelled like the Marlboro Man after a month on the range.

"How do you know you're not interested unless you see what you're missing?" She brought her hands to the bottom of her skimpy top, threatening to expose herself.

Bennett jumped from the chair, threw the remnants of his sandwich into the wastebasket, then checked his watch. His clothes had another ten minutes until they were dry, but he would spread them out on the backseat if necessary. He moved toward the bank of dryers.

"Oh, come on, old man. Can't get it up anymore? Maybe you just haven't been with the right girl—"

As soon as her hand touched his upper arm, he swung open the dryer door, which knocked her away.

"Watch it, asshole."

Bennett shoved his damp clothes into his Wal-Mart bag and headed for the door. What was wrong with this world? When had the fairer sex become so hostile? So aggressive? So foulmouthed? When had young girls become sexual predators?

"I was going to give it to you for twenty-five," she said from behind him.

Bennett spun wildly, nearly losing his balance. His breath was coming hard.

"Change your mind, daddy?" The smirk on her face was repugnant.

"I had a daughter your age once," he said, feeling dizzy now, hearing his voice waver. "Her good-for-nothing boyfriend got her pregnant and then he killed her."

The girl's brown eyes squinted and she took a step away him. "Hey, don't freak out on me, grandpa."

"Is that what you want for yourself?"

She laughed uncomfortably. "All I want is twenty-five bucks."

"Did you get your diploma?"

She blew air out of her lips. "What are you, a truant officer or something?"

"Just how young are you?"

Her smirk returned. "How young do you want me to be?"

The sadness Bennett felt for this girl was so heavy he feared it would crush him to the floor. Was everyone like this? What had happened to them all? Was there no decency left in this whole country?

"Where are your parents?" he asked.

"Fuck off."

Bennett turned, pushed open the Laundromat door, and got in his car. He set his sights on Des Moines by nightfall. If he made it there with his soul intact, he'd consider that gravy.

CHAPTER 14

"This had better be good," Roxie said, standing over Bea with her arms crossed over her chest.

Bea pursed her lips. "You won't be disappointed. Sit down, both of you."

Ginger rearranged several stacks of newspapers on Bea's desk and made a spot for her latte. Roxie grabbed a chair from one of the sportswriters' desks but had to brush off what looked like tortilla chip dust before she took a seat.

"We could get in serious trouble for doing private research at the paper," Ginger said, lowering her voice even though the sports department was empty save for the three of them. "You know they're looking for even the tiniest reason to dump us all."

"What's your point?" Bea asked.

"My point is I hope this doesn't take too long because I have to be somewhere at ten."

Roxie and Bea waited for her to elaborate.

"It's nothing. Just a consultation," Ginger said.

Roxie's mouth fell open. "*Another* one?"

Ginger replied calmly, "Let's see how principled you are when it's *you* going through early menopause."

"You're not going through menopause," Bea said,

shaking her head and clicking away at the keyboard of her desktop. "How many hundreds of people have to tell you that before you believe it?"

Ginger made a noise in the back of her throat that conveyed how insulting she found that remark.

"Well, it's true," Bea said, looking over the tops of the eyeglasses she wore at the computer. "We've gone over this before."

"At least a dozen times," Roxie said.

Bea removed her glasses and let them dangle from a chain around her neck. "None of your doctors—not your family physician or your gynecologist or your psychiatrist—"

"Psych*ologist*," Ginger said. "There's a distinct difference."

"Okay then," Bea said. "Your *shrink*—none of these people think you're going through menopause, early or otherwise. You told us they said you have none of the physical symptoms that come with the change of life and that you're a woman in her prime."

"I know what their tests show," Ginger said. "But it's my body and after two kids and seventeen years of marriage, I think I *know* my body."

Bea shook her head. "Fine. This won't take but a minute, Granny Garrison." She perched the glasses on the bridge of her nose again and went to town on the keyboard. She angled the computer monitor so everyone could see.

Roxie started reading out loud. "'Richard Luis Rousseau, D.O.B. October 24, 1973, Newport, Rhode Island.'" Her eyes scanned down. "Graduated from a prep school in Connecticut, business degree from Yale. What's CPSI of Berkeley, California?"

Bea was happy to answer. "According to the secretary of state's office, CPSI is Celestial Pet Superstores, Incorporated, and Richard Rousseau is listed as the principal."

"This guy owns the Celestial Pet stores?" Roxie looked impressed. "Well, that would explain why he had a driver, I guess."

"Isn't that where Josie won the grooming contest?" Ginger asked.

Bea nodded.

"So *that's* how they met." Ginger squinted and nodded slowly, piecing it all together.

"Yeah, that's Romeo, all right," Roxie said, pointing to the Yale senior portrait displayed on the computer screen. "He's improved with age."

Bea turned the monitor back toward herself. "I'll go over the highlights—or lowlights—of our man's biography." Bea cleared her throat. "This guy has a couple drug arrests under his belt, including a six-week stay in a Milwaukee jail, and a big ole juicy attempted vehicular homicide charge from 2002."

"Jesus!" Roxie said. "Did it go to trial for homicide? Did he cop a plea?"

Bea shook her head. "No—charges were dropped. Just like the drug charges he faced as a nineteen-year-old and then again in Thailand about eight years later. His daddy owned a huge import/export company, made tons of money, and had friends in high and low places. So little Ricky got to forgo the whole pesky justice-system thing."

Ginger's eyes went wide. "His dad was in the Mafia?"

Bea looked over the tops of her spectacles. "You watch too much HBO," she said. "But," Bea went on, "here's the most awful part. In the vehicular homicide incident, this Rousseau guy apparently got wasted at a party and took a girl on a motorcycle ride. They crashed, and the girl went into a coma and she stayed there for seven years!"

Ginger brought a hand to her mouth.

"She died just a few weeks ago," Bea added. "The newspaper coverage was pretty scant, but the girl's father—a guy named Bennett Cummings—ripped Rousseau a new one right on the front page of the *New York Times*. Take a look."

She turned the monitor so they could read the headline:

RHODE ISLAND MOTORCYCLE TRAGEDY LINKS TWO NEWPORT DYNASTIES

"It's a pretty wild story—seems the Rousseaus and the Cummingses were yacht-club types and had known each other forever. The accident basically ruined everyone's lives. Rousseau was in the hospital for months. His father died of a stroke while Rick was in rehab. The girl withered away to nothing in a nursing home."

Ginger blinked back tears. "God, that's just awful."

Roxie jolted straight up in her chair. "And this is the guy who's dating our Josie?"

Bea pulled her mouth tight, as if she were going to cry as well. "That's him."

"We've got to warn her!" Ginger stood up. "This is terrible! This guy's worse than that pothead, what's-his-name!"

"Wayne?" Roxie offered.

Ginger shook her head.

"Billy? Randy? Spike?"

"That's him," she said. "So what do we do now?"

Bea leaned back in her office chair. "Do you guys know where Josie is this weekend?"

Roxie and Ginger looked to each other and shook their heads. Ginger sat back down, deflated.

"God, I feel awful," Roxie said, dropping her head. "I've been so caught up in my own drama that I haven't even called her. Maybe she's at her parents'?"

Bea shook her head. "I called them."

Ginger was aghast. "You did?"

Bea nodded. "Then I called her sister, Beth, and after delivering her version of *Can This Marriage Be Saved?* she finally got around to telling me she had no idea where Josie was."

"I would just die if anything happened to her," Roxie said. "Did you try her cell?"

Bea rolled her eyes. "Of course I did. She's not picking up."

The three women sat in silence for a moment.

"You know, I think I really need to say something at this juncture." Roxie looked at her friends. "This Rick Rousseau dude was a lowlife, I got that. But that was seven years ago. Maybe he's changed. Maybe he really regrets what happened and has straightened up. He seemed like a very nice guy the other night in front of her apartment."

Ginger nodded. "He's a corporate CEO now, after all."

Bea winced. "News flash—lowlife and corporate CEO are not mutually exclusive occupations."

"Well, sure," Ginger acknowledged. "But nobody's said what we're supposed to do with all this information. Do we act on it? Do we warn Josie? Do we wait and see what happens? What?"

"I think it all boils down to how we see Josie," Roxie offered. "If we think she's going into this relationship fully informed and with a level head—and that she's capable of taking care of herself—then we should back off and let her handle it."

They all stared at each other.

"There's always the back-door approach," Bea said, a sparkle in her eye.

Ginger shook her head. "I've got a real bad feeling about this."

"I haven't said anything yet!" Bea protested.

"Yeah, but you're going to, and I don't think I'm going to like it."

"Just hear me out, Ginger. You too, Roxie." Bea leaned forward in her chair and rested her elbows on her knees. She looked like a woman's basketball coach dispensing orders in a sideline huddle.

"Let's say we bypass Josie and go right to the source of the problem—Rick Rousseau himself. Let's say we approach him—in a nonconfrontational way, of course—and tell him we're on to him, that we know who he is and what he's done."

Roxie frowned. "I'd hate to see what you consider nonconfrontational, Bea."

"Maybe we could all go for drinks? Or even dinner?" Ginger sounded markedly more enthusiastic.

"Oh, right," Roxie said, laughing. "We just introduce ourselves as Josie's psychotically nosy coworkers and tell him we want to interrogate him to see if he's worthy of our friend. Now that's an offer any man would jump at!"

Bea looked up from her crouch, smiling. "This is a first, ladies! I do believe we're all on the same page."

For a woman who'd had precious little sleep the night before, Josie was damn near perky all day Saturday. It was probably the newness of everything—the staggering beauty of the ranch, the way Rick looked at her and touched her, Rosa's food. Honestly, the woman's homemade cinnamon rolls made Josie see the face of God, and her chicken enchiladas with mole were nearly as sensual as Rick's bedtime story. Josie decided that before she left on Sunday evening, she'd ask Rosa if she had a recipe for eggplant Parmesan.

She and Rick spent the entire day walking and talking their way through the ranch, taking breaks only for lunch and an afternoon snack of lemonade and Rosa's fresh-baked oatmeal raisin cookies. Within the first five minutes of her tour, Josie knew the word "ranch" didn't do justice to the place. The word conjured up images of the old TV show *Dallas*—a flat, brown, fenced-in world with big, bleached horns of Texas Longhorns mounted over the fireplace. Rick's place was the Garden of Eden in comparison.

He showed her everything. The tour of the main house began right after breakfast, sixteen rooms on two floors that managed to combine history with modern comfort. All of the guest rooms featured antiques, though none were as spectacular as those in Rick's suite. He told Josie why—those furnishings once belonged to Madame Toulouse herself.

"We have a lot to live up to in that bed," Rick said, with a laugh.

The great room on the first floor featured several worn leather couches grouped around a huge stone fireplace. The walls were decorated with bits of the ranch's history—framed pages from Madame's diary of household purchases, early sepia-hued photographs of men with handlebar mustaches standing with their horses and carts in front of the house. There were also dozens of oil paintings from Sonoma's most respected painters. Josie was particularly intrigued by a painting of two lovers, sneaking a kiss in a vineyard at dusk. Something about the tenderness in the man's embrace made her sigh.

"Romantic, huh?" Rick stood at Josie's side as she studied the painting. "It's one of my favorites."

Josie slowly turned her head to look at Rick. She might as well admit it—she was in love with him. At that moment, he was focused only on her, as if she were all that mattered. She loved that. She wanted more of that.

"It's not just the painting—this whole place screams romance," she said. "You should rent it out for weddings."

That suggestion seemed to please Rick. A huge smile spread over his face. "You ain't seen nothing yet," he said, grabbing her by the hand and taking her outside.

He walked her around the first-floor veranda, where wicker tables, chairs, and rockers were grouped under huge ceiling fans. Ropes of wisteria twisted and tangled their way through the wrought-iron railing. When Rick took her arm and guided her down the front steps and onto the lawn, Josie was awestruck at the vision. The thick green carpet sloped hundreds of feet in front of the house and ended at a stone wall that divided lawn from vineyard. Beyond the wall was a line of live oaks, and beyond that was nothing but pure Sonoma Valley vista—scraggy mountains and green vineyards as far as the eye could see. Samhain Ranch was more than a retreat, it was a world unto itself.

The dogs stayed close, running and wrestling and sniffing. "I think Genghis is going to turn up his nose at Dolores Park after being here for a weekend," Josie said.

"He can come as often as he likes." Rick looked

down at her, smiling. Those were the same green eyes that had mesmerized Josie from the moment she saw him. But today his eyes seemed deeper, darker. Maybe it was because she knew him now, she knew who he was.

Rick gave her a tour of gardens overflowing with herbs, tomatoes, raspberries, and figs, plus a variety of trees, including apple, lime, and lemon. He showed her the delphiniums, and the hollyhocks, roses, ferns, snapdragons, geraniums, and dozens of plants with names Josie couldn't remember five seconds after Rick told her. He took her hand and pulled her up to stand on the stone wall, then pointed out over the rolling hills of grapes. He explained to Josie how the vineyards were laid out and how each area would yield grapes destined for a particular type of wine. He took her through the olive grove and said she could take home cases of their olive oil if she wanted. He took her on a tour of the pool and poolhouse, plus the tennis and basketball courts, where they found Teeny shooting hoops and listening to his iPod.

"Beautiful morning," Teeny said, removing his earbuds. He stood in place and bounced the basketball, catching his breath. Josie caught the way Teeny's eyes flashed with a question when he scanned Rick's face.

"The most beautiful in recent memory," Rick said to his friend. "Want to take a stroll with us?"

"Nah, you two don't need me tagging along." Teeny smiled at Josie. "So you like the place?"

"Yes," Josie said simply, knowing superlatives weren't needed. "I sure do."

Next, they hiked up to the staff housing at the far north edge of the ranch, a line of about a dozen small houses with tiny well-kept yards. It was where Rosa and her husband and children and their children lived. It looked like a miniature subdivision, Josie thought.

Rick showed her the charming three-bedroom guest cottage and the newer barn—a huge structure divided into a section for cars and farm vehicles and a section that had become Rick's custom-made gym. Rick offered to take her through a workout, but with one glance at the free weights, she asked for a rain check.

Next he took her to the horse barn, where she met Tom, the only cat on the ranch who liked people. He rubbed up against her ankle and purred, undeterred even when Genghis sniffed and poked at him with his paw. Then they went out to the pasture to meet the horses—a paint, two Appaloosas, and three quarter horses. Rick saddled up a couple of the mild-mannered geldings and they took an hour-long trail ride, Chen and Tara tagging along happily. Genghis kept his distance from the intimidating beasts.

When evening rolled around, they returned to the suite and took a shower together, kissing and soaping and laughing. Rosa served them dinner on the veranda—scallops with angel-hair pasta, a baby greens salad with walnuts, and then pears and cheese as dessert.

While Josie sat there in the spacious, comfortable rocker and sipped her tea, it occurred to her that the entire day—through every glorious moment of that remarkable day—Mrs. Needleman's words had echoed through her head:

"*. . . you must be brave enough to embrace what you've asked for.*"

Josie had asked for a lot when she wrote that list, and here he was, sitting next to her in the last golden light of the day. He was a survivor, a seeker, a lover—

a man who'd been through hell and back and decided there had to be a better way.

No wonder Mrs. Needleman had sensed he was in danger—Rick had barely made it out of his twenties alive! And Gloria's prediction that Rick would need Josie's forgiveness? The old lady had been dead-on there, too.

Josie reached over and took Rick's hand. He smiled at her. It was bizarre to think that she'd only known him for a couple weeks, because it felt like they'd been in each other's company forever.

"Did you name this place, or has it always been called Samhain Ranch?"

Rick tilted his head. "Interestingly, Madame herself named it and it stuck."

"Isn't that word associated with witchcraft?"

Rick brushed his thumb across the top of her hand.

"From what I've read, the word 'Samhain' comes from the ancient Celtic word for 'summer's end,' a harvest festival that doubled as their festival of the dead. It eventually became All Hallows' Eve, and then Halloween in modern times. Wiccans consider it a Sabbath, so, yes, you are absolutely right."

"It's the perfect name for a place so magical."

"I think Madame was definitely on to something," Rick said, his smile spreading. He leaned in toward Josie. "But I'll tell you a secret."

She moved closer. "I love secrets."

"There's another definition of the word that I think is a better fit, and the more time I spend here the more I'm convinced it's what Madame Toulouse had in mind."

"Tell me."

"Well." Rick paused to kiss her cheek. "Samhain was also the time for 'taking stock' of the year gone by and giving thanks for all you have. It was a time when the supernatural world was separated from our world by only a thin veil, and the connectedness of all life was recognized. That's how I think this place got its name."

Josie stretched her neck to close the space between them, and left a soft kiss on his lips.

"Excuse me."

Teeny stood over them looking sheepish. "I seem to have rotten timing and I apologize," he said to Josie. "Hey, Rick, can I have a moment?"

Rick finished the kiss and patted Josie's knee. "Be right back."

Josie took a sip of her tea and looked out at the last bit of dying light beyond the hills. There was a restorative energy in this place. There was a power here, and it was joyful and reassuring, something that filled her with calm.

But she shuddered with a realization—she could have easily gone her whole life without experiencing this. She could have gone a lifetime without meeting Rick. It would have been so easy—and so likely. She would never have known what she'd missed, or even that something this wonderful existed.

The thought made her feel quite lonely.

The sound of Rick's agitated whisper caught her attention. She got up from the chair and went to the corner of the veranda, where she could peek around the side of the main house. Teeny and Rick stood near the kitchen door, under a light over the doorway.

"It's probably nothing," she heard Rick say.

Teeny shook his head, obviously distressed. "We can't take anything for granted," he said. "Something about this smells bad, Rick, and—"

Teeny had sensed her spying. Josie pulled her head

back around the corner. She closed her eyes hard, silently cursing herself for being so nosy, then tiptoed back to her chair.

Rick was entitled to privacy, she told herself. He'd already bared his soul to her, what more did she want? Besides, it was probably just business.

She heard Rick's footsteps as he returned to the front porch. "Sorry," he said, a frown on his face.

"I'm the one who's sorry!" Josie blurted out. "I shouldn't have been eavesdropping!"

Rick laughed, resting his hands on the arms of her chair and bending toward her. "Sweetie, you're in my house and in my bed and in my life, so there is no such thing as eavesdropping. I don't have anything to hide from you, and I never will."

Josie nodded, biting her bottom lip.

"Do you trust me, Josie? Please answer me truthfully."

"I do." There was no question in her heart. "But Teeny wanted to talk in private, and he seemed upset . . ."

Rick stood up and returned to his rocker, moving back and forth a couple times before he spoke. "Teeny can be overcautious at times, which isn't a bad thing."

"This is about your security?"

"Yes, it is." Rick's voice sounded weary.

Josie sat up straight. "Is something wrong?"

Rick rubbed his chin, as if he weren't sure how to answer. He studied Josie a long moment. "Margot Cummings's father wants revenge for her death—the eye-for-an-eye kind of revenge. He wants me dead."

Josie's jaw dropped.

"And Teeny thinks he's already on his way here to kill me."

CHAPTER 15

She'd finally gone to sleep. It had taken Rick four hours to convince Josie that Bennett Cummings could not get to him, and that there was nothing to worry about.

Earlier Rick had asked Teeny to join them on the porch and the two of them spelled everything out for her—the exact nature of Cummings's threat and how many people were on Rick's security payroll at the ranch, at work, and at his home in Pacific Heights. They explained to Josie how the motion and heat sensors worked and the exact location of all the security cameras. He confessed that the Lexus was custom designed, bullet- and bombproof. He gave her the combination to the gates at Samhain and at his place in the city.

Teeny described to Josie how he'd been keeping track of Cummings's activities all this time. He explained that the old man hadn't been seen in four days, that the word was he had the flu but Teeny didn't believe it. He said that even though Cummings's leased jet was still in a hangar and he hadn't purchased air or rail tickets under his name, he could have traveled under an alias or by car.

Teeny even told Josie how she herself had been the

subject of an exhaustive security check before Rick accepted her invitation.

"Do you remember the day you barged into corporate headquarters?" Teeny asked her.

Josie sniffed. "I did not barge—I was wearing a visitor's badge," she said.

Rick went on to tell her that he was reviewing her background report the very moment she showed up outside his office door.

"But you had a big stack of papers in your hand," she said, confused. "You could put my life story on a Post-it note."

It was then that Teeny shot Rick a look of helplessness, and Rick told him he'd take over from there. Teeny said good night, and Josie hunkered down to hear the most difficult part. Rick explained that they had to be sure she wasn't connected to Margot's father, a chemical company owner named Bennett Cummings. He said her background check included information on her whole family, her friends, her boyfriends, her job history, her finances, and everything in between.

When he was done, Josie got up without a word. She left the porch and wandered off into the night. Rick gave her about fifteen minutes to be alone, then found her sitting on the stone wall under the big live oak, crying softly. His dogs lay near her dangling feet. Genghis sat, resting his head on her leg.

"I understand you're angry," he said, approaching her slowly before he perched next to her on the wall.

The dogs were thrilled to see him, even if Josie wasn't.

"Don't give me the silent treatment. I'd much prefer it if you called me names and cussed me out."

Josie turned to him then, her face catching the

moonlight. Her cheeks were streaked with tears. "Is there anything else?" she asked quietly.

"What do you mean?"

"Is there anything else you need to tell me?"

"No."

"Nothing? Are you absolutely sure?"

Rick sighed, knowing he'd come this far and he had no choice but to let go of the last morsel, as much as it pained him. "There's one more thing."

Josie swiveled on her butt so that she faced him, then crossed her legs. "This ought to be interesting."

"You're pissed. You have a right to be—I violated your privacy. But I was explaining to you how careful we are, that the reason I'm not overly concerned about Bennett Cummings is because we do our homework, without fail."

"This is an awful lot to digest in just one day," she said.

"I know." Rick reached for her hand but she pulled it away.

"You spied on me and my family and friends," Josie said, shaking her head. "You're carrying around so many secrets I don't see how you can stand up straight. And if I have a relationship with you, I'll be a part of all this."

"I understand."

"This is way over my head," Josie said. "My last boyfriend was normal—he designed computer software and played in a pickup basketball league. Wait— you already know that, don't you?"

"I am who I am, Josie. That's what I've been trying to tell you all day—this is the whole package. I know it's a lot to accept, and I know it isn't everyone's idea of a Prince Charming."

"Good Lord," Josie said, wiping her cheeks. "Look,

Rick, there's only one thing that's a deal-breaker for me. It's the part about the children."

"What children?" he asked. He had no idea what she was talking about.

"If you are getting ready to tell me you really did get someone pregnant or you haven't taken care of a child you brought into this world, I'll just—"

"No, Josie. There are no kids. No pregnancies. I'm asking you to believe me."

Josie waited a moment before she continued. "You know, everything else you've done was reckless and stupid and selfish. I get the picture. And you've paid a horrible price for all of it. But you never once set out to destroy someone else."

Rick nodded soberly.

"But men who deny their own children are the lowest of the low. It's unforgivable."

"I agree."

Josie chomped down on her bottom lip and hugged her arms close across her chest. She searched Rick's face in the moonlight, looking for what, he wasn't sure, but he was happy to let her stare as long as she needed. He had nothing to hide.

"I believe you," she said eventually. "So, what's the one last thing you have to tell me?"

Rick sighed. "You'll be the sixth person in the world to know this."

Josie didn't seem impressed. "Yeah?"

"I'm chairman of a nonprofit called the Meadowbrook Foundation. It pays the medical bills of severe head injury patients without insurance coverage."

Josie squinted at him. "A foundation?"

"I hired an executive director to keep it running so I can stay behind the scenes. I don't want any recognition."

"That's it? That's the one last thing?"

"Yes."

She uncrossed her arms and let her hands fall in her lap. Very quietly she said, "It's a way of remembering Margot, isn't it?"

"It is."

"So why that name?"

"We crashed on Meadowbrook Lane. I thought it would be as good a name as any."

Josie continued to study him, her face slowly relaxing, her frown subsiding. "You sure that's the last thing?"

"Positive."

"Come on." Josie hopped up from the wall and reached out her hand. They walked in silence up the lawn and toward the main house, the dogs running alongside. They climbed the stairs to the balcony outside Rick's suite. When they reached the door, Josie looked up at Rick, her face stricken.

"I have my own secret," she whispered. "I won't feel right until I tell you."

"Whatever it is, I'm listening."

"I ordered you from the universe."

Rick laughed, not sure he'd heard correctly. "You want to elaborate on that a bit?"

Josie gave him a crooked smile. "It's a long story, but I interviewed this old lady for her husband's obit, and when I was leaving she told me that before the next morning I needed to make a list of the exact qualities I wanted in a man and send it to the universe."

"Interesting," he said.

"I finished typing it into my laptop just before I walked into the Celestial Pet grooming salon, the morning we met."

"That's very romantic."

Josie laughed. "It's spooky, is what it is." She took a deep breath. "This lady also told me that it would take courage to accept the man I had requested."

Rick raised an eyebrow. "No kidding?"

"And then she came into the paper the other day to tell me she sensed you were in danger."

Rick stiffened. "Who the hell *is* this woman?"

"Mrs. Gloria Needleman, eighty-four, of Cayuga Terrace."

"Josie. Josie. Josie." Rick pulled her into his arms and squeezed her tight. "Someday, when we tell our grandkids about how we met, they'll think we're completely crazy."

"Maybe they'll be right," she said.

All that had taken place hours before, and now Rick lay in the dark, Josie asleep at his side. In his last few moments of consciousness, he made his list for the day. He was grateful for the gift of communication. He was grateful for the freedom that came with honesty. Once again, he was grateful for Josie.

Gwen had been taught not to cry. She was told that it spoiled her ivory complexion and made her eyes red, her lids puffy, and her nose obscenely swollen. Crying didn't flatter even the most beautiful of women, as her mother used to tell her. Extraordinary women, she said, knew the most important accessory was composure. The way to catch a rich, powerful, and handsome man was to be beautiful, intelligent, *and* serene, even if it were only on the outside.

Oh, really? Gwen thought, looking into the mirror. *Go fuck yourself, Mother.*

She peered closer into her huge bedroom mirror, attempting to assess the damage caused by too much wine and a two-day temper tantrum. She turned her face to catch the light. She looked undone. Hungover. Ruined. No man would want her like this, and certainly not Rick Rousseau. He didn't want her at her very best.

Gwen ran a hand through her knotted hair. It was a shame, really. A waste. She was thirty-two, and she'd thrown away the very best years of her life chasing a phantom. Her mother had advised her to never give up on Rick Rousseau. She told Gwen that he was too perfect a catch to let get away. Her mother had laid it out like this: very rich men who make their mistakes early in life were the ones worth pursuing.

Wrong again, Mother.

Gwen stumbled across the luxurious white carpet of her bedroom and down the hallway. She veered into the study, and fell into her desk chair. She rooted through the drawers, creating havoc in her perfectly organized home-office environment.

She knew she'd hidden Bennett Cummings's personal cell phone number somewhere. It wasn't exactly something she could put into her BlackBerry or leave lying around her condo, now was it? If Worrell ever found out Cummings had written to her last year—and she hadn't reported it—Gwen would be out on the street. Worrell was insane when it came to loyalty. He was insane when it came to Rick.

She remembered how, the day she was hired to run Meadowbrook, Worrell pulled her aside and said he'd always have his eye on her. He explained that Rick's trust in her was conditional, dependent on one thing and one thing alone—Worrell's opinion.

That man was such an ass. She hated him. She hated Rick, too. She hated him for not wanting her.

Well, fuck you, Rick, she thought. *Good luck find-*

ing some other love-struck sycophant to run your stupid foundation. It's not like she'd taken the job for the professional challenge—she'd taken it for *him*!

A dry sob escaped from Gwen's throat, which promptly turned into the hiccups. Where was that damn thing? Where had she put it? *Hiccup!*

Her fingers touched a small piece of cardboard taped to the back panel of the bottom desk drawer. Aha! Now she remembered. She was so cunning! *Hiccup!* Maybe she should look into a position in the intelligence community.

Her hand emerged from the drawer clutching a standard-sized business card, off-white, embossed with two large letters in an elegant script—*BC*. On the back was a handwritten series of numbers.

Of course she couldn't use her home, office, or cell phone to place the call, which meant she'd have to find a pay phone somewhere. The idea was so retro she quivered. Gwen ran into her bedroom and dressed as quickly as she could while still looking present-able. She slipped on her David Yurman watch, her Ed Hardy sneakers, a pair of silky Versace drawstring pants, and a classic Armani cashmere hoodie. She tied her hair up into a sleek knot at the back of her neck, shoved a ball cap on her head, and slipped on a pair of Dolce & Gabbana sunglasses big enough to cover any sign of a mental breakdown.

She walked about eight blocks, through the Pacific Heights neighborhood. Intentionally or not, she found herself in front of Rick's house—a modern, four-story glass and stucco structure surrounded by gates and fences and the best digital security money could buy. She'd been there only once, and she'd been stupid enough to think Rick had invited her for something more than work. His living room was built for romance, the entire city spread out like De-Beers diamonds in the dark. But they sat at a small table and discussed the legalities of endowment planning.

Gwen charged down the hill. She noticed a small bar and grill at the dividing line between chic Pacific Heights and the more commercial Cow Hollow neighborhood. She spied a pay phone on the sidewalk.

Gwen pulled out the business card, then put about six quarters in the coin slot, figuring that should at least get her started. She dialed. After two rings a recorded message activated. It said, "Leave your information. I shall call." *Beep.*

Brief and to the point. Gwen appreciated that Cummings didn't waste anyone's time. That's probably how he got so rich. Gwen left her name, the public phone number, and a tantalizing hint of what she had to offer him. She waited in the booth for ten minutes, feeling awkward as people walked down the street and stared at her. She supposed her wardrobe didn't exactly mesh with the demographics of a woman who relied on public phones. Cummings didn't call back.

Perhaps that was for the best, Gwen thought, sliding open the phone booth door and trudging back uphill. She wasn't entirely sure what she'd say once she reached him. She knew Cummings hated Rick for what he'd done to his daughter, his only child. She knew Cummings wanted revenge. She knew Rick had destroyed Cummings's life, much like Rick had just destroyed hers. Perhaps they could offer each other some kind of assistance.

It was the only way to make it in this world, her mother had always said—eat or be eaten. Those were her only choices, right?

* * *

"Absolutely not."

Josie looked at him with that now-familiar expression of acceptance. Big eyes. Barely discernible nod of the head. Little smile. In general, he loved Josie's generous, forgiving nature. At that moment, however, it annoyed the hell out of him.

She'd just asked him if he'd take her on a motorcycle ride. The request had been harmless enough, he supposed, but now he was fighting off a rush of dark fear roiling in his gut. His body had begun to tremble. Just the idea that he'd ever put Josie on the back of his bike made him nauseous. The idea that she would wrap her arms around him—the way Margot had—and rely on him to keep her safe made him sweat. The idea that he'd be holding her life in his hands—all that goodness and laughter and sweetness—made him want to run out of the barn like a madman.

"It could be a really short ride," she said. "I've never been on a motorcycle before."

He watched Josie walk up to the Harley-Davidson, trace her fingers along the shining chrome and the supple leather. She gripped the handlebars and pretended she was gunning the engine, which made her laugh. Then she looked up at him with those impossibly gentle gray eyes and smiled.

"Maybe someday?" she said.

"God, Josie. I don't know."

She nodded and walked toward him. When she stopped before him and looked up into his face, Rick knew she expected him to embrace her, but he couldn't. He just couldn't do it. Suddenly, he felt alone. Walled in. Paralyzed by the fear.

So Josie embraced him. She slowly wrapped Rick in her arms, one around his waist and another up high on his back. She just hugged him. She didn't try to talk him into anything or tell him any lies about how she trusted him with her life. She just hugged him tight, and didn't let go. Eventually, his arms pulled her tighter.

Rick wasn't sure how much time went by, the two of them standing there holding on to each other, the sound of the tractor off in the distance, the friendly tomcat rubbing against his ankle, the rhythm of Josie's breath.

But it was enough time for him to reach the still place inside him. It dawned on Rick that he had a woman who cared for him in spite of everything. A woman who was strong enough to hear the truth and loving enough to forgive.

Eventually, Rick raised his hands to Josie's soft curls and he stroked her hair. He lowered his lips to the top of her head. "Josie," he whispered.

"I'm right here."

He supposed that was the miracle. She was still there.

"If we ever did go for a ride, hypothetically . . ."

"Yeah?" Josie raised her head and smiled at him.

"We'd have to stay on the ranch. I wouldn't feel comfortable taking you on the road."

"That sounds fun."

"Well, it might not be," Rick said, feeling his agitation escalate again. "We could get miles out in the vineyard and I'd ask you to get off and walk back."

"Why would you do that?"

"Because I could freeze. I could decide that I couldn't go another inch."

"Lucky for you I've got a strong pair of legs."

He chuckled, aware of how her optimistic nature soothed him, cut through the nonsense. "Everything about you is strong, girl."

"So do you want to give it a try with me?" Josie grinned at him. Rick knew she was asking for a bike ride but reminding him of their promise to each other.

Suddenly, Teeny appeared in the doorway to the gym and leaned up against the wall. He'd just finished his cardio and was soaked in sweat, and the tender concern on his face meant he'd overheard at least part of their conversation. In fact, Rick wasn't one hundred percent certain the wetness on Teeny's cheeks was from his workout.

Without a word, Teeny walked over to the shelves on the far wall of the south barn and pulled down an iridescent purple helmet with a visor that Rick had never noticed before.

"This ought to fit," he told Josie, tapping her on the shoulder.

Josie whirled around in delight and grabbed the helmet, shoving it down over her curls. Teeny adjusted the chinstrap and gave the top of the helmet a pat.

"How do you feel?" Teeny asked.

"Like a real Harley mama," Josie said, her grin spreading. "How do I look?"

Teeny shook his head, laughing. "You didn't happen to bring any black leather and fringe with you, did you?"

She shrugged. "Forgot to pack it."

Teeny winked at Rick. "The bike's ready to go, man."

But Rick wasn't. It took every ounce of strength he had to stay put, feet planted on the concrete floor, and not run for his life. He didn't think he could do this.

For the first year after the accident, the memory of the crash would loop through his brain dozens of times a day, debilitating him mentally even as he fought to heal physically. The memory was always the same.

The rain on his face, the rush of the drugs and beer in his bloodstream, the woman's warm, living body pressed up to his back.

Then the guardrail would appear in the headlight. The bike would lose traction as he tried to make the sharp turn. In that split second he would recognize that he'd been going so fast that there was no way out.

The impact. The blackness. The pain. The self-hate.

"So what do you think, man?" Teeny asked.

Rick stared at him, remembering how one day he simply had to stop wishing he could rewrite history and focus on retraining his mind instead. He would visualize the rain cool on his face, the clarity of his sober mind, his responsible speed, his smooth control around the hairpin turn. Then he would visualize returning Margot safely home.

Only then could Rick begin to believe his life had value, that he'd been allowed to live for a reason. That's when he got squeaky clean—even going off pain meds. That's when he set up the foundation, moved to San Francisco, and started his company. That's when he'd begun to live, for the first time.

Rick knew the fear that was trying to strangle him at that very moment wasn't real. It was only another creation of a negative mind, and he would not let it run him.

"Let's do it," he said, taking a step toward the Harley.

"Are you sure?" Josie asked.

"Hell, no," Rick said. "Let's go before I chicken out."

Des Moines was only 158 miles behind him, and Bennett hadn't planned to stop in Lincoln, Nebraska. It was only mid-morning—too early for lunch and a couple hundred miles before he would need a fill-up. But the Skylark was acting funny, lurching a bit when he pressed the gas. So he pulled off at the first truck stop/diner complex he saw, appreciating the serendipity of the situation as the neon words MECHANIC ON DUTY flashed against the dreary sky.

The mechanic was a friendly, middle-aged man missing most of his teeth, who informed Bennett that the Buick's fuel pump had seen better days. He told him it would take at least $500—paid in advance— and a couple hours to fix. Bennett promptly paid in cash, and the man's eyes widened. "The bean soup is the only thing worth ordering up at the diner," the mechanic told him by way of appreciation.

Bennett walked the hundred or so yards between the garage and the sprawling roadside restaurant and convenience shop. On the way through the main double doors, he witnessed what no longer even startled him—an unfolding human drama of the most sordid kind. A young couple were insulting each other. She kicked him in the shin. He called her a "ho," and left her standing on the sidewalk. He drove off in his car with her screaming after him, informing him he "ain't shit." Just another day in America.

Bennett went inside and leisurely reviewed the scant offerings on the magazine rack, and selected the most recent issue of *Fortune*. He paid for his purchase and took a window seat in the restaurant. He ordered a cup of coffee, but passed on the highly recommended bean soup.

A thud on the window caused him to look up from a rather tedious article on the newest struggles of credit consortiums. The shin-kicker had just slammed her forehead against the glass. Her eyes were clenched shut, her mouth was open, and her shoulders shook.

Bennett didn't hear any sound, so he decided the glass was either soundproof or she was in the midst of a silent scream.

He flipped the magazine page, appreciating the sleekness of the latest Mercedes sedan. The glass shook with a pounding.

Bennett looked up and sighed. The girl on the sidewalk was banging her clenched fists on the window, and everyone in the place could hear her wailing now. He saw the hostess tell the manager to call the police.

Bennett rose from his booth. "She's with me," he told the management. "Give me just a moment to calm her down. I assure you the police aren't necessary."

By the time he reached the sidewalk, the girl had fallen to her knees and had redirected her fists into the concrete. He touched her shoulder.

"Young lady, stand up."

She shook her head wildly. The colorful beads woven into her hair clicked together like a wind chime in a storm.

"Stand up now," Bennett said, more forcefully. He put his hand under the arm of her jacket. "If you don't get a hold of yourself the management is going to call the police. I recommend you do what you can to avoid that."

The girl looked up at him, disdain twisting her mouth. "I don't need nobody's sympathy."

Bennett glanced around, noting the crowd that had begun to gather. "Pardon my candor, but I think a hysterical black girl abandoned at a truck stop in the middle of Nebraska might want to take advantage of any offer of assistance."

Her lip curled. "How do you know I'm abandoned?"

"I watched him leave," Bennett whispered. "Please, come inside where we can finish this conversation."

The girl then turned her head and saw the audience, now several truckers deep. She jumped to her feet and wiped her face with her palms, suddenly in agreement with Bennett. She picked up her backpack and swung it over her shoulder.

"I'm not what you think I am," she said in an angry whisper, walking past Bennett as he held the door for her. When Bennett motioned toward his booth, she sat, but not before shaking her head with contempt and giving him a warning. "Don't ever touch me again," she hissed. Once Bennett had taken his seat, she leaned across the booth and said, "I am a strong and proud woman and I don't want nobody's damn charity. This is my problem and I will come up with my own damn solution."

Bennett smiled. "Understood. In the meantime, would you care for something to eat? I hear the bean soup is excellent."

"Um, you can go faster if you want," Josie said loudly, peering over Rick's shoulder to the speedometer, watching the needle hover between the numbers ten and twenty.

"Nope. This is good," Rick shouted, his body still rigid as a board in her arms.

Josie hung on, enjoying her bumpy crawl down one of the hundreds of dirt lanes crisscrossing through the vineyards. "What section are we in right now?" she asked.

"It's still the chardonnay. We're getting ready to go into the reds—we have a cabernet and a merlot past the split-rail fence."

The dog pack raced by them, kicking up the dust. The motorcycle continued to chug along. Josie sighed and turned her head so she could rest her cheek on

Rick's strong back. She squeezed him tight, and let herself smile.

"I love you," she whispered, not nearly loud enough for him to hear. "I love you, Rick Rousseau."

Josie's smile widened. She was riding on the back of a Harley through her boyfriend's vineyards! Okay, there wasn't enough wind to blow back her hair, but it was still a picture-perfect moment. How was it possible that in less than a month her entire world had been transformed? That night on the Celestial Pet sidewalk seemed like it belonged to some other woman entirely. She supposed it had—the woman back then was the prelist Josie Sheehan. But the girl with her thighs wrapped around a thousand pounds of steel and leather was the postlist Josie Sheehan—the girl who'd placed her order with the universe and was now a thoroughly satisfied customer.

She made a mental note to review that infamous list when she got back to the city, because she felt certain Rick hadn't failed to measure up in any category.

A funny, respectful, generous, intelligent, deep-thinking man who is passionate about his work? Check.

Loves dogs? Check.

Spiritual? Enjoys nature? Oh, yes.

Overcome obstacles in his life? Puh-lease!

And the imaginative, passionate, sensual man she'd always dreamed of? The mad kissing skills? The eyes that revealed his soul? The go-all-night-ability? Yes, yes, yes, and yes!

Well endowed? Ha! In his pants *and* his nonprofit!

"Everything okay back there?" Rick yelled.

Josie laughed. If the weekend had taught her anything, it was that she could love a man who met all her requirements, yet was terribly, irretrievably flawed. Funny how that worked out.

"Perfect!" she shouted back.

CHAPTER 16

The girl hadn't said much for the last two hours. Not that additional conversation was necessary once they'd established the ground rules for the trip: if he tried to touch her or disrespect her in any way, she'd kick his ass to the Pacific Ocean.

Bennett had always been a fan of straight talk.

He dared a glance her way and found her sleeping, her right cheek pressed up against the window glass. He pegged her for about twenty, maybe slightly older. She was dressed like any other young kid he'd seen on the road—jeans and a tight T-shirt layered over an even tighter T-shirt. Her denim jacket was clean. Her high-top sneakers looked new. Her black hair was braided tight at her scalp but hung loose to her shoulders, dotted with purple, white, and blue beads. She had beautiful, almond-shaped eyes, clear skin, and nice teeth. Not that he'd seen her smile.

He wondered if she was a college student. Or if she had a job. He couldn't place her accent. The only jewelry she wore was a pair of cheap gold hoop earrings.

"Keep your eyes on the road," she said, her face still pressed against the glass.

The road ahead was Interstate 80, same as the road behind. And that's how it would remain all way to San Francisco. Bennett looked out the window and saw nothing but flatland. At times during the day he'd felt like Jonah, swallowed by some great beast of the grasslands, its innards alien and stark.

"My name is Bennett," he said. "What's yours?"

The girl sat up in the passenger seat and scowled at him.

"Look, mister, I would've never accepted a ride with a stranger unless I had to. I'm smarter than that." She wagged a finger at him. "I weighed the risks and benefits and made my decision. But I'm not weak and I'm not stupid. Never have been. Never will be."

"I see that."

"So don't fuck with me."

"It is not my intention."

She stared at him in silence for a moment. "What is your intention, then?" she asked, her hostility mellowing to distrust. "Why did you buy me lunch? Why did you offer to drive me west?"

Bennett kept his eyes on the road as instructed. "You clearly needed assistance. We've all been there at some point in our lives."

The girl reached up and fingered the gold-fringed Mexican flag hanging from the rearview mirror, along with his pine-scented air freshener. She laughed. "If you're Mexican, then I'm Vanna White."

Bennett smiled. "I borrowed the car from a friend. I'm of German heritage."

Her stare nearly burned a hole through the side of his head. "Do people call you Benny?" she asked.

He laughed. How ridiculous it would sound if anyone in his life addressed him so casually! Even Julia. Interestingly, he'd hardly thought of Julia in the last several days. It was as if she were part of a life that no longer existed for him. "Ben or Benny would be fine," he said.

"My name is LaShelle."

"Nice to meet you, LaShelle."

"Thanks for the ride, Benny."

"Of course."

"Mind if we listen to music?"

"I'm not sure what stations are available out here."

"Oh, I brought my own," she said, reaching between her feet to root through her backpack. She shoved a CD into the slot in the dashboard, adjusted the bass level, and relaxed in her seat.

The thumping was so severe that Bennett expected to look in his rearview mirror and see Skylark parts scattered over I-80's westbound lanes.

"Nice speakers!" LaShelle said, bobbing and weaving to the pounding beat.

Bennett kept his hands on the wheel and his eyes on the road while LaShelle sang along to lyrics that, from what he could deduce, warned of big changes coming. He liked the sentiment.

"What is this song called?" Bennett shouted.

" 'Big Shit Poppin'!' "

How prophetic, he thought.

Late that night, in a motel room on the Colorado border—and across the hall from LaShelle—Bennett took out his Rand McNally map. He already knew what the pages would show, but he wanted to savor it: revenge was three days away. Big shit was about to pop, indeed.

Josie didn't show for the six A.M. walk with her friends. She had no choice—she was exhausted. Rick brought her home about ten the night before and stayed until three in the morning. How was a girl supposed to survive a seventy-two-hour emotional, spiritual, and sexual roller-coaster ride and still be interested in a break-of-dawn Monday morning hike?

So she took Genghis out on the leash for a quick lap around the block instead, knowing she looked as rough as she felt, and hoping she wouldn't run into anyone she knew. She stepped in a pile of dog doo in the middle of the sidewalk. God, how she hated irresponsible pet owners! By the time she got back to her apartment, she had less than an hour to get herself together and get to work.

As she was drying her hair, Howie showed up at her apartment, wanting to talk about Beth. Josie sat with him on the couch, her hair still wet on one side, and listened to him vent and cry. She assured him that giving her sister another chance was the smart thing to do. Howie hugged her, told her what a great listener she was, and reminded her that the family was going out to dinner that night for her father's birthday. She arrived at the paper a whole hour late with only half of her hair styled.

Of course, Bea was the first person she saw when she entered the newsroom.

"Sorry I didn't make it this morning," Josie said, hardly able to look her in the eye.

Bea cocked her head and twisted her lips. "You should check your voice mail more often, Joze. We've all canceled for the week."

Josie felt her eyes widen. Not once in all their years of friendship had they canceled their walking date for an entire week. A couple days, sure, like when everyone accompanied Ginger to divorce court. But a week?

"What's wrong?" Josie said, the guilt sending her heart rate through the roof. She'd disappeared for days on end and had no idea what she'd missed in her friends' lives. "Oh, my God, did Roxie get fired?"

Bea shook her head. "The Spanish Inquisition doesn't meet until Wednesday, but Roxie's plan is to continue her pedal-to-the-metal freaking out until then. And one of Ginger's boys was picked up by the police late last night for trespassing and curfew violation, so she's taking a couple days off to deal with him."

Josie stood frozen in the center aisle of the newsroom as Bea spoke, people weaving by them to get where they needed to go. She felt numb with remorse, ashamed for abandoning her friends for a man—especially when they didn't even know she had one!

"Look, Bea, I've got something I need to confess—"

Bea touched her arm. "Why don't you save that thought until we all get together again next week? I'm sure whatever it is, Ginger and Roxie wouldn't want to miss it." Bea smiled. "It can wait a few days, right?"

Josie squinted, trying to figure out why Bea would turn down an exclusive. That wasn't like her. Josie had the feeling she'd missed much more than Bea was letting on.

"But—"

"I'm late for an editorial meeting," Bea said. "Talk to you later, okay? I like your new hairdo, by the way."

"Ooo-kaay." Josie watched Bea take her usual speed walk through the newsroom. Then she raised a hand to the still-damp left side of her head.

A college intern bumped Josie's arm in passing and coffee splattered down the front of her white blouse.

At that point, Josie admitted to herself that she may have just wrapped up the most stellar weekend of her life, but the week ahead wasn't looking so hot.

* * *

"Just wanted to update you on where we stand on this lovely Monday morning."

Rick motioned for Teeny to come in the living room and have a seat. He took the large rectangular package from him, pleased with how it had been bundled in several layers of bubble wrap under the brown paper.

"This is great, Teen. Come on in."

It wasn't often that Rick took a day off, but he decided to cut himself some slack that particular morning. As it happened, the weekend with Josie had required physical—and emotional—skills he'd either ignored for many years or had never used at all.

And he was worn out.

Teeny took a seat on the white leather couch and crossed his legs, launching right into it. "Let's see, Bennett Cummings is officially MIA, your brand-new girlfriend knows everything about you, including the security codes to your properties and how much you're worth—to the penny—and Gwen Anders just turned in her resignation."

Teeny held out a single sheet of Meadowbrook stationery. Rick reached for it, immediately reading the four terse lines of type followed by Gwen's elegant signature.

He groaned. "I told her this wasn't necessary."

Teeny shrugged. "She showed up bright and early and left it on your desk. Didn't have a damn thing to say to me when I asked her what was up."

Rick frowned, then handed the paper back to Teeny. "I'll call her."

Teeny shrugged. "You can do whatever you like, of course, but I have a feeling our girl Gwen is serious. I've never seen her look as ragged as she did today." He shivered. "Scary."

Rick laughed and sat down in a chair across from Teeny. "So what's the latest with Cummings?"

"Nothing—that's the problem. Nobody's seen him at his estate. Nobody's talked to him. He's not used a credit card or conducted a bank transaction or made or accepted calls to his cell in five days."

"Maybe he really is—"

"Not in any hospital we can find."

"All right, Teen." Rick sighed. "What do you suggest we do?"

His friend looked around Rick's Pacific Heights home. "You could stay in here for the rest of your life. You know, watch TV and take naps."

Rick smiled. "That may be what's happening today, but it's not what I plan to do with the rest of my life."

"Oh, yeah? You got plans I don't know about?"

Rick got up from his chair and went to the bank of windows, knowing that when he said aloud all he'd been thinking that morning it would sound like crazy talk. He knew Teeny wanted him to be happy, but more than that, he knew his friend wanted him to be safe and sane.

"I plan to ask Josie to marry me." He kept his back to Teeny, and waited for the response he knew was coming. When he didn't receive it, he turned around. Teeny had fallen against the back of the couch and was cradling his bald head in his hands, as if he were trying to keep his brains from falling out.

"I'd like to find a ring by the end of the week," Rick continued. "Something simple but so stunning it will blow Josie away." When Teeny still had no comment, Rick went over to him and leaned in his face.

"Don't try to talk me out of it."

Teeny shook his head. "Wouldn't dream of it."

Rick sat back down. "You think I'm moving too fast?"

Teeny's hands fell from his head and he smacked them down on his knees. "Fast?" He laughed. "Fast would be if you'd known her for a couple years. This is warp-speed shit, Rick. You've only known her for a couple of *weeks*!"

Rick nodded. "So you don't like her?"

Teeny shot up from the couch. "I *love* her, man. She's great. I'm not questioning the who of this situation, I'm questioning the when."

"I don't need more time. I know it's right. I know she's the one."

"Okay." Teeny held up his palms in surrender and sat back down.

The two stayed silent for a long moment. Teeny finally said, "If you believe it's the right thing, then it is."

"Thanks."

"And you know I'm not one to shy away from high-end jewelry shopping, so count me in." Teeny got up again and headed for the door.

"Hey, wait a second." Rick reached in his jeans pocket and pulled out a small piece of memo paper. He glanced at Josie's handwriting and smiled at the memory—Josie had jotted this information down before Rick left her place much earlier that morning. She had been naked and twisted up in the sheets, her cheeks and chest flushed and her eyes sleepy. Rick handed the same paper to Teeny. "Check on this woman's story for me when you have a minute. I'd appreciate it."

Teeny took the paper, frowned, and read it aloud. " 'Gloria Needleman, age eighty-four, Cayuga Terrace'?" Teeny looked up with a theatrically sly smile. "We gonna get a ring for her, too?"

Rick ignored him. "Apparently, this lady warned Josie that I was in danger and advised her that being my girlfriend would require forgiveness."

"What the hell?" Every trace of humor was gone in Teeny's expression. "How do you know this lady?"

"I don't know her, that's the point. I have no idea who she is."

Teeny folded the paper and stuck it in the pocket of his jacket. "So how does Josie know her?"

Rick laughed. "She interviewed her a few weeks back for an obituary about her husband, and the lady gave her some advice for the lovelorn on her way out."

Teeny shook his head. "I don't like it."

"That seems to be your mantra lately," Rick said, patting him on the shoulder. "I want to head over to Josie's this afternoon. I thought I'd surprise her with dinner when she gets home."

"What are you going to do, break in?"

Rick chuckled. "She gave me a key."

"Well, it's nice to know she's as lax with her personal safety as you are." Teeny sighed. "I'll pick you up at four."

"It was stupid of me to fall for it, I know," LaShelle said. "He told me he had a producer friend in L.A. who would record a demo for me. That's where we were headed when he dumped my ass in Nebraska."

"I'm sorry, but I don't know what a demo is," Bennett said.

LaShelle laughed. "It's a CD with a few of your songs on it—you know, a *demonstration* of your talent."

"Of course."

"You're such a nerd, Benny," she said, playfully

punching him on the arm. "What did you do back in Rhode Island, anyway?"

Bennett smiled, noting how she'd just violated her no-personal-contact rule. "I recently retired from a chemical manufacturing corporation. I worked there for forty-five years."

"Shit!" LaShelle said. "How did you survive a job that boring for that long? I worked a couple months at a Taco Bell and I thought I'd die."

Bennett laughed. "It's amazing what you can get used to."

LaShelle smirked. "That's not how I plan to live *my* life, I can tell you that." She shook her head and raised her chin. "I'm going for it, Benny. I'm getting my ass out there and I'm taking on Los Angeles and the world and one day you're gonna be hearing my shit everywhere—on the radio, in movies, on TV."

"I know I will."

"I'm gonna blow up fast. Overnight, Benny."

Bennett assumed that blowing up was a good thing in the music business, unlike his line of work. "That kind of determination will take you far," he said.

LaShelle was suddenly quiet. Bennett looked out of the corner of his eye to see her wipe a silent tear from her cheek. Her swagger had wilted as quickly as it had blossomed.

He decided not to push her. She was a smart girl, and clearly, reality had long ago stuck a toe into the door of her dreams. Determination was important, but it wouldn't pay the rent, and she knew it. Dreams wouldn't keep her belly full.

Bennett didn't have to ask—LaShelle had no one waiting for her in Los Angeles. She didn't even know how she'd get there from San Francisco. She was scared to death. And alone.

Margot had never experienced that kind of fear or isolation, he realized. She was given everything she desired, sometimes even before she knew she desired it. Margot was never forced to rely on her own drive and talent.

His palms tightened on the Skylark's vinyl steering wheel as the truth hit him—his little girl died without a true passion. By trying to ensure her happiness, Bennett had kept her from life's most basic joy—chasing one's own dream.

LaShelle opened Bennett's road atlas and said, "We should be in Salt Lake City by six or so."

He nodded, taking a moment to swallow down the sadness. "Any preference for dinner tonight?" he asked.

LaShelle stared blankly out the windshield. "Anything but tacos."

This time he was prepared for the attack he knew was inevitable.

First, he set the package on the hallway floor, carefully propping it up against the wall, away from the expected point of collision. Next, he set the groceries on the other side of the door. He slipped in the key, turned the knob, and raised a bent knee to the front of his body for protection.

"Off!"

Genghis was already sailing through the air. He bounced off Rick's shin.

"Sit." Rick scowled at Josie's dog, trying not to laugh while being firm. It was difficult. The Labradoodle made him laugh every time he looked at his goofy face. Rick shook his head in wonder—for a woman who seemed so desperate for a dog grooming a few weeks ago, Josie sure hadn't been in a hurry to take him in for a trim. At this point, Genghis had the canine equivalent of dreadlocks, which only made him look funnier.

"All right. Good boy." Rick bent down and rubbed behind his ear, then gave him a bite-sized dog biscuit he had in his pocket. Genghis continued to sit. He was rewarded with another biscuit.

Rick entered the apartment and smiled. It looked just like it had when he left in the middle of the night—unkempt. He could see into her bedroom, and noted that her suitcase was lying open on the floor, stuff spilling out. He hadn't even given the poor woman time to unpack, he'd wanted her so badly.

Rick got the painting in safely, placing it in the center of the dining table, out of Genghis's reach. Then he put away the groceries. He got Genghis's leash on him and took him for a quick walk around the block, occasionally acknowledging the large Lexus crawling along the street next to him. Rick couldn't imagine what life would be like if, someday and somehow, Bennett Cummings was no longer a worry. He'd sure love to find out.

Rick gave Teeny a nod and a wave when he got back to the apartment. Teeny rolled down the automatic window.

"Page me when you're ready to go."

Rick nodded. "Thanks, Teen."

Back in the apartment it was first things first. He went through Josie's CD collection to find some inspiring tunes, and, after a brief shock at the sight of a bootleg live Clay Aiken recording, he found just the thing. Rick immediately went to work, Nat King Cole crooning from the living room.

He arranged the flowers in a nice glass vase. He sliced the tenderloin into thin strips, washed and sliced the cremini mushrooms and shallots, and rooted through Josie's spice cabinet, relieved that she had tarragon and nutmeg, because he'd forgotten to buy both. He started the water for the noodles.

Rick straightened the living room. His search for the perfect place to hang the painting took him into her bedroom. The sight of the disheveled bed sent a wave of heat through him. He couldn't help himself— he buried his nose in the cool white sheets, smelling Josie and himself, their love and their sex, all blended together, like it had been all weekend.

Rick knew he was acting a fool. He was a fool in love. It was the most exhilarating experience of his life.

He decided to display the painting over the living room fireplace mantel, where Josie had hung a mirror. He would rearrange things later to her liking, but decided to go for maximum impact when she walked through the door.

He vacuumed and set the table. Then he looked at his watch and decided it was time to undress for dinner, an activity that held Genghis in rapt attention.

Ten minutes later, just as he was melting butter in a large skillet and singing, "'I'm happy as a king, and foolish though it may seem, to me that's everything . . .'" he heard the door open.

He didn't know who was more excited—him or the dog.

Genghis greeted her happily at the door, along with the strains of Nat King Cole's "The Very Thought of You" and the scent of what Josie swore was home-made beef Stroganoff. This could mean only one thing: Her mother had moved in. Now wouldn't that be the perfect end to a perfect day?

"Welcome home, baby."

Josie shouted with surprise. Her boyfriend—yes, her *boyfriend*—stood in the kitchen doorway wearing nothing but a huge smile and a barbecue apron sporting the words DINNER IS READY WHEN THE SMOKE ALARM GOES OFF.

Her hand went to her mouth. She laughed. A few seconds later, she was in tears.

"Did I scare you?" Rick came to her and put his bare arms around her. "Maybe you don't like this kind of surprise. I should have—"

"Oh, my God!" Josie pointed to the wall over the fireplace. "What is that doing there?"

"We can move it wherever you'd like."

She clutched her chest.

"I hope I didn't scare you."

Josie threw herself against him, planting a big kiss right on his beautiful mouth. He didn't scare her. He astounded her. This surprise was thoughtful, fun, and so damn romantic it made her cry.

She pulled away from his embrace. "Nobody has ever done something this wonderful for me," she said, trying her best to stop blubbering. Her eyes moved from the painting to the table set with flowers, candles, and a tablecloth. She cried harder.

"Ah, Josie." Rick hugged her again and kissed the top of her head. "This is nothing. It's the kind of thing you should get on a regular basis."

Josie shook her head and rubbed her sloppy tears all over the front of his apron. "Nobody's ever gone to this much trouble for me." She looked up at him, his gorgeous green eyes filled with concern. "Nobody's ever set the table like this. Nobody has ever cooked naked for me!"

"I am wearing an apron."

"And the painting—Rick, I can't accept that!" She shook her head. "It's too much. It's too valuable."

Rick frowned. "Do you love it?"

"Yes!"

"Then it belongs here. It belongs with you."

Josie just stared for a moment, unable to think. "Rick, I don't know what to say. Thank you. Thank you for all of it. I'm blown away. And I love you." She kissed him again, but only briefly. "Is something burning?"

"Oh, hell," Rick said, racing back to the kitchen, his hard and thoroughly naked man-ass on display for her viewing pleasure.

"We're good!" Rick called out. "The butter just got a little brown!"

Josie felt her dog's stare, and she looked down at Genghis. "I know," she whispered. "I'm in shock, too. If you had opposable thumbs I'd ask you to pinch me."

Rick came back into the living room, wide-eyed. "Do you realize you just said you loved me?"

After a moment of panic, Josie figured there was no point in denying it. "I did. And I do. But it wasn't the first time I told you."

"No?"

Josie giggled. In her wildest imagination—which would put anyone else's wild imagination to shame—she'd never dreamed that this life-changing moment would take place with a naked man in an apron. Then again, she'd never imagined that the most important moment of her life would feel so effortless, so normal.

She went to Rick and reached for one of his hands. "I told you I loved you when we were on your motorcycle yesterday, out in the vineyards."

Rick frowned. "I didn't hear you."

"I whispered it into your back," she said with a shy smile.

"That would explain why I didn't hear you."

"I whispered it because it's what I was feeling at that moment—I just had to say it or I would explode. But I didn't think you were ready to hear it."

Rick tilted his head and looked down on her, wonder on his face. "But I am ready, Josie."

"You are?"

"Yeah. Can you say it again?"

She laughed. "I love you, Rick. You've changed everything, instantly, and I'm so glad we found each other. I really love you."

He reached up and tenderly stroked her cheek. "I started to fall in love with you the second you and Genghis walked into the grooming salon."

"Seriously?"

"Oh, yes."

"And how do you feel about me now?"

Rick chuckled, then leaned down and kissed the tip of her nose. "I adore you, Josephine. Everything is more beautiful in your company. I marvel at how perceptive you are and how you make me laugh. I trust you completely, and that's coming from a man who hasn't trusted anyone but Teeny in a long, long time."

Josie nodded.

"I can't get enough of the way your body feels in my hands and how you smell and look and taste. I love you, and it gets bigger and stronger every day we spend together."

"It really does," she said.

Rick's gaze fell to her lips. He lowered his head and put his mouth on hers. She closed her eyes and let the sensation run hot through her center, amazed at how their kisses kept advancing to the next level, how with each new secret they shared or every additional layer they peeled away, their kisses grew deeper and wiser. That particular kiss was the bomb—hot, sweet, grateful, hungry, hopeful. The beef Stroganoff would have to be refrigerated.

There was a pounding at her door. Genghis barked.

Josie pulled away, frowning, annoyed that someone had the nerve to disrupt her blissful surrender.

"Are you expecting anyone?" Rick asked.

"No. Were you?"

Rick laughed, looking down at his attire, or lack thereof. "Only you, dear."

Josie went to the door and got up on her tiptoes to look out the peephole. "Oh, *shit*," she hissed, slamming her eyes shut and doubling over in distress. After taking a second to calm herself, she looked at Rick and said, "My whole freaking family is here. You should probably put on some pants."

CHAPTER 17

When was the last time Gwen Anders had felt desperate?

Never.

Therefore, Gwen had not prepared in advance for the day she found herself in desperate need of male attention, for someone to recognize her intellectual complexity, her shrewd approach to finance, and her impossibly firm buttocks.

Regardless of her lack of preparation, that was where Gwen was that Monday evening, in the lobby bar of the St. Regis Hotel. She'd been telling herself that she just needed to get out, do some top-shelf people-watching, munch on a few wasabi peas, and sip on a decently prepared cocktail or two while contemplating her next move. In reality, she was just plain desperate for someone to tell her she was the most beautiful woman they'd ever seen, which made her no better than the dozen other well-dressed thirty-somethings alone or in a gaggle of girls, their perfectly made-up eyes darting around the room, the fear barely concealed in each playful flash of seduction. Their prey: the visiting millionaires returning from a day of dealmaking.

After a half hour of this unpleasantness, Gwen was ready to leave. Yes, she'd recently been rejected by the man of her choice, tossed aside for a chunky obituary writer named *Josephine,* of all things, as she'd discovered while in Rick's office that morning. (The man shouldn't leave his background checks open on his desk like that.) And yes, due to that humiliation, she'd been forced to resign her position. But she was still Gwen Anders. She would rise above it all.

She took a last sip of her ginger-pomegranate cosmo and prepared to leave. The desperation in that bar had a foul smell to it, clashing terribly with her Acqua di Parma perfume. She had just reached for her purse when she saw him.

Tall. Mediterranean. Black hair combed back and long at the collar. Patrician nose. Wide mouth. No suit for this man—he was in jeans and a wrinkled linen jacket over a wrinkled cotton button-down. He moved with the grace of a man who was in full command of himself and his world, despite the fact that he looked like he'd just spent a couple days on a plane, in coach.

In an instant, Gwen no longer felt desperate. She felt alive. When the man casually turned her way she knew he'd already seen her, possibly even selected her before he'd entered the hotel lobby. He seemed like a man who carefully calculated all of his chance encounters.

She couldn't help it—the left corner of her mouth curled and her eyelids grew heavy.

He headed right toward her. He sat down without an invitation. And with an accent thicker than a tipsy Antonio Banderas, he said, "You are an exquisitely beautiful woman."

Gwen laughed as she got up to leave. She strolled through the lobby, certain that he was admiring her audacity and her impossibly firm buttocks in equal measure.

He caught up with her on the sidewalk. The evening was windy and she felt her hair blow around her head like a halo.

"I would like to photograph you. That is all." The sincerity dripped from his words and his dark eyes.

Gwen laughed again and signaled for a taxi.

"Please do not deny me," he said.

That's when it hit her—she didn't need this man. She didn't need any man. She had herself. That's why she had come here tonight—to remind herself that she was still everything she had always been, even if Rick Rousseau didn't want all that she was. Gwen hadn't been desperate for a man's attention after all—she'd been desperate to rediscover her self-respect.

She got inside the cab, knowing that as of right that second, her days of wine-soaked self-pity were officially over.

"Please do not go," he said, his last plea before she reached for the door handle.

"Have a pleasant stay in San Francisco," she said, slamming it shut.

Gwen asked the taxi driver to wait for her at the public phone booth in Cow Hollow. She got the same terse voice mail. She left an equally brief message: "This is Gwen Anders. Disregard my previous message. It was a terrible mistake."

"I forgot."

That's what Josie said as she opened the door to her mother, father, brother, sister, brother-in-law, niece, and nephew.

"How could you forget Daddy's birthday?" Beth said, adjusting Chloe's position on her hip.

The crowd began to push into her apartment.

"I didn't forget his birthday—I just forgot we were going to dinner."

Donald shot her a doubtful look. "Since when do you forget about a meal?"

"Were you in the middle of cooking something?" Josie's mother sniffed the air, then headed into the kitchen.

Her father was on his way to the sound system. "Nat King Cole?" he asked.

Beth stopped in the center of the room, raising her eyes to the painting. She spun around abruptly. "Oh, my God, Josie's getting ready for a date! And where in God's name did you get this gorgeous painting? It almost looks *real*!"

Her mother poked her head out of the kitchen. "Whose beef Stroganoff recipe are you using? It looks delish!"

That's when Rick came out of her bedroom.

"It's his recipe," Josie said, pointing. "And his painting."

Rick was wearing a pair of jeans, sneakers, and a cotton sweater over a T-shirt. He smiled graciously, and didn't miss a beat.

"Hello, everyone. Mr. Sheehan, nice to meet you." He extended his hand and approached Josie's dad. "I'm Rick Rousseau." Rick moved seamlessly over to Josie's mom. "Mrs. Sheehan. I'm Rick. I've heard so much about you." He kissed her cheek.

An openmouthed Beth was next. "So nice to finally meet you, Beth." He touched her shoulder. "This must be Chloe. Oh, and hello, Howie. Is this Calvin?" He moved toward Howie, shook his hand, and touched the younger child on the head.

"I'm Donald," Josie's brother said, extending his hand to Rick. "We apologize. We didn't mean to—"

"It's my fault entirely," Rick said, addressing everyone. Genghis had stopped sniffing and jumping on the new arrivals and now sat at Rick's feet. "Josie had no idea I'd be here—I surprised her with dinner when she got home from work."

"Oh . . . my . . . God," Beth whispered, her eyes huge.

"We were headed to the Olive Garden for my birthday party," Josie's dad said, shoving his hands in his trousers. "The one down at the Stonestown shopping center. They have unlimited breadsticks. Ever eaten there?"

"It's a *galleria,* Dad," Beth corrected him.

"It's a shopping center with a frilly name," Josie's father said. "I ought to know—I put in half their plumbing. So, would you like to join us, Rick?"

Rick looked pleased by the invitation and turned to Josie for the go-ahead. She was shocked. Rick had met and charmed everyone in her family in less time than it usually took her to get Genghis to stop humping their shins.

She smiled at Rick, thinking he was the bravest, strongest man she'd ever known.

"I'd be honored, sir," Rick said to Josie's dad.

"Let me get my keys," Josie said.

"We can fit you in the van," her dad said. "Plenty of room for everyone."

On the way out the apartment door, her mother leaned into Josie's ear. "He's wonderful!"

Beth grabbed her sleeve and whispered, "Don't mess this up, whatever you do."

A few hours later, around a large round table and

stuffed to the gills with pasta and a prearranged chocolate birthday cake, the Sheehans began pulling out gifts and cards for Josie's dad. Josie hadn't had time to get him anything, which her dad must have seen in her panicked expression.

"Don't even worry about it," he told her, patting her hand. "To see my girl happy is the greatest gift a father could ask for."

Josie's dad raised his wine goblet and said, "Here's to another year of life's unexpected adventures." Everyone joined in the toast, Rick with his water glass and a wide smile that was all for Josie.

"I know you're exhausted." Rick opened Josie's apartment door and shielded her from the spastic dog. "You relax and I'll take him for a walk."

"Are you sure?" Josie looked surprised.

"Of course."

"What about Teeny? Shouldn't he know you're walking around at night?"

Rick laughed. "He's right outside, Josie. Didn't you see him a few tables away at the restaurant?"

Josie's mouth opened. "For a man that big, he can sure keep a low profile."

"I'll pass along the compliment." He kissed Josie's cheek and retrieved Genghis's leash and a plastic bag from the coat closet. "Anyway, who needs Teeny? I have a Mongol warlord for protection."

Josie glanced at the panting Labradoodle and sighed. "I'm pretty sure he likes you better than me now."

Teeny got out of the car and joined Rick. They laughed and talked as Genghis sniffed and did his business, Teeny going on and on about how nice the Sheehans seemed. They'd completed one leisurely lap around the block when the hairs on the back of Rick's neck began to stand on end.

He peered around in the darkness, seeing nothing unusual. A car door slammed a few buildings down. Jazz floated down from an open apartment balcony door. But something wasn't right.

"We need to go back, now."

"What's wrong?" Teeny abruptly stopped walking, his hand going to his waistband.

"I don't know. But it's something."

"Let's go."

Teeny jogged with them back to the apartment building and up the stairs. They found Josie's door unlocked, and Rick berated himself for not only leaving her alone for too long but for not locking the door when he left. *What was I thinking?* Teeny went in first, sweeping the room with his gun drawn.

"Josie?" Rick called out. He strained his ears, relieved to hear the shower running in the bathroom. "I'm sure everything's okay," he said to Teeny, heading toward the bedroom.

"I'll stay here for a couple more minutes."

Rick opened the bathroom door a crack. "Josie? Did you fall asleep in there?"

No answer.

"Josie?"

He flung open the door, fearing the worst—*Bennett Cummings has taken the only thing that ever mattered to me.*

He threw open the shower curtain.

Josie was curled on her side, legs drawn up, head on a little plastic bath pillow, sound asleep. He reached down and touched her warm throat and felt her heart beating strong and slow.

He turned off the water and grabbed a towel from a hook on the back of the door.

"Josie, baby. Time for bed."

"I told you, Lloyd," she muttered, slapping his hand away. "I don't wanna have lunch with you ever again."

Rick chuckled, loving that she dissed old boyfriends in her dreams. He gazed down on her, shaking his head. He had no idea he could love anything or anyone as much as he loved the woman curled up in the bathtub. She looked so soft and pink and vulnerable. An image flew into his brain—his baby, suckling at one of those perfect round breasts.

Rick drew in a breath, overcome with the power of that image. He wanted babies with Josie. He wanted a family. He wanted to try. And Josie was at the center of all that longing, all the dreams he'd barely admitted to himself.

With a kind of deadweight clarity, right down in his gut, he knew the only problem with loving someone was fearing you'd lose them.

Rick gently tucked the towel around her, pondering the physics of his challenge. He didn't think he could lift her up from that angle. He'd have to get her to her feet first.

"Stand up, Josie. I'll tuck you in."

She didn't stir.

"Everything okay in there?" Teeny called from the living room. Rick stuck his head out the bathroom door. "She fell asleep in the tub. Want to help me lift her out so I can carry her to bed?"

Teeny shoved his gun back in his waistband, laughing softly. "You don't pay me enough, Rousseau."

By the time Teeny had entered the bathroom, Rick had completely wrapped Josie in the towel, snugly overlapping the corners at her chest.

"I'll get her upper body," Teeny said, slipping a big arm under her back. "You get her legs."

The two of them gently lifted Josie from the tub, Teeny transferring her full weight to Rick's arms the instant he could turn her.

"Thank you," Rick mouthed to his friend, heading for the doorway and turning sideways to get through.

"You sure got your hands full with this one," Teeny whispered. "Good thing I've been kicking your ass in the barn."

Rick smiled at him.

"Page me in the A.M."

He nodded good night to Teeny and carried Josie to the bed. He laid her down and grabbed another towel from the hall closet. Carefully, he tried to dry her curly hair, so thick and heavy that his effort seemed pointless. So he just wrapped the towel around her head as snugly as possible, and removed the damp towel from her body. He tucked the sheets and comforter under her chin.

He kissed her on the mouth.

Suddenly, her arms were around his neck and she was kissing him back. "I want you," Josie whispered, taking her lips away long enough to speak the words. "I want you so bad."

Rick began taking off his clothes, hoping Josie hadn't just invited Lloyd into her bed.

"I love you, Rick," she said, her eyes now open. "I think I fell asleep in the shower."

"You did, but I got you now."

She yanked the towel from her hair and pulled back the covers. "Yes, you do."

Rick dove into her. She was warm and damp and eager. He let himself disappear in her heat and her moans, rolling with her, laughing, kissing, sucking and licking her soft body. At some point, he found himself with a handful of her wet curls in his hand as he took her from behind, wild with his need, his hand cupping her belly.

He drove himself to an orgasm, feeling Josie pulse and tug on him from inside her body. This was heaven. She was his heaven, and his love. He would never let anything happen to her, ever.

Gwen refused to come to the office, and instead asked Rick to meet her for a cup of coffee. Teeny drove him to the Market District café and, after checking the inside of the restaurant, took up residence on the bench out front.

"Do you ever get tired of being followed?" Gwen asked, nodding her head toward the windows.

"Someday it won't be necessary, but right now, it is."

Gwen nodded, looking down into her espresso. "I probably owe you an explanation."

"I'd rather you just retract your resignation."

She smiled slightly and shook her head. "I need to move on. It's time."

There was something different about Gwen today. She was more relaxed than he'd ever seen her. Her edges were softer. He studied her face, and saw an openness there he'd never noticed. "This isn't about the financial losses, is it?"

"No, though I truly believe I failed you on that count." She took a sip from her tiny cup. "It's about me, Rick. You can't be oblivious to the fact that— since I laid eyes on you—I've wanted you to want *me*."

Rick was surprised. After five years of innuendo, he wasn't prepared for a direct hit like that. "Yes, I'm aware of that."

"But you never did want me, did you?" She asked it without anger and waited patiently for him to answer.

"No. I didn't."

"Why?" Gwen entwined her hands into a tight ball and tapped the table. "I'd like to know."

Rick pondered that for a moment, then said, "I saw everything you were, Gwen—a beautiful, accomplished, brilliant woman. But none of it appealed to me."

She laughed hard, pointing her chin to the ceiling as she howled.

"I'm being honest with you," Rick said, admitting that what he'd just said did sound pretty ridiculous. "I wanted nothing to do with women—not after what I'd done to Margot. It took me a long time to trust myself again, to trust myself with a woman."

Gwen sat with that information, looking down at her hands, then all around the café. Eventually her gaze returned to Rick. "There's something I've wanted to ask you for years."

"Now's the time," he said, giving her a friendly smile.

She didn't smile back. "Do I remind you of Margot? Is that why you had no interest in me?"

Rick fell back against the café chair, raising his eyebrows in consideration. It was true that both women were elegant, tall, slim, blue-eyed blondes. But Gwen was far more reserved in her personality, while Margot had been a party girl. Yet, Gwen had a point.

"Maybe a little," he conceded.

She nodded. "So tell me about her."

Rick frowned, not following the conversation. "Margot?"

"No, silly," Gwen said, playfully slapping Rick's

forearm. "Josie. Your girlfriend. Tell me—why her and why now?"

He got goose bumps. Gwen had no way of knowing about Josie.

"Fine, I admit it," she said with a shrug. "When I left my resignation on your desk I saw her background file lying right there on top of everything—color photo and all." Gwen gave him a smile. "So fire me."

Rick was angry—at himself. It had been an oversight to leave that out for anyone to see, but as he recalled, his thoughts Friday afternoon had been on how to get Josie to the ranch for the weekend, not on tidying up his workspace.

"I'm all ears, Rick," she continued. "If beauty, brains, and success didn't do it for you, I'd sure like to know what did."

Rick shut his eyes for an instant, drudging up patience he didn't feel. What was the best way to tell Gwen that he'd found a woman who surpassed her on all those counts, and more?

"Come on, please explain it to me," Gwen said. "I am dying to know what kind of key it took to unlock the virtuous Rick Rousseau." Her smile did nothing to hide her angry sarcasm.

"She fits me, Gwen." Rick wanted this to be quick and kind, but stern. He wanted to put an end to this conversation. "We chose one another. Why is a private matter between Josie and me. I'm in love with her. I know you will find a way to respect that."

After a flash of bewilderment, Gwen's expression returned to the blank pleasantness she usually displayed. She reached for her bag.

"I wish you nothing but happiness," she said. "If you need my assistance finding a replacement, I'd be happy to help."

"Thank you." Rick stood up when Gwen did. "Good luck to you, Gwen." He held out his hand.

She took it. She kept her hand linked to his for just a second longer than she should have. Rick ended the contact.

Looking slightly embarrassed, she asked, "I can still count on you for a recommendation?"

"Anytime."

"Good-bye, Rick."

She walked through the café, out the door, and past Teeny without acknowledging his presence. When Rick arrived on the sidewalk a moment later, Teeny was laughing.

"What's so funny?"

"Oh, you know," he said, letting go with a great sigh. "I was just thinking what excellent taste you have in women."

Rick felt his face expand in a smile. "Will you be my best man?"

Teeny looked down at him, his eyebrows arched high on his forehead. "On your wedding day and every other day," he said.

"Feel like hitting Tiffany?"

Teeny laughed. "I thought you'd never ask."

"I'd like to keep going if you don't mind."

"You wanna drive all night?" LaShelle looked shocked by Bennett's suggestion. "You got a woman waiting for you in San Francisco or something?"

Bennett had to laugh. "No." It did give him pause, however, that LaShelle had begun to ask questions. Perhaps giving her a ride had been a mistake. Maybe he should have dropped her at the closest bus station and been done with her.

"Didn't mean to pry," LaShelle said, pursing her

lips. "It's just that we're a long way from Rhode Island."

"We are," Bennett said.

"So, you got family in California?"

"Just someone I know. It's business, really."

LaShelle wiggled her head around on her neck, disdain in her eyes. "Something ain't right about you, Benny."

He let go with a little laugh of surprise, but in his gut he felt apprehension. "We all have our imperfections," he said.

LaShelle nodded. "Uh-huh, well, let's start with your clothes."

Bennett was offended. "What in the world is wrong with my clothes?"

She rolled her eyes. "Number one, they ain't you. You look like you're dressed up for Halloween or some shit. You don't belong in those clothes. Nothing about the picture fits together."

"Oh, really." He was becoming quite amused by the exchange.

"Come on now, Benny. A man who carries himself the way you do, talks like you, has table manners like you? And a haircut and nails like yours?" LaShelle looked him up and down. "You're in good shape for an old man, and it's not the rough hands and hard work kinda shape, either. I bet you work out with a personal trainer."

"Interesting theory," he said.

"And *that* kind of man don't appear in public in a monster truck T-shirt, drivin' a trifling Buick with a Mexican flag hangin' off the rearview."

Bennett chuckled softly. "Well, I certainly appreciate the compliment, if that's what it was."

"Ha!" LaShelle crossed her arms over her chest.

"That wasn't no compliment. What I'm saying is, I'm on to you, Benny. Don't know what it is, but I know you're a man on a mission and you sit over there every day, mile after mile, stewing over it."

"I'm just trying to get where I need to go."

"Uh-huh." LaShelle sighed. "Anyway, I don't want to get all up in your business. All I know is you wouldn't hurt a fly, Benny. That's really the only thing I care about."

Bennett gulped. "Thank you for your vote of confidence."

LaShelle laughed.

They sat in silence for about five miles, when out of the quiet came the voice of an angel. " 'He's a man on a mission/Sent to make things right/Drivin' as far as he has to/ If it takes the rest of his life.' " The words were followed by her humming a bittersweet melody.

"What's the name of that song—and don't tell me it's 'Big Shit Poppin'.' "

She giggled. "I don't know what the name is. I just made it up."

Bennett was no expert on popular music. His tastes ran more to Mahler's *Fifth Symphony*. But he knew a lovely singing voice and a catchy melody when he heard them, and he'd just heard them from LaShelle.

"Can you sing more? Maybe even finish what you just started?"

LaShelle reached between her feet into her backpack and pulled out a ragged spiral notebook, covered in doodles and lettering that looked like street graffiti. "I got about seventy songs in here that I wrote. You pick a topic and I probably wrote a song about it."

Good God, he thought. He just might be sitting in the car with the world's next Diana Ross! Upon closer examination of the notebook cover, he learned he was sitting next to LaShelle Davis, 112 College Avenue, Apt. 10, Indianapolis, Indiana.

Bennett cleared his throat. "Have you written anything about a father's love for his daughter, by any chance?"

LaShelle cocked her head away from him in surprise. "Damn if you didn't pick the one subject I know nothing about."

They drove all night. LaShelle sang a selection of music ranging from gospel hymns to country and western ballads, many of which she'd written herself. Bennett felt his heart stir when she sang a Billie Holiday song. He was grateful the darkness hid his face.

After they stopped for a quick bite to eat and a fill-up, LaShelle turned on the passenger-side light and finished writing the song she'd started hours earlier. She sang it in its entirety, then said, "It's called 'The Ballad of Big Bad Benny.'"

He laughed, and she joined him. Bennett hadn't laughed like that in years—seven years, to be precise.

They reached Reno at about two A.M. LaShelle had slept for a few hours and woke up refreshed. They had breakfast, filled up again, and were heading back to the car.

"Toss me the keys, Benny," LaShelle said. "You kick back for a while. We'll be in San Francisco before you know it."

Bennett didn't know what had come over him, but he gave her the keys. "You have to fiddle with the shift when you put it in reverse," he warned her. Once back on the highway, he was asleep in minutes.

CHAPTER 18

There wasn't much spring in anyone's step that morning. They sat listless under a palm tree at Dolores Park, watching the dogs play. Roxanne shared her bad news first: After her lawyer said she had no recourse if fired, she'd decided to quit the paper before they axed her. Ginger went next: Her son had gone from honor student to juvenile delinquent overnight, and she felt like the world's worst mother. Bea then admitted she felt weighed down with the knowledge that they had to act on Josie's behalf, and soon.

"I'll do it by myself if you'd prefer," Bea told them, noting their lack of enthusiasm. "I can handle it alone."

Roxanne shook her head. "No doubt, but we don't want this Rousseau guy pissed at Josie."

"I can be as subtle as the next person," Bea said.

"You have many wonderful qualities," Ginger said, "but you're about as subtle as a two-by-four upside the head."

Bea sniffed. "Fine. Then we'll do it together. But you have to be ready to roll when I tell you we're on. Can you do that?"

Ginger nodded faintly.

Roxanne sighed. "In a couple days, my schedule

will be as open as it could possibly get for a human being—no job, no one to date, no reason to live."

Ginger patted Roxie on the shoulder. "Listen, if it makes you feel any better, I heard a rumor that they're going to cut half the editorial staff in the weekend and features departments, so I may be next."

"I heard that, too," Bea said. "But I didn't want to upset you."

Ginger laughed. "How could it upset me? I don't have any more 'upset' left in my tank! My husband left me for a girl I swear still wears a training bra. My sons are headed to death row. And I'm starting to get jowls."

Bea groaned. "Please spare us."

"I am! Look!" Ginger raised her chin and patted the underside of her jaw with the top of her hand. "I'm starting to look like Hillary Clinton in the last days of her primary campaign!"

The air filled with cracking sounds when Roxanne stretched her neck. "Sorry. Just getting rid of some tension," she said apologetically.

"All right, then. We need a strategy," Bea said.

In a weary voice, Roxanne said, "What do you have in mind?"

"Do you have any suggestions?"

Roxie looked up, sighing. "Yeah, Bea. My suggestion is we drop this whole thing before we alienate Josie forever. This is her life we're fucking with. She has a right to privacy. She has a right to choose the man she wants to have a relationship with. I just can't wrap my brain around how this is okay to do to my best friend."

Bea nodded gravely. "I have an answer for that."

"You have an answer for everything," Ginger offered.

"Rick Rousseau is not a Spike or a Randy or a Billy or a Lloyd," Bea said. "Those guys were losers and jerks, but compared to Rick Rousseau, they're Eagle Scouts." She stopped and wrapped her arms snug around her knees, lowering her voice. "Rousseau is bad news. He's a drug addict. His girlfriends have a tendency to end up in comas. But I really think the combination of his money and his looks has Josie blinded."

"That would be awful," Ginger said.

"This is Josie's pattern," Bea continued. "She brings a guy she barely knows into her life and expects happily ever after. The worst that's happened so far is that the guy breaks Josie's heart and steals a few of her kitchen utensils. But her latest boyfriend is on a whole new level of rotten."

Roxanne nodded. "Fine. Let's just get it over with."

Bea smiled with relief. "I've been thinking that Rousseau would have too many opportunities to cancel on us if we made plans in advance, you know, like if we invited him for a drink or something." Bea waited for feedback, but didn't get any. "So I'm thinking we just surprise him."

Roxanne raised an eyebrow. "Like run up to him on the street and yell *boo*?"

Bea wasn't amused. "We know where his office is and we know he goes to Josie's, right? So how about we wait for him to show up at one of those places, and catch him before he goes inside?"

"You mean another stakeout?" Ginger asked, obviously not loving the idea.

"Don't you think it's a little dicey to ambush a CEO at his own corporate headquarters?" Roxanne asked. "Security tends to frown on that kind of thing."

"Then Josie's place it is," Bea said.

"When?" Ginger and Roxanne asked in stereo.

"Keep your phones with you at all times. I'll let you know."

About fifty miles outside of San Francisco, LaShelle went silent. Bennett tried to engage her in conversation a few times, and failed each time. She was a fine driver, he'd noticed, and anyone else would assume she was concentrating on the increased traffic. He knew better.

She was gazing into the black hole of her future.

"We should probably stop and get some rest," he said. "Pull off at the next hotel you think might work."

"But it's almost morning. We're almost there."

Bennett nodded. "Tomorrow's a big day. We should get some rest and a nice hot shower, maybe wash our clothes."

LaShelle glanced over at him, her eyes sparkling in the darkness. "I don't know why you decided to help me back in Nebraska, but I appreciate that you did. Thank you, Benny."

"You're welcome," he said, suddenly fighting back a wave of sadness. He would miss her, he realized. She'd been good company. Maybe one day she would come to visit him in prison. "I know you're going to make it, LaShelle. I am sure of it."

She nodded curtly. "Here's a place," she said, taking the exit to a Hampton Inn.

LaShelle was equally taciturn later that afternoon as they drove into the city. Eventually she asked, "Do you have any ideas about a good place to drop me?"

"I do," Bennett said.

"I really hate to ask you this, after all you've done for me—"

"I'll give you enough money to get started," he said. "It would be my pleasure."

LaShelle's tears streamed down her face. "I think fifty ought to do it," she whispered. "I can take it from there."

Bennett smiled and nodded. "Fifty it is."

He followed the signs to the San Francisco International Airport and parked in the short-term lot. LaShelle frowned at him. "You leaving me here?"

"Not exactly. Get your bag, please."

Bennett opened the trunk and pulled out the little package he'd prepared for LaShelle that morning—a check for a million dollars, drawn from his private account, stuffed into a Hampton Inn envelope along with information the bank would require to verify the transaction. The envelope was tucked into the freshly laundered monster truck T-shirt, tied with a string he'd found in the glove compartment. Bennett shoved the bundle into his flannel shirt, closed the trunk, and went around to where LaShelle leaned up against the Buick.

"Do you have ID?"

One of her eyebrows rose high on her golden-brown forehead. "You Homeland Security now?"

Bennett laughed, linking his arm with hers and urging her ahead. "No, but those very same gentlemen will require you to have identification to board a plane, and that's what you're going to do."

She ripped her arm away from him. "You are *not* putting me on a plane back to Indianapolis! I'm not going back there! I don't care if I have to work at Taco Bells from here to Mexico—I ain't never going back to that hellhole!"

Bennett nodded soberly, knowing he'd reacted similarly the last time business required travel to the Hoosier state. "Of course not. I'm putting you on a plane to Los Angeles."

Her eyes went huge.

"Isn't that where you were headed, LaShelle?"

She swallowed hard, nodding.

"Then that's where you'll go." He held out his elbow again. "Shall we?"

Bennett paid cash for her ticket at the Virgin America counter. He walked with her to security, but before they parted, he handed her fifty dollars in cash. "Here you go," he said.

She took the money, folded it, and put it in her front pocket. LaShelle kissed his left cheek. The kiss matched her voice—it was that of an angel.

"I'd like you to have this, too." Bennett pulled out the prepared package. "Just a little something to remember me by."

LaShelle looked at the monster truck T-shirt and laughed, shaking her head. "You're such a nerd, Big Bad Benny." He watched her shove the shirt inside her backpack and zip it closed. He sighed with relief.

"Well." She looked around anxiously. "I should probably go."

"You should."

"Is there some way I can reach you? I'd like to pay you back the fifty as soon as I get settled."

Bennett shook his head. "Everything I've given you today is a gift, not a loan. If the nature of my gift should shock you, please be advised that it's the real thing."

She frowned. "You talking about the cash or the T-shirt?" she asked.

"Both." He touched her hand. "There's only one thing I ask of you."

LaShelle cocked her head. "What's that?"

Bennett said the words to LaShelle that he'd never

once uttered to his own daughter. "Never give up on your dream. Promise me you'll never give up."

She looked surprised, but smiled. "Okay. I promise."

LaShelle hugged him quickly and disappeared into the human cattle call that was airport security. He caught her eye one last time and waved good-bye. She waved back. Bennett retrieved his suitcase from the trunk of the Skylark before he headed to the car rental lot and the end of life as he knew it.

Josie hadn't yet used any vacation days for the year, so after her deadline Tuesday afternoon, she asked her city editor for the rest of the week off. "I could really use a few personal days," she told Ken.

He looked baffled. "To do *what*?"

"Personal stuff," Josie said, trying not to be offended that her boss assumed she had nothing to do. Of course, she wasn't going to correct him. Ken didn't need to know she planned to sleep, do laundry, go to the grocery, finally take Genghis in for his first free grooming, and spend some time with her sister—all the stuff she hadn't gotten around to because she'd been having nonstop incredible sex with the man she loved.

Plus she wanted to have that man over to her place for dinner again Thursday night. He said he had a surprise for her.

"You never take personal days," Ken said, still confused.

"Yes or no, Ken." Josie put a fist on her hip.

Ken swung around in his desk chair and tapped on the computer, checking the newsroom staffing schedule. "Yeah, sure. Looks like I can pull one of the interns off night cops and have them cover for you. You expecting anybody interesting to die this week?"

She laughed. "I'm an obituary writer, Ken. Not a psychic."

"Well, go have fun. Just swear to me you'll be back Monday."

Josie rubbed her fingers on her temples and pretended to go into a trance. "I see myself on Monday . . . back at my desk . . . gulping bad newsroom coffee . . . looking harried and overworked . . ."

"That's my girl," Ken said.

On her way to her car, she had the most wonderful realization: Josephine Agnes Sheehan had a life! She was taking personal days! She was happy!

Josie smiled to herself, pleased that if she were to drop dead right that minute, at least there'd be something to write about.

CHAPTER 19

Bennett had been in town for only a day when he decided to proceed. The furnished villa Milton had purchased for him more than two years prior had been adapted to meet his peculiar needs. The location was perfect—set back from the road, hidden behind a gate and trees, and solidly constructed. In the last few weeks, Milton had arranged for the home to be stocked with nonperishables, booze, and every amenity Bennett could desire. He'd arranged for it to be cleaned and polished from top to bottom.

Milton had always been a stickler for detail. And Bennett knew that when this ordeal was over, his lawyer and longtime friend would manage the resultant scandal as well as anyone could. Milton would also be a comfort to Julia. What more could he ask for?

Bennett's attention went to the surface of the large dining room table, where he'd laid out all the tools of his new line of work. Somewhere in the jumble of hats and wigs, glue-on mustaches, guns, Mace, a portable GPS, maps, his car rental agreement, stacks of cash, and other miscellany, Bennett knew he would find that cheap, no-frills, pay-as-you-go cell phone Milton had purchased for him. If his lawyer had to reach Bennett, this was the way he'd do it.

To Bennett's shock, he turned on the phone to find he had three messages, one from Milton and two from an unfamiliar San Francisco number. He listened to Milton first: an Indiana woman named LaShelle Davis had cashed a million-dollar check from Bennett's account at a Los Angeles bank. Milton had approved the transaction, because everything seemed to be in order, but he needed to speak to Bennett as soon as possible.

Bennett smiled and thought, *Good for you, LaShelle*.

Then he listened to the other messages. The first one said, "This is Gwen Anders. I have valuable information regarding Rick Rousseau." Then she gave him the unfamiliar number. The second message, also from Gwen Anders, advised him to disregard the first one. Bennett laughed. What kind of ridiculousness was that?

Bennett called the number. After sixteen rings, a man answered, and said it was a pay phone.

He tossed the cheap plastic cell phone back to the table, thinking that Gwen Anders had certainly picked the wrong time to play him for a fool.

There was a polite knock at her door. Because Gwen was expecting a FedEx delivery and was chatting on her cell phone, her guard was down. She opened the door, smiling.

Directly into the barrel of a handgun.

The man knocked the phone from her hand and stepped inside.

"Pick it up. Then hang it up," the man whispered. Gwen did as she was told. "Gotta go, Mom. Sorry." She snapped the phone shut.

"Get inside."

Gwen's body began trembling as her mind struggled to reconcile the aristocratic New England voice with the ridiculous appearance of her assailant. The man was of medium build, in cheap clothes, and it looked like he was wearing a fake wig and mustache, of all things.

She gasped. *"Bennett Cummings?"*

He kicked the door shut behind him. "At your service."

"But . . ." Gwen didn't know if the realization should make her less frightened, or more so. "I told you to disregard my message."

He flashed a cold smile while keeping the gun trained on her forehead.

Oh, God, what have I done? Gwen began to have trouble breathing.

"This won't take long. Just give me your valuable information and I'll be gone."

"It's nothing. It isn't even important," she said, her eyes darting to the gun and then to his face.

"I beg to differ, Miss Anders." Cummings took a step closer. "It's pure serendipity, and serendipity is always important."

Gwen frowned and shook her head. "I don't understand . . ."

"When you called I was already on my way here. See how interesting that is?"

Gwen tried to back away but bumped into a small hall table, knocking over a vase of fresh flowers. She jumped. Then she stared at all the broken glass and spilled water. If only she could grab a piece with a jagged edge . . .

Click. The cold steel of the gun tapped against her left temple. She straightened.

"What do you have for me, Gwen?"

She swallowed hard. This was a nightmare. How could she have done this to herself? To Rick? She closed her eyes and tried to drag some oxygen into her lungs.

"If you lie, I will know, and I will kill you." The pressure against her temple increased. "Don't think I won't."

"Rick Rousseau has a girlfriend," she sputtered, her eyes flying open. "He started dating someone and it's serious. He says he loves her."

Cummings tilted his head to the side, obviously puzzled. "And this girlfriend is not you, I assume."

"No." Gwen's body began shaking violently. Black spots swam in her vision. She thought she might throw up. "I'm not feeling well—"

"Give me everything you know about her," Cummings said, spinning Gwen around and wrenching an arm behind her back. He pushed her toward her antique secretary in the living room, where she had paper and pens neatly arranged. "Write everything down. You have thirty seconds."

Bennett sat at the wheel of his rental, parked three buildings from the girl's apartment. Surprisingly, the narrow one-way street had become a veritable hub of activity. Not only was Rousseau inside the apartment having dinner, his bodyguard sat in a black Lexus out front. In addition, there seemed to be three women crouched in the dark behind a tree just east of the girlfriend's apartment building. Bennett was perturbed. He would prefer to exact his revenge with less of an audience.

He was preparing to call it a night when who should exit the building but Rick himself, walking an oafishlooking dog. The bodyguard joined him and they strolled down the sidewalk, past the figures crouching behind the tree. Maybe he'd been too quick to judge the evening a total waste.

He rolled down his windows and strained his ears.

"Nice night for a proposal." Teeny tucked his hands in his pants pockets while strolling next to Rick and Genghis. "Wouldn't you agree?"

"Don't rush me," Rick snapped. "She's just started dinner."

"It was an innocent observation."

Rick laughed. "Well, back off. I think you're more nervous than I am."

Teeny ran a hand over his bald head. "This is as close to proposing to a woman as I'll ever get—I'm a wreck."

They got about halfway down the block when Rick noticed Teeny tense up. He kept strolling, but there was no longer anything casual about it. He was on alert.

Teeny whispered to Rick, "Not a life-and-death thing, man, but prepare yourself."

"Cummings?" Rick asked.

"You wish."

"What the hell does that mean?" Rick tried to look behind him, but Teeny grabbed his arm.

"Eyes front and keep moving," Teeny said. "Dog ladies at two o'clock."

"Rick Rousseau!"

Rick took a deep breath and turned toward the voice. Three women stood on the sidewalk, jaws set firm, feet apart. The oldest and biggest one—Bea Latimer was her name—was clearly in charge.

"We're Josie's friends. We need to talk to you," she said.

Rick nodded, noting how glad Genghis was to see them. "You obviously know *me*," he said, then gestured toward Teeny. "This is my associate, Timothy Worrell."

Teeny produced a charming smile. "It's nice to be formally introduced, ladies."

"A pleasure," the redhead named Ginger Garrison said. Bea's eyes flashed at her with reprimand.

Rick decided to defuse the situation with hospitality. "I'm visiting Josie right now, as you know, so why don't we all go up to the apartment? I'm sure she'd love to see you. She's told me all about you."

"That sounds very ni—" Ginger stopped herself mid-sentence.

"This isn't a social visit," the youngest one said. Roxanne Bloom narrowed her dark eyes at Rick menacingly. "We're concerned about Josie's safety. We don't think you're good for her."

Rick admired Roxanne's candid approach. Truly, he welcomed the show of devotion from all three women. It was a comfort knowing they had Josie's back. The problem was, this was supposed to be a quick walk, not a meeting of the UN Security Council, and he hadn't planned to leave Josie alone for long.

"She's been hurt before," Ginger said. "She has this habit of falling in love with men who aren't good for her—which is nothing unique to Josie, of course, because most of us have done that at one time or another. In fact I spent eighteen years married to someone who—" Ginger stopped in mid-sentence and gave her hair a nervous fluff. "The point is, we think you're her latest mistake."

"And by far the most dangerous," Bea added.

Rick transferred the dog's leash and plastic baggie to Teeny and said to the women, "Please walk with me a minute. I'd enjoy the company." He turned and resumed his pace.

Bea raced to his right side. The two other women positioned themselves at his left. Teeny walked behind them, with Genghis and the plastic bag, trying his best not to snicker.

When the group turned the corner, Bennett made his move. He powered off the automatic interior lights to the car and stepped out. He gingerly opened the car's back left passenger door and left it cracked. He slipped across the walk and into the building, taking the stairs as fast as he could. He found the door to apartment 2A unlocked. He tiptoed inside, relieved that the music would provide some cover for his movements. The girl was in the kitchen, her back to him, humming and chopping, completely oblivious. Completely vulnerable.

Rousseau was a fool.

Bennett was behind her in seconds. He jammed the needle into the back of her thigh while putting his hand over her mouth. He wrenched the chef's knife from her hand and held it to her throat until she stopped fighting. Almost instantly, she went limp in his arms.

Bennett balanced the girl against him, threw the knife on the floor, and prayed he was fit enough to drag her deadweight down two flights of steps and out to the car without being spotted.

Why couldn't Rousseau have chosen a smaller woman?

"We know all about you," Roxanne said.

"I see." Rick walked slowly and nodded. "What in particular do you see as a threat to Josie's safety?" he asked.

"You're joking, right?" Ginger looked insulted.

Rick studied all of their faces and shook his head. "Look, if you ladies are attempting to scare me away, you're going to fail. Simple as that."

Bea laughed bitterly. "We're giving you a chance to bow out gracefully and leave Josie alone. If you don't, we'll tell her everything we know about you, and we'll call the police."

Rick nodded patiently. "What would I be charged with, I wonder?"

After a moment, Ginger said, "Incomplete disclosure at the start of a relationship."

Teeny burst out laughing. "If that's a punishable offense, then I know a whole bunch of people who should be in maximum security without the slightest chance in hell of parole."

Roxanne snickered. "Yeah, me, too."

Rick smiled to himself.

"This is not a joke, people." Bea's voice was angry and she laid her hand on Rick's upper arm. Everyone stopped walking. "You've been in jail at least twice for drug possession with the intent to distribute. You killed a woman because you thought it would be fun to operate a Harley while drunk and high. Talk about someone who should be serving a life sentence!"

Rick blinked. His insides felt sliced to shreds. He glanced quickly at Teeny, who was no longer amused.

"Find some other woman to date, Rousseau." Bea wagged a finger at him, tears forming in her eyes. "Better yet, do the entire female race a favor and don't date at all. Whatever you do, just leave Josie alone."

"Real subtle, Bea," Roxanne mumbled.

"There's no need for subtlety." Rick kept his voice soft. "The truth is the truth, and everything Bea just said is the truth. In fact—" Rick felt Teeny's hand on his shoulder, and he didn't know if it was to calm him or recommend that he shut the hell up. It didn't matter, because Rick planned to continue until he'd said all he needed to say.

"In fact, I did exactly what Bea suggested. I didn't date anyone after the accident, not for seven years." Rick smiled sadly. "I didn't trust myself—I'd been a spoiled, selfish, reckless rich kid who didn't give a damn about anyone. After the accident I decided to change my life, but I was scared shitless that I'd somehow hurt another woman. So I stayed away from them. I concentrated on becoming an honorable person, instead."

The women stared at him, slack-jawed.

"But then I met Josie, and she changed everything." Rick looked into all of their faces. "Your friend is an incredible woman. She knows that story Bea just told, and a hell of a lot more. And she's already forgiven me. She's decided to give me a chance."

"You told Josie about your past?" Ginger looked stunned.

"Of course I did. I love Josie. She deserves to know everything there is to know about the man who wants to marry her."

"WHAT?" Roxanne waved her hands around. "What did you just say?"

"Nice going, Ace," Teeny said.

"You're lying." There was disgust in Bea's voice. "You two only just met."

"Then don't take my word for it. Let's go get this out in the open." Rick turned back toward the corner. "You know, Josie told me about the vow you all took," he said.

"She did?" Ginger scowled at him, then immediately began tapping her fingertips against her forehead, which Rick found odd.

"The four of you agreed to be happy without men in your lives, correct?"

"Damn right," Roxanne said.

"Well, Josie wasn't sure how and when to tell you about me." Rick smiled. "Now I understand her hesitation."

Teeny snickered under his breath. Rick started walking at a fast clip.

"You're really going to ask her to marry you?" Roxanne nearly had to jog to keep up with Rick's up-hill march.

"Do not say anything to her. I mean it," Rick said. "You can put me through the meat grinder all you want but you *will not* ruin that moment for her. Are we clear?"

Bea frowned at him. "I still don't believe you."

Shaking his head, Rick stopped walking again, reached into the inside pocket of his jacket, and pulled out a small black velvet box. He opened it under the streetlight. The women were nearly blinded.

"No way," Roxanne whispered.

"Oh, my God," Ginger breathed. "Tiffany!"

Bea peered close. "Two carats?"

"Three," Teeny said. "Emerald cut with two ba-guettes on either side. Platinum setting. The matching wedding band is just as stunning but has simpler lines—perfect for daily wear."

Rick snapped the box shut, nearly catching the tip of Bea's nose in the spring hinge. "Shall we go get your answers, ladies? I don't want Josie to think some-body kidnapped me." They all rounded the corner, then charged up the hill. When they reached the build-ing, Rick gestured for the women to go ahead of him. "You first. I insist."

As he spoke, Rick noticed a dark-colored sedan traveling the wrong way down the street. A shiver went up his spine.

Bennett gasped for air as he drove through the streets of San Francisco. Every few seconds he'd glance at the GPS readout for reassurance. This town was a maze of steep hills and baffling intersections and he only had twenty minutes before the effect of the tranquilizer would wear off. If he could just get into the underground garage of the Presidio villa, everything would be all right. Bennett glanced at the rearview mirror, checking on the sleeping girl. She was doing better than he was. She seemed to be resting peacefully, while Bennett was in need of traction and an oxygen mask. Thank God he'd prepared a method for transporting a limp body up the private elevator and into the house, even if he'd intended the body to be Rousseau's.

The girl moaned softly, but didn't move. The GPS said he had six miles to go. Bennett's heart pounded and his hands perspired so badly they were slipping on the rental car's steering wheel.

It had begun. It could not be stopped. He had kidnapped Rick Rousseau's girlfriend. It wasn't his original plan, but a last-minute change in direction wasn't necessarily a sign of weakness.

After all, which option would inflict the most injury on Rousseau? That single instant of comprehension for him, when Bennett put the gun to Rousseau's head and prepared to pull the trigger? Or days of guilt-soaked agony and torture of the soul, Rick knowing that he'd allowed his woman to be stolen and probably killed?

Plan B, obviously. It was genius. It was the ultimate payback. Bennett was only sorry he couldn't hold the girl hostage for seven years before he killed her.

Now *that* would be eye for an eye.

. . . you wouldn't hurt a fly, Benny.

Bennett slammed his fist against the cheap steering wheel. Damn! How he wished LaShelle had kept her opinions to herself! If forty-five years in business had taught him anything, it was this: If you doubt your success, then you'll fail.

Ginger was the first inside Josie's apartment. "I don't think she's here," she said, confused. "Did she go somewhere?"

Rick cocked his head, the adrenaline rushing through his body. Teeny dropped the dog's leash, pulled out his gun, and pushed past everyone to get in the living room.

"Stay back," Rick said, motioning for the women to retreat to the hallway. "Josie?" he called out, over the music. He ran to the sound system and turned down the volume. "Josie?" he repeated, even louder.

Teeny swept the kitchen, the bedroom, the bathroom. Genghis sniffed at a knife lying on the kitchen floor.

Teeny ran back to the living room, shaking his head to indicate he hadn't found her, his face twisted with grief.

"What the hell's going on?" Bea stepped inside the apartment and walked right up to Teeny. "Why the hell do you have a gun?"

"Has something happened to Josie?" Roxanne yelled. "Should we call the police?"

"I've got a real bad feeling about this," Ginger whispered.

Rick took a second to gather his thoughts, but there was only one thought to gather: Bennett Cummings had Josie.

He was sure of it.

CHAPTER 20

Bennett needed a stiff drink. Lifting the girl from the car and propping her in the rolling office chair had just about done him in. His heart raced. Perspiration soaked into his shirt. Bennett made himself a vodka and tonic, and settled into a comfortable love seat.

The girl tried to kick her legs again, and Bennett was pleased to see the ropes holding nicely. As a sailor, he'd always prided himself on his knots. Never once, however, did he suspect he'd use his yachting prowess to tie a girl to anything, let alone an office chair on wheels.

She tried to scream, but her mouth was muffled by the balled-up washcloth held in place with a kitchen towel. He'd used a colorful pink scarf he found in the closet as a blindfold. The overall effect looked less menacing than a hostage scene from a movie, but it would have to do.

"It would be to your benefit if you'd relax," Bennett said in his most soothing voice. "If you are calm and quiet, you will be allowed to move freely in the guest suite. You can have something to eat or watch movies. You'll be quite comfortable. I just finished preparing everything for you."

The girl kept wiggling.

"However, if you continue to struggle, I'll have to leave you bound and gagged for the several days I plan to keep you here. Is that what you'd prefer?"

The girl screamed and thrashed violently. Bennett got up and made himself another drink. His hand shook when he added two jiggers of Ciroc.

He was aware that from here on out, things would be unpleasant. There was no avoiding it.

Within minutes of Josie's disappearance, Teeny had the security team's emergency plan in place, everyone aware that Josie Sheehan's safe return was the only objective. Teeny spoke to several of his associates in Rhode Island, demanding that they come up with something—anything—that would provide new information on Bennett Cummings's whereabouts.

Two FBI agents and two San Francisco Police Department detectives talked quietly in Rick's kitchen. Josie's apartment was now a crime scene. The FBI had already issued an APB for Josie and Cummings, along with a vague description of a late-model, dark sedan. Rick had provided police a detailed statement about the nature of his relationship with Bennett Cummings, the threat he'd received, and his suspicions that Josie had become his target. Bea had already arranged for the *Herald* to run a front-page story on Josie's disappearance in the morning edition. Police had put out a bulletin to be aired on the late news that very same night.

In the midst of all the activity, a detective had taken Rick aside and asked, "If you were so concerned something would happen to her, why did you leave her alone?"

There was no satisfactory answer to that question.

There never would be. Rick had asked himself a hundred times in the last three hours how he could have let this happen, and with each passing minute the black tentacles of self-hate got tighter around his throat. Certainly, Josie's family over there on the sofa wasn't comforted by the fact that Rick had only intended to take the dog out for a few minutes. They didn't care that Rick had assumed he himself was the target, not Josie. The truth was, he had left her alone—and took the bodyguard with him!—and now she was gone. He had failed to keep her safe.

Rick now understood that the uneasy feeling from earlier in the week had been his intuition talking. When he'd raced back to Josie's apartment to find her asleep in the tub, that was his warning. Yet he didn't listen. *He didn't fucking listen!*

"Come here a minute, man." Teeny wrapped his arm around Rick's shoulders and guided him past the dozens of people gathered in his living room and into the study, shutting the door behind them. "Don't go there on me, Rousseau," Teeny said. "Don't you dare go there."

Rick stayed silent.

"If you want to get Josie back, then you stay right here, you stay alive and aware, do you hear me?" Teeny got down in his face. "You keep your mind sharp and your thoughts positive. That evil self-destructive shit has no place in your world anymore. It doesn't belong here. Josie deserves better from you."

"Like she did earlier tonight, when I left her."

Teeny put both his hands on Rick's shoulders, shaking him. "I don't want to have to kick your ass, but I will. Stop it. *Now*."

Rick took a deep breath. "I hear you," he whispered.

"Good." Teeny straightened and smiled. "Now, here's the good news, man. One of my sources came through for me, found out that Cummings drove at least part of the way in his gardener's car. We got a plate and a description."

"Good," Rick said.

"We're going to find her," Teeny said.

Rick nodded. "I know we will."

"That's what I'm talking about."

There was a knock on the study door. It was Bea. "Excuse me, Teeny, but you just got a call on your cell. She says it's important."

Rick and Teeny hurried back to the dining room, where Teeny had set up a kind of command center. He grabbed the phone from the glass tabletop.

"Worrell," he said. A second later, frowning, he handed the phone to Rick. "It's Gwen Anders," he whispered. "She's hysterical."

Rick took the phone. He didn't have a spare second for her. "I can't talk right now," he barked.

"Rick! It's my fault! I did it! I just saw the news report about Josie Sheehan being abducted!" Gwen began to sob.

"What?" Rick stopped breathing. "You have Josie?"

"No! No! Cummings came to my house and put a gun to my head! I told him about Josie! I told him she was your girlfriend! It's my fault!"

Rick handed the phone back to Teeny as Gwen sobbed. "Send somebody over there to get her," Rick said. "She has a statement to make."

Teeny looked incredulous. "What the hell does Gwen Anders know about Josie's disappearance?"

"She told Cummings all about her."

Teeny's eyes flashed. *"Fuck!"*

Rick kept his voice down so Josie's family couldn't hear him. "Just get Gwen over here so she can talk to the cops."

Rick turned away. There was so much blistering rage in him right then that he wanted to throw something across the room just to see it explode. He needed something to crush, to smash, to rip apart with his hands. He wished it could be Gwen.

She'd cried so much in the last few hours that the blindfold was soggy. Her mouth was dry and her jaw hurt from being forced open with the gag. Her wrists were rubbed raw from whatever kind of rough rope he'd used to restrain her. Josie had to pee so badly she didn't think she could hold it another second. And whatever drug he'd given her had made her terribly nauseous.

She heard nothing. No sounds of a TV or water running or someone walking around. Nobody breathing. Wherever she was, it smelled clean, like a hotel. But it had none of the background noise of a hotel, just a faint sound of cars in the distance.

"Have you decided to cooperate?"

Josie would have hit the ceiling if she hadn't been tied down. He must have been next to her the whole time, staring at her! She nodded her head as much as she could, given the restraints.

"Here is our agreement." The man came very close, and Josie could smell his alcohol-saturated breath. "You will do what you're told. You will not scream or try to escape. I have a gun and I plan to shoot you at some point, but the better behaved you are, the longer I'll delay the inevitable. Do you agree?"

Josie didn't care much for that arrangement, but she nodded.

She felt the man move behind her and his hands touch the back of her head. The blindfold fell away and the light hurt her eyes. The gag went next. Then the man started cutting the ropes. As soon as she was able, Josie jumped to her feet and tried to run. She slammed straight down into the carpet. The office chair was still tied to her ankles.

"So impatient."

Josie twisted her body to look at him. He certainly looked the part—in his sixties, distinguished, arrogant, filled with hate, a handgun in his belt. "You must be Bennett Cummings," she said

He smiled as he cut the ropes from her feet. "You know about me."

"Yeah," Josie said, wiping the drool off her chin and rubbing her jaw. "You're the psycho who's after Rick."

"Charming way to phrase it," the man said, gathering the cut ropes off the floor. "Of course, you've left out a few pertinent details."

"I know about Margot. It was an accident. Rick is a good man."

When Cummings straightened up, his eyes were filled with loathing. "You poor, gullible, naïve, stupid thing." He shook his head, then placed the pile of rope on a nearby side chair. He yanked the office chair away and put it up against the wall. He pulled the gun from his belt, cocked it, and pointed it at her. "Get up. I'll show you your accommodations."

Josie scrambled to her feet, but her legs felt like Jell-O. She almost fell, but he caught her.

"Miss Sheehan, my back cannot withstand dragging you around any more than I already have, so please try to stay on your feet." He turned her body around and shoved the gun into her right kidney. "The bathroom is this way."

Josie relieved her bladder, noting the sore and bruised spot on the back of her thigh where Cummings had jabbed her with a needle—the last thing she remembered before waking up bound and gagged. She splashed cold water on her face and swished out her mouth. She also ran water over her scraped and bloody wrists and patted them dry with a fluffy white towel. There were no windows in the bathroom, just a small linen closet and truckloads of the finest marble and granite money could buy. Wherever she was being held captive, it was top-of-the-line all the way.

Josie took a moment to steady herself before she opened the door. She breathed deep. The reality was that Cummings had a gun. She didn't—and even if she did, she wouldn't know how to use it. So she would have to find another way to deal with him. Josie figured the longer she stayed missing the more intense the search for her would become. So she had to stay alive as long as possible, doing whatever was necessary, until Rick found her.

That was her plan.

A wave of sorrow hit her. She knew Rick would be insane with worry. He was probably blaming himself. She wished there was a way to reassure him.

"Hurry up in there."

Josie opened the bathroom door to find Cummings waiting, gun still drawn. "There is no way out of here, of course," he said. "I'll give you a complete tour. That way, you won't waste the precious remaining hours of your life looking for a way to outsmart me."

"Sounds fun." Josie noticed how Cummings eyed her injured wrists and looked away quickly, as if the sight disturbed him.

Josie decided to keep him talking. "So, you were expecting me?"

"I was expecting your boyfriend, actually. But I decided you'd be more fun."

"What did you shoot me up with?" Josie pointed to the back of her leg.

"Just a generic animal tranquilizer I purchased off the Internet. You shouldn't have any long-term side effects—not that you'll need to worry about that." He smiled and used his gun to herd her into the other room. "You must be famished. I know I am."

Rick rubbed Genghis behind the ears, comforted by the warm weight of the dog's body up against his legs. Taking advantage of the moment of privacy, Rick bent down and buried his nose in the dog's fur, inhaling the mellow sweetness of Josie's scent. He wondered how long her essence would cling to the dog's woolly coat.

He gathered all the strength left inside him, and willed himself not to break down.

Teeny quietly entered the study. "Gwen wants to talk to you."

"I can't stand to look at her," Rick said, his face still buried in Genghis's curls. "Get her out of here as soon as possible."

"She's giving the FBI some decent information," Teeny continued. "Apparently, Cummings came to her place wearing a mustache, wig, and ball cap. She described his clothes in detail. And based on what Gwen's said, it sounds like he's carrying a 45.-caliber semiautomatic."

Rick looked up. "Does Gwen know where he is?"

"No," Teeny said.

"Then she's useless." Rick straightened up in the leather chair.

Teeny had the saddest look on his face. "She wants to apologize."

"Not necessary."

The door opened. Gwen stepped in. *Who does she think she is?* Rick averted his eyes.

"I am truly sorry," she whispered. "What I did was selfish, conceited, and petty. I have no excuse."

"Forget this, Gwen," Teeny said. "I think you should go."

"Wait." Rick stood up, noticing for the first time that Gwen looked like hell. Her head was bowed in shame. He'd never seen her with a single hair out of place, let alone a disheveled mess. She seemed more human to him this way.

Rick sighed, closing his eyes from the weight of the truth. That's all any of them were—human. And to be human was to be a fuckup just waiting to happen. All of them. Without exception.

"Damn you, Gwen," he said.

She nodded, the tears coming. "I don't expect you to forgive me. I'll never forgive myself." She turned to go.

Rick cursed under his breath. He must be crazy. "Come here," he said. She turned to him and he opened his arms to her. He patted her on the back as she sobbed.

"I didn't want anyone to get hurt!" Gwen wailed. "Oh, my God! I am so sorry!"

Teeny's eyes were huge as he looked down on the unlikely drama. Rick managed a weak smile, then pushed Gwen away. He'd suddenly thought of something so obvious it was ridiculous.

"Hey, Gwen, how did Cummings know he could come to you?"

Gwen blinked. "He wrote me before Margot died. He said he was interested in a mutually beneficial business arrangement." Gwen's eyes flashed to Teeny. "I decided not to tell you."

"Jesus," Teeny whispered.

"Here." Gwen dug into the front pocket of her sweatpants and handed Rick a business card. "After you told me you were in love with Josie, I left a message at this number. I wanted to make you pay."

With his eyes locked on Gwen's, Rick's hand shot up into the air, the card trapped between two of his fingers. Teeny snatched it and ran out the room.

He stared at her, shaking his head slowly.

"You probably hate me," she said.

"I don't," Rick said, suddenly exhausted down to the marrow of his bones. "Nothing good ever comes of it."

By the time the sun came up, Josie had quite a few things figured out. First, she knew she was stuck like a bug in a glass jar. All doors were locked solid with numeric keypads and pass codes. All the windows had been welded shut and coated on the outside with an opaque film that kept her from getting a sense of her location. She couldn't even tell if she was on a ground floor or twenty stories up. She'd seen Cummings carrying a small flip phone in his pocket, but otherwise there were no telephones, no computers, no way to reach the outside world. Even the TV in her suite had no live signal—just a DVD player and a stack of movies.

Also, it was obvious to Josie that Bennett Cummings wasn't a hardened criminal, and certainly not a natural-born kidnapper. Bennett couldn't bear to look at the red marks on her wrists. With each mention of how he planned to shoot her, he sounded more and more like a bad actor in a low-budget movie, like he had to impress himself with his diabolical plan as much as he needed to impress Josie. Cummings was nervous. He'd had about six drinks the night before, and he paced for hours. Josie watched him from a crack in her bedroom door.

But there was one other thing she sensed—Bennett Cummings was stuck, never allowing himself to grieve the loss of his daughter. Josie had spent the last eight years looking into the face of grief, so she knew what she was talking about. He was still so angry he couldn't see straight, and he thought revenge against Rick would make his loss easier to bear. It didn't work like that, of course, but you couldn't tell that to someone when they were caught up in their hate the way Cummings was.

Josie couldn't help but wonder if this whole mess might have been avoided if Bennett Cummings had found a way to grieve. That's when it hit her—maybe conversation would be the only weapon she'd need.

"I hope you're not planning a doomed escape attempt." Cummings said that as he walked from the kitchen and dining areas of the house to where Josie sat in the fancy living room. He handed her a to-go cup of convenience-store coffee.

Josie looked around her. The place was something out of *Architectural Digest*. Josie figured that if she had to be kidnapped, this was a swanky way to be imprisoned—modern, sleek furniture, bamboo floors, geometric art, a slate waterfall built right smack in the middle of the room. It would probably be stunning if the sun were allowed to shine through the huge windows.

Josie studied Cummings as he walked toward her and took a seat in a matching leather and chrome chair. He seemed tired.

"I'm not planning my escape, Mr. Cummings," she said. "I was just thinking of Margot."

His eyes flew wide. She saw his pulse beat against the thinning skin of his throat. "She's not yours to think about," he snapped. "You do not have permission to do so."

Josie shrugged. "It's just that the only things I know about her is what Rick told me. I was just wondering what kind of person she was."

Cummings glared at her. He was a very smart man. Josie suddenly questioned her approach.

"She was beautiful. Intelligent. Funny. And then, after your boyfriend got through with her, she was sad, limp, gray, and brain-dead." He produced a sneer. "Any more questions?"

Josie swallowed. "Do you have any pictures of her with you?"

He didn't move. He didn't answer.

"I was just curious."

Cummings remained stone-still.

"I'm sorry. You'll have to forgive me," Josie said, making her voice as kind as she could. "You probably don't know this, but I write obituary feature articles for the *Herald,* and I've learned that talking about a late loved one can be cathartic for the family. I'm embarrassed—it's just a reflex, I suppose, and I do apologize."

Without comment, Cummings got up from the chair and left the room. Josie was about to groan out loud at her own stupidity when he came back, a copy of the morning *Herald* in his hand. He threw it down on the coffee table.

"Of course I know about you, Miss Sheehan." He laughed. "Everyone in San Francisco knows about you this morning."

Josie's lips parted in shock. She reached for the paper. Top left, above the fold, the headline read:

HERALD REPORTER MISSING,
POLICE FIND SIGNS OF ABDUCTION

As much as she hated to admit it, the article tickled her. The headline was relatively snappy. The piece was well written yet did not clue in Cummings about the methods the police were using to investigate the crime. Editors had chosen a photo of Josie and Genghis in Dolores Park, one that Bea had probably given them, and Josie's hair looked great. Friends and family offered a $500,000 reward for anyone with information that led to an arrest. There were quotes from her mom and dad, Beth, Rick, and Bea. The article described her as a woman who was cherished, missed, and fretted over.

Josie looked up, her eyes locking on Cummings. She would get out of there alive. She had no doubt. Because that was Josie's beautiful life they were talking about in the paper, and she wanted to live it.

Josie began to sob. At first it was legitimate—she was humbled by how rich her life was, how fortunate she was to be loved the way she was. But after a few minutes, Josie noticed how her crying affected Bennett Cummings—he looked terribly uncomfortable. So Josie cranked it up a notch, wailing about her family and her dog and how all she wanted was a chance to have a happy life. She cried until Bennett Cummings couldn't stand it anymore.

At the twenty-four-hour mark, investigators had made progress on some fronts but were stymied on others. An airport bureau cop spotted the 1998 Buick Skylark with Rhode Island plates in the short-term lot. The vehicle had already been towed to SFPD's forensics services division, but so far, there was no evidence linking the car to Josie's abduction. Police were viewing hours of security-camera footage that might have captured someone walking either to or from the car. But nothing yet.

The cell phone number Gwen Anders had provided was a prepaid phone from a Minneapolis wholesaler, paid for in cash about a year earlier. There was no way to determine who had purchased it or was using it. However, the FBI had begun pulling cell tower records to see if the number had connected with any of the area's sixty-plus towers within the last week, which could, at the very least, narrow down a search area.

Rick knew investigators were moving as fast as they could. He had no complaints. The San Francisco police detectives and the FBI agents were doing their jobs well. It just wasn't fast enough for him. It wasn't good enough—because they still hadn't found Josie.

Her parents were holding up remarkably well. Though Josie's dad reassured him they didn't blame Rick for their daughter's disappearance, her mother's eyes told him the real story—he'd better get Josie back to them in one piece. Genghis moped around Rick's Pacific Heights home, obviously missing his owner. Once Josie was home safe, Rick would be happy to tell her that her dog was a devoted companion, after all.

He worried about her. He pictured her tied up and gagged and left without food or water. He worried that Cummings might hit her. Rick feared Josie would give up on him, decide he wasn't coming for her. The idea of that took him to the very edge of insanity.

He had to get out of the house. He grabbed Teeny and Genghis and they walked from one end of Pacific Heights to the next, mostly in silence, up hills and back down, for more than two hours. They were about three blocks from home when Teeny's phone rang.

Rick watched him nod and say, "You're kidding." Teeny's eyes shot to Rick. "Absolutely. Thank you."

"They have a two-block radius for us," Teeny said, his smile out of sync with the shock on his face. "A call was placed from the phone two days ago, about an hour before Cummings showed up at Gwen's condo. They've pinpointed the call as coming from the Presidio District."

Rick's heart began to pound.

"Whatever you're thinking, don't think it," Teeny said. "They're putting together a hostage-recovery team, part FBI and part SWAT—"

Rick was already halfway down the block.

"Rick!"

CHAPTER 21

"Here."

Josie wiped her cheeks with a fresh tissue and nodded pitifully, accepting the hot chocolate from Cummings. She took a sip while Cummings collapsed in a kitchen chair. He put his head in his hands. She didn't blame him—she'd cried all morning, then taken a nap, cried all afternoon and into the evening. She could hardly stand herself.

"Are you all right, Mr. Cummings?" she asked.

His head moved back and forth in his hands.

"Can I do anything?"

She heard him laugh, his face still hidden.

"What are you thinking?"

He slowly raised his head. The display of sorrow on his face made him look twenty years older, like a man on his deathbed. Josie was startled by the change.

"I was just thinking about my drive here from the East Coast," Cummings said. He fell back against the chair, his hands limp in his lap. "I kept running into young women who needed help—a waif in a coin laundry somewhere in the Midwest, an overwhelmed mother in a Wal-Mart. I drove a young woman named LaShelle all the way from a Nebraska truck stop to

San Francisco and then put her on a plane to Los Angeles. She wants to be a recording artist." Cummings laughed to himself. "I gave her a check for a million dollars to follow her dream."

Josie's mouth fell open. "That never happened to me at a truck stop."

Cummings gave her a weak smile. "I just now realized what that was all about."

"It was about Margot, wasn't it?" Josie bit her bottom lip. "You weren't able to save her, were you?"

"No. I was not."

"But you could save one of these women."

Cummings shrugged.

Josie knew she had to tread lightly with this next part. "When someone dies young, it rocks everyone off kilter. It's hard for us to understand why someone who'd hardly lived had to die. It's not right and it isn't fair."

Cummings looked at her, nodding his head faintly.

"What do you regret most, Mr. Cummings?" Josie knew she was pushing it, but if she could get him to open up, she might be able to neutralize some of his rage. "Was there something in particular that you wished you'd said or done with Margot while she was alive?"

Cummings's eyes flashed. "Miss Sheehan, an obituary writer does not a psychoanalyst make."

She laughed. She couldn't help it. There was something about Bennett Cummings that she liked. He had a wry sense of humor. He was very smart. And he was utterly lost. He was a man who seemed to have everything, but was lost anyway. And lost people did desperate things.

Josie hoped to God she wasn't already forming an unhealthy affection for her kidnapper.

"All I know is people can torture themselves after their loved one is gone, worried they failed them somehow." Josie wrapped her hands around her mug of hot chocolate, searching for the right words. "I've noticed that for some people, that's where most of the pain comes from—their own guilt."

"You are quite astute, Miss Sheehan." He got up from the table, and Josie assumed he was done with her lecture. But he was back in a moment, a fresh vodka and tonic in one hand and a BlackBerry in the other. He turned on the device and swung his chair closer to hers.

Josie was treated to a slide show of Margot's life, a life of an American princess. It boggled the mind how privileged she'd been. "She was extremely pretty," Josie said, meaning it.

"She looked just like her mother," Bennett said.

"You haven't mentioned your wife." Josie sat quietly while Bennett scrolled through additional photos of his daughter. "Is she still alive?"

"She's dead, for all practical purposes."

Josie frowned. "I don't understand."

He turned to her. At this proximity, Josie could see all the wrinkles in his skin, all the broken blood vessels on his cheeks and in his eyes. He looked worn out.

"I thought Rick was done with women." Bennett looked directly into Josie's eyes. "Tell me how this thing between you came about."

Josie smiled slightly, aware how he'd turned the tables in an instant. "Rick had been alone since the accident, yes. But something very special happened when we met—it was an attraction that seemed bigger than both of us. We fell in love."

"Do you trust him?"

Josie nodded. "I do. Absolutely."

Cummings chuckled. "You know, looks fade and money is not the answer."

Josie tilted her head, intrigued. "I'm aware of both those things, Mr. Cummings. Yesterday you told me I was naïve and stupid. Well, I'm not."

"Then allow me to tell you a story," Cummings said, standing up. "I think you'll find it illuminating."

She followed him into the living room, where he stood before the waterfall. He stared down at the tiny lights that danced under the clear water.

"I'd known Rick Rousseau since he was a toddler. His father was a decent enough man—a good businessman. His mother was beautiful but she died young. I knew Rousseau's type. Too pretty. Too charming. Too wild. The male equivalent of my daughter, really." Cummings smiled sadly. "I didn't give him a second thought until Margot came home at Christmas break of her sophomore year, four months pregnant."

"I see," Josie said, vaguely uncomfortable with where this was going.

"Do you?" Cummings paused, looking down at her. "It was Rousseau's baby, Miss Sheehan. He got my daughter pregnant and didn't have the decency to own up to his responsibilities. He was a coward. My wife took Margot to the clinic and got it taken care of, though at first the doctor said four months was too far along. Through it all, Rousseau was nowhere to be found."

The bottom of Josie's belly dropped. Her brain buzzed. *"What?"* That was the only comment she could muster.

"Margot was never whole after that, always so sad. She told me later that she regretted her decision terribly, that she should have had the child but was afraid."

Bennett shook his head. "Rousseau came back into her life almost a decade later, to finish the job he started. And even then it took another seven years! But he eventually got what he was after." Cummings looked at Josie, his eyes filled with tears. "He killed my little girl."

Josie could do nothing but stare at him, searching for some indication that this was a trap. All she found was a very sad old man who had lost his entire family—his wife, his daughter, and his grandchild—by one man's hand.

"But." Josie swallowed, breaking her eye contact with Cummings. "He swore to me he never got anyone pregnant and that he had no children."

Cummings chuckled. "I wonder what other lies he told you." He shook his head. "Miss Sheehan, you truly are a fool if you think Rick Rousseau is a decent man."

She ran into her suite and slammed the door shut. She fell on the bed and cried. She cried for Margot and her parents. She cried for Rick—how could a man be so corrupt? How could he have lied to her like that? With all the trimmings? With such sincerity? How could he be so sinister?

But mostly, Josie cried for herself. Cummings had been right. Bea and Ginger and Roxie had been right. She was gullible, naïve, and so very stupid. She had really thought Rick loved her. She had fallen for it. Again!

She pounded her fists into the fancy bed linens, the rage pouring through her as it all came back to her—those days at the ranch walking hand in hand, all those talks she believed were heartfelt, deep, and true, all those hours she'd spent in Rick's arms, and under his spell. It was too much to bear.

* * *

Bennett sat up the entire night, drinking and thinking and listening to poor Miss Sheehan in there, her heart in tatters.

What would killing that poor girl accomplish? She was somebody's daughter. How would another young woman's senseless death fix anything? He drained his drink, suddenly fascinated with the nature of his self-loathing, so foul and so dark. He shuddered.

Bennett couldn't save Margot. And now he couldn't save himself. It was too late. Even without homicide, the kidnapping alone would send him to prison for the rest of his days.

But he could save Miss Sheehan.

Bennett looked at the clock on his BlackBerry, noting that it would be dawn soon. Enough was enough.

A soft melody passed through his mind like it was carried on a breeze. It was catchy, but a little bittersweet. It was his song.

You wouldn't hurt a fly, Benny.

He entered her room on unsteady legs. For a moment, he panicked at the sight of her limp body. Had she done something to herself? Had there been side effects from the tranquilizer? How could he have done that to her in the first place? When Miss Sheehan mumbled in her sleep, he sighed, greatly relieved. Bennett shook her shoulder.

"Let's go," he said. She bolted awake, blinking at him in terror. She scrambled to a sitting position.

"Don't shoot me. Please."

"I'm not going to shoot you. I'm going to take you home. I've inconvenienced you long enough."

He reached down for her and pulled her to a stand, leading her toward the living area. Without warning, an explosion blew one of the side doors right off the hinges, the force of the blast so severe it rocked them backward. Through a rolling wave of dark smoke, at least a dozen men in riot gear swarmed into the house.

"FBI! Hands up! Step away from the hostage!"

Bennett did what was demanded of him, and within seconds he was thrown to the floor, the crushing weight of a boot pinning his head in place.

She saw Rick instantly. She knew him by the way he moved, the elegant way he was built. As he cleared the smoke, Josie watched him coming right toward her, a look of joy on his face. It was so convincing. Maybe he really did care for her, in his own way. But she wanted more. She wanted the whole thing—a man who was good deep down, a man she could trust.

Never again would she let this happen to her.

"Are you hurt? Thank God! Josie? Did he hurt you?" Rick's hands grabbed her upper arms. "Baby, look at me!"

"I'm fine," she said, watching the police drag Cummings to his feet. "He didn't hurt me at all."

Rick crushed her in his arms. His body trembled against hers. He kept saying her name over and over, kissing her hair and face. *"Josie. Josie. Josie."*

She was relieved when the paramedics peeled Rick off her and forced her onto a gurney. She didn't know how she'd ever be able to look him in the eye again.

CHAPTER 22

Josie collapsed into Gloria Needleman's plastic-covered couch and looked around the room, thinking that this was where the whole saga began just a little over a month ago. She showed up for an interview that day and left with a plan to change her life.

Not for the first time, Josie wondered if things would have been better if she'd never written that list, never met Rick, and never fallen so deeply in love.

She balanced her elbows on her knees and sighed. Maybe a grand life adventure wasn't all it was cracked up to be. Maybe Josephine Agnes Sheehan was destined to live a dry, boring life in the company of a Labradoodle. Maybe she wasn't supposed to find love. Maybe she'd messed with destiny, and she'd be paying for her impudence the rest of her days.

"Drink this. It will fortify your soul."

Mrs. Needleman suddenly appeared at Josie's side, and her words startled Josie. The old woman had gone into the kitchen a few minutes ago to make tea and Josie had forgotten all about her.

She squinted up at Gloria. "Did you spike it or something?"

The old woman laughed and sat down next to her.

"Heavens, no. It's just good old-fashioned black tea—loose leaf, mind you. Now, drink up."

Josie took a cautious sip of the hot liquid and set the cup and saucer on the side table. She let her head fall into her hands.

Gloria patted her back in rapid, gentle taps. "The important thing is you weren't harmed, and that man is behind bars."

Josie shook her head back and forth, feeling her hair fall down around her like a curtain. She'd come here to ask Mrs. Needleman for advice, but now all she wanted to do was get back under the covers and hide, her preferred mode of existence for the last week and a half. She hadn't left her apartment except to walk Genghis. Her family and Bea, Ginger, and Roxie had been her only visitors.

"You have to see your young man."

"I can't," Josie said, her face still covered by hands and hair.

"Nonsense! We've already seen how courageous you are."

Dear God, Josie was sick of that word. Where had courage gotten her? She'd been courageous enough to write the list, ask Rick for a date, chase him down, accept him for who he was, and survive a two-day kidnapping ordeal—and where had all that taken her? Right back where she started, where she always seemed to end up—alone, a man gone from her life, without her soul mate.

The only difference was that this time, it hurt so bad she didn't know if she'd ever bounce back.

Josie raised her head and glanced over at Mrs. Needleman. The old woman's knowing expression made her so uncomfortable she couldn't sit still. "May I use your bathroom?" Josie asked.

Mrs. Needleman pointed an arthritic finger toward the hallway. "Second door on the right. Take all the time you need, dear."

"Thanks." Josie bolted to the hallway but didn't make it past the first door on the right or the left. She stopped in her tracks. The hallway was covered with framed photographs. Josie had to blink a few times to make sense of what she was seeing—Gloria Needleman, marrying people, on the beach and in gardens and on the courthouse steps. In backyards and on sailboats and in a rooftop garden, the wind whipping her dress around her skinny legs.

The photos were in color and black-and-white, and they showed old couples with canes, college students, middle-aged people with kids. The people were black, white, Chinese, Latino, and everything in between. The dress code was white satin, jeans and boots, or hippie chic. The photos were dated from the 1960s through the first decade of the twenty-first century.

Josie's mouth fell open.

"Yes, I am a certified marriage officiate in the state of California," said a warbly voice at Josie's side.

She jumped. *God, this lady has a habit of sneaking up on me!*

"But—" Josie stared down at the wrinkly face with the fierce eyes. "I don't get it. You're a preacher or rabbi or something?"

Gloria laughed heartily. "Why, I do happen to be ordained in a nondenominational faith. I'm also a notary public. But the point is I've been given a gift, and it's my duty to use it."

"Your duty is to go around marrying people?"

Gloria laughed again. "My duty is to connect people, to use my gifts to gently guide people toward love."

Josie squinted. "So you're a real matchmaker?"

The old woman shrugged.

Josie returned her attention to the wall, searching for something that would help her understand why she suddenly felt angry. She turned abruptly toward the old woman. "You set me up with Rick? This was your plan all along?" Josie felt herself shaking she was so mad. "You had no right to do that, Gloria."

"No, no, dear girl. I didn't know Rick existed as an individual. Please, come sit down with me again and I'll try to explain."

Josie felt as if she were sleepwalking as Gloria led her back to the sofa.

"When you came to see me after Ira died, I knew instantly that you were my next assignment."

Josie laughed. "I know I'm going to regret asking, but who exactly gives you your assignments?"

Gloria giggled the way she did sometimes, narrow shoulders shaking and hands clapping in joy. She looked like a young girl. "On that particular day, *you* gave me the assignment, Josie."

She shot her a dubious look.

"I saw how you bristled when I talked about my happy life with Ira."

"I bristled?" Josie sat straighter. "I don't recall bristling."

"I could feel how lonely you were. And I sensed that you were on the cusp of finding your beloved, but were going to need a little, well, *encouragement*." Gloria paused and reached out for Josie's hand. The old woman's skin felt papery and cool to the touch. "I saw that yours would be a special case."

Josie glanced at the ceiling, trying to be polite but losing the battle. She'd come here for help. More of Gloria's gobbledygook was the last thing she needed.

"I should probably go." Josie began to stand up, but Gloria held on to her hand.

"You should sit still and listen if you know what's good for you."

The reprimand in Gloria's voice was startling. It reminded Josie of the nun who taught her in fourth grade, the one who regularly made Josie stay after to clean the chalkboard with warm water and stinky liquid soap.

"I sensed that without some extra attention, you and your love would pass each other by, never find your chance for happiness in each other." She patted Josie's hand. "I could not let that happen."

Josie tilted her head, puzzled. "I had a similar thought once, sitting on the porch at Rick's ranch."

Gloria smiled softly. "You don't say?"

"I remember looking out at the beautiful view, feeling truly in love for the first time in my life, and then, *bam!* I knew it was a miracle that we'd found each other. It would've been so easy for Rick and me to have never met. It seemed the more likely outcome, really."

"Exactly."

Josie looked at Gloria for a long moment. "So writing the list put me in the right frame of mind? It helped me see Rick for who he was when we met? It made me bold enough to go after him?"

Gloria's eyes lit up. "Perfectly put."

Josie shook her head vigorously to regain her focus, and stood up from the couch. She paced across the living room, her heart ready to burst with the disappointment and loneliness. She spun around and pointed at Gloria. "But you were wrong—he wasn't the one!" Josie knew her voice sounded shrill but she didn't care. "I'm right where I started, only exponentially more miserable!"

She didn't want to cry anymore. All Josie wanted from this visit was some comfort, not a whole new round of confusion.

"Tell me why he's not the one for you." Mrs. Needleman patted the clear plastic. "Come. Sit back down and tell me about it."

Josie sighed, shuffling back to the couch. She told Mrs. Needleman everything—the details of Rick's past, his solemn promise to her that he'd never gotten any woman pregnant, his claim that he would have moved heaven and earth to be a good father if he had. Then she shared Bennett Cummings's tragic story of his daughter's pregnancy, abortion, and death.

"Rick lied to me," Josie said simply. "I could overlook everything about his past—every selfish and harmful thing he'd ever done—because he never set out to harm anyone. And I told myself he had changed! I *trusted* him! How gullible can a girl be?"

Mrs. Needleman nodded solemnly. "So what did Rick say when you gave him a chance to explain?" Gloria blinked, waiting for Josie's answer. When it didn't come, she asked again. "What did your young man say when you told him this story?"

Josie tilted her head and stared in disbelief. "I never asked him. I haven't spoken to him since he busted the door down to save me."

Mrs. Needleman folded her hands neatly in her lap. "But he's tried to contact you?"

Josie swore the old lady was trying not to smile, and she didn't appreciate her attitude. "Several times a day. But I'm not returning his calls."

"I see."

"What's the point?" Josie asked, growing more pissed off by the second. "I've learned my lesson for good this time. I don't want any more men in my life.

Why bother? They'll only use you and lie to you and then leave you."

Gloria made a tsk-tsk sound behind her teeth. "So, refresh my memory, dear. How exactly did Rick use you?"

Josie froze. That was an interesting question, and she decided to organize the list of offenses in her mind before she shared it with Gloria. Unfortunately, her mind went blank.

"Josie?"

Rick had made her laugh. He had taught her what it felt like to make love. He had put her safety and happiness above his own. He'd chosen her to be the one woman he'd confide in, trust, and love. He had told her she was sexy and beautiful. He'd given her that gorgeous painting, simply because she'd liked it! He'd enjoyed her eggplant Parmesan. He'd even cooked for her—naked.

Dear God, he even liked her *dog*.

"Uh . . ." Josie said.

Gloria smiled cheerfully. "And when exactly did he leave you?"

Josie felt her eyes go big. She didn't say anything.

"Is there any chance that Rick wasn't lying to you at all?" Mrs. Needleman's eyes got that laserlike focus that made Josie uncomfortable. "Is it possible that he was truthful, and you are the one who left him, and for no good reason whatsoever?"

Josie remained quiet, but the inside of her head was roaring.

"How will you ever know if you don't communicate?"

That was enough. Josie jumped from the couch and grabbed her bag. She headed for the door, the tears streaming down her face. Her hand trembled as it grabbed the doorknob.

"Don't blow it, dear girl."

She spun around—Mrs. Needleman was once again right up against her. Josie shook her head. "If I go to him, he'll tell me what I want to hear. But how will I know what's real? There will always be this little voice in my head telling me I made the biggest mistake of my life trusting him again. I'll always be waiting for the next shoe to drop."

Gloria nodded. "Well, then there's only one last-ditch option."

"What's that?"

"Follow your instincts. Have faith in love."

Josie's hand slid behind her back, where she rooted around for the doorknob.

"Ira and I weren't perfect. Oy! Far from it." Gloria shrugged. "There were times I couldn't stand being in the same room with that man."

How convenient that Gloria skipped over that part for Ira's obit, Josie thought.

"Oh, but how I loved him." A smile spread over Gloria's wrinkled face and her eyes mellowed. "Many times I would look at Ira and feel a sacredness in our being together. I knew he was my soul mate, the other being handpicked by the universe to help me grow into fullness on this earth."

Josie was taken aback. "That's pretty deep," she said, slowly turning the knob.

"Ira was my beloved. And I have reason to believe that Rick is yours." Gloria's eyes bored into Josie's widening gaze. "Some mystics say that if you are lucky enough to find your complementary soul, the Divine steps in to create a third entity—a spirit companion, if you will—whose only job is to watch over the two of you."

Josie swallowed hard. She pulled the door open a crack. "Nice idea."

"But if you turn your back on your beloved . . ." Gloria pressed a hand to her heart, as if overwrought by what she was about to say. "Dear girl, if you consciously turn away from your beloved—the one designed to love your human heart into perfection—then the spirit companion leaves you. It never returns. And the goodness that was meant to be will never come to pass."

Josie blinked a few times, letting the words sink it. Great, she thought. Not only had she failed spectacularly in love—yet again—but this time she'd also managed to tell her guardian angel to fuck off and die.

"Go to Rick. Talk to him. Afterward, if you know in your gut that Rick is not your beloved—" Gloria poked a finger into Josie's belly, "then tell him so and be on your way. It is your choice."

Josie felt her shoulders sag. She nodded slowly and sighed, yanking her bag higher on her shoulder. "All right, Gloria. Maybe I'll talk to him. I guess it wouldn't hurt to get some closure, one way or the other."

"That's the spirit!" Gloria slipped something into her hand. Josie stared at the words on the business card: *The Reverend Mrs. Gloria Needleman, Universal Spiritual Church; Notary Public; Wedding Officiate; Mensch. Payment Plans Available.*

Josie laughed. She half expected Mrs. Needleman to tell her she was pulling her leg.

Instead, Gloria leaned close. In a conspiratorial whisper she said, "I'm already booked solid for June."

* * *

Gloria was right. Josie was being hardheaded. Rick deserved a chance to explain. Hadn't Josie once promised him that she'd be kind and forgiving? These last ten days had been filled with nothing but grief, anger, betrayal, and general nastiness, and she hated the way it made her feel.

By the time she reached her friends at the top of the hill at Dolores Park, she'd made her decision. There would be no going back.

The women stopped dead when she appeared, not only because they didn't expect her, but because of Genghis's drastic change in appearance. They stared in disbelief, mouths open, eyes big.

"Jesus H!" Bea shouted. "Did he have a fight with Edward Scissorhands or something?"

"He's bald," Ginger whispered. "He looks—I don't know—like a big Vienna sausage with legs."

"Gee, thanks," Josie said.

Lilith growled and snarled at Genghis, a male dog she did not recognize. Roxie cracked up laughing. "What the hell happened to him?"

"I got him clipped yesterday."

"More like skinned," Bea corrected.

Ginger gasped. "Is this what Celestial Pet gives you for free? Because if it is, I think you should go ahead and spend a few bucks."

"Okay. I know he looks strange." Josie could add guilt to the long list of negative emotions she'd been wallowing in. "I took him to this little place off Twenty-first Street on a whim, when we were out walking. I tend to do impulsive things when I'm depressed."

Ginger shook her head in dismay. "For the love of God, go shopping next time, Joze—you can always take a pair of shoes back to the store."

Roxie tilted her head. "I've missed you. I'm glad you're here." She gave Josie a quick hug.

"I've missed you guys, too," Josie said. "I wanted to tell you that I've thought about it, and I'm going to talk to Rick."

"Thank God!" Bea shouted, jumping up and down in her Reeboks. Martina must have thought it was some kind of agility exercise because she jumped with her, barking with joy.

Roxie and Ginger threw their arms around Josie and rocked her back and forth, squealing with excitement. Everybody's leashes got tangled. An oncoming dog walker opted to take a wide detour around the chaotic group, while Lilith snarled.

"I *knew* I could talk you into it," Bea said, when she finished jumping.

Josie picked a strand of Ginger's hair from her lips and said, "Mrs. Needleman did that."

"Really?" Bea looked hurt.

"But you helped," Josie quickly added. "And so did you two." She peeled Ginger and Roxie off her shirt.

Ginger began fanning her flushed face. "Rick is an absolute gem of a man. And Josie, he loves you. Isn't that the God's truth?" Ginger looked to Roxie for confirmation.

"Damn right," Roxie said. "That man adores you, Josie. He's been like a lost puppy without you since the kidnapping. He blames himself for putting you in danger—he thinks that's why you're angry with him!"

"Well, it's not," Josie said quietly. "Like I told you, something else has been bothering me, but I realize I can't figure it out alone—I need Rick's help."

Ginger sighed. "If you two get back together, it will be the most romantic thing I've ever witnessed in my life."

"The kidnapping wasn't Rick's fault," Bea said.

"It wasn't anyone's fault," Josie added.

"The hell it wasn't!"

Everyone was stunned by Bea's outburst.

"It was *my* fault!" she said, raking her fingers through her spiky hair, her voice filled with anxiety. "If it weren't for my interfering, Rick would have been with you! You wouldn't have been a sitting duck!" Bea's lips began to tremble. "I'm so sorry, Josie. Please try to forgive me."

"Oh, Bea." Josie went over to the now thoroughly crying woman and gave her a warm hug. "I am blessed to have friends who love me enough to worry about me. Just, next time . . ." Josie gave all of them a thin smile. "Come to me directly if you've got concerns, okay?"

"Of course!" Ginger said.

"And you won't hide something important again, no matter how melodramatic we get with our vows and promises," Roxie said, grinning.

"Never," Josie replied.

"But there won't be a next time, right?" Bea's voice sounded worried. "You're going to work it out with Rick, right? You're not going to let him go."

Josie looked around at the anxious expressions on her friends' faces and laughed.

Roxie looked appalled. "You almost let a man like Rick Rousseau walk out of your life and you think it's funny?"

"You can't do that," Ginger said, her eyes big. "Go after him, Josie!"

"Do whatever it takes." Bea's voice became hushed and she grabbed Josie's arm. "Give it everything you've got. Beg if you have to."

Josie stared at them. The same women who had

spent years scolding her for throwing herself at men were now demanding she throw herself at a man. "You've done a complete one-eighty on me. What's up with that?"

"We're talking about Rick," Bea said, quite seriously. "Josie, this man is not one of the Spikes of the world."

"He's not a Lloyd," Roxie said.

"He's not even a Wayne or a Randy or a Billy or whoever that guy was who stole your turkey baster when he moved out."

"I haven't thought of Lester in years," Josie said.

"You finally got it right. That's what we're saying." Bea shook her head. "So don't fuck it up now."

Josie smiled at her friends, knowing she'd heard that piece of advice more than once lately. "I'll try to reach him sometime this afternoon."

"He's at the office until four."

Josie stared at Bea, who looked sheepish. "How would you know that?"

"We've been keeping in touch," Bea said with a shrug. "You know, in case you might need him for something."

Josie laughed.

"Not that I'm going to get in your business ever again," Bea added. "I swear."

"I think it's time for some new vows," Ginger said, a mischievous smile taking over her face. "Pile on, girls." She stuck out her hand. Bea slapped hers on next. Then Roxie. Josie went on top.

"I promise to give myself a break—not be so afraid of being forty and alone," Ginger said. "And I promise to be a better friend to all of you."

Bea jumped in next. "I promise to be there for all of you however I can, but from now on I'll offer my assistance from a respectful distance—and only after it's requested."

Everyone giggled.

"I vow to try harder to let go of the past," Roxie said, with a sigh. "I'll try not to be so hacked off all the time."

It was Josie's turn. Unlike the last time they did this, she didn't feel compelled to put on an act. Unlike the last time, she had no clever commentary.

Josie looked into the faces of the three women in the circle and said, "I vow to take stock of my blessings every day, and that includes all of you. Thank you for being my friends."

The women pumped their hands in unison and reached to the sky with a celebratory *whoo-hoo!* They linked arms and walked, laughing, their dogs running free. Except for the muzzled Lilith and the frightened HeatherLynn, who finished peeing on Ginger's shoe, then demanded to be picked up.

Rick awakened from the stillness of meditation. The instant he opened his eyes, Josie was there. At first he thought she was a mirage, and that, like a dying man in the desert certain he'd found water, Josie had come back to him—his salvation at long last.

His cell phone rang. It was Teeny. "Yep, I see them. Tell the front desk I'll take care of it."

"Good luck," Teeny said.

Rick stood up and walked out from the shade of the ginkgo tree. He jogged across enough of the lawn to know this was no mirage. Coming up the front walkway was the only woman he'd ever loved and a dog he decided had to be Genghis, only nude.

"Over here!" he called out. "Josie!"

It was Genghis all right. The dog saw him, raced

his way, sailed through the air, and body-slammed him, only to sniff Rick's zipper once he'd regained his footing. But the Genghis Rick knew was gone—he had to be half his former size.

He stared at the dog in disbelief—he looked like a lamb after shearing. Rick could see the Labradoodle's entire face, and for the first time he could put together the tongue-lolling smile with the crazy happy little brown marble eyes. It was like meeting an old friend for the very first time.

Josie came to stand near them. She was wearing a short denim skirt, a little blue T-shirt, and sandals. Her hair was pulled back from her face, and fell down to her shoulders. She looked so pretty he could hardly breathe.

Go slow . . . be cool . . .

"Please don't tell me Celestial Pet did this to him," Rick said, trying not to laugh.

"I know. It's pretty awful. It wasn't your store." Josie took a step closer, her cheeks reddening with embarrassment. "I took him to Bev's Canine Beauty Barn on Twenty-first Street."

Rick sucked in his lips and bit down, trying with all his might not to bust out laughing. "Why did you do that?"

Josie's eyes narrowed. "Because I was so angry it made sense to me, that's why. I didn't take him to Celestial Pet on purpose, out of spite. I wanted you to be hurt and offended that I didn't use my free service."

Rick nodded as though her logic were sound.

"Stupid, obviously." Josie sighed and looked around the lawn. "Rick, can we talk?"

"Absolutely." He gestured toward the shade under the ginkgo tree. "Step into my office."

They walked side by side for a moment, and he

gestured for her to take a seat on one of the buckwheat cushions.

He didn't see it coming. The force of the attack caught him off balance and he staggered backward, nearly falling to the ground.

Josie's bag hit the grass and she jumped up, body-slamming him, much like her dog had just done. She grabbed him and kissed the hell out of him. She clung to him, her legs wrapped around his waist and her arms around his neck. She smothered him with her kisses, her apologies, her tears.

Rick couldn't breathe, but it didn't matter. If he had to die, this would be his preferred method of crossing over.

He stumbled back and hit the trunk of the tree. With one arm Rick braced himself against the bark. With the other he squeezed her bottom.

It would have been one of the best moments of his life if Josie wasn't crying. But she continued crying and kissing and clutching at him like her existence depended on it.

"Hold on a minute." Rick somehow managed to get his lips away long enough to gasp for air. "Wait. Just a—"

"I'm so sorry!" Josie grabbed him on either side of his face. "I've been horrible. Childish. Downright mean. Rick, forgive me!"

Rick tried to nod his head, but he had little range of motion in her grip.

"Oh. Sorry." Josie unhooked her legs from his waist and slid down the front of his body. She pulled down her skirt and smoothed her hair. "I've missed you. I didn't realize how much till I saw you. I got carried away."

If measured in pain and regret, the last ten days of

Rick's life had rivaled the worst days after the accident. For the last ten days, Rick had walked around like a zombie, aching for Josie's company, her laugh, her love.

Right after the arrest, Rick assumed Josie hated him for not protecting her from Cummings. It was some comfort when his newest friends—Bea, Ginger, and Roxie—told him there was something else bothering Josie, but that she refused to discuss it. They assured Rick that Josie would come around, and suggested he give her some space.

He'd never had platonic women friends before. He had no idea it could be so handy.

"Feel free to get carried away with me any time you want, Josie," Rick said.

She nodded. "I've been afraid to come to you." She looked down at the cushions. "Can we sit?"

Rick took her hand and pulled her down on his lap. She patted his arm and then moved to the next cushion over. "With my other relationships, I never used to come out with stuff that bothered me. I held it in— and look where that got me." Josie took a deep breath. "Rick, I want to do things differently with you. I came here today because we need to clear the air between us. Can we do that?"

"Yes." Rick nodded. "But first, I have to ask—have you been okay?"

Josie nodded. "Yeah. I'm fine physically. Mentally, it hasn't been horrible. At first Cummings scared me, but he wasn't all that bad."

Rick raised an eyebrow.

"He was just a guy who couldn't mourn the loss of his daughter. For seven years, he'd focused all his energy on hating you." Josie took a breath. "I think he figured out that no matter how many of Rick Rousseau's girlfriends he kidnapped, Margot wouldn't be coming back."

"I only have one girlfriend," Rick said. "I don't plan on having any more, ever."

Josie looked down and fiddled with some clover, a faint smile on her lips. It took everything in him not to touch her.

"Rick, Cummings told me that Margot came home pregnant on Christmas break of her sophomore year." Josie raised her eyes to him. She looked sad. "Did you know about that?"

Rick froze, the question jarring him. "No. Why?"

"She was four months along when she had an abortion. The baby was yours."

Rick felt his body go rigid with denial. It couldn't be! "Margot never said anything about a baby," Rick said, his calm a cover for the chaos inside him. "I think Cummings was mistaken."

Josie pursed her lips. "Didn't you date her in college?"

Rick rubbed his jaw, not sure their activities constituted "dating," but it was the euphemism of choice on every college campus, everywhere. "Yes. I dated her for the last part of our freshman year, then again in the fall of our sophomore year. And she never said a word to me about being pregnant."

Josie's shoulders sagged.

Rick leaned his head against the tree trunk, trying to breathe. There was something about this that wasn't right—something more than being told he'd fathered a child he never knew existed. Something at the back of his mind was screaming that it didn't make sense.

Then it hit him, and he laughed out loud with relief. "That baby was not mine, Josie."

Josie frowned at him. "How do you know?"

Rick leaned toward her. "Did Cummings say Margot was four months along at Christmas?"

Josie nodded. "He said the doctor initially refused to perform the procedure because she was too far along."

"Josie." Rick reached out for her hand. "Listen to me. It wasn't my child. I need you to believe me."

He saw how she struggled—it was broadcast all over her face. She wanted to believe him. She was willing to believe him. But it was hard.

"That was the only thing . . ." Josie's chin quivered. "It was the one thing I told you I couldn't handle, Rick."

"I remember. And I'm telling you the truth."

Josie looked deep into his eyes and nodded. "All right," she said. "I'm going to trust my instinct here and believe you." She smiled sadly. "I want to believe you."

"Would it help if I could prove it?"

"How in the world could you do that?" She leaned away from him, confused.

Rick chuckled and shook his head at the irony. "I never thought I'd turn into Chatty Cathie about all this, but remember when I told you I was in jail twice—once in the States and once in Thailand?"

Josie nodded.

"I was in jail four months before Christmas of that year. I couldn't have gotten her pregnant."

Josie sat up straight. "Are you absolutely sure?"

"Sweetie, I was a guest of the city of Milwaukee from late August to the beginning of October, when my dad finally got the charges dropped. I was three weeks late starting the semester at Yale, but the registrar let me in anyway—yet another problem my father managed to make go away."

Josie blinked.

"Margot may have claimed I was the father, but I wasn't." He watched Josie's face, relieved by her tentative smile. "I can have my arrest records by the end of the day."

"I don't need records, just your word," Josie whispered, the tears gathering in her eyes. "Mrs. Needleman told me that when I talked to you I'd know whether I could trust you, right here." Josie took one of Rick's hands and pressed his finger into her belly. "She was right. I will never doubt you again, Rick."

He fell into her, and she welcomed him into her arms. After the initial rush of relief, Rick grabbed her and pulled her onto his lap. He kissed her softly, letting his lips tell her all the things words could not do justice—that she was the love of his life, the glue that held all the good things together.

Genghis began to lick Rick's face, ruining the moment. They both started laughing.

"I think he's jealous," Rick said.

"No. He's just missed you." Josie touched Rick's cheek. "He's started sleeping by the door. He's been waiting for you."

"Thank you for coming to talk to me." Rick propped her up on one of his knees. "Don't ever be afraid to ask me about my past—or my present or future for that matter. There's nothing I don't want to share with you."

"Really?" Josie bit her bottom lip. "You love me like that?"

Rick chuckled. "Would you like to know just how much I love you?"

Josie nodded, her eyes sparkling.

"Let's stand up for a minute." Josie jumped to her feet and pulled Rick up. "Now, close your eyes for me." She did. "Keep them closed."

Rick dug into the front pocket of his shorts, pulling

out the little velvet box he'd been carrying around since the night his proposal was interrupted. It seemed like years ago.

He got down on one knee. He opened the box and offered it up in his right hand. Genghis plopped at Rick's side. Clearly, this was going to be a team effort.

"You can open your eyes now, Josie."

She gasped, and her hands flew to her mouth in astonishment.

"Will you marry me? Will you try this with me?"

"I will!" she shouted, half laughing and half crying, staring at the ring in awe. "I think I'm about to get carried away again," she said, just before she pounced on him.

CHAPTER 23

The August air was clear and cool, and a few clouds floated across the blue sky. Samhain Ranch was in full bloom, the grapes plump and round, the fig trees heavy with fruit, the gardens bursting with outrageous color and scent. The one hundred or so invited guests mingled on the lawn and sipped champagne, their laughter rising and falling on the breeze. Dogs and children weaved in and out of long skirts and tablecloths. Josie couldn't help it—she'd been spying from behind the thick vines of the guest cottage's second-story balcony, and she couldn't tear herself away.

It was her wedding day. Who would have ever imagined that Josephine Agnes Sheehan's wedding would look like something from a storybook? Who would've imagined she'd be marrying a man like Rick Rousseau?

Frankly, who'd ever imagined Josie getting married, period?

"There's not going to be a wedding if you don't finish getting dressed!" That was Beth, yelling from downstairs.

"Josie, we can't find your father's cummerbund!"

That was her mother. "He might have left it at home! Sweet Mother of Jesus!"

"Psst." Josie turned in surprise to see Rick perched on a bedroom windowsill.

She laughed in surprise, her heart soaring at the sight of him. "How in the world did you get up here? You're not supposed to see the bride before the ceremony!"

"Too bad." Rick took a few strides toward her, but stopped abruptly. "My God, you're beautiful."

Josie stepped in from the balcony and faced him, immediately feeling his lustful gaze burn her skin. She wore only her white stockings and garter, satin heels, and a white lace bustier and panties. She put her hands on her hips. "Well, I sure hope you like what you see because you've just ruined your big wedding-night surprise, Rousseau."

A huge smile spread across Rick's face and he rubbed his close-shaven chin. "I'll pretend like I've never seen it before. I swear." He chuckled. "But, since I've already ruined it, would you mind just turning around for me? Just once?"

Josie did a half spin, raised her arms, and wiggled her hips like a hula dancer. When she turned back around, Rick looked flushed.

"You okay?"

"No," Rick said, hopping down from the windowsill and adjusting his tuxedo trousers. "I don't think it's appropriate for a guy to get married with a raging hard-on. It may even be against the law."

It was Josie's turn to admire her betrothed. Rick's hair was neatly trimmed and combed back from his strong, handsome face. His mellow green eyes smoldered in contrast to the pure white of his tuxedo shirt and white tie. They also matched the green of the two serpent heads peeking up from the collar. The perfectly cut black Armani jacket and trousers gave him a sleek, sophisticated look. The entire ensemble was topped off by his worn running shoes and no socks.

Rick saw her expression. "Don't worry. I'll change into my other shoes—I just didn't want to climb the trellis in those things. No traction."

"Of course," Josie said, smiling. They held each other's gaze for a long moment, saying nothing, each savoring the vision of the other. She felt it. She knew it. Rick was the one for her. She was the one for him.

"I finished my vows this morning," he said, a touch of pride in his voice. "And everything's loaded up in the limo."

"That's great."

Rick came closer and reached for her hands. "Are you okay, sweetie? You seem a little quiet."

Josie nodded and said she was fine, but the tears started. "I'm blown away by all this, Rick! My God— we're getting married!" She blotted at her eyes. "I can't start crying now or I'll never stop!"

"It's okay, baby." Rick pulled her close and cradled her in his arms. He held her carefully, aware of her complicated hairdo and her makeup. He kissed the top of her head with the utmost caution. "You know you can always tell me anything, no matter what it is." He paused. "Are you having second thoughts?"

Josie pushed herself away and stared at him with wide eyes. "Are you freakin' nuts?" she asked. They both laughed loudly. "Are *you* having second thoughts?"

"Hell, no. I am the happiest man that ever lived."

"Who are you talking to?" That was Beth shouting again, only this time she sounded much closer. "Oh, my God! Get out!" Beth yelled, pointing an accusing

finger at Rick and retreating from the bedroom door.
"Mom! Rick snuck into Josie's room!"

"What?" her mother screeched from downstairs.
"Beth, get down here and help me with this godfor-
saken, muddy-mettled rascal of a dress!"

Rick raised an eyebrow. *"Henry V?"*

"Hamlet."

"I'm outta here." His hand slipped from Josie's
grasp and he hurried to the window.

"Hey, Rick?" she called after him.

He turned, halfway over the windowsill.

"Thank you." Josie didn't know why she said those
particular words, but they were what needed to be
said.

"For what, sweet Josie?"

"For agreeing to have that cup of coffee with me. I
know saying yes wasn't your first instinct."

Rick tilted his head. She watched his smile tighten
as a wave of emotion swept across his face. For a moment, she thought he was going to cry, too. "Thank
you for asking me," he said, swallowing hard. "I know
it wasn't your first instinct, either."

Josie nodded.

Rick blew her a kiss. "I'm going to spend every day
showing you how happy I am to have you in my life."

"Josephine Agnes?"

Josie turned to see her mother and Beth in the hallway, holding Josie's wedding gown aloft. Behind them
were Roxanne, Bea, and Ginger, in matching moss-
green gowns accented by matching expressions of
amusement. Bea dramatically crossed her eyes, sucked
in her cheeks, and made a peace sign over Beth's head.
Josie laughed.

"Do you want to get married or not?" Her mother
nodded at the yards of cream-colored satin carefully

draped over her arm. "Rick's photographer friend is getting antsy. You're in your underwear. Your father has no cummerbund."

Josie glanced toward the window again, but Rick was gone. She ran to the balcony in time to see him, in his tuxedo and running shoes, sneaking across the lawn to the main house. An agitated Teeny waited for him, gesturing wildly.

Josie felt the happiness start with a little flutter in her belly. It raced through her heart, where it gathered force and speed, and blossomed into a huge smile.

She turned to the women in the doorway. "Let's get this party started!"

Because Mrs. Needleman turned out to be about four feet tall, even in her orthopedic dress shoes, Rick and Teeny had to build a wooden dais for her to stand on during the ceremony. They'd draped it in a white table-cloth and stuck flowers all around it, and it had looked fine at the time, but seeing her standing there now, a book of poetry in her hands, Rick realized Mrs. Needleman looked like the decorative topper to an oversized wedding cake.

He couldn't help but laugh.

Teeny leaned down and whispered in his ear. "Don't you dare start that, man. It's more contagious than crying."

Rick was saved when the string quartet struck its first chord of the Bach Air. It was time.

The bridesmaids began their procession across the lawn, one by one, down a center aisle of manicured grass. Beth came first, beaming with happiness. She was followed by Bea, who looked thrilled but moved as if she hadn't worn a dress in forty years, which, according to Josie, she hadn't. Roxanne was stunning with all that dark hair pulled up at her neck. Ginger was her usual knockout self but looked like she'd been poured into her dress, which might explain why his photographer buddy Lucio hadn't taken his eyes off her the entire day.

Then there was Josie.

Rick swallowed hard, his heart bursting at the sight of his beautiful bride. If he thought Josie had looked good in lingerie, it had been a warm-up for this. She was stunning as she walked slowly toward him on her father's arm.

Josie was nervous—he could tell by the way she blushed. But it only made her more radiant. She was all smiles, soft curls, and sparkling eyes. Her curves were wrapped up in a floor-length, sleeveless dress as elegant as it was uncomplicated. It suited her perfectly. It suited the setting.

When Josie reached him, Rick pumped her dad's hand, then guided Josie to their place in front of Mrs. Needleman. Rick stole a quick glance at Josie before the ceremony began, and winked at her. She giggled.

He tried his best to stay in the moment, but the truth was, it all went by in a blur. Mrs. Needleman said a few sweet and kind things about the two of them, adding that destiny had had a hand in their union. Despite all of Rick's worries, when the time came for him to say his vows it went off without a hitch. Josie got so choked up when he spoke of how her love had brought him back to life that Beth shoved a lacy handkerchief in her hand.

Josie's vows were similarly short and sweet. She said that no one could change the past, and that today was all any of them had. She promised to treat her husband with honesty and kindness and to greet each day they shared with gratitude. At that point, Rick held out his hand so Beth could pass the handkerchief.

Mrs. Needleman said a few more words, but Rick hardly heard them. He was too focused on his bride's beautiful face, on those delightful lips that he'd be privileged to kiss for the rest of his days.

He truly thought he heard Mrs. Needleman say he could kiss the bride, so he did. As soon as his mouth landed on Josie's, the laughter erupted all around him, Teeny's guffaw the loudest. Rick popped up his head in embarrassment.

"Who am I to stand in love's way?" Mrs. Needleman said with a dramatic shrug. "Go and be joyous. Know you are protected and blessed in your union."

"So that's it?" Rick asked, to more laughter, including his wife's. This wasn't going as smoothly as he'd planned, but then again, the fact that he was getting married at all was a surprise. A surprise of the sweetest kind.

"So can I kiss her now?" Rick whispered. Mrs. Needleman nodded and Rick dove into his love, his wife, his life. A moment later, they were walking across the lawn hand in hand to cheers and hoots. Bea let loose with one of her Superdome-worthy whistles.

After the bride and groom spent an hour or so eating wedding cake and sipping champagne with their guests, Rick escorted Josie to the Harley. It was parked at the top of the lane, festooned with white sparkly streamers. While the guests took their places along both sides of the road, Rick helped Josie gather her skirts and straddle the back of the bike. He fastened the helmet under her chin and kissed her nose. They might only be cruising to the end of the dirt road, where their white stretch limousine waited, but he would take no chances.

Rick didn't miss the irony: They were headed to the North Pole via Finland, then Russia, and a week at sea on a nuclear-powered icebreaker, yet, for him, this short motorcycle ride would be the most difficult leg of the journey.

"You want to try this with me?" Josie asked.

"More than anything."

She smiled at him. "I have a feeling it's going to be a grand adventure."

Rick kissed her quickly and put on his own helmet. Her arms reached around his middle as he revved up the Harley engine. Under a shower of flower petals and best wishes, Rick and Josie rode off into their future, moving at a cautious fifteen miles an hour.

Gloria Needleman rested her head against the back of a wicker porch chair, propped her feet on a matching stool, and adjusted an uncomfortable twist in her support hose. She closed her eyes. It had been a glorious day—one of the most delightfully tender ceremonies she'd ever officiated—but, without a doubt, Josie and Rick's wedding was not the end of this assignment. It was just the beginning.

I'm getting too old for this drek, Gloria thought, sighing.

"Fifty bucks says she's pregnant in a year."

Giggles erupted from Josie's friends when the oldest one, Beatrice, made that observation, which was likely correct.

Gloria cracked open an eye just enough to study the women undetected. They sat not more than fifteen feet away on the front porch of the main house, the late afternoon sun casting a golden glow over them, their matching dresses fluttering in the breeze from the ceiling fan. Their shoes were off. Their faces were happy and relaxed.

It amused Gloria how these women thought it was a coincidence that they'd befriended each other at the newspaper and stayed together all these years despite their obvious differences. Gloria knew better. She knew that people entered your life to help you learn the lessons you needed to learn, and Josie and her friends were no exception.

"Wrong again, Bea," said the dark-haired beauty named Roxanne. "I say it'll be nine months to the day. Just watch."

Gloria shook her head imperceptibly. This Roxanne had driven them all to the ranch yesterday in a car advertising that she vomited on all men. It said so right on her bumper sticker! The girl thought she had it all figured out—at the age of twenty-eight, no less. Oy! Was this one ever in for a shock!

The gorgeous Ginger chimed in next, and Gloria watched as she stretched out a pair of legs that went from here to forever, as the men back in her day would say. But goodness, the woman's bridesmaid dress was tight! It was a wonder she could breathe!

"I don't care when it happens for Josie, just so long as it does," Ginger said, pulling at the sleeveless bodice of the dress. "Today was so romantic it almost— I'm saying *almost*—makes me willing to believe in love again!"

Gloria chuckled to herself. The comely Ginger wouldn't know romance if it bit her in the tuchus. Which it was about to do. The dear girl was so afraid of being over the hill that, if she wasn't careful, she would miss her chance to be over the moon.

"I bet I know what made you a believer," Bea said,

with enough of an edge that Gloria knew a punch line was coming. "Casanova the cameraman!"

"Excuse me?" Ginger sat up straighter.

Roxanne nodded. "Your gawking radiated so much heat I worried the wedding party would spontaneously combust."

Ginger eyed Roxanne with suspicion. "Really? What about you and the new puppy head-peeper Rick invited here today? You two sure got chummy real fast."

"That was business," Roxanne said, pulling back her shoulders. "Eli is a pet behaviorist and he's going to help me with Lilith's aggression issues."

"It was business for me, too," Ginger said. "Lucio is going to take a portrait of me and HeatherLynn."

"Fine," Roxanne said.

"Wonderful," Ginger said, draining her drink. "Does anyone know if they're still serving mimosas?"

Gloria giggled. Roxanne and Ginger were less prepared than most she'd dealt with. The women had been hurt so badly that they'd become resistant to enchantment. They were skeptics at a time when embracing the mystery would come in handy. The stumbling block for Roxanne was anger. For Ginger, it was fear. And from the beginning of time, anger and fear had been love's most formidable foes.

Not that there was any way to prepare for meeting your beloved, Gloria knew. There was no training for that sort of thing. It happened once in a lifetime—and that was if you were very, very lucky. Or had help.

In a nutshell, that's why she couldn't retire. Not quite yet.

"Mrs. Needleman, did you fall asleep? Do you want to go to your room and rest a little before dinner?"

Gloria opened both eyes to the vision of Beatrice's concerned face. It was a kind face. It was a wise face.

It was the face of a smart-ass who couldn't keep her nose out of other people's affairs.

No wonder Gloria liked her.

"Help me up, dear," she said. Bea was so strong she nearly shot-putted Gloria over the porch railing and into the gardens below.

"Sorry," Bea said.

"No worries." Gloria patted her arm, thinking now was as good a time as any for Bea's first lesson. "Finesse, Beatrice. The more subtle your intercession, the better. Keep that in mind."

"Uh, okay, sure." Bea took Gloria's elbow and helped her down the back steps, past the kitchen entrance, and down the walkway to her first-floor guest room.

Once the women made sure Gloria was settled, they told her they'd come by in three hours to take her to dinner. When Josie's friends turned to leave, Gloria tapped Ginger on the shoulder.

"Yes?" Ginger asked, smiling.

It broke Gloria's heart that a woman as pretty and good-hearted as Ginger had spent the majority of her adulthood with the wrong man. A real *schnegegi,* she'd heard. It happened more often than anyone dared admit, and, in Gloria's opinion, it was one of the greatest of human tragedies. But in Ginger's case, the problem was fixable.

"My dear girl, could you stay a moment?" Gloria asked in her sweetest old-lady voice. "There's a little something I'd like to discuss with you."

Read on for an excerpt
from Susan Donovan's next book

THE NIGHT
SHE GOT LUCKY

Coming soon from St. Martin's Paperbacks

Ah, romance.

Lucio propped the limp body of the latest fainting
bridesmaid against his chest, then reached up under a
resplendent amount of green chiffon fabric until he
found the back of her knees. He lifted her, pulled
her close, and turned toward the guesthouse, where
he'd learned she was staying. Lucio knew he should
concentrate solely on the placement of his feet on the
stone walk, but the allure of Senora Garrison's exposed
bosom and satiny throat were impossible to resist. So
he alternated. He looked at his feet on the stones, then
at the glorious swells and slopes of the woman in his
arms. He carefully placed his feet on the doorstep, then
appreciated the graceful curve of her dangling arm.
The stairs, her cute little nose. Kicking open the door,
her trim waist.

It was too much for him. The instant Lucio entered
the upstairs guestroom—even before he could place
her on the bed—he lowered his lips to the satiny warm
skin below her jaw line. He kissed her there, gently
flicking his tongue against her pulse. She would be
fine, he knew. She simply needed to loosen her dress.
So Lucio placed her on top of the coverlet, rolling her

away enough for him to reach the zipper. Slowly, he pulled it down, and with the release of each stainless steel tooth, more of the woman's taut skin was revealed to his appreciative gaze. Lucio's breath quickened as the inches of flawless pink revealed themselves between her shoulder blades, around her ribs, along the straight, delicate spine, and lower, lower, to the top of what was proving to be perfectly rounded buttocks.

With great care—and an unexpected surge of self-discipline—he eased her onto her back, making sure the dress covered her bare breasts but did not hinder her breathing. He brushed her left cheek with the back of his fingertips.

"*Te fuiste, mi amor*," he whispered. "Wake up, love. You left me for a moment. Breathe now."

She stirred.

"That is good," he said, suddenly aware of a strange sizzle in the air, an electric rush moving through his body. He glanced to check if a breeze ruffled the curtains. But there was nothing.

Then Ginger sighed, her dainty pink lips parting ever so slightly, and Lucio felt it again, stronger this time—a wave, a disturbance in the air, a question and its answer tucked inside a crackle of energy. Ginger's eyelashes flickered. His self-control had been short-lived.

"Forgive me," Lucio said as he lowered his mouth to hers. "But I must."

He kissed her. Her lips yielded to his gentle pressure, opening to him. Lucio groaned in bliss, the energy coursing through him, the kiss building, surging, growing hotter and hotter . . .

Until she struck him.

The thud of her palms against his chest knocked the wind from his lungs. Lucio prevented himself from falling off the edge of the bed and managed a smile. "Sleeping beauty awakes!" he said, bowing slightly.

"You freakin' pig!"

With that pronouncement, Ginger sat up abruptly, her thick auburn hair askew, her dress falling far south of modesty. She choked in outrage, yanking the dress up past a set of stupendous breasts all the way to her clavicle. That's when she screamed.

In the two decades he'd roamed the globe as a nature photographer for *Geographica Magazine*, he'd dealt with hysterical females of every size, shade, nationality, and demeanor. They'd cursed him in a variety of tongues—Mandarin, Punjabi, and Cajun French initially came to mind—and in a variety of exotic settings. The Nepalese highlands. Kenya's Rift Valley. Under a canopy of strangler fig vines over the Upper Amazon. But he couldn't remember any of them being as desirable as Ginger Garrison. There was something beguiling about the woman—quite tall but, oh, so feminine. He guessed she was in her mid-thirties, at the peak of mature beauty, with fiery hazel eyes and delicate hands, one of which was, at that very moment, flying toward his face, palm flat and open.

Thwack!

The guestroom door flew wide, and Lucio immediately recognized the cavalry as the other two bridesmaids in the wedding party: an older, mannish woman named Beatrice Latimer and a little dark-haired cutie named Roxanne Bloom. Though he would have preferred it the other way around, Roxanne was in a bulky bathrobe and Bea was in a camisole and panties.

"What the fuck?" Bea said, balling her fists at her sides.

"Allow me to introduce myself." Lucio rose from the bed and headed toward the neutral center of the room. "I am Lucio Montevez, but those who know me well call me Lucky." The women did not seem impressed. "Your friend fainted on the walkway outside, and I brought her here to recover."

"We don't care if you're the pope!" Roxanne's eyes flew wide. "We heard Ginger scream and we're calling the police!"

Lucio tried not to laugh. "There is no need, I assure you."

"Really?" Bea took a step toward him, and by the looks of the woman's defined quadriceps, she meant business. "Because it sure looks like you just assaulted her." Bea pointed at Ginger. "Her dress is open. She looks unraveled. That scream was the real deal. Your luck has just run out, dude."

"Wait." It was Ginger. She fumbled with the dress, clutching it to her chest as she reached around her back to find the open zipper. Then she blinked, quickly shook her head, and touched her lips. Her eyes shot toward him. "I couldn't breathe. I remember I saw you step out from behind the roses, then everything went black." Ginger's jaw slackened. Her hand fell to her side. And she stared at him in shock.

Ginger's friend had been right—she looked unraveled. Lucio certainly hadn't meant to unnerve the woman to this degree. It was only a kiss.

"You said you were waiting for me," Ginger whispered, horror in her eyes.

"I did."

"Then you said something in Spanish. What was it?"

"I merely explained that you'd stolen my heart."

Ginger's eyes went wider still. "You kissed me."

"I had hoped to wake you," Lucio said, smiling. "I am happy to see it worked."

"Ever heard of a cold cloth on the forehead?" Roxanne asked.

Lucio laughed. "This has been a rare pleasure, ladies. Please let me know if you should need further assistance."

He headed toward the door, looking back long enough to see the loathing in Bea's sneer and the distrust in Roxanne's narrowed eyes. Ginger, however, was once again touching a pair of lips that had drifted into a dreamy smile.

With a nod, Lucio headed down the steps and outside, a smile of his own spreading across his face. Without a doubt, loosening the dress of the hazel-eyed, auburn-haired Ginger Garrison had been the most pleasant surprise of the last three months.